HOLD ME
Instead

ANDREA D'ALESSIO

Edited by J. Berry Editorial

Cover Design and Art by Ink and Laurel

Proofread by Dot The i Edit

ASIN (ebook): B0FFGLGXDR

ISBN (paperback): 9798998889400

For my husband, who has always known my vaginismus doesn't define me, even when I struggled with it myself.
I love you so much.

CONTENTS

CONTENT NOTES

The female main character, Charlie, in *Hold Me Instead* has vaginismus. Throughout the book, her experience with pelvic floor dysfunction, as well as treatment for it, are explored. Her case was not caused by trauma. Please keep in mind that everyone's experience with pelvic floor dysfunction is unique, and treatment in this book is not meant to be used as medical advice.

Below you will find a list of topics that may be difficult for some. *Hold Me Instead* is intended for adult readers 18+. It depicts explicit language and open door intimate scenes. Additionally, you will find:

- MMC's father recovering from a severe heart attack, including some hospital visit scenes

- Anxiety and mental health representation

- Alcohol use

- A character disclosing her experience with breast cancer

- Discussions of a manipulative past relationship (off the page)

- Discussions of a cheating relationship (off the page)

- Discussions of having to put an animal to sleep (off the page)

Author's Note

As children, dreams are uninhibited, nothing seems out of reach, and the possibilities of what "could be" is thrilling. By the time we're adults, the messages around us, whether through those close to us or what society loves to cram in our faces, chips away at our resolve. Life throws new obstacles our way, seeing what will make us crack, or even break. Yet while we may be in pieces, we are still us. The fragments, the chunks that might tear down from time to time, they still exist, and they matter. Those moments allow us to examine parts of ourselves more closely, to strengthen who we are as we build ourselves into the best versions we can be. The beautiful thing is that we're always growing, there's always room for us to change and shift. The foundation will only get stronger.

My dream of writing a book had gone dormant until just the right time in my life. When I started working on the Elmwood Falls series, Charlie's story wasn't going to be the first, and she was going to be a physical therapist who treated pelvic floor dysfunction but didn't have a condition herself. When I shared some of my plans with my psychotherapist, she asked, "What about Charlie having vaginismus?"

Still early in my own treatment at the time, with shame weighing me down, I was terrified by the notion. But as the saying goes, do what scares you.

I'm so glad I faced that fear. Charlie's crush on Zachary proves desires exist and are valid, even with vaginismus as a steady companion. The result is a story about acceptance, love, and trust—both with a partner and with yourself. Writing it helped me remember how many things define a person—how many different pieces define *me*. Passions and dreams are part of the tapestry, and with our personal struggles, everything weaves together into one lovely, unique design.

I wrote this story for myself, to view my own struggle with vaginismus more objectively. To help me shed the shame and own the narrative. But I also wrote this for those going through something similar. If you're reading this and experiencing pelvic pain, I hope you feel less alone. There *are* medical professionals out there who understand, who care, who continue to learn and listen to patients. Don't give up searching, and find someone close to you who will be your support system. Everyone's case is different, and while this book discusses treatment options, it's not all that exists, and may not even be what you need specifically. But know that there are options!

If you're reading this and haven't experienced pelvic floor dysfunction or something similar, thank you for taking the time to read and learn. For people with pelvic floor dysfunctions who've been told to just deal with the pain, simply knowing there are others out there willing to listen and understand and validate these experiences can mean everything. Also, this goes far beyond pelvic floor conditions, but you get what I'm saying. And if you're reading this and have a partner struggling with pelvic floor dysfunction, thank you for recognizing that your partner is worth it, and that a relationship can actually grow stronger as you work through it.

It took me a long time and *multiple* doctors to find the ones who knew what I was experiencing, who knew who to direct me to for treatment. And I know for some it's even harder to find that proper care, especially for Black women, people of color, and the trans community. So please, continue to advocate—for yourself, for those you love, and for those you don't know.

I hope this book helps you remember that you're more than one thing. That you're able to let go of something that has too much power over you. That you can hold onto something beautiful instead.

With lots of love and appreciation,
Andrea

CHAPTER 1

Charlie

HIS HEART ATTACK WAS all her fault.

Charlie Harris startled as a muffled alert squawked over the PA system, and then the waiting room was quiet, a cloak of urgency lingering. She crossed her ankles, the squeak of her berry-pink tennis shoes a piercing echo through the chamber of tiles.

She strangled a sob. "Get it together," she whispered.

Her fingers clenched the crumpled coat on her lap, cool raindrops slipping off the waterproof material onto her palms. She focused on her breath, a rhythmic ticking from the empty nurses' station outside the room joining the chorus, where a small witch figure on a broom tilted back and forth like a metronome. Her eyes darted around for a distraction among all the beige. A dozen empty burgundy chairs spruced up the small room, cushions dulled from years of concerned loved ones. The only other person in her vicinity was an older woman a few seats down, asleep with her head cranked back on a sigh, mouth open.

Charlie shifted, her veterinary scrubs a staticky scrape against the fabric seat. She contemplated leaving the woman alone versus being the stranger who startles her awake. Considering it might require a physical nudge to the shoulder, the latter seemed too unsettling. Besides, if this woman could manage to rest, surely there was a way Charlie could too.

1

Leave her alone.

She dropped her face in her hands, elbows to her knees, and groaned softly. She'd believed Daniel that morning—he'd assured her he was fine, despite the sheen of sweat on his forehead and exhaustion etched in his face. She should have insisted he go home, "fine" or not. The week's busy schedule had clearly affected him, all further hindered by her prearranged personal day. If she hadn't added time off this week, this could've been prevented.

*If she hadn't, if she had, could've, should've...*She could do that dance all day.

Charlie struggled to swallow and traced divots in the armrest with a trim, bare fingernail. It hardly registered that he was here, down the hall, just through the double doors. The dreamlike state of the day had been filled with pet appointments, as though nothing traumatic had happened that morning. As though her boss hadn't been lying there on that stretcher with an oxygen mask, shockingly frail, rushed out of his clinic by EMTs. God, the helplessness of that moment...

Her gaze fell on the oversized painting in the small room, positioned like a picture window to a meadow. Tall grasses and wildflowers were swathed in golden rays, the colors homogeneous and dulled. It was likely stationed there for years, a totem to clouded hope for anyone seated alongside it.

"You got the time?"

Charlie blinked at her waiting room companion, who smiled back as though she hadn't been snoring softly a moment earlier.

"Um." Charlie fumbled her jacket for her phone. *Five texts and two missed calls.* "Quarter to eight," she said.

The older woman hummed and shifted in her seat. "Any of the doctors been by recently?"

"Not since I arrived, no." Charlie quickly scanned the missed calls, one from her mother and one from her cousin, Amber.

"Not even the young hot one?"

Charlie looked up. "Uh...no?"

The woman snorted. "Little bonus I've found to hanging around here. He's a dish. Mint?"

She held out an open tin, a hint of a watch band peeking from the cuff of her shirt. The scent of roses followed her motion.

"I'm good, thanks." Charlie couldn't help a small smile as an ache pinged in her chest.

She reminded Charlie of her late grandmother, making friends wherever she went, always finding a way to engage others in conversation. This woman probably agreed with Nana's motto: "*Ask someone for the time or have the chance to provide it. People need one another, Charlie.*"

The woman snapped the tin shut with a nod, mints rattling as she stuffed them in her purse, then busied herself with a magazine.

Suspicious to find herself smoothly dismissed—Nana would never wrap things up that easily—Charlie clicked to her texts from Amber.

Amber: *Ignore my call, here's the skinny...*

Amber: *The Jackass of All Jackasses reached out thru my website. Wants to commission a custom child's rocking chair.*

Charlie frowned, the thought of her ex-boyfriend, Bobby—whose real name was rarely worth uttering—was unwelcome on a normal day, even after four years.

Amber: *Should I say no?*

Time stamp of twenty minutes later.

Amber: *I should say no...*

Time stamp of five minutes later.

Amber: *I'm gonna say no.*

Charlie tapped out a reply. He'd already done enough damage, wasn't fair to take down Amber's dream too.

Charlie: *Take his money! And don't deprive his innocent child of your handiwork.*

Dots appeared immediately, signaling Amber's reply.

Amber: *Innocent? That kid is doomed.*

Charlie snorted with a small shake of her head.

Charlie: *Don't curse the kid already, Amber.*

Amber: *[shrug emoji] Anyway, I don't think he realizes it's me.*

Charlie: *Your picture's on your site...*

Amber: *Right below my name! He really is a dipshit. Look at that, my fee just went up!*

Charlie chuckled. She could always rely on her cousin's loyalty and levity. But no matter how many marks her ex scored in the bastard category, she wasn't about to let that cost Amber business as she nudged her woodworking off the ground. Plus, unlike her cousin, Charlie had a little more faith in humanity that the kid could grow into a decent human.

Amber: *You home yet?*

Charlie's fingers hovered over the phone. This week was taking its toll. While Amber was unaware Charlie had taken a day off, she needed her now.

Charlie: *Actually just got to the hospital. Daniel had a heart attack this morning.*

Amber: *Oh shit.*

Charlie: *They did surgery as soon as he got here.*

Amber: *How is he?*

Charlie: *In recovery, it went well thankfully. Haven't seen anyone yet, though.*

Amber: *Wow...*

Another moment passed, then:

Amber: *How are you?*

Charlie swallowed. It was all surreal. He'd been operated on that morning. But the person through those doors, down the hall, couldn't be Daniel Lee—the one who'd cheered her on through vet school and attended her graduations like a proud parent. Who jogged *every* morning, the same two-mile stretch he'd run for decades, even in a Wisconsin winter. Who twirled his granddaughter around and let his grandson cling to his back.

She typed a simple *I'm ok* in reply, the statement as numb as she felt. She'd worked hard to see all their scheduled patients, staying open well beyond their Saturday 4 p.m. closing time to do so. She'd allowed work to consume her, as though he'd gone home with a common cold. But it didn't sit right. Not when she pictured the man who'd mentored her the last decade of her life and what he'd gone through today. Hell, he and his wife treated Charlie like one of their own children—their daughter was like her big sister.

There was nothing comforting in following through with it all. Daniel had endured a freaking heart attack, and Charlie had stayed at work. He'd undergone intense surgery, and she'd barely arrived before visiting hours ended. And here she sat, building up the nerve to see him. She couldn't go to his room. No matter how she looked at it, she was his employee, his co-veterinarian. She wasn't family—definitely *wasn't* his daughter.

Another buzz in her hand.

Amber: *Is Zachary in town?*

The breath whooshed from Charlie's mouth. Daniel's son was an entirely different story. Seeing his name sent a shot of adrenaline through her so unexpected her entire body warmed. She fanned the messy knot of brown hair resting at the nape of her neck. The black shirt under her scrubs became too much, so she shoved the long sleeves up her forearms. *Shit.* She might see him. Why hadn't that thought crossed her mind? It'd been, what, five years?

Shut up, Charlie, you know it's been six.

Amber: *I bet he's fucking gorge now.*

Ugh, me too.

"You a doctor? Nurse? Or is that part of your costume?"

The older woman's voice shook Charlie back to her surroundings, and she shoved the phone in a coat pocket like she'd been caught ogling a photo of the man in his presence. She looked up, briefly surprised at the questions until she remembered her Halloween scrubs and cat ears headband. Didn't matter it was the weekend before, Halloween costumes could be celebrated all month as far as she was concerned.

"I'm a veterinarian," Charlie replied. "Dressed up for my patients. So today, I guess I'm also a cat," she said, touching the headband in her frizzed hair. Her forced, nervous chuckle faded quickly at the unnecessary admission she'd dressed in costume for the animals—not for the amusement of clients or coworkers. She cleared her throat, hoping it erased her ridiculousness.

"Oh, how lovely," the woman said. She sorted through an endless treasure trove in her purse before producing a tiny brush, then swiped at the wispy grays of her hair, her hand following to pat them in place. Seemingly unconcerned about Charlie's penchant for Halloween or the wealth of thoughts performing a mosh pit in her brain.

"You...been here awhile?" Charlie asked, then immediately cringed.

What was fair game to ask strangers in a hospital waiting room that didn't hit a nerve? Or, apparently, sound like a bad pickup line? Better question, why did she feel obligated to converse? Couldn't they just sit in awkward silence? If Nana were here, Charlie wouldn't have to ask herself these questions, what with Nana's constant chatter.

"Waiting for my honey to get off his shift. Should be along any moment now." She applied her lipstick, compact mirror in hand, blotting tissue ready to absorb excess red paint. The woman had to be early seventies, and she rocked the bold shade like it was made for her.

Charlie had never been able to pull off red lipstick—it always seemed too jarring against her own fair, rosy skin. Though, they did have similar skin tones...

The woman smoothed a hand down the front of her striped blouse, then unbuttoned another button, expertly positioning the shirt against her collarbone with practiced, red-tipped fingers that matched her lips.

"Here for family?" she asked, looking up with a soft smile. She radiated happiness, a demure look emphasized by her confidence.

Charlie wanted to be her when she grew up.

"My boss." She hesitated, her brow furrowing at the impersonal title. "I've worked with him for almost ten years. He had a heart attack."

The woman tittered. "My husband survived two of his own. The damn cancer got him."

"Oh. I'm so sorry."

The woman shrugged. "Life is shit at times." She looked beyond Charlie. "And then it's great again." A smile lit up her face that, for a fleeting moment, suggested love or romance could arrive at any point in life.

A man with styled white hair wearing dark blue scrubs stood at the entrance to the narrow room. "Ready?" he said.

The woman stood and gave Charlie a pat on the shoulder as she walked to the hallway. "My best to your boss, dear. Hang in there. Oh!" She stepped back into the tiny room and whispered, "This gentleman coming down the hall isn't the young hot doc I mentioned, but he's certainly a looker. Ah, if men are your preference, that is," she added with a smile. Then she was gone, the fragrance of roses lingering.

Charlie didn't have to wait long for the reveal—a man appeared in the hall beyond the waiting area and stopped in her line of sight, staring ahead at the double doors. His black hair was short, the wavy length on top mussed as he gripped it. A charcoal bomber jacket cloaked broad shoulders, his posture long and lean. He wore dark blue jeans that hugged thick thighs, and even a quick glance revealed a solid ass. In fact, it deserved a second look. He had his father's frame. Taller, sure—*wait, hold up. Not the ass part. Or the "thick thighs," Charlotte!*

There was no mistaking that the man in front of her was Zachary Lee.

That old, familiar flutter plucked at her organs, threatening a tango of nausea and giddiness. He turned his profile her way, hands on hips as he stared at his feet. His tawny skin tone was the same as Daniel's, but the rest was so *Zachary*. His profile sent her heart—no, her heart*beat*—into overdrive, that jawline one of his most powerful features. With the help of a grin she remembered so well, he was captivating.

Not that he was smiling now.

Head down, he walked into the waiting area, seemingly unaware of her. The smell of fresh rain on fabric enhanced a warm, earthy scent emanating from him, bursting through the dwindling floral air. He moved past her to the far corner of the room and folded his six-foot self into a chair, sinking with a look of despair.

Charlie faced forward, knee bouncing as she stared at the painting. If only Mary Poppins could help her hop into that framed meadow. Maybe she hadn't given it enough credit—she'd prefer frolicking freely through monochromatic fields over this anxiety-ridden, hormone-addled swirl of emotions.

This was silly—they knew each other. She should say something. Acknowledging him made perfect sense. Perhaps he didn't recognize her, and when she said hello, he'd swoop her into one of his tight, all-consuming hugs, and they could sigh in companionable relief. She'd been on the receiving end of his embrace only once, but it was one she'd never forget.

She dared a glance out of the corner of her eye. He leaned forward, forearms propped on his thighs, hands clasped between his knees. Eyes drilling holes into the tan tile floor. It was more than despair. He looked...*angry*. Not that Charlie could fault him. Unfortunately, it was a look she remembered all too well, their last encounter imprinted on her mind. Dread kicked every other feeling out of the way as she realized she was probably the last person he wanted comforting him. Though she still didn't know why.

"Stop staring at me, Harris."

Charlie's eyes bolted forward, her breath frozen, as his deep voice skated over her arms and smacked her in the chest.

She was right. That tone was definitely full of anger. Toward her.

CHAPTER 2

Zachary

TODAY COULD FUCK ITSELF in its warped asshole.

While it didn't surprise him to find her here, recognizing Charlie Harris after all these years, *sensing* her, only irritated him more. He couldn't determine what had clued him in while barely looking her way, but he felt the weight of her stare. It went more than skin-deep, and that was a firm no-entry zone for Zachary Lee.

"How you holdin' up?" she asked.

His breath tripped as her soft voice slammed into him, knocking his thoughts into even more of a jumbled mess.

A whole year. That was the last time he'd heard his father's voice, after Zachary had signed the divorce papers. Their brief conversation was a hollow memory—*"Zachary. How you holdin' up?"*

"Fine."

"Good, here's your mother."

He scoffed. Maybe Charlie was more like his dad than he realized. More so than him.

Zachary kept his gaze on a muddy streak across the tile. "Fine." It came out gruff, his disdain echoing in the quiet. It emboldened him somehow, made him feel justified in his anger. What his anger was about at that moment, he wasn't sure. But he gripped it like a lifeline.

The universe excelled at highlighting his shortcomings. After a punishing morning run failed to ease life's bullshit, the jarring call about his father had only disoriented him further. He'd had enough wits about him to throw some shit in a bag and load up his old dog for a drive from Chicago that took twice the normal time—all to wind up in a stifling waiting room with the woman who represented his terrible life choices.

She slid her hands along her thighs, tapped her knees, and interrupted the silence once again. "Scary morning, huh? Must've been awful getting the news over the phone."

He leaned back and grunted at Charlie's gentle approach.

Unfortunately, the news about his father being rushed to the hospital came from an uncharacteristically harried voicemail, adding to the pall of everything. He'd pushed his sister to that tactic, he knew, by ignoring her earlier attempts to reach him, ultimately delaying himself from getting on the road. His grip had finally eased on the steering wheel once he got the update that his dad was stable and in recovery.

A sharp squeak on tile drew his attention as Charlie crossed her ankles, the bright purply pink tennis shoes a punctuation to his thoughts. He released a long breath, running his hands through his hair, squeezing the misted strands as though that would squash droplets of memories.

Charlie cleared her throat. "The nurse told me his room's through those double doors out there? Jeanie called the office to let us know the surgery went well, but I haven't heard many details."

When his mom's name fell from her lips, he finally gave Charlie more than a glance. The features of her face were sharper, matured over their years apart, yet still soft. Her nose and round cheeks were red against her fair skin, no doubt from the chilly autumn rain. She wore little makeup, a trait he remembered about her, though something brightened her eyes, staring from her wide tortoiseshell glasses. She remained still, as though she was holding her breath. A surge of remorse coursed through him at her obvious discomfort, then amplified when he noticed her Halloween scrubs and cat ears. Leave it to Charlie to be festive at the clinic. *Damn her and her charming sense of humor.*

No, he corrected himself, *goofy. Not charming.*

Not that the distinction made much difference where she was concerned.

"Halloween's not for another week," he said.

Her nod was slow, uncertain. At least she was breathing and blinking now.

"You wore that today?" he asked—accused.

She perched on the edge of her seat, ready to bolt. "*Yee-es*," she said, lengthening the word into two syllables.

Her eyes darted over him, studying, while he studied her.

Damp wisps of brown hair clung to her face, and small flyaways dried haphazardly, creating a wild nest for the cat ears on her head. The frizz had always bothered her, he recalled, humid Wisconsin summers making the carefree tendrils regularly present.

The comfort their presence brought him made him instantly *un*comfortable.

He cleared his throat. "Not very professional, dressing in costume for work." *There, regained control.*

Her eyes narrowed for the briefest moment. "It's just a headband. Besides, nothing wrong with being a little playful on the job." She followed up her response with a too-serene smile. It was a far cry from her normal beam that sparked energy into a room.

Zachary shifted, disturbed he could distinguish between her smiles and intrigued at this glimpse of her bold side. As far as he was concerned, their friendship had ended the moment he'd moved to Chicago—he'd barely paid her a passing thought since then. Sure, the latter was largely due to what his father had told him right before he left town. But the fact she was here didn't surprise him. He wasn't going to avoid the woman, but he wouldn't pretend they were still friends either.

He tapped his fingers on the armrests. "Isn't it family only right now?"

"I don't think—"

"You aren't family, Harris. No matter how much my dad insists otherwise."

The silence that met him was satisfying for a split second. A split second, before those wide eyes blinked rapidly away from him, and her confident posture melted. Just a fraction, but it was enough.

He closed his eyes and turned his face. *Dick move.* They hadn't seen each other in years, and this was how he treated her? She was here to check on his dad. To support his family. Something he knew she did regularly, whether she had ulterior motives or not. *Which is also bullshit. She doesn't have a bad bone in her body.*

It really sucked that he liked her—he sure didn't care for himself right now.

He huffed, muttered quiet curses, then said, "That was uncalled for." It was lacking, but it was the level of apology he could pull from the pit of shit that was his life lately.

She swallowed a few times, then released a quiet, shaky breath, the blinking finally slowing. He stared at his shoes, his attention to her subtle movements putting him on edge.

When he wasn't talking to her, or seeing her, for that matter, he could hold on to his anger. For six years, apparently. But now it all felt...pointless. Today wasn't her fault, not even this heightened awareness of her. *That* had to be due to the instability of the day, some grasp at a positive feeling, or familiarity.

"Your energy reminds me of Mrs. Van Der Wier's pug," she finally said.

A surprised chuckle brewed, but he muzzled it. "That's a name I haven't heard in a long time," he said. He pictured the wrinkly white pup with its permanent scowl, always emphasized by the pet clothing Mrs. Van Der Wier chose for the day. "Which outfit?"

"That velvet smoking jacket. For sure."

This time, he smirked. "He *hated* that thing," he said.

"Mm, always looked his angriest in it," she said.

He groaned on a small chuckle, knowing her dig was still generous. When he looked up, she was watching from the corner of her eye again, biting the inside of her cheek. Pink flushed over her face and down her neck. She wanted to say something else, her energy palpable, wrapping around him in the tiny room. The feeling reminded him of their easy rapport, and suddenly, the grudge he held against her—that wasn't *for* her at all—evaporated. In its place was an urgency to mend their friendship, something he desperately needed. What he didn't know was whether it was just because he needed *hers* specifically.

"My *Yeh-Yeh* had a heart attack when he was fifty," he blurted.

Zachary hadn't been born yet to see his grandfather through that time, but the incident had scared his dad enough to start running daily. To encourage Zachary to focus on heart health. He hadn't realized that had been in the back of his mind until now.

Charlie opened her mouth as if to speak, but the speedy tap of heels interrupted, his sister appearing in the hall. Zachary leaped to intercept her and squeezed past Charlie. His shoulder bounced off the framed painting that threatened to consume the room, and she pulled her knees close and knocked into her chair. But they narrowly avoided contact with each other.

He stepped into the hall and caught Sandra's elbow, and she startled to attention, weary gaze wide as she took him in. She pressed her lips together, then flung her arms around him.

"You're here," she said into his chest, holding tight. Her floral perfume, though faint, soothed with familiarity. He felt her release a deep breath before stepping back. "Have you gone in yet?" she asked, voice low.

"No, just got here. Needed a moment."

She nodded, her dark brown eyes less vibrant than normal. "I stepped away to call Jay, check on him and the kids. And...needed some air."

Mascara marred her tawny skin. Her signature curling iron waves fell limp, her black hair nearly straight in its low ponytail. Even her ivory top was wrinkled, untucked from sleek maroon pants.

"You okay?" he asked softly.

"It's been a shit day." Her eyes filled with tears as she shook her head. "Thank God he's alright, that they got him into surgery when they did. He was really lucky," she added on a whisper.

Zachary swallowed, rubbing his hand up and down her silky sleeve. He hadn't stopped to consider how close it had been. The image of the last time he'd seen his father, the *hurt* on his dad's face, flashed through his mind. Pain caused by stupid choices Zachary had made.

"Vivi immediately sat down to make him a card. Alex, of course, then had to scribble one of his own. Jay said it resembles the poop emoji, but Alex claims it's a puppy."

Zachary blinked to attention, affection now on Sandra's face as she talked about her husband and kids.

"I'm so grateful Dad will actually see the cards," she choked.

Zachary felt his throat tighten, but croaked, "Yeah, you know how much Dad gets a kick out of shit."

Sandra's laugh burst free, eyes watery as she tilted her head his way. A tired smile lingered. "I'm really glad you're here." She straightened, dabbed the corners of her eyes with her fingertips, and walked toward the double doors. "Alright, let's go."

"Wait." He cleared his throat. "Sandra, hold on—"

"I'll pull Mom out of the room if you want some alone time. He's sleeping, but still."

The sound that escaped him could only be described as a growl—fitting, since he felt like a disgruntled animal. Emotions were confusing and fuck expressing them. "I'll hang out here for Mom. Besides, it's rude to make people wait," he taunted.

His sister squinted with a scrutiny that was effective as a high school counselor. "What?"

He pointed inside the waiting room where Charlie sat, pretending to focus on her phone.

"Charlie! I didn't know you were here." Sandra rushed over to Charlie, who stood for a welcoming hug. "Did you text me?" she asked, pulling back with concern.

"No. I, uh, haven't been here long. Figured I'd run into you at some point," Charlie said.

Sandra whipped back to him, eyes alert. "Were you nice to Charlie?"

An abrupt laugh escaped him. His sister waited, eyebrow raised. She knew he harbored residual issues regarding the practice, though he'd never divulged them all to her.

Charlie rubbed her currently pinched forehead, but said nothing in his defense. Though she wouldn't have a reason to, would she?

He flung his arms wide, frustration as exposed as his palms, but kept his tone measured. "What is this, kindergarten?"

Sandra shrugged. "You *are* acting like a child in regard to Dad. Figured all your tendencies to revert back might be kicking in."

He crossed his arms, then realized the pouting gesture for what it was and moved to lean against the wall, using every effort to appear casual. "I don't know what you're talking about." *Thirty-five years old and I feel like a kid. Weird "big sister" powers.*

Sandra full-on grinned, and some of the tension left his body. If nothing else, their stupid quarrel made her happy for at least a moment.

"Jay must hate all this counselor bullshit," he mumbled, even though he knew full well his brother-in-law loved that about Sandra. It seemed like every part of her that needled Zachary growing up only made Jay fall harder—like when Zachary was eighteen and she analyzed aloud in painstaking detail Zachary's high school relationships "for thesis research," only to have then-college-boyfriend Jay turn to her and say, "Do mine next." True love, where your quirks and flaws were plated in gold.

They don't make relationships like that anymore.

Charlie touched Sandra's arm. "Do you need food? I just wanted to check in, see what I could do," Charlie said, interrupting the sibling bickering.

Zachary's gaze traveled over her short frame, and the curves fitted to her scrubs. She gripped a raincoat against her body, its stripes of bright colors a cheerful contrast to the gray scrubs, the top of which was printed with cats holding jack-o'-lanterns and wearing witch hats. Upon closer inspection, he noticed some cats held signs that read We Choose Treats!

God damn it, charming she is.

"Thanks, but Jay distracted the kids by cooking up a feast tonight, and I managed to force some cafeteria food on Mom. Much as I've tried, I think she's staying here for the night."

"Does she need anything from home?" Charlie asked.

He rubbed his chest, unsure why it suddenly ached.

"No, you're sweet to ask. We're doing alright at the moment. Unless this dope needs something." Sandra turned to him. "Are you coming home with me?"

"Staying by Jordan." His eyes darted to Charlie, who barely glanced his way, then back to his sister. He was pretty sure Charlie wasn't eager to help him, anyway. "I don't need anything. Assuming I'm the dope you meant."

Sandra smirked.

"Then I'll check in with you tomorrow. Let me know if anything comes up," Charlie said, continuing the conversation as though Zachary wasn't involved.

Sandra stopped her. "Did you want to see him?" she asked Charlie softly.

"No, no. You three should have this time with him."

"He's asleep, but Mom would love to see you. You're family, you know that."

Zachary stiffened at Sandra's words, noting Charlie's similar reaction. Without looking at him, Charlie nodded.

"Okay. I'll pop in for a minute," she said.

"Great. You coming too?" Sandra asked.

He shook his head. "Gotta make a call first. I'll be in shortly," he lied.

"Okay...Don't go anywhere, Z." Sandra looped her arm in Charlie's, and they headed through the double doors like the best of friends. Like women who were there for each other.

Like family.

While Zachary stood alone, watching them go—his sister, and the woman who'd take over his dad's veterinary hospital in his place.

He cursed softly, scrubbing a hand over his clenched jaw.

Charlie didn't look back, which was actually for the best—she wouldn't like what she saw in him anyway.

CHAPTER 3

Charlie

"CHRIST ON A CRACKER," Charlie cursed through gritted teeth, rubbing the crown of her head. She pressed her chest to the floor, ass in the air, and scooted from under the table.

"Dr. Harris, what in the world are you doing?" Maura's tone suggested a hands-on-hips stance, her work-mom role one she took as seriously as being office coordinator at Elmwood Falls Veterinary Hospital.

Charlie stretched for the On switch, and the newly powered device hummed to life. "Just adding some final touches," she said. She stood, pleased to see the projection of the ghost dog, Zero, flying around the wall. "Hm, maybe we should've gone with an entire *Nightmare Before Christmas* theme," Charlie muttered. She gasped and whipped around. "Oh my God. Why did I decide a *ghost of a dog* was a good idea for a veterinary hospital!"

Maura angled her head, sigh implied. "People know the movie, they'll get it. Besides, it's very spooky, a ghost-ridden lab."

"Right, right." Charlie released a noisy breath, curving her lips into a smile.

As expected, Maura stood in the doorway, hands on hips, wearing her trusty Halloween sweatshirt. The faded black crew neck had screen-printed ghosts flying through a graveyard, the quality only slightly cracked. She fit right in with the ghosts dangling from lights and tucked around operating tables and kennels. A new accessory, however, was a fuzzy orange headband nestled in her wavy, shoulder-length gray hair. With every slight movement, two green springs with googly eyes bounced around her head.

Charlie laughed. "I like the new addition."

Maura knocked a spring out of her face. "The grandkids picked this out." The eye hopped back, and she swatted it again. "Well, that'll get annoying."

"I love it. But secret's safe if that headband goes missing for the day," Charlie said, moving toward her.

Maura chuckled. "Are you kidding? Wouldn't dare risk their wrath when they stop by." She pointed at Charlie's cat ears. "I made the mistake of mentioning yours, and next thing I knew, they showed up at my house with this."

"They know you'll do anything they ask."

"Yeah, it's going to be a problem as they get older," Maura said, her voice almost wistful.

"Like it isn't already?" Charlie chuckled. She rubbed at the fading ache on her head, slowing as she took in the concerned look on Maura's face. A few inches shorter than Charlie's five foot four, Maura adjusted her stance, maintaining eye contact.

"How long have you been here?" Maura demanded.

"Not long..."

Maura narrowed her gray-blue eyes. There was a secret power in the wrinkles decorating her fair skin, more a measure of her perceptive abilities than her seventy years.

Charlie shrugged. "Wanted to get a jump start on the schedule, see what we need to shift around. Since Dr. Fletcher's only available a few more days—"

"I said I'd go over that with you, Charlie." Maura said softly.

"I know." Charlie rested her head against the doorjamb. "I couldn't sleep last night, and really, it felt better to be here. Stay busy, I guess."

"You spent all your free time here this past week as it is," Maura said. "You can't keep that up."

Charlie nodded, her brow sliding against the wood frame. "This is the first village trick or treat Daniel will miss." His strong runner's form had looked frail in the hospital bed, well beyond his sixty-five years. "He looked like he'd aged ten years in a week, Maura."

Maura averted her gaze. "I was wondering if you stopped by the hospital last night."

"I barely saw him the first time. I needed..." Charlie swallowed.

Maura nodded, then patted Charlie's arm. "Why don't you get some fresh air? It's a beautiful day, smells wonderful after the rainy week. Buy a coffee or something."

Charlie looked at the wall clock. "Trick-or-treating starts soon—"

The back door burst open and smacked the wall.

"Sorry!" a voice rang through the hallway.

Charlie and Maura hustled toward the employee entrance, slowing at the sight of Charlie's cousin using her body to softly close the door.

"Amber? What are you doing here?" Charlie asked.

Amber Harris whipped around, long golden-brown hair spinning under a bowler hat. "Hi!" she said, arms outstretched, a coffee in each hand. Her mauve lipstick grin was partly visible behind a green apple dangling in her face.

"What in the...?" Charlie started.

Amber straightened, showing off a black suit coat, buttoned over a white dress shirt and red tie. "I'm that portrait!"

Maura chuckled. "*The Son of Man.*"

"Yeah! Today I'm calling it *The Daughter of Man*," Amber said with a shrug. "Oh, shit, Maura. I didn't grab you a coffee."

Maura waved her off. "I was just telling Charlie she should get one, so your timing's impeccable. Here, take her outside at least." Maura's firm grip scooted them along. "Don't come in until you see trick-or-treaters. Coming our way, not clear across the park," she clarified, then closed the door on them.

"She's a strong little thing," Amber said, handing over a cup. "And knows you well."

Charlie took a sip, relishing the maple latte. "I don't know what you're talking about," she muttered.

Amber scoffed. "Yeah. Like you wouldn't spot a kid way across the park going the *opposite* direction and rush inside to prep as though they'd be here in three minutes instead of half an hour."

Charlie took another sip, ignoring the accuracy of that statement.

"Oh!" Amber reached into a deep coat pocket and pulled out a small brown paper bag with the telltale white stamp of a cake. Her naturally husky voice deepened playfully. "Brought you this too."

Charlie grabbed it and peered inside, the cinnamon sugar sweetness of Dorothy's Bakery tickling her nose. "Snickerdoodles!" she squeaked.

"Figured you could use the pick-me-up," Amber said.

"I'll be on a sugar high after all this. You brought me a bunch!" Charlie said, a bite already in her mouth. "Ohmigod," she managed.

"You don't have to eat all of them now."

"Ha!" Charlie replied, already reaching for a second.

"You can bounce off the walls with all the kiddos then," Amber said, chuckling.

Charlie grinned. "So how'd you do this?" She poked the dangling apple on the hat's brim.

"Oh! Lots of glue." Amber nodded seriously, and the apple hat bobbed with her. "Most importantly, a fake apple."

Charlie shook her head, feeling lighter. "I love it. Should've known you'd do something creative."

Amber flicked her straight locks over her shoulder, then tipped the hat's brim and bowed, her bangs smooshed against her olive-toned skin. "Thank you," she said. "Thought it'd be a good way to promote Cleo's art classes. Even though I keep forgetting the name of this painting. Don't even ask me who the artist is."

Charlie chuckled. "Did she dress in theme too?"

Amber frowned. "No. Well, to be fair, I didn't really mention my idea."

"Ah. Don't you have to get over there to help set up?"

Amber juggled three jobs: one working for her childhood best friend Cleo at her shop on Main Street, another as a waitress at the Italian restaurant Arturo's—also on Main Street—and most recently, her own woodworking business.

Amber sighed. "Cleo kicked me out. Said I was 'unhelping' and to come back later."

Charlie snickered, savoring the cookies as she took in the final minutes of quiet.

The veterinary hospital was a stand-alone red-and-brown brick building and shared a parking lot with an antique shop and an eye clinic.

The antique shop had an apothecary table in their front window with cauldrons and vessels fuming from dry ice, while the optometrist's blinds were closed, two sets of blinking robotic eyes peeking through. Together, the three businesses formed the tip of the triangle that was Elmwood Falls Village—EFV—the quaint downtown of Elmwood Falls. All shops in their half-mile radius prepped for locals and nearby residents, amping up Halloween window decorations each year. It was the vet hospital's tradition, since Daniel had opened its doors, to have a haunted house, and Charlie and the team had been determined to see it through.

She released a rough breath, her recent visit to see Daniel ingrained in her mind. He'd been asleep, breath steady, brow furrowed. Jeanie had never hugged her so tight, her eyes tired and red, new frown lines taking up firm residence. The reality of it all was even more...real.

Charlie closed her eyes and inhaled, the smell of ozone and damp crushed leaves as comforting as a flannel blanket.

"Alright, I've let it go long enough."

Charlie looked at Amber. "What?"

"You doing okay? And don't give me any 'I'm fine' bullshit. Seriously, how are you?"

Shoulders hitched, Charlie stared at Village Park beyond their lot. Normally bustling with joggers and cozy picnics, or hosting movie nights and concerts in the summer, the pristine green lawn was quiet, cleared of activity before the annual EFV trick or treat got into full swing. The peaceful setting did nothing to ease her mind. There was so much to do, to arrange while Daniel was out, and no matter how many extra hours she'd put in this past week, they were swamped. In fact, standing outside thinking about it wouldn't help any. She took her extra day off, and look what happened—Daniel had endured a heart attack, overworked, not leaning on Charlie enough. If she dwelled on that though, it led her to *why* she'd taken the extra day, and that her cousin still had no clue.

"I'm exhausted," she finally said. "Worried about him. Thankful he's alright. Stressed because there aren't a lot of independent veterinarians available to fill in." Charlie shook her head. "I'm a lot of things right now."

Amber put her hand on Charlie's arm. "You don't *need* to be here right now, Charlie."

"I do, though. Otherwise, I'll spiral. Besides, we have to figure out schedule changes. We're booked through the holidays, and we really don't want to cancel on our clients."

Amber hesitated. "Yeah, but it's okay to rest, especially after last week. Take time to process what happened."

Charlie stepped away from her cousin. "He's okay, Amber. I can't let the practice fall apart while he's recovering. I couldn't face him if that happened. Can you imagine?"

Amber angled firmly toward Charlie, that damn apple twitching in front of her face. "I want *you* to be okay too."

"I'm good," Charlie rasped. She cleared her throat and forced a smile. "Really. I want to be here, it feels right." She looked to Amber, eager to show her determination—except the apple dangled between them. "It's hard to take you seriously right now."

"I have no idea what you're talking about," Amber said cheekily.

"Very funny," Charlie said, smiling as Amber wrapped her in an extra tight hug. Charlie's shoulders loosened, and as they stepped apart, she nudged her cousin. "Hey, if you hang around a little longer, you'll probably see Logan."

Amber's playful shove in return moved Charlie a foot. "You mean, *Dr. Fletcher?*"

A laugh broke from Charlie as she steadied. "That's the one."

"I'm very tempted."

"Oh, I know. He's only with us a few more days, and then he's on vacation. So you better make your move soon."

Amber grinned. "Who says I haven't?"

Charlie gaped. "Did you?"

"No. I didn't. I was trying to feel him out." Amber hummed a moment. "If he's leaving town soon, this seems like the perfect time. You're positive he's not seeing anyone?"

"No one. He's going on this trip solo too."

"Gah, he's getting better by the second! Oh, I see little monsters in the distance."

Charlie followed her line of sight across the park and spotted clusters of people starting their trek down Main Street.

"I better get back to Cleo. Don't go in there too soon, Maura's probably standing guard at the door." Amber grinned.

"Yeah. Thanks for the goodies."

"Stop by after, okay?" Amber gave her a quick smack on the ass, then hopped into a light jog toward Cleo's shop. "See ya later, sport!"

Charlie swiped at air, too slow to get her cousin back, but the family endearment lightened her mood further.

When they were kids, Charlie and Amber had played on the same recreation soccer team, coached by Amber's dad. Watching professional sports with Uncle Carl had resulted in the girls observing a lot, especially in the way of commentating. When a young Amber had asked why players and coaches smacked each other on the butt, her dad had replied that it was a way to show camaraderie, almost like calling the other person "buddy" or "sport." Little did he know his daughter would try it on her own teammates, literally calling out "Go get 'em, sport!" as she tapped a player on the ass. Her dad had quickly shut it down, explaining that wasn't something they could freely do.

It stopped in the game, but the two girls found it hilarious and continued it personally.

Charlie did a slow walk to the edge of their parking lot, then immediately went back to the building. This had been plenty of time outside. As soon as she touched the cold metal handle of the employee door, a memory hit her with such force, she felt transported to when she'd worked for Daniel during high school. It had been overcast, a chilly autumn weekend much like this one. She'd held open the door as Daniel rushed inside, carrying a box of puppies he'd found on his doorstep that morning. Zachary followed closely behind, wearing her favorite navy hoodie of his and holding a single pup wrapped in a towel, his focus intent as though he was counting each breath.

She could still hear the newborn squeaks, remembered watching in awe as Daniel handled the situation smoothly, without skimping on the care of any patients scheduled that day. He was her hero, guiding her and the rest of his staff through the care the animals needed. Charlie had known since she was a kid that being a veterinarian was her dream, but that moment had solidified it as a calling, holding the helpless little pups and nursing them back to health. And, she recalled, the look on Zachary's face had displayed what she felt. He was early in his vet schooling, but the two had been stationed side by side whenever they worked together, until each and every pup had found a family.

It was possible because of Daniel, because of his love and care for any animal under his watch, and it fostered a strong team around him who ensured the same. One that kept the practice running even when their fearless leader fell ill.

She opened the door and walked inside, laughter carrying through the small hospital as more staff gathered to prepare for trick-or-treaters. It was true—this didn't fall on her alone. But she'd be damned to let anything falter while Daniel was gone.

CHAPTER 4

Zachary

GIGGLES ECHOED THROUGHOUT ELMWOOD Falls Village like some eighties movie come to life. A toddler dressed like a clownfish exited the veterinary hospital with a group of costumed children and waddled past Zachary, tail fin wiggling. The kids joined a handful of skeleton-clad adults who waited in the parking lot with a brown dachshund wearing a hot dog bun costume. They refilled thermoses from a carafe in their little red wagon stacked with winter coats. The temperature was expected to plummet that night for a short stint, and Zachary recalled when he was six and had to wear a snowsuit over his costume to combat the weather. He had been disappointed no one saw his Woody costume and thought he was just a regular cowboy. So the following year, he'd planned to be the Stay Puft Marshmallow Man and wear his giant coat under his costume. Instead, it was a beautiful seventy degrees, and he'd walked around like a saggy balloon. Zachary had come to understand global warming at a young age.

His attention snagged on two families passing in the park. One family dressed like a team of superheroes, and the other parents wore everyday coats, while the kids ran around as a tiny witch and a dragon. The parents were spunky, their laughter and shouts reminding Zachary how close-knit the community was. The Village was the heart of the city of Elmwood Falls, part of a fairly large Midwest metropolis, yet the likelihood of running into someone you knew was high, giving the feeling of a small Wisconsin town.

Zachary stood at the edge of the Elmwood Falls Veterinary Hospital parking lot. There were countless people from his past he might encounter today. Plenty he hadn't talked to since he'd moved and would be fine never seeing again.

But what unnerved him most was going inside the small red-and-brown brick building where he'd grown up, learned from his father, and worked alongside him. The place where his dad had told him he was giving the practice to Charlie.

"Come on, Uncle Zachy!" His niece Vivi yanked his hand. "It's a haunted house!"

A sheet of black fabric covered the entrance, attached to the wide white sign that read VETERINARY HOSPITAL in fading black letters. A scarecrow propped open the front door, and monster music carried across the lot. Vivi halted, tapping her toes and flinging her arms, the wings of her iridescent butterfly costume flapping in time.

"What are you doing, Vivi?" he asked, arms crossed like a bodyguard.

"We did this"—*tap, tap*—"for our Halloween dance class!" She turned in a slow circle with zombie arms timed to growls in the song, then busted a kid-version "Thriller" move, her straight black hair swinging back and forth.

"Wow, Viv, is that what you learned this week?" Sandra stopped beside Zachary, setting down a wriggling Spider-Man Alex.

"Yeah!" Vivi shouted, then bolted to the front door.

"Hold it!" Sandra hollered at Vivi, then turned toward the park, eyes scanning. "Where the hell is Jay?"

Vivi held still, her front half already hidden behind the curtained doorway.

"I'll find him," Zachary offered, eager to delay his venture into the past, but the man himself appeared just in time.

Jay Wang sauntered toward them, tray of coffees in hand. His black hair was faded on the sides, the top slicked just off-center. His warm beige skin was already flush with pink from the biting wind.

"Here's some reinforcements." Jay handed a drink to his wife and turned to Zachary. "Black coffee, right?"

"Thanks," he grumbled. How Jay remembered his drink, he had no clue. They hadn't had coffee together in years. He took a sip, the liquid sending extra warmth through his chest.

Jay lifted his cup in acknowledgment. "Figured we could all use the boost."

Zachary nodded. "We've been doing this what, three hours?"

Jay chuckled, and his grin grew at whatever he saw on Zachary's face. "Oh. You're serious? No, only an hour."

"*One?*" Zachary's sleep had been shit lately, which had caused him to trudge over to Sandra and Jay's with low energy as it was, disappointing Alex when he showed up in a navy hoodie and jeans. His nephew had gifted him a sword for the day, satisfied Zachary met the qualifications and could participate in the festivities.

His sister wore her hair down with a gold crown lent by Vivi, and the kids allowed her to wear a chunky cream sweater, jeans, and trendy brown hiking boots. Jay was polished in a plum jacket over a black thermal and blue jeans, his black knit derby shoes fresh with a white sole. He twirled around the scepter Alex had given him for the day. Both of them had managed to prep their kids and themselves for trick-or-treating. Zachary had only showered because he'd forced himself on a run first thing that morning.

"Jay, can you grab Viv?" Sandra said, bending to wipe Alex's nose.

Zachary snagged her cup just before it toppled.

Jay located their daughter, now only visible by the one leg extended outside the black curtain of the clinic, and jogged over to her. He stooped and gently tugged her back outside, movements animated. As she walked inside with her dad, Vivi's smile grew as if she was about to embark on her young life's greatest adventure.

How the two of them managed to make this Halloween as normal as possible for the kids was beyond him. Sandra looked exhausted from the emotionally draining week, and Jay was bouncing around, trying to anticipate anything and everything. To Zachary, that seemed like wasted energy when life apparently thrived on an ambush approach.

"I'm tired!" Alex cried out, arms hanging low for emphasis.

"Woah, he looked like you right there," Zachary said to his sister, chuckling as Alex walked in small circles, swinging his candy bucket out to the side.

Sandra stood and grabbed her coffee, downing large gulps. "I wish this was spiked," she muttered.

Zachary smirked. "We can leave, you know? Or..." He hesitated, weighing the options. "I can finish up with them, if you two want a break."

Sandra bit her lip as she considered, hair whipping her face in the crisp breeze. She shook her head. "No, it's okay. We made it all the way to this point, only have these three stops left. Besides"—she smirked, adjusting the crown—"you're not getting out of going to see Dad."

Hospital visits weighed him down. He did better when he could move, could physically do something. Sitting there while his father rested wasn't it. His visits thus far had been brief, often timed to avoid being alone with his dad awake.

He focused on his nephew, now seated on the ground as he sorted candy into small piles on the asphalt. Zachary squatted beside the toddler, surveying the loot. Almond Joys were piled with blue Jolly Ranchers, Tootsie Rolls with Snickers. Kit Kats with red Jolly Ranchers. He smiled. "Which are your favorite, buddy?"

Alex placed a Reese's down and pointed to it, then pointed at the blue pile, and the red. Then reached into the bucket for more.

"Yeah, it's hard for me to pick just one too." Zachary grinned up at his sister, surprised by her soft smile. He cleared his throat, then tussled Alex's short black hair. "How about a piggyback ride through the haunted house?"

"Mmkay," Alex murmured. He supervised as Zachary returned the candy to the bucket, pointing a tiny finger at each remaining piece. Once the candy was safe, he pushed himself up and held out his arms.

Zachary stood with Alex secured to his back, those little hands gripped tightly around his neck. "Let's do this. Hey, you okay?" he asked Sandra.

She nodded, eyes pooling, and looped her arm through his. "I'm just really glad you're here."

"Me too!" Alex shouted into Zachary's ear, energy rebooted.

Sandra laughed as Zachary winced a smile, but he still tickled Alex into shrieks of laughter as they walked inside.

Cheesecloth hung from the lobby ceiling, softening the glow of overhead lights. Ghosts floated above the gray front desk, and a giant

Frankenstein stood guard, holding a robotic pumpkin with a black cat popping up and down. Zachary heard Alex gasp at the sight, then felt his legs straighten and stretch as he tried to slide off his back.

"Slow down, bud," Sandra said, following him over to the monster. She spoke softly to him, and he stared, wide-eyed.

Each of the patient rooms had a different monster theme and glowed with purple and green lights, staffed by employees who handed out candy. Zachary caught sight of Jay and Vivi as they disappeared into a room that greeted them with a witch's cackle.

"Oh my word, Zachary Lee. It's been too long!"

Zachary turned, immediately wrapped in Maura's embrace, her head barely reaching his chest. After a tight squeeze, she held him at arm's length.

He smiled down at the woman who'd known him since birth. "It's good to see you, Maura. I like your new look," he said, knocking a squiggly eye springing around her head.

Maura gave his cheeks a light pinch. "Still a smart-ass."

He smiled. While years had added laugh lines and wrinkles, Maura was as sunny as always. She had to be close to seventy now, but exuded the energy of a cycling instructor.

"How's your father today, dear?" she asked softly, keeping their conversation private.

"Same. Longer rounds of staying awake. Mom's with him now, and we're going by after the kids are done."

"Mhm." She studied him. "How about you?"

"I'm fine." He shrugged. *Did it really matter right now?*

She narrowed her eyes. "Have to take care of yourself, you know. Was just saying the same thing to Dr. Harris. You know her, bleeding heart for these animals, just like your father. She'd probably sleep here just to make sure we could function as close to normal as possible."

He huffed. "The schedule's packed, I'm guessing?"

"Oh, yes," Maura tittered. "Tomorrow and Tuesday we've sorted. Dr. Fletcher's been amazing, stepping in. Have you met him? He's manning the 'haunted lab' area."

"No, I haven't."

"He's wonderful. Works mostly at the emergency hospital, but he's filled in for your dad and Dr. Harris from time to time. He knows our routine, and the clients love him."

Zachary looked away, irritation growing at this faceless guy who'd swooped in, covering patients *and* volunteering for the community event.

"Dr. Harris and I are trying to figure out the rest of the week after he's gone. You know how these graduates are getting multiple offers, so they're all snatched up. Plus, we're not the only ones short-staffed in town. I'm sure you're experiencing the same in Chicago—"

"I can do it."

Maura paused. "Do what?"

Zachary looked around, as though a neon sign would flash Good Idea! at him in support. Instead, a ghost fell free of its adhesive and floated from the ceiling onto the desk. He met her gaze. "I'll fill in for my dad."

Maura clasped her hands around his. "Oh, Zachary, really? Dr. Harris will be thrilled," she added quietly.

That sounded like a stretch.

"Are you sure that'll be okay with your team?" she asked as she walked over to the fallen ghost and stuck it to the front of the counter.

He looked at Maura and considered telling her the news. She was like an aunt, and a master at getting things out of him. Under these circumstances though, he held strong.

"This is a perfect time, actually," he said. "I'm not expected back for a while." *Or ever.*

Miraculously, Maura didn't question him further. Instead, she squeezed his hands again. "Zachary, that would be amazing. Having you back?" Her eyes misted, and she patted his cheek.

"We may have to hold off on those," he teased as he pointed to her hand on his face, secretly appreciating the affection.

"Nonsense." Maura added a pinch, then turned and greeted more trick-or-treaters.

His mind raced, struggling to make sense of his offer. He could easily slip into the role, help out, make up some excuse for taking time away from Chicago. It was good for him to remain busy. Keep everyone off his back about being home. Speaking of...he looked around and realized he'd lost Sandra and Alex.

Maura grabbed his shoulder. "Maybe you'll catch Dr. Harris? She's manning the *spooky* operation tables. I'm sure she'd love to hear the news from you."

"What news?"

Zachary turned to find Charlie emerging from the front desk. Today, her hair was twisted into a braid, with flyaways that floated in a halo effect. The cat ears were back, this time with the added touch of drawn whiskers and a triangle on the tip of her nose. She wore a snug midnight-blue knit sweater, depicting a black cat with gold eyes and a full moon, tucked loosely into a pair of high-waisted jeans. Her eyebrows raised above large glasses frames, this pair a solid black with a slight cat-eye style.

Those subtle details were intentional, and apparently, he knew to look.

"Is Daniel okay?" she asked.

Zachary straightened, the concern in her voice gutting him. "Yes. But I'm going to fill in for him. Here. Starting this week." Firm, to the point. *No need for emotions to get involved*.

"We have Monday and Tuesday covered," she replied, voice thin.

"Great. I'll start Wednesday."

She glanced at Maura, who was busy cooing over a family's bumblebee toddler and their matching golden retriever. "I don't think that's necessary," Charlie said.

He stepped toward her, his over half a foot difference in height causing her head to tip back. She widened her stance and put her hands on her hips. Slid them down her sides. Then crossed her arms.

"Look," he said. It took less effort than expected to soften his voice. "You're in a bind. Let me help out until stuff settles. We both know things only get busier with the holidays. It'll be even harder to find someone available on short notice."

She turned her head, probably to decide how to tell him to "shove it" amid children, but suddenly, Maura gripped both their arms, whipped open the half-door by the front desk, and shoved them behind it.

"Charlie, we're low on candy. Would you mind grabbing the extra bags I stashed in the kitchen? Take Zachary with you so you can sort out details. It's so wonderful having you home." Maura smiled at him and tossed her hands in a shooing motion.

He started to walk, but stepped on Charlie's heels. She hopped forward and gifted him a deadly scowl, and he raised his hands in apology. A huff and a whole lot of muttering poured from her as she turned and hustled down the narrow, dimly lit hallway, cackles and howls carrying from a speaker in the back.

Zachary followed to the small staff kitchenette. It was as outdated as he remembered, with pairs of plain, orange-hued oak cabinets above, and below, a small white tile countertop. Peeling black-and-white laminate flooring was bathed in a green glow from an illuminated skull set atop the fridge, but he barely registered that before realizing Charlie was bending forward and reaching so far into the lower cabinets, he was sure she'd find Narnia.

He shook his head slightly when he realized she was still muttering to herself, guaranteed it had to do with him and not how far she had to search for that candy, with her nicely rounded ass in the air.

He slammed his eyes closed and turned toward the doorway as though he'd caught her stripping. Then *that* idea raced through his mind, and suddenly, the kitchenette was stiflingly warm. This was Charlie, an old friend. He knew her when she was basically a kid. Not that their three-year difference was significant anymore.

"Maura's got quite a grip on her," he landed on. *Yes, neutral territory. That's good. Just stop* looking *at Charlie.* He swallowed. *Was my voice lower than normal?*

The cabinet door smacked shut, followed by a cool breeze as Charlie brushed past him.

He smirked, the chill in her demeanor not what he was used to from her, but certainly a distraction he was interested in seeing. In only a few strides, he caught up and landed in the office she shared with his dad.

Huh. That was something he hadn't considered in his hasty decision to work here. Seeing her day-to-day was one thing, but knowing they'd have lumps of time where they'd be crammed in this tiny room together...He couldn't decipher the odd jolt of energy it sent through him.

She closed the door, muffling Halloween tunes and sugar-filled shrieks.

He looked around the cramped room. Two solid wood desks were positioned under windows on adjacent walls, ensuring plenty of chair collisions. Both computers cycled through screensavers of pets in costumes, and the plain white window shades were drawn so the lamps draped in cheesecloth cast an eerie glow. There were piles of boxes stacked in the corners, and around one desk in particular—his father's.

He sighed. "Dad's still doing this with the files?"

Charlie plopped the bags of candy on her desk, then turned to face him. "This is actually better than it was," she said, arms crossed again.

"Better?" Zachary looked around the room in disbelief. Veterinary magazines were strewn on top of a few boxes, papers on *and* in between them. Never files for the patients, his dad would assure him. "*Just financial bullshit, I know where everything is,*" he'd say. It made Zachary's chest tighten.

"Please tell me he's had someone sort the important stuff," Zachary muttered.

Charlie stared at Daniel's desk, brow furrowed. He waited.

"You working here. It's obviously temporary," she said finally.

"Obviously." He could've toned down some of his disgust.

Her eyes jumped to his. "No one's forcing you to do this."

He held up a hand with a small nod of apology. "I'm here to help."

A beat of silence, then, "Tomorrow, noon. We'll meet while I'm on lunch."

"I can come in the morning, stay for the day."

She was already shaking her head. "I told you we have tomorrow and Tuesday covered."

"Yes, well, *this* looks like plenty to get a jumpstart on," he said, gesturing to the boxes.

Her gaze followed, and she nodded in relent. "It's a frightening pile."

"That's putting it lightly."

He saw a quick tug of a smile, but she straightened her face and her stance. "Zachary, are you really going to work *with* us?"

Her intentional phrasing made him pause. He was particular about work, and he didn't doubt that she remembered him rambling on about what he'd do differently from his father. He'd often push the envelope to try and introduce new things, only to be met with resistance. So it was a fair question. As far as his answer...he realized it wasn't so simple.

"I'm here to help," he said again.

Her eyes darted between his, then she turned back to the desk, muttering once more. She scooped up the bags and stepped toward him.

"Tomorrow then," she said.

"Tomorrow."

Silence.

Charlie flicked her fingers from beneath the giant bags of candy. "You may go."

He dipped his head, fighting a smile. "Nice costume, by the way. Looks familiar." He gave a little flick to a cat ear. "Although, this is new," he said, his fingertip adopting a mind of its own, grazing her soft, whisker-painted cheek. As though it hadn't been six years since seeing each other. As though they were still friends. As though he had every right.

"Sorry," he whispered, though he found the move hard to regret.

Charlie froze, eyes wide, and then blinked rapidly. She threw in a scoff, scanning his body. "Yeah, well, great job with yours. Get a toy sword and call it a day, huh?"

He looked down, having completely forgotten about the sword Alex insisted he wear. Tucked into his belt loop, the plastic thing was so lightweight and short against his long legs, it hadn't phased him. *Good thing I didn't lose it, little guy would've been crushed.* But he scoffed in return. "All a knight in shining armor needs."

She burst out a laugh, a one syllable sound that made him uneasy. "Of course that's all you think you need. An accessory. You can't even open the damn door!" She yanked the handle and swung open the door with a clumsy juggle of candy, and marched into the hall.

Zachary slowly pressed his fist on the doorjamb as he watched her, his body sliding to lean against it as his fingers went to his hair. Music and voices carried from the rest of the building, sounding much happier than the little bubble he'd just been in.

"Oh, and Zachary?" Charlie barely turned her body his way but definitely directed her glare. Her eyes scanned him, and she straightened, but the severity of her look had lessened. "I'm running the meeting, remember. This isn't an opportunity to jump back into the way things used to be." With that, she left.

The reminder she was the woman taking over the practice smacked into him. Yes, she should take the lead. She was determined to do so. But that didn't mean he couldn't have a say in *his father's* practice.

His fingers slid together with the memory of her soft skin.

It didn't matter how long he'd been gone. He was ready to prove he was needed.

Chapter 5

Charlie

Charlie cut through the short path in the park. Large maple trees with vibrant bursts of orange and red dotted the area, a view that normally stopped her in her tracks. Now there wasn't time to admire its beauty, with the cool air fueling her frustration and speedy steps. This was no cozy fall evening for Charlie.

"'*Here to help*,' yeah," she muttered.

She emerged on Main Street, where shocks of yellow from slender ginkgo trees alternated with black wrought iron lamps along the sidewalk. Their warm light buzzed as dusk settled, and the breeze bopped the witch hat and pumpkin paper lanterns hanging on the posts. Century-old red and cream brick buildings lined the road, housing small businesses, new and old, some there for decades. She passed the floral shop with the bridal shop upstairs, waving absentmindedly to the owners, and marched to Cleo's Local Goods.

She pushed open the door to laughter carrying through the empty shop, a melodic harmony to the bell announcing her arrival. The sugary smell from Dorothy's Bakery next door permeated the air.

Great. She wanted to vent, but the mood inside was softening her edge. And triggering her need for more cookies.

"Hi!" Amber appeared from the back, costume intact. She weaved through display tables garnished with bats and crows, but despite the apple blocking her face, Charlie saw her smile drop. "What's wrong?"

"Zachary's back," Charlie blurted.

"Oh! *Ohhh.*" Amber guided Charlie to a small counter where they served customers samples of local teas for sale. She poured Charlie a cup. "Spill. Not that tea," she joked, chuckling at herself but steeling her expression when Charlie gave her a pitiful snort.

Charlie took a sip, warmth seeping through her as cinnamon and ginger danced on her tongue. She inhaled the spicy scent, reminiscent of eating apple pie in an orchard, her shoulders settling. "He's going to fill in for Daniel."

Amber clapped. Then stopped. "This is bad?"

"We haven't worked together in years."

"That's okay! You two got along so well, I'm sure you'll fall into a rhythm right away."

"I'm going to be in charge this time."

Amber wiggled her eyebrows, indicated by the slight bob of her hat. "Exciting."

Charlie groaned. "You don't understand. He has a very specific way of doing things. He used to tell me all the things he'd change if he were in charge, and he'd argue with Daniel constantly."

"You're not Daniel, though. And Zachary's been gone a long time."

"None of that matters."

"Why?"

Charlie flicked a hand with a small huff. "That kind of stuff doesn't just go away."

"Alright. So you might bump heads a bit. Or you won't. There's a lot on everyone's minds right now, maybe Daniel being sick will unite you or something."

Charlie turned the cup in a slow circle on the countertop. As slowly as Zachary's finger had trailed over her skin, his delicious scent delivered right to her nose while he dared to look adorable wearing a toy sword, likely to appease his nephew.

She shivered. "He's irritated with me for some reason."

"What? Why?"

She had her guesses, but she couldn't be sure. They'd never talked about it.

Amber leaned toward Charlie and stilled her futzing with a firm touch. "How could he hate you? Maybe it's a misunderstanding. That's possible, right?"

Charlie shrugged.

Amber nudged her shoulder. "You know what I think? All the feels are back."

"What!" Charlie scoffed. "No. Definitely not."

Amber let out a gleeful chuckle. "How does he look? I'm guessing he aged well, and that's part of the problem. Like you didn't think he could get any hotter?"

Charlie spun off the seat and approached a tea towel display. "Why would that make a difference?" Her fingers trailed over the fabric, screen printed with snowflakes and the words Stay Out Of My F*cking Kitchen. Maybe she just needed to buy him a candid towel as a welcome home gift to help get the point across.

"Uh, when it comes to your job, nothing frazzles you. You've run that office no problem when Daniel's been on vacation in the past."

Charlie whipped around. "Are you saying I'm frazzled? I'm not frazzled."

"Sure, is that why your voice sounds like it's about to crack? Or break into hysterical laughter any second?"

Charlie took a moment to compose herself. "Yes, okay, he looks great. And still amazing in navy hoodies, damn him." That detail had *not* skipped her attention.

Amber sputtered a laugh. "What?"

"But that has nothing to do with it! I'm telling you, something happened when he left, and he hasn't let it go. His attitude was immediate, even at the hospital."

"You saw him at the hospital? The first night?"

"Yes."

"And you didn't tell me?!"

"I did tell you! In my text."

"Wait, wait, wait. You mean the very detailed one you sent when I asked how you were doing? You responded 'I'm okay. Saw him. I'm home now.'" Amber crossed her arms.

Charlie winced. "See, I said I saw him..."

Amber rolled her eyes. "Yeah, right, definitely. How was I supposed to decipher that message?" She turned off the electric kettle and closed the tea canister. "So, how is he? All manly and grown? I know you were all about that jawline, but did you get a look at his ass?"

Charlie clenched a stack of embroidered cloth napkins. "He has one now, if that's the question."

Amber hooted. "You *totally* checked him out!"

"Hey, I still maintain he has a sexy jawline."

"That's just because it houses a smile that makes you swoon," Amber sang.

"You know, if I wasn't already feeling transported back to high school around him, this conversation would definitely do it."

"Oh, come on. When's the last time you actually talked about a guy? That wasn't Daniel?"

Charlie grimaced, her gaze finding Amber. "That's unsettling."

"You're telling me."

"Gah, you're a shit," Charlie said, shoving her way toward the seasonally themed candle display along the back wall. Maybe determining which fall scent matched her personality would calm her nerves. If Amber ever stopped cackling.

"Amber, leave Charlie alone," Cleo scolded, appearing from the back room.

Charlie's mouth dropped as she took in their friend. Cleo's tall, graceful frame was draped in a silvery-blue leotard with a wide neckline that exposed her dark brown skin. Short sleeves puffed around her shoulders, and elbow-length gloves glittered. A full tulle skirt floated to her calves like a dreamy waterfall.

"Oh my God, Cleo." Charlie breathed.

"Doesn't she look amazing?" Amber said.

Cleo gave them a modest smile, her lips painted a deep berry. "Sasha made this for the community production of *Into the Woods* last year." She swished the skirt slightly, and a crown sparkled on top of her loose, buoyant black curls.

"Wow. It's gorgeous," Charlie said.

Amber sighed, hands landing on her hips. "I thought you two were taking a break?"

Cleo feigned nonchalance, tidying up a table. "With the holidays, figured we might as well spend the time together. Nice and easy." She glanced around the shop, her deep brown eyes bright, silver glitter covering her eyelids. "Who's ready for a drink?"

Amber narrowed her eyes, looking between Cleo and Charlie. With a huff, she jerked her thumb toward Cleo. "She's closing up early. We're meeting Magnolia at River Bites. Join us, we can all gripe together! Free pretzel bites to any table in costume."

"Speaking of, you two are helping me with a costume next year," Charlie said.

"Is that a yes?" Amber asked. She tossed Charlie's cup, then bounded around the counter.

Charlie checked her watch. "I should go home and feed Toothless."

"Nice try. It's too early for her dinner," Amber said. She nudged Charlie toward the door.

Once they stepped outside, Cleo locked up behind them.

The crisp, chilled air snapped against Charlie's skin. She tugged at her sweater, surprised how unaffected she'd been on her walk over. "I left my stuff at the clinic," she said, turning toward the park.

"Oh no, no." Amber grabbed Charlie's arm. She marched them in a half-circle to face River Parkway. "If you go back, next thing I know, you'll be texting me from home."

Not a bad plan. "But my wallet," Charlie said.

"Walter's known us since we were in diapers. He won't let you go thirsty. If you still haven't added credit cards to your phone"—Amber gave Charlie a side-eye, then shook her head—"I'll spot you tonight."

"Face it, Amber will get you there no matter what," Cleo said as she wrapped her sweater closed, skirt blowing around her.

"You at least need to eat something," Amber protested as she tugged Charlie along. "This'll be good, though. We'll come up with a plan to help you manage Zachary."

Amber was right—Charlie handled things smoothly when Daniel was out of the office in the past. Unfortunately, it was hard enough finding relief veterinarians to step in when they had planned vacations, let alone when someone was sick. Logan Fletcher often filled in, but from time to time, they had a new face around the office. She could treat Zachary like a new employee. It had been years—enough time had passed that they could start over. They didn't *really* know each other anymore.

A trick-or-treat banner stretching across the cobblestone road *thwipped* in the breeze, and strands of hair whipped her face. She brushed at her cheek, her hand slowing, remembering his soft touch, the warmth of his fingers. His focus on her face. The clench of his jaw as their skin slid together in the smallest of places, though she felt it zing through her entire body. How quickly her mind traveled to what it would be like to reach up and hold his hand there, to lock eyes, to trace his lips.

She blinked rapidly, coughing to disguise her uneven breathing. As much as she preferred to be curled up on her couch with Toothless and a bowl of popcorn watching *The Office* play episode after episode, going out was a good idea. She needed to reset. Get her shit together. Steel herself against the week ahead. Her crush on Zachary was in the past, and what mattered was the practice. To keep it running for Daniel, herself, the patients, and the community.

And to prove to Zachary she could handle it.

***

Inhale. Fourteen and a half. Sixteen if she counted the lights. With her eyes closed, Charlie knew that's how many ceiling tiles stared down at her as she lay on the physical therapy table. It had become a calming technique over the years of her vaginismus treatment, but it couldn't quite calm her today. Not when she knew what waited for her at work.

Zachary Lee.

Exhale. She fanned her face and flapped the patient gown as she fought off immediate sweat. It had been a while since she'd had one of her spirals, their frequency lessened by psychotherapy and the anxiety meds she'd finally started. Her stress was high since Daniel's heart attack, with thinking about him and putting in nearly fourteen-hour days, checking labs, messaging clients, and catching up on notes. Zachary working in proximity could short-circuit her. Her brain already struggled to connect the dots between her high school crush and the irritable, sexy man—*Like, hello, Time. You did nice things with a person's physique.* But she felt him assessing everything that needed tending to during his stint at the practice.

A knock sounded, jolting Charlie back into regulated breathing.

"Hey there, Charlie. I have a student shadowing today. Do you mind if she joins your appointment?" Ali Porter peeked into the room.

"Sure, no problem." Charlie took another deep breath as she stared at the ceiling, mentally preparing.

Her physical therapist blew in with a focused and determined energy.

"Charlie, this is Morgan. She's working toward her degree as an OBGYN. Morgan, this is Charlie, a patient who's been with us for a few years now."

Charlie smiled back at the young woman, who appeared at her side. Morgan wore sky-blue scrubs, her chestnut hair pulled back and golden-brown skin free of makeup. She leaned against the wall, effectively giving Charlie space.

"Thanks for letting me join today," Morgan said.

"Of course," Charlie replied.

This sort of training didn't bother her. In fact, it made her feel like she was contributing somehow. Ali ran a successful full-service physical therapy clinic in the city, one of the few offices where pelvic floor treatment was available.

The widespread belief that a woman's pain was "normal" and could be fixed with medication or "dealing with it" ran deep, and finding actual proper care was difficult. Charlie had heard it plenty of times over the years. If she reflected on it, the reality made her vibrate with anger. That didn't even include dealing with insurance, like her recent procedure, where nondoctors denied coverage for something her obstetrician recommended she have done, simply because *they* didn't think it necessary. Charlie knew the word Botox is what threw them. It angered her that they would turn down something to help her medically, even after appeals, simply because in their minds they linked Botox to elective vanity care.

Ali set her thermos on the side table and rolled a stool next to Charlie. "How are you?"

"Doing well." Charlie smoothed the gown needlessly, her knees bent over a bolster.

"How's the body?" Ali asked as she opened Charlie's file, tucking a strand of blonde hair behind her ear. Her gentle demeanor and no-nonsense approach made the environment comfortable and safe.

"Body's good. Doing my stretches, some yoga." Charlie tapped her thighs, surprised at the rush of nerves. She'd been seeing Ali for years, started off twice a week for appointments, until she could wean off to weekly, then every other week. Now she was down to once a month, aside from this—a follow-up to her recent Botox injection.

"Bowels?"

"Still normal." Her work with Ali helped her body relax and ease up on stress all around.

"And the dilators?"

Charlie nodded. Those good old dilators, solid plastic for clinical work. "Much better since the Botox."

Ali's blue eyes sparkled with a bright smile. "Wonderful to hear," she said, jotting more notes. She set aside her file, rolled the sleeves of her checkered knit sweater up her fair skin, and reached for the massage cream.

Charlie watched Ali's methodical work on her inner thighs.

"Take a moment, relax a little. You feel a little tight," Ali said. "You okay?"

Charlie released a breath. "Stress at work."

"Ah." Ali waited another moment, checked again. "Okay, that's better." She worked on the muscles, then reached for an exam glove. "Alright, let's check the tissues." With her gloved index finger covered in lubricant, Ali carefully inserted the digit into Charlie's vaginal opening. She probed and stretched the tissues inside, holding a spot where Charlie felt a hint of that telltale burning pain.

"Do you usually start manually?" Morgan asked.

"Depends on the patient and where they're at," Ali said. "Charlie's come a long way. Since she's jumped to such a large dilator size, this works best for her."

Each person is different, all her therapists reminded her.

Charlie swallowed. "My very first appointment, Ali couldn't even insert her pinky because the pain was so intense."

"Really? Wow, you've made so much progress," Morgan said kindly.

Charlie had tried a number of different doctors over the years, her hope fading with each one, until she'd finally found a gynecologist who not only knew what she was struggling with—that it wasn't merely *in her head*—but also knew how to help. No penetration of any kind could happen at that point, tampons included. Once all her friends had started using them, it had seemed like a rite of passage, a sign of being older and mature. Going through high school without being able to offer a tampon to a friend, or sneaking a pad into the bathroom and tucking used ones low in the garbage can, had added a thick layer of embarrassment. As an adult, she knew people had their preferences. But she'd at least wanted to have a choice.

Now here she was, having worked her way through four dilator sizes that could be inserted relatively pain-free.

"Tissues feel great." Ali had switched to the dilator without Charlie batting an eye, which was a major improvement.

"Awesome," Charlie murmured.

"She had a muscle that moved and blocked anything from entering," Ali explained to Morgan. "This follow-up is soon after the Botox injection, but I'm not feeling the wall."

Thank God. "You know, my OB said it happened even when they put me under for the injection," Charlie said.

"Oh, wow," Morgan said.

That day had been a struggle for many reasons, especially in securing Amber's older sister as her driver while only divulging she was having a procedure with anesthesia. Brooke was oddly distracted that day as it was, so somehow, the stars had aligned and bought Charlie time. She hadn't talked to Brooke much since.

That next day, Daniel had experienced his heart attack.

"You've made *major* strides," Ali said, putting everything away. "Keep up with those stretches, your dilator work. Keep doing what you're doing. And work on here." Ali tapped her own forehead. "When you're ready to take that step, you'll know."

Charlie nodded, the words familiar, sinking in a little more than last time. "Thanks, Ali."

Ali gave her a small wave as she left.

"Nice to meet you," Morgan and Charlie said at the same time. They smiled, and as the door closed, Charlie released another breath.

She was close, she knew it. She'd been chipping away at the emotional and mental struggles that accompanied the physical, each little step unlocking when it was ready. It felt like the final thing was the anxiety surrounding her condition, to release the fear of an intimate relationship.

One day, the objective Charlie would overpower the subjective. One day, she could move past what she lost with her ex, the man who made her believe any sort of healthy and mutual intimate relationship wasn't in the cards for her. A man who worked around her physical condition for his own satisfaction, instead of working *with* her to show he cared. He hadn't cared, not really.

After years of working through this, Charlie knew her vaginismus didn't define her. Instead, she had to believe it made her stronger.

CHAPTER 6

Zachary

ZACHARY PUNCHED IN THE code for his buddy's garage door and ducked inside when it opened halfway. He paused for quad stretches, rolled his neck, then stepped through the interior door into the mudroom, where he was greeted immediately by a wet nose to his thigh.

"How's my girl?" Zachary squatted, grateful for Maple's greeting as the old dog swathed his face with kisses. "Did you just wake up?"

"Her hearing may be going, but her sense of smell is not," Jordan called out.

Zachary grinned and nuzzled Maple's soft ears, the floppy one getting an extra squeeze, before he took off his shoes and met his friend in the kitchen.

Jordan stood at the stove in a black T-shirt and sweats, pans sizzling, the gray quartz countertop featuring potato peels and mushroom scraps.

"I only did a twenty-minute run. Did you get up right after I left?" Zachary's mouth watered as he scanned the scrambled eggs and sausage. A *ding* drew his eyes to the air fryer, tucked below cherry wood mid-century modern cabinets.

"Mind getting the potatoes?" Jordan asked.

"What's the occasion?" Zachary removed the crisp, diced potatoes and set them on the counter.

"Was hungry," Jordan said with a grin. "There's enough for you, don't worry."

"I should be the one making breakfast," Zachary muttered.

"Nah, maybe another day. Help yourself." Jordan loaded up his plate, then propped his hip against the counter as he ate.

Zachary draped his running jacket over a blue sloped chair and sat at the round wooden table, while Maple settled beside him on stiff hindquarters. "Thanks for feeding her last night. I didn't expect to be gone so long."

"No problem. Senior dinner hour, I get it. Besides, we got some good bonding in, didn't we, Maple?" Jordan said.

Maple looked between them, then slowly laid down.

Zachary petted her silky head. "You're up next."

Jordan chuckled. He rubbed a hand over his curly high-top fade, his short-sleeve shirt exposing a *MADRID* tattoo in a typewriter font on his dark brown skin. "How was trick-or-treating?"

"The kids'll be running on sugar for weeks," Zachary said.

"Where's your candy?" Jordan pointed to Alex's toy sword by the mudroom.

"Yeah, completely forgot. Wore it to the hospital and back here," Zachary said.

"Aw, that's sweet."

Zachary rolled his eyes and chuckled. "Mm. How was your shift? Did you close?"

"Yep. The bar was the busiest it's been. People spilled onto the patio even though it was forty degrees and they were half dressed. Halloween itself will be crazy, though."

"You working that too?"

"Not at the bar, no. Thankfully. Mel has backup costumes planned if employees don't wear their own."

"You lucked out."

"I know better than to work for her on Halloween. She dressed me like her personal doll when we were growing up as it was. Damn older sisters," he said with a grin.

Zachary smiled. "Remember how she designed T-shirts for our moms to wear to football playoffs?"

"Remember? Pretty sure my mom still has hers!"

"Yeah, yeah, mine probably does too."

Their laughter faded. Jordan crossed his arms and ankles as he leaned against the counter, his bartending ear in full swing. "So. How's he doing?"

Zachary shrugged. "He was awake this time. The kids got him to smile a bit."

His friend nodded, then studied him for an extra moment, holding the silence. "Well, my shift starts soon, but we should go out tomorrow, grab a drink."

"You work at the hospital today?"

"Yeah, at noon."

Jordan was a full-time nurse at the children's hospital but pulled a shift or two each week at his sister's bar. He'd heard general stories about the kids Jordan treated, and honestly, it would weigh on Zachary to witness that constantly and then watch a bunch of adults piss life away.

"I don't know how you do it, all the varied hours. It's like a switch flipped when I hit my thirties—if I'm out til bar close, I'm hungover for two days. Just from being out late."

"Mm, yeah. You prefer the five-days-a-week, morning-til-night routine."

"Well." Zachary scrubbed a hand through his hair.

Jordan shrugged. "Gives me a different sort of energy, I guess. Helps to be around adults and their messy shit for a change. Seriously though, it'd be good for you to get out a bit, not just with your niece and nephew."

"Hey, they share candy with me."

Jordan chuckled, and Zachary stood to get food for Maple. Sensing his intention, she wobbled into a sitting position, her face somehow innocent and youthful despite the spray of white around her eyes and nose.

"I uh...I'm gonna fill in for my dad," Zachary said from the counter.

When he glanced over, Jordan was staring at him, eyebrows raised.

"I learned they're pretty swamped and haven't found someone to step in. Can't have them cancel all those appointments."

Jordan nodded slowly. "Do they know you were let go?"

Zachary cleared his throat. "No, not worth mentioning yet."

"Sure." He paused. "This is a temporary thing?"

Zachary set down Maple's food, then shoved his hands into his pockets. "Of course it is."

Jordan just nodded again.

"What?"

"Nothing. I think that's great."

Zachary shrugged. "Seemed like the right thing to do." He shifted his feet, uneasy under his friend's scrutiny.

"Well, you're welcome to stay here as long as you need." Jordan held up his hand before Zachary could argue. "You know that. You and the old girl." He nodded toward Maple.

She stared between them, panting happily, then returned to her food.

Zachary smiled and rubbed a hand over his mouth. "Thanks. Does it come with breakfast like this regularly?"

"In your dreams, man," Jordan said as he slapped Zachary on the shoulder.

"Thanks for...all of this."

"Anytime." Jordan nodded. "Alright, I have shit to do before I clock in. Drinks tomorrow. You can fill me in."

"I pretty much did."

Jordan gave him one more look.

"Yeah, alright. Where, Mel's place?"

"Not this week. But we should at some point. She'll want to see you while you're in town!" Jordan called as he headed toward his room.

While you're in town.

As though Zachary were here for a casual visit. A friendly passing through of his hometown to catch up with old friends. Not because his father had undergone a serious heart attack. Staying with his best friend eased some strain of being back. He wasn't a burden to Sandra, and while his mom would love to have him, he didn't need to be in the same house as his father.

Thank God his father would get to go home.

His phone buzzed. He pulled it from the pocket of his joggers and went to the guest room, Maple at his heels. Furrowing his brow, he saw a text from Bella Mazzolari, the one mutual friend he still shared with his ex-wife.

Bella: *So you know how I said I'd only share if it's something important?*

She followed it up with a screenshot from Anna's social media account that showed his ex-wife, smiling brightly for the camera, nestled against a man gazing at her with adoration. In Anna's arms were two small puppies with matching red bow collars around their short sandy fur. They sat on a bright white couch, in a bright white room, perfectly staged decor around them. If a picture could encapsulate Anna's dream life, both social media and reality, it was this one.

But the caption sealed the deal.

"Everyone, meet the love of my life, Xander. He swept me off my feet this summer! We've been enjoying a private start to our relationship, taking time away from the spotlight to form a solid base to our relationship, and I couldn't be happier. I'm so excited to announce that this handsome face will be joining my father's clinic as their new veterinarian! And I'm sure you're all dying to know—we were fostering these two little bundles of joy and are thrilled to say that we FAILED! We've officially adopted Percy and Gus, four-month-old Labrador Retriever siblings. The four of us can't wait to share our new adventures with you!"

Zachary stared hard at the words, hashtags blurring, as fragments of the post processed one at a time. Another buzz pulled him from his daze.

Bella: *You probably met him already? I wanted you to have a warning in case their relationship hadn't been exposed at the clinic. Am I too late?*

Bella: *Also, hi! Should've started with that...*

Zachary: *Hey, Bella. Haven't met him. They actually let me go.*

His phone rang.

"What the hell? When?" Bella's voice was groggy.

"About a week ago."

"That timing can't be legal!"

"It's not worth it. 'At-will' and all that. Got my severance, and I needed to get out of there anyway."

Bella released an exasperated, growling huff. "I don't like it."

He checked his phone. "It's so early by you."

"I know," she whined. "I've got a photo shoot with some of the girls for this fancy liquor. Have to leave soon and get across town before the stupid LA traffic gets terrible. Wait, it's almost six? I'm already screwed."

"Sounds great."

"Yeah. I really love it here," she said earnestly.

He chuckled.

Born and raised in Wisconsin, Bella had spent the last few years living in Los Angeles after appearing on a reality show called *Is This Love?*, competing for the love of that season's bachelor. She'd made it to the final five and became a social media darling. At a Chicago skincare company's grand opening event, she and Anna had connected and bonded over their Midwestern roots in the influencer world.

"Hey, I'm sorry it all went down like that," Bella said.

"It's fine. It's better this way. Things were too..."

"Toxic?"

He sighed. "Yeah. Besides, I've got other shit to worry about." He gave her a quick update about his dad and being home.

"God, what a shitty couple of weeks." A beat. "Does Anna know about your dad?"

"No. No reason to tell her."

"Hm." She brightened. "Hey, I'm coming home over the holidays. If you're still in town, we should meet up."

"Yeah, that'd be great."

Maple rested her head on his knee until he ended his call. He scooped up her forty pounds, and she curled at his side on the bed. Sighing, he ran his fingers through her soft, golden-red coat. He'd adopted her when she was about seven years old, not long after losing the dog he'd had since he was ten. Maple reminded him of his late pup, from their similar flowing fur down to the strip of black on their backs. He hadn't expected the instant connection with Maple, though. She'd been his bright spot the last few years, through the more tumultuous stages of his failing marriage and then divorce. Deep down, he wondered if Maple had been the final nail in the coffin of their marriage. Anna had thrown a fit when he'd brought home a dog considered a senior when she was hoping for a "cute puppy" to help boost her already successful online following. For home decor and personal care products.

Maple was his golden ticket. He'd definitely picked the right female companion.

Charlie would understand his draw to Maple. She'd always had a passion for rescues, had volunteered through high school. He guessed she'd only grown more passionate—and not just because of how she handled him yesterday. That defiant look in her eyes. Her determination to put him in his place. Those funny cat ears. The painted whiskers.

Maple sighed, content beside him, and he settled closer.

At some point, he should clear the air with Charlie. He'd thrown her for a loop, offering to work with them. And he hadn't been himself at the hospital.

Hell, he hadn't been himself for years.

***

Showing up early at his dad's practice was an escape. His mother wanted him at the hospital, and Sandra had suggested he entertain the kids after school. While he loved those little energy-suckers, being around animals was what he needed. So instead, he'd showered and headed to work. For now, his family suspected he had personal business to take care of. It didn't feel necessary to tell them he was filling in for his dad. Not yet, at least.

Maple joined him for support and to win over everyone, especially when he knew how unsettling his presence might be for some. Unaware of her responsibility, Maple was unabashedly happy to receive the kisses Maura rained all over her head as they stood with her behind the check-in counter.

"My, you're even more beautiful than your pictures! Such a stunner." Maura held out a dog treat to the old pup, who chomped it eagerly. When Maple sat panting, a huge smile on her face, Maura laughed and handed her another.

"That was her plan all along, you know," Zachary said, shaking his head with a smile.

"This old girl deserves it," Maura said.

"Yeah, don't I know," he said softly.

"Your dad still brings the dogs in from time to time." Maura gave Maple a final fluff of the ears and sat in her chair, only to have Maple scoot closer and rest her chin in her lap. "Oh my, such a love bug."

Seeing family—and those considered as much—love on Maple, slowly stitched up little pieces of his heart. Really, who could resist her sweet face?

"Maura, can you call the Pipers and coordinate a time for tomorrow to squeeze in Snow? Even if it's over lunch." Charlie flew in from the hall, avoiding looking at Zachary. She must've heard his voice because there wasn't an ounce of surprise at him being there early.

Maura's expression softened as she looked at Charlie, still petting Maple's head. "You've already shortened your lunch tomorrow."

"Shoot, that's right." Charlie chewed her bottom lip, her eyes scanning the walls in thought. "End of day, then."

"Dr. Harris," Maura said, her stern voice quiet.

Charlie's hair was pulled back in a low knot. Her scrub top of the day was a vibrant pink that matched her sneakers, the words You Gotta Be Kitten Me! printed across the front. Something inside him was pleased to see her cheery work attire continued beyond the holiday.

Why that was important, he had no clue.

"They've been through so much, I want to get Snow back on track," Charlie insisted.

Zachary watched a look of understanding pass between the two until Maura nodded in agreement, despite Charlie bending over backward for clients. It was a move he knew well from watching his father. But at this point, they couldn't afford to run themselves ragged. How could he leave here knowing Charlie was overextending herself?

Maura turned to help a client, and Charlie slowly faced him. Light makeup, mostly whatever made her eyes extra vivid behind her glasses. Those eyes looked tired, and he sensed an instant camaraderie, a feeling that frankly had no right being there.

"Zachary," she said.

"Harris."

She gave him her best *watch it* look, which disappeared when Maple trotted over to sniff her hand.

"Oh my, are you Maple?" Charlie cooed, crouching to greet his dog. "Aren't you sweet?" Maple licked her cheek, a gesture that heated Zachary in a way that only confused him.

His voice finally clicked into gear. "How'd you know?"

"Grandma Jeanie loves to show photos of her," Charlie said, petting Maple's crimped ear.

Right. He swallowed hard, watching Charlie whisper to Maple. "Thought I'd bring her by today while I got started."

Without giving him a glance—he couldn't blame her, his dog was the best—she replied, "Thought we were meeting at lunchtime."

"Considering the state of our office, figured it couldn't hurt to organize a bit."

"*Our office—*"

"Okay, Dad's side. His mess of a desk."

Charlie gave Maple a kiss on the head and stood. Zachary's eyes stayed locked on the spot where her lips had landed as Maple sauntered to him and sat. His fingers gently touched the top of her head, and all he could focus on was that Charlie's lips had been there last.

Yes, that is where her lips were. That's what happens when you kiss. Your lips touch a spot on someone—in this case, my dog. These are facts.

Why those details about Charlie stood out to him, though, when Maura had done the same thing moments before, was beyond him. Watching Maura, he'd been hit with a warmth through his chest only family could generate. Watching Charlie, that warmth burned into a sizzling heat that shot through his body and made his palms sweat.

His eyes refocused on Charlie, who'd been talking this whole time.

He cleared his throat. "What?"

Patiently, she repeated, "Dr. Fletcher is here today, so you'll have to work around him if he's in the office."

"Ah, right. Dr. Fletcher."

"Did you meet him yesterday?"

"No."

"Okay. He's great. He's stepped in before, during vacations, that sort of thing."

"I've heard."

Charlie raised her eyebrow, but when he didn't expound, she turned toward the hallway.

Zachary signaled Maple to follow, and he hustled after Charlie as though he'd lose her in the small building. He glimpsed her swaying hips before she disappeared into the office, and the narrow hallway felt empty, despite a tech who gaped at him as he passed.

A poster board taped to the wall stopped him, Maple following suit. It held a layout of the vet hospital and its parking lot, tags pinned in various spots with labels like Dog Treats, Bandana Tent, and Grill Tent.

Zachary's eyes widened. "Grill Tent," he muttered. He glanced next to the poster board at a sheet titled EFVH 40th Cookout Sign-Up. "Harris. Don't tell me the cookout's still on."

Charlie popped out of the office, and Maple's tail wagged. "Of course it is. Why?"

Zachary pointed to the form. "That's two Sundays from now."

"Yeah."

"Dad just had a heart attack."

Charlie furrowed her brow. "I know."

Zachary flipped his hand at the sheet. "We don't have time for this."

"We?"

"This can't be high priority right now."

"It's the fortieth one."

"So?"

Charlie returned to the office, voice taut as she said, "We've got it handled."

Zachary followed. Maple scoped out the room, sniffed a dog bed next to the desk, and promptly curled into it.

Charlie watched, her smile slight. "She got comfy quickly."

"She sleeps anywhere. Charlie." Her eyes shot to his. "Who cares what number cookout this is?"

"Zachary, *forty years*. That's a huge deal for your dad."

"Yeah, well, he won't be here for it, so what does it matter? Things happen. We've got enough on our plate, people can deal."

Charlie stepped closer. "This isn't just for the community. We do this for the practice."

He rolled his eyes. "The effort to put it on can't be worth the one or two extra clients we get, or the little money we earn from food."

"Remind me how long it's been since you've attended one of these."

He hesitated, taking the opportunity to remove his coat. "Some...years."

"Uh-huh. Did you know we bring in local vendors geared toward various pet services?"

"Again, supporting the community." Zachary crossed his arms, warding off her approach.

She took another step, coming toe-to-toe in the stifling room. "Yes, they get exposure. And they donate goods for a raffle, where all the proceeds go toward our Dale Fund."

"Dale Fund?" Zachary straightened at the mention of his childhood dog.

"Yeah. The program we started to help cover medical costs for pets in dire need. Strays or clients who need financial assistance."

He relented. "Okay, well, that's a nice addition to the event."

Her eyes brightened, determination fueled. "There are even a few game tents, also sponsored by people in the community, who lend their time to help us bring in more funds."

He grunted.

"And did you know that the rescue we feature typically ends up with applications for almost all the pets they bring?"

His shoulders dropped slightly. "I can get behind that."

Charlie crossed her arms, the phrase on her shirt perfectly framed. "Which tends to bring us more than 'two extra clients.'"

"Look, I get it, it's clearly more than what Dad started it as. It's impressive, actually," he grumbled. "Maybe we can just postpone it. People will understand."

Charlie straightened her glasses, lavender wafting up to Zachary's nostrils. "We're moving forward as planned. It's under control, everyone knows the drill. And it helps set us apart from all the corporate-owned clinics."

Again, he wasn't needed. Zachary tamped down the swirling emotions at the realization that the practice had grown, and he hadn't been part of those changes. But the woman in front of him certainly was, with her wide hazel eyes and frizzing hair that looked soft to the touch.

Zachary leaned forward, her small intake of breath catching him off guard as he narrowed the distance. It was her hair, that sweet, earthy lavender scent, inviting him closer. "This fund..." His voice sounded rough, his lowered tone accidentally...intimate.

Charlie nodded, her eyes bouncing between his, scanning his face.

"Named after Dale the Dog?"

"Yes," she whispered.

Zachary's eyes traitorously looked at her soft lips, the pale pink slightly parted.

Charlie swallowed. "Seemed only right, honoring the beloved Lee dog."

His eyes bounced back to hers as he straightened. "Did you name it that?"

She stared at him in silence for a beat. Finally, she nodded.

Why it mattered, he wasn't sure. His fingers twitched. He tamped down a sudden urge to reach out and touch her. To maybe hug her. But he and Charlie didn't have that type of arrangement. Or friendship. *Acquaintance.*

She turned toward her desk and flipped through a file absentmindedly.

"Well. Let me know what you need from me."

Charlie whipped around. "For the cookout?"

"Yes."

"You'll still be here?" Her mouth opened and closed. "Uh. Are you taking a leave of absence from work in Chicago?"

"I'm taking some time to help out my family."

"Right but—"

"Don't worry about it, Harris. Not your problem."

"If it means you working here, then it is. I thought you were only coming in this week."

"I never said that."

"That's what…" She blinked rapidly, bit her lip as she shook her head slowly. When she spoke again, her mind likely racing, her voice was quiet. "Why'd I think that?"

"Maybe you were *hoping* for that."

The whimper she let out made him squirm, her despair palpable. She swallowed. "How long will you be in town, Zachary?"

The nerves that radiated from her balanced him. "Long as we need."

CHAPTER 7

Charlie

It was too much to process. Her emotions were running the paces.

Also, Amber was right. All the feels were rushing back, and she felt her inner teenage crush rear its bumbling head. For a moment, her mind went rogue. Zachary, sliding his hands around her waist and pulling her to him, unable to wait any longer to kiss her senseless. It had been *years* since that fantasy last surfaced.

How was that cocky half-grin as hot as his full-on smile? And the stubble on his jawline? She'd been indifferent to facial hair before but had a feeling he could grow a beard down to his clavicle and she'd offer to oil it for him.

Shit. Thoughts of oiling him up would *not* help.

She gulped. "I didn't think you'd be working with us beyond this week." As though repeating the sentiment would help.

He shrugged broad shoulders, the waffle cotton of a long-sleeve navy thermal flirting with his lean muscles. "Makes sense to, don't you think? I can take Dad's spot until he's no longer out of commission."

"You'll stay *that long*?"

"Jesus, you don't have to sound so repulsed by the idea," he muttered.

If only repulsed *was what I was feeling.*

"How many weeks out are you booked solid?"

She squinted at him. Considered lying, except he'd learn the truth soon enough. "Two months."

"Then I'll make sure you're set at least until then." He brushed his hand over his head, and she registered the tousled strands as they flipped against his forehead.

"Uh-huh," Charlie replied numbly. "Oh!"

Dr. Logan Fletcher's appearance in their office startled them both. Maple merely raised her head a few inches and studied their new visitor.

"Whoa! Full house we have here." With an easy smile, Logan reached out his hand toward Zachary. "Logan Fletcher."

Zachary shook it, voice firm. "Zachary Lee."

Logan's blue eyes brightened. "I've heard so much about you!"

She watched Zachary's face harden at Logan's obvious comfort.

"Nice to finally meet you. I always enjoy working with this team." Logan gestured toward Charlie with a wide smile that had made him the cover of the local emergency veterinary hospital pamphlet. His focus fell to Maple, who perked at his approach. "Hello there, aren't you a lovely lady?" Logan said as she gave him a sniff and lick of approval. Maple rested her frosted face between her two front paws, and he turned a genuine softness back to Zachary. He was like a shiny penny, his blond hair and chiseled jawline—and strong veterinary skills, of course—fresh and around for only a while. "Really glad to hear Daniel's doing alright. Charlie mentioned you'll be stepping in for him. I'm sure he's relieved."

"Yes. Charlie and I have everything under control," Zachary said.

Charlie shivered. He said her name with such intent. She'd replay it in her mind if she wasn't so irritated by him upending everything. His decision to work with them, no end date in sight. An early arrival, despite her insistence. Frustration about the cookout she had completely under control.

She wanted to yell at whomever told him navy was his color while running her hands over the soft weave of his shirt, reveling in the contours of his chest.

If she wasn't careful, he would bulldoze his way through the practice. She'd given herself a pep talk that morning, determined to focus on work and handle Zachary's presence for the week. A few days of him helping out wouldn't equate to enough time for him to rock the process. But longer? There was no way he'd be able to help himself. Such confident comments from him in his one-sided standoff with Logan reminded her to stick to her plan.

"Logan, Zachary will be shadowing a bit today."

That brought Zachary's attention back to her, his eyebrows slowly rising. She swore she saw a smirk tug at his lips. "Shadowing," he murmured.

She waved at the boxes. "And handling some paperwork." She steeled an assertive look at Zachary. "The kitchenette has a little table that should work just fine."

"No, no, you work in here," Logan said. He stepped between them to clear the few things he had at Daniel's desk. "I don't need much space, you know that, Charlie. I'm only here through tomorrow. He should have access to the office."

All the while, she couldn't tear her gaze from Zachary's, awareness brightening his saddened eyes. That had definitely been a smirk in hiding because now it appeared in full splendor, punctuated by laugh lines that cited his amusement at her frustration.

She clenched her fingers. Logan was only being accommodating—the man never made waves—but paired with Zachary rolling in like the boss's son, it rankled.

She managed a smile. "Thank you. I have to get into surgery." She moved toward the door and called over her shoulder, "See you at lunch, Lee."

***

"Oh, dear God." Charlie stood in the doorway, the tired gray carpet covered in piles.

Zachary sat at Daniel's solid oak desk, chin propped on his hand, flipping through paperwork. At the sound of her voice, he glanced up, then looked at his watch. "That went fast."

"So did this explosion," Charlie said as she stepped around the stacks, balancing her lunch high as though that'd help her avoid making a mess.

"Careful!"

She glared but made it to her desk without incident. "Please tell me this will be gone by the end of the day."

"I can't promise anything," Zachary said, returning to the pile in front of him.

Charlie scoffed. "We can't work like this."

"Why didn't Dad delegate anything to Maura?"

Charlie sighed. "He passed on a couple things to her, but he doesn't include me in any of it either. We tried to convince him numerous times."

Zachary muttered to himself, then said, "How do you stand being in here?"

"Guess they became part of the room for me too."

He glanced at her desk. "Never mind. Makes sense now."

"Hey!" Charlie looked at her desk, slightly offended. Sure, there were piles, but they were *organized* piles, one on each side of the desk. She knew where everything was, and the keyboard and mouse pad were visible, unlike Zachary's. She glanced at the rest of the office. "I'm not liking *this* at all."

He spun his chair around to face her. "Have you two really never talked about it? Discussed a better system—wait, I mean discussed *a* system because this sure isn't one." He hesitated. "He trusts you, he'd hear you out."

Charlie paused, her hummus and celery halfway to her mouth. He'd barely forced out those words. "I've brought it up, yes. He acted like he had things under control, though. Switched conversations..."

"How can you run a business like that?"

She almost nodded in agreement to what she thought was hypothetical, then realized he was actually *asking* her. "Wait, what? I'm not involved in anything beyond paperwork pertaining to the patients I treat."

Zachary crossed his arms and leaned back in his seat. "Doesn't bode well for the future. There's no proactive spirit in that. How could he feel comfortable leaving the practice to you?"

The hummus slid off her celery, landing on her desk with a tiny *blup*. This was the first time the two of them had discussed the practice transferring to her.

She waved the now naked vegetable at him as she swiveled her chair his way, a few feet of frustration hovering between them. "How dare you suggest that I wouldn't take care of this place?"

He shook his head. "Dad's planning on retiring in what, a couple years? Why isn't some of this on your plate now?"

Charlie had mentioned this exact concern to Daniel. She knew full well she had plenty to learn. Treating pets? Her dream career. Working with the community? She had a good rapport with people. But the business side of things? The finances? Looking at spreadsheets and dealing with money was the most unexciting task she could think of, but that didn't mean she had a problem learning it. She was well aware owning her own practice was a large undertaking and had forced her way through a business degree for that explicit purpose.

"That isn't for you to decide," she said through gritted teeth.

At some point, the two of them had leaned forward in their rolling chairs, knees inches apart in the tight space. Zachary's hands gripped the armrests, while Charlie still waved that piece of celery in the air, her other hand squeezing her thigh.

"Heyyy, Dr. Harris, Dr. Lee." Their lead tech, Jasmine, stood in their doorway. "I'm just gonna close the door, give you some privacy." With a sheepish grin, she shut the door.

Charlie and Zachary locked eyes. He leaned back, and she crunched loudly on celery, quickly shoveling in another piece covered in enough hummus to make up for what was already in her mouth.

She watched from the corner of her eyes as he rubbed his forehead. This wasn't the Zachary she remembered, the one who came home from college for the summer to find an eager sixteen-year-old working for his father, who was just as eager to talk with her about all things animal related. She'd picked his brain, and he'd happily taught her some new things he'd learned in school. She could admit she'd looked up to him, and he'd shown pride at filling that role. He'd also listened to her stories about working at the animal shelter with a genuine sincerity. She'd gained a friend who cared as much as she did.

This Zachary seemed...lost.

"Look. I'm..." Zachary sighed. "I shouldn't have gone there. I know this isn't your doing." He gestured to the mess around them.

It was a start. "I mean, this is actually *your* doing," she said, pointing to the stacks covering the floor.

She immediately regretted it, making light of the moment instead of pursuing what was actually going on here. Her therapist would probably agree, but she shoved the thought from her mind as soon as Zachary met her eyes, that hint of a smile playing on his face.

"Well, before I run out of time, let's go over some things." She turned toward her desk and grabbed her notebook. She had a list of general information they shared with new employees, but she'd jotted down additional notes she knew Zachary would appreciate.

They discussed changes in protocols since he'd last worked there and a rundown of new staff. He wasn't familiar with their software, so Charlie made a note to have him briefed when he came in on Tuesday. Because, of course he was.

"Daniel's off day is still Wednesday, just not this week. Maura rearranged some of the appointments we had to reschedule, once we learned you'd be here. We'll start with a staff meeting, to get you acclimated with everyone."

"Fine," he said.

She looked at the time and stood. "This will be gone by end of day, right?"

He looked at the paperwork. "We'll have cleared floor space."

Charlie shook her head.

"Hey, before you said something about corporate-owned clinics. Has it been bad here?"

"Yeah. I have friends I went to school with around the state, at least half of them have had their clinics purchased. One was by a smaller company, and it was pretty seamless. But the others were snatched up by—"

He leaned forward. "Neptune Corp?"

"Yes!"

"Damn. They bought the clinic nearest ours in Chicago. Nearly unrecognizable. Would've been bad for business, but our clientele has very specific taste and the corporate mold didn't work for them."

"That's lucky, then."

A knock sounded at the door. Maura peeked her head in. "Special delivery for the Lee family." She walked in, a foil-covered casserole dish in hand, and set it on Daniel's desk.

Zachary slid back like it would bite, the chair crunching over papers. "What's this?"

"The Schmitt family dropped it off. Mrs. Schmitt had an appointment this morning and heard you were here. Went home and baked your family a casserole. They send their best."

"Oh, well, that was...nice."

"Yes, dear," Maura soothed. "Want me to put it in the fridge?"

"No, no, I got it. Thanks." He stared at the dish as Maura left the room.

Charlie hesitated near the door. "You okay?"

"Yeah." Zachary furrowed his brow. "It's nice to see people are looking out for them, you know? My dad doesn't have many relatives here from Hong Kong, and the few that are here live in Illinois. I haven't even seen them in a long time; though, that's partly due to my ex. But I bet it's been a while for him too. I'm just...glad he's got all this love and support around him."

He stared at the gift, his expression adorably confused, a glimpse of his younger self showing. Charlie walked the few feet toward him, then placed her hand lightly on his shoulder.

He startled. His focus went to her hand, then traveled up to meet her eyes. The sadness there threatened to choke her, a vulnerability she couldn't remember ever seeing from him.

"You sure you're okay?" she asked softly. His frown lines weren't as deep as the ones when he smiled, but she stifled the urge to trace them just the same.

His eyes widened, and she worried her thoughts were written on her face. Just as quickly, he quirked the slightest half-smile. "All good, Harris. This is a very nice gesture. Mom and Sandra will be touched." He picked up the dish and stood, gesturing it toward her. "After you."

Charlie moved to the hall, her feet automatically taking her toward the kitchenette. "Wait," she muttered, whipping around. She was headed the other direction.

He was right behind her, his eyes zipping up her body to meet hers. She let out a nervous laugh, making to move around him, now hyper-aware of each and every step she took. It felt like she was taking exaggerated tiptoes, her arms tempted to balance at her side. *Move like your human self, Charlie, not a cartoon.* He pressed his back to the wall and let her pass, but she felt the intensity of his gaze.

She suppressed a shiver. There was something unfinished about walking away right now. Or maybe she just didn't want to? It was probably a strong desire to cover up her ridiculous walk.

"Zachary," she blurted. When she looked back to find him still standing there, watching her, that shiver reappeared, this time sending a parade of warmth through her body.

He raised his eyebrows, seemingly unashamed that he'd been caught.

"You can fill in for your dad at the cookout." She sensed his reflex to protest, so she continued. "The grill tent. Pretty straightforward. Should be easy enough for you to handle." She smirked as his eyes narrowed, feeling like she'd regained a little of her footing. To avoid giving him a moment to object, she hustled into room two.

CHAPTER 8

Zachary

"Anna."

"Oh, Zachary!" His ex-wife flung her arms around his shoulders, then glided her way into his downtown Chicago apartment.

He reluctantly closed the door, if only to prevent his neighbors from being part of whatever this fiasco would be. She'd reached out the night before, asking if there was a time she could see him. Considering Bella's tip-off, she must have been doing some sort of damage control, despite his inactivity on social media. Since he needed to grab things for work, he'd told her she could swing by his apartment during the one hour he'd allotted himself there.

"So. What's up?"

She paused by the edge of his sparse, plain kitchen and turned to face him, one perfectly manicured hand clutching her designer purse strap, the other holding a small handled bag. Her light brown eyes were wide with concern, her face and copper hair done up and perfectly placed. "Brought this for you."

He took the bag and peered inside, finding a wild, smoky loose leaf black tea, packaged by a small business in Los Angeles. His favorite. Coincidentally, one they had shared during her first social media influencer business trip to the West Coast. "Oh, thank you."

"I heard about your dad. How is he?"

Zachary reared back slightly. *How is he?* She had no relationship with the man. "He's doing fine. Recovering."

She nodded, free hand to her chest. "Thank God."

"How'd you find out?"

"I'm surprised you didn't tell me yourself."

His laugh sputtered. "You are?"

She looked at him like he was adorable. "Of course. It's not like we have bad blood between us. We're still friends."

Zachary raised his eyebrows.

Anna pouted, her lips dark pink against a machine-generated tan. "*I* consider us friends."

"Yeah, that's why you so generously fought for the house, the car, and as much of my money as they'd allow."

"Money you earned working for my father," she said firmly.

"Fucking Christ," he muttered. "It's been real, Anna." He reached for the door, but her words stopped him.

"Speaking of Dad," she said. "He's hired someone new, but you should know, none of it had anything to do with you."

He shook his head. "What?"

Anna huffed, popping her jean clad hip to the side, heeled boots on display. *Always a pose. Always intentional.* At one time in his mind, always sexy. "The vet happens to be my boyfriend, my new partner. But none of it had anything to do with letting you go."

The residual taste of his breakfast sandwich staled in his mouth, and his gut churned. "Sure, Anna. Okay."

"I'm serious, Zachary," she said with a huff.

He nodded. He really didn't know how much he believed her, but he knew it wasn't worth a fight. He needed to move on.

"Fine. Didn't have to come all the way over to tell me that," he said, opening the door.

She sighed again, then stopped in front of him on her way out. "Bella told me you knew, and I just felt like it was right to talk to you in person."

"I don't know what we cleared up, but I'm good. I've gotta get going, so..." He gestured toward the hallway.

Anna swayed out the door with one last pleading look, her eyes softer. "I really am glad your dad is okay." She added a small smile, then clicked away in her boots.

Zachary shut the door. There, at the end, that had been the Anna he'd fallen for in college. He'd felt her sincerity, surprised to realize he even appreciated it. A part of him missed their friendship, but she did everything she could to smother that version of herself from view. Eventually, that also meant Zachary.

He tossed the tea, which now felt more like a "sorry my dad fired you" consolation than a "thinking of you and your family" gift, on the counter. Pulling out his phone, he walked toward the living room. It felt empty without Maple there to curl next to him on the charcoal fabric couch or to lie on the orthopedic bed at his feet as he sat in the swivel leather armchair.

"Hi!"

"Bella Mazzolari, did you ream out my ex-wife?" Even though she couldn't see him, he couldn't help but smirk, knowing full well Bella was incapable of such a thing.

She released a full-body laugh. "Yeah, sure. I mean, I guess I did scold her a bit. Seriously though, the timing on her post was not cool."

Truth.

"Wait. Why do you ask?" Bella asked.

"She just stopped by my apartment."

"Nooo."

He laughed. "Yeah."

"Wow. Damn, I made it easy on her, didn't I? She knew you already knew about the boyfriend too."

"She wanted me to know that wasn't why I was fired," Zachary said.

"Good Lord," Bella muttered. "Why would she even suggest such a thing?"

"Guilty conscience?"

"Ha!"

He didn't want to consider the possibility that was why he'd been let go. Had his ability as a veterinarian really not been worth more than whomever Anna was dating?

"Hey, you still there?" Bella asked softly.

He scratched his head. "I know you're not in the veterinarian field."

She jumped in when he didn't continue. "Definitely not. But I love animals!"

His laugh was clipped. "Am I a good veterinarian?"

There was silence on the other end, and he immediately felt stupid for asking the question. For wondering about it so badly he'd ask a friend who had no idea of his ability.

"Never mi—"

"Zachary Lee. The only thing all this shit with Anna and her dad proves is that it is completely, one hundred percent *for the best* that you're no longer working there. They're caught up in some weird internet world of fancy veterinary clinics, including her father. That doesn't sound like the priorities of an animal hospital I'd trust for my pets."

He nodded slowly, staring out the large living room window at the high-rise across from him. He pressed his head to the pane of glass and looked down, splashes of red and yellow courtyard trees visible below.

"As for your abilities in your career? Yeah, I don't really know. I did hear of all the special acknowledgments over the years because Anna loved to brag about them. You also made my great-aunt feel very taken care of when she brought her dog to see you. That goes a long way in my book."

He'd forgotten about that.

"Thanks, Bella."

"Hey, anytime. I'm just sorry my conversation with her sparked an ambush."

"Well, she did acknowledge what was going on with my dad too."

"She did? Sorry, yeah, I...I may have let that slip."

"It's alright. She brought tea. Which probably wasn't so much about my dad because..."

"Because it's Anna."

"Yeah."

"Yeah. Ugh. Hey, looks like I'll be in Wisconsin a little sooner than I thought. I'll keep you posted? Would love to see your face. And I feel like I owe you dinner?"

They wrapped up their call. As he shut his apartment door behind him, though, he felt a sense of relief. This time, heading back to Elmwood Falls felt like going home.

***

"Are you gonna keep the gift?" Jordan took a sip of his beer.

Zachary sipped his taster, the orange and spice of the pale ale refreshing. "Yes. I love that shit—they make a mean tea. I can separate her from it." He paused. "Maybe this batch will just taste a little petty."

Jordan bellowed with laughter, then lifted his amber ale taster in a toast. "Good riddance. Hopefully, you're finally done."

"Been a year since the papers were finalized, and we were over well before that."

Zachary eyed his friend. Anna had been a different person when they'd first married, but once he'd announced their split, Jordan had been vocal about his support. Apparently, he hadn't been in the Anna Fan Club. Zachary had appreciated the support from family and friends—well, the friends he still spoke to—but when they voiced their dislike for her, he questioned his judgment.

It didn't matter anymore. It couldn't. He'd moved on, was done with anything serious—he wouldn't make that mistake again. In fact, this was the first time in ages where he felt like he was really considering what he wanted. Getting out of Chicago seemed to help him clear his head.

"What'd your dad say when you told him you'd be filling in while he's out?"

"Nothing." Zachary glanced around the brewery. The large warehouse space was divided, the back reserved for brewing and the front for the taproom with wooden high-top tables and booths over a concrete floor.

"Did you actually tell him?"

"Believe it or not, I did. Right before I left the hospital last night."

"Giving him ample time to actually talk about it with you then," Jordan said sarcastically.

"That wasn't the end of it," he grumbled.

Jordan laughed again. "Ah, Z. Lay it all out there. Rip off the Band-Aid. You both will be happier once you clear the air."

He knew he needed to. Years of hardly talking to his dad was sad enough, but continuing the charade well after his divorce, and with his father's health scare...it was losing its edge. The memory of when he'd approached his dad about working for his father-in-law, wanting to explain how that had evolved, still weighed heavily on his chest. Yet, it seemed like his dad had planned to give the practice to Charlie all along.

"Why do I have to be the one to do it?"

Jordan shrugged. "I don't know. But it feels like the right move, doesn't it?"

"My mom just wants one of us to make the move. She doesn't care who."

"I bet, especially with you home."

"She even told me I could move back in with them while I figure things out, if I want."

"Aw, her baby boy is back." Jordan chuckled and tossed back a lager. "I'm guessing everyone's excited to have you back at work?"

Zachary sat back in his chair and tapped his fingers on the table. "Not quite."

"Did you already piss someone off?"

"Why does that even come to mind?"

"Come on, Z. You were never shy about what you'd do differently if you were running your dad's place. I can't imagine that's changed. Especially after working for such a hoity-toity family for years."

"Maura seemed genuinely happy to see me."

"That's the office manager, right? The one who's been like an aunt to you?"

"Yeah."

"Right. So, basically, family. She doesn't count."

"There's been turnover, some new people. It's a really capable team. One of the techs taught me their software this morning, but I'd bet she knows as much as Maura. Everyone's really on top of things."

"Uh-huh."

"Just ask the question you really want to know."

"Okay. How are things between you and the woman taking over things?"

Complicated. "She doesn't want me there."

"Right. And the scowl on your face?"

Zachary felt the tension in his jaw, tried to relax his face, and realized he had no idea how. "Look, I can admit I haven't been...my best self around her."

Jordan smacked the table, throwing his head back with a laugh. As the cheerful noise finally faded, he wiped under his eyes dramatically. "Wow, thanks for that. I needed it."

"You know, I'm really starting to wonder why we're still friends, considering you seem to have such a low opinion of me."

Jordan gave him a light punch to the shoulder. "Listen. For as long as I've known you, you've wanted to be a vet. Talked my ear off about how you couldn't wait to have your own patients, to work alongside your dad."

Zachary swallowed the memory.

"You've always been passionate. Even when you talked about things you'd do differently, it was obvious you just wanted to keep things progressing."

He shrugged. "Why wouldn't we want to do that?"

Jordan nodded slowly. "When you started working with Anna's dad...I don't know...The way you talked about it changed."

Zachary considered that. "I was learning their way of doing things. Just like when I did my rotation."

"No, that's not what I mean. I heard less about animals and more about image, I guess. What they expected of you."

"That can't be right."

Jordan held up his hands. "Yeah, what do I know? You go off and work for a man whose practice has received national attention. A place that poured a shit ton of money into an expensive clinic and weirdly elaborate parties for their wealthy clients. Then you come home to your dad's small practice, where people from all around the city bring their pets because they know they'll get true mom-and-pop care. You're barreling in as if you haven't been in an entirely different world for more than half a decade." He leaned closer. "I know you. You don't do anything half-assed. That certainly includes your job. But at this point, what's familiar is what you've been doing lately, not what you grew up learning."

Zachary was quiet. Was that how things had been? Is that what people saw when they looked at him?

"You guys used to be friends, right?"

Zachary nodded.

"Yeah. You'll come back to us." Jordan gestured a stout taster in salute to Zachary. "There's hope for you two yet."

CHAPTER 9

Charlie

DAPPLED LIGHT FELL ON the smiling face of the tan pit bull mix, tongue spilling from his mouth as he patiently obeyed the command to sit.

"Got it. Okay! Such a good boy, Humphrey," Amber cooed over the sturdy dog as she held her camera, its thick strap across her body. The dog gleefully danced in circles.

Charlie grinned. "He's a fan of yours."

"Gah, he's so cute." Amber squatted and scratched the pup under his chin. She laughed as he slowly sank to the ground—careful not to disrupt the affection—and exposed his belly for more scratches. "You're an awesome guy, aren't you? I wish you could live in my apartment, but my landlord would flip."

"When's your lease up?"

Amber rolled her eyes at Charlie. "You're ridiculous." She took a beat as she looked back at the dog, then said, "January."

"Hmm." Charlie watched the two as Humphrey tugged on a rope toy Amber dangled above him. Chances were high that Humphrey would still be available by then, but Charlie figured it best to keep the thought to herself.

"You have so much energy, I love it! You'd be a great running partner, wouldn't you?" Amber rubbed her hands along Humphrey's face and placed a kiss on his head. The dog scooted closer, nuzzling his body against hers, and Amber looked at Charlie and mouthed, "Oh my God."

"So freaking sweet," Charlie said.

"Can you imagine your mom meeting him?"

Charlie snorted, knowing full well her love for animals didn't come from Penelope Harris. Not that her mom disliked them—it was more so a fear of them. Even a chipmunk in the yard would send her running inside the house.

"I bet you'd turn Auntie Penny around, Humph," Amber said, laughing when he licked her face. "God, that's so wet." She wiped her cheek as she stood, his panting gaze following her every move, until his mouth closed, head slightly tilted. "Oh no, did I insult you? Charlie, did I insult him? I didn't rub it off, bud, I rubbed it *in!*"

Charlie laughed at her cousin, who squatted and gave the dog more pets out of guilt, just as the owner of the rescue joined them outside.

"How'd our boy do?" Cory stopped next to Charlie, hands on hips, as he watched Amber practically roll around with Humphrey. "Maybe she'd be interested in doing a foster-to-adopt?" he murmured to Charlie.

"Maybe in a couple months," she whispered back.

Amber reluctantly stood, grabbing her camera and sliding through the digital photos. "Think we have all we need, Cory." She grinned, spinning the camera around to show Humphrey laying on his back, tongue dangling, as he stared at her hopefully.

"He's a cutie," Cory said. "Brian fell in love with him when we pulled him from the shelter, but we can't add to the brood right now. The wedding's a few months away."

"Uh, not to mention your four other dogs," Charlie said.

He shrugged. "You get it. How many animals have you fostered for us now?"

"Yeah, they're addicting." She sighed, feeling it like a smile that stretched to her toes. Nothing like a trip to her favorite rescue for a little mood boost.

"Cory, I'll have these to you before the cookout," Amber said.

"That's awesome. And thanks for checking on our two seniors, Charlie. I wasn't expecting you to still come our way with everything going on."

"You're so close by," she said. *And I needed to get out.* Stepping away for lunch was unusual for Charlie, but bumping into Zachary every half hour was throwing her off-kilter. And they weren't even through week one. "Besides, it's rejuvenating to come here." She smiled at Humphrey, rolling in the dirt.

"Well, we're looking forward to the event. Give our best to Daniel when you see him?"

"Definitely."

"Thank you, both. Alright, Humphrey, you ready for a walk?"

The dog started his hopping twirls, and Amber followed Charlie to the parking lot.

"You've been oddly quiet," Amber said.

Charlie tugged her fleece jacket tighter as she reached her blue sedan. She faced her cousin, whose brown hair was pulled back into a stylish ponytail, her bangs framing her face. Amber had that effortless way about her, whether working out or working. Or wearing an apple in her face. In her high-waisted straight-leg jeans and a loose-fit mustard sweater, she looked like a model of a photographer in a fall setting, her appearance complementing the few autumn leaves still clinging to the branches.

"We were busy."

"Sure, fine, whatever." Amber crossed her arms, gaze quizzical. "How's Daniel?"

"He's doing well, all things considered. It'll be a slow recovery."

"Hm. And how are things with Zachary?"

Charlie bit the inside of her cheek. The steady flow of traffic was more appealing than her cousin's prying gaze. Zachary had seamlessly worked himself into the fold the day before, his first official day, well received by staff during their morning meeting. She didn't want it to feel so natural having him back, but she sensed it irritated him how smoothly it went too. On the plus side, she was able to step out during her lunch and meet Amber at the rescue. "Well, he's going to be here at least through the cookout."

"Really?"

"Probably longer. He claims he can work with us until Daniel comes back."

"No shit."

"Yeah." Charlie gripped her head. "I don't think I can handle that, Amber."

"Because of his hotness?" Amber nodded sagely.

She groaned out a laugh. "No! Because he'll be watching everything I do, and after a couple weeks—maybe only one—he'll squeeze in his way of doing things. I just know it. He's already wearing his white coat every day, even though Daniel loosened on that years ago." Though, the white coat mostly bothered her because he looked delicious in it.

"Then tell him to knock it off."

"I don't have the 'won't take bullshit' gene. You and Brooke got that."

Amber snorted. "Brooke isn't half as good at it as me."

Charlie couldn't help the chuckle that came out, but it turned into a small whine. "I don't know what's wrong with me."

"I do. You've got the hots for him."

"Amber..."

"It's true. You always straighten out staff when there's an issue, and you've had no problem voicing concerns to Daniel directly. I guess there's a small chance it's just a warm-up period. You know, to be comfortable around him again. But my money's on the hotness."

"I hate you." Charlie unlocked her car door and opened it, tossing her tote bag inside.

"Oh, you wound me." Amber laughed. "That's a pitiful insult, even for you."

"Shut up."

"So when can I meet him?"

"You're not helping."

"Brooke knew him in high school. I bet she's got some dirt on him."

"That's just playing into it all the more. I'm an adult woman now." She settled into the driver's seat. "I can handle this."

"Sure. Yeah. That's what this whole conversation proves." Amber stepped back as Charlie closed her door, then tapped on the window.

Charlie hesitated but rolled it down. "What? I have to get back."

Amber rested her hands on the open window frame, her trim, midnight-blue nails gripping the edge. "You're going to be fine. It'll probably be a smoother transition than you think. You'll hardly run into each other with the schedules you keep, right?"

Charlie released a breath through puffed cheeks until they deflated.

"I bet you won't even notice he's there."

Charlie let out a short "Ha!"

"Hey." Amber poked her. "Saturday. Drinks with everyone."

"Everyone?"

"Yep." Amber wiggled her eyebrows. "Even Brookie will be joining us. Thank God, because she won't tell me what's going on, but I *know* there's something."

"That sounds great, actually."

Amber squealed. "Sweet. Whiskey Nights. Seven thirty on Saturday. We'll get a table." She leaned into the car and gave Charlie a peck on the cheek. "Love you, cuz!" She trotted away before Charlie could say a word.

Charlie took a minute, contemplating. An actual girls' night out was long overdue and would be a welcome way to tune out everything else. To forget about...people. The thought alone eased her return to the office. Maybe they'd have a nice few days to wrap up a weird and stressful week, and she and Zachary could shake this awkward reunion.

CHAPTER 10

Zachary

"So how long did you say you'd be in town for?"

Zachary kept his eyes away from the client and instead on her Maltese, whose bright pink bows bobbed in the way of an ear inspection. "No end date at the moment. When was Muffin's last checkup?"

He could easily check the paperwork, but it was better to keep this woman distracted.

"A year or so ago," she purred, tilting her head so her blonde waves could swing over her shoulder. Her elbows rested on the small exam table across from Zachary, the low-cut top of her shirt creating a display. "How long has it been since you've been back?"

On a night out, he'd have no problem with the obvious signs she was throwing his way. But today, and at work, he wasn't feeling it. It could be due to the strain at the practice—they were overbooked, and at rates he'd discovered hadn't been updated in ages. Could be the major health scare with his father, which he still hadn't processed. Could be that he didn't have a job to return to.

Or could it be his current *boss*, the woman who made him run hot and cold?

She'd been oddly quiet the day before—unnerving. His second full day in rotation with them had gone smoothly, but she'd kept her distance. He'd watch her smile and laugh with staff, but barely nod to him in passing. Just as well, since he'd been completely focused on *not* fucking up so he could prove his presence there was the right one.

Today, she'd waltzed into their office from the morning storm, wearing that brightly striped raincoat, and he'd felt a sense of relief as she joked about it raining cats and dogs. She even chuckled at her own words as she said them, knowing how well-worn they were. Her enjoyment had made him smile. Then she'd informed him he'd incorrectly entered notes into the server, which pissed him off not only because he'd spent extra time double-checking his work, but also because she was the one to catch it. Then she'd revealed a scrub top with rainbows and kittens and puppies, and he'd *literally* felt his blood pressure drop. Being around her was like a hit of cardio.

"Dr. Lee?"

He'd been inspecting the dog on autopilot, preferring his own thoughts to this ill-timed conversation. He fumbled for her last question.

"Uh. It's been about six years," he answered. He stepped to the computer and entered some notes. "We'll run a full blood panel on Muffin since she's due, make sure everything is good. But otherwise, she looks healthy."

The woman walked over and placed a hand on his forearm, her chilled, pale fingers spearing the sleeve of his white coat. "I really appreciate it. I'd love to take you out for a drink, help you get reacclimated to the area. Maybe tonight?"

"Thanks, but I can't." He glanced at her with a quick smile, then back to the monitor.

"How about tomorrow night?"

"Thank you, but no, Ms..." He scanned the screen, trying to locate her name.

"Please, call me Anna."

Hell, no.

He cleared his throat as he closed the file. "Thanks for the offer, but no. Jasmine will be in shortly to get bloodwork, and we'll be in touch. About Muffin." He closed the door on her open mouth. Grateful to find Jasmine in the hall, he gave her the update and hurried to his office.

That was the last appointment for Friday, but he'd be sticking around a few more hours. He still had his dad's paperwork, and apparently, plenty to fix from the day before.

Rounding into the office, he stopped in his tracks, finally registering the quiet. The sound of shuffling footsteps as techs cleaned up faded as he looked into the small room.

Charlie had a hip to her desk, her arms tight against her stomach, staring out the window as wind whipped the trees. One hand moved up and down the opposite arm in a soothing motion. The gray of dusk cast a filtered glow, highlighting the mess of her loose ponytail. The sight of her made him hold his breath. She was the stillness and, yet, embodied the storm. He didn't want to break the spell, but he needed to know what cast it.

"You sure do make good use of the view," he said. Immediately, he regretted the simple words, which were no match for the glistening hazel eyes that turned his way. Without thought, he was standing next to her. "Charlie?" He said it softly, reverently. Not wanting to add a wave to whatever had rocked her.

She looked into his eyes, blinking rapidly to fight back tears. Their honey and green hue was amped up to amber and moss, the muted light hitting her from the side, her lashes damp and richly dark. Light pink splotches dotted her face, and Zachary reached out to touch her arm.

"Hey, Harris, what's wrong?"

She shook her head slightly, not moving away from his touch. She closed her eyes for a moment, took a deep breath, then let it out. "We lost a patient today. Eighteen-year-old cat. His dad—this sweet old man—has been sick, and his caregiver brought the cat in today." She let out a sad laugh, using it to step away from Zachary. "It's never easy. Not sure why this one's hitting me so hard."

Zachary watched her tug her hair free and whip it into a knot on her head, swiping under her eyes as she cleared her throat. Suddenly, all he could picture was high-school Charlie, the first time she'd been assisting at the clinic when an animal was put to rest. He didn't know her well at the time, but he remembered everything about her in that moment—the teal scrubs, black metal glasses framing glistening eyes, the way she bit on her lip to stay composed, like it was a test to pass. All he'd wanted to do was hug her and tell her it'd be okay.

He didn't do it then, but watching her hands shake as she picked up her glasses and wiped the lenses, he could hold her now.

Zachary moved slowly, not wanting her to bolt, but giving her time to voice if she wanted space. Instead, her hands stopped moving, her eyes aimed at her desk. She bit that lip again, probably trying to fight whatever emotions wanted to burst free. He placed his hand gently on her shoulder, and when she leaned into his touch, guided her to face him and pulled her close.

Although he told himself she needed the comfort, as soon as she was in his arms, he realized how selfish the act had been. *He* needed her touch—when Charlie's arms went around his waist, he released a contented sigh. That subtle scent of lavender wafted off her hair, and as he slid his hand up and down her back, she let out a wobbly breath. While it must have been in relief, the sound triggered satisfaction in him that he'd succeeded in caring for her, and he felt a surge of pride. His hold on her tightened.

"Oh, no." Charlie pushed back from Zachary. "Oh, shit, Zachary..."

"What?" He was confused by her flustered state, eager to rewind a few seconds.

She opened her desk drawer and yanked out a wipe. "Great, I messed up your perfect coat. And your perfectly tailored button-down. For crying out loud, don't you own other colors..."

He stared dumbly at her hands as she gripped his navy shirt with one and blotted furiously with the other. Her eyelashes fanned over damp cheeks, her nose pink.

And her cheeks burned red. "We had an old dog with an anal gland abscess right after the cat. I didn't expect..."

"Nothing I'm not used to," Zachary said, his voice oddly rough to his own ears.

Her blotting slowed, and she pulled back to observe the wet patch on his coat and shirt. She pressed her lips together, then offered a consolation pat on his shoulder. "You know what?" She tossed the wipe into the small garbage bin, then shoved folders around her desk like a TV background actor, needing direction. "You were too pristine anyway. You probably manage that like, every day, don't you?"

He stilled her, his hand on her elbow. "Hey. I'm sorry you had a shit day."

She sighed and looked at him with a tilt of her head. She seemed to give in to some secret decision as she said, "I appreciate your kindness."

He laughed, surprised by her formal response. Her answering smile stretched full across her face, and Zachary's breath stuttered. She looked at him like he mattered, like she enjoyed the person he was. Like she was really seeing him. A lightness eased his shoulders, as though she had whisked away everything that weighed on his mind. She had to know how much power her smile held, and yet, the glimmer of affection he saw in her eyes told him she had no clue. She was just being Charlie.

A spark of lightning filled the room, pulling their attention to the window. They watched it for a moment, silent, and he found himself counting in his head until the thunder rumbled.

"To be honest, the cat made me think of your dad." Charlie said it softly, still looking out the window. Zachary focused on the rain as it cascaded along the pane of glass, afraid taking too deep of a breath would stop her. "I was with him the first time. I'll never forget how caring he was, to the pet, to its family. Even to me. He provided this *warmth* to everyone, like he was wrapping the entire moment in a loving blanket. I've always strived to live up to that."

Zachary knew. He knew when it had been Dale's time, how much he'd wished his dad had been there beside him.

"I think I missed him today," Charlie said, her voice cracking. "Which is silly, he's alright. He's going to be alright." Though a statement, there was a hint of a question to her words.

It was true—he was doing well, considering. But his doctor had hinted at a long recovery. Something the Lee family hadn't really dissected yet.

For now, Zachary could answer Charlie as honestly as possible.

"He's going to be okay. They're making sure of it. And you know my dad, he won't let it be any other way."

Her eyes softened, her smile fond as she faced him. "Daniel's as stubborn as he is kind."

He grunted, uncomfortable with the truth. "That's for damn sure. They're um, treating him for hypertension. Thinking stress led to all this."

Her eyes darted between his. "He's been working too hard. See, I knew I shouldn't..."

She hadn't voiced the rest of her thought, but it started much like his own. Like, *if I'd never left...* Not her, though. What could she have done? He wanted to touch her hand in reassurance. Thank her for being a good partner to his dad. For looking out for him. He wanted to apologize for his actions and words. But he didn't want to scare her off. He slipped off his white coat and draped it over his chair, her eyes tracking his movements.

"I'm going to fix my files in the system," Zachary said.

"Oh! Great."

"Jasmine wrote up notes on what I need to do."

"Yeah, she's an expert at it. Keeps us all in line."

"I, um, I did have a couple questions, if you have a minute?"

He had no clue what he wanted to ask her. Jasmine's instructions were *very* clear, even using one of his mistakes as a detailed example. At the risk of feeling stupid, he wanted her nearby more.

For the next half hour, he managed to find enough to keep her around—including making more mistakes in front of her, which was *not* part of the plan. It gave him plenty of time to memorize the flicks of her wrist as she pointed at the screen, the square shape of her bare fingernails, how small her hands looked next to his. Just when he found himself about to comment, to measure palm to palm—what was *wrong* with him?—she scooted back in her chair.

"Wow, I didn't realize the time. I need to feed Toothless." She moved to pack up.

"Toothless?"

"My cat." She draped her purse over her raincoat and gave him a look. "You gonna be alright finishing this on your own?"

He scoffed. "I could finish this in my sleep."

"That's what we might accuse you of," she said, heading to the door. He laughed, and she stopped just before disappearing into the hall. "You know, Jasmine has a lot on her plate. We don't have time to hold your hand, Dr. Lee."

Zachary dipped his head, grinning. "Understood, Dr. Harris."

"Hm," she hummed, a smirk playing.

The room bounced with light, and a clap of thunder sounded, this time closer.

"Yikes. Okay, I should really go," she said.

"Be careful," he said. "Um. Of course you will be. It's just...habit. Dad says that to us all the time."

"I know," she said softly.

"Right." He tapped his desk, brow furrowed at the thought that his dad went around saying that to other people. Come to think of it, he couldn't remember the last time he'd heard his father say it. The habit had been instilled in Zachary since he was little, so it had felt natural to do it with Anna. By the time they were married though, she'd rolled her eyes at the sentiment, getting insulted that he thought she wasn't a great driver. Embarrassingly, he'd never considered the words from that point of view before. Saying them now, to Charlie, he felt an entirely different meaning attached. Possibly the one his dad had meant all along.

"Zachary?"

He looked up at her.

"Thanks."

He swallowed with a small nod.

"Goodnight." Her smile was small, but the sadness from earlier had lessened.

"Night," he said, the word soft.

She stepped backward into the hall until she was out of sight.

Though she definitely wasn't out of mind.

CHAPTER 11

Charlie

ANOTHER RESTLESS NIGHT, THOUGH this one wasn't consumed by concern for Daniel's health or the practice. Instead, this restless night bulldozed in with the storm.

And thoughts of Zachary.

She couldn't get comfortable, not when every time she closed her eyes she pictured his, gazing at her with such concern, wanting to help in some way. In his protective embrace, she'd been eager to accept it.

His hugs were better than she remembered.

Toothless had been no help as Charlie had paced, gazing at her through sleepy golden eyes from her curled up spot on the bed. The sleek black cat did offer a snuggle session when she'd finally crawled in beside her. After one too many position adjustments on Charlie's part, though, Toothless had abandoned her to sleep in the living room. Which left Charlie physically alone, wishing further that those powerful arms and woodsy scent were surrounding her again.

***

She went into Saturday morning determined to be normal—which basically meant not giving off vibes she'd been up all night thinking about him. So when she arrived early, confident from her pep talk on the drive over, she was thrown to see a Dorothy's Bakery pastry bag and coffee on her desk, a small note propped up against them.

It's never too early for cookies. Z.

Charlie snatched up the bag, releasing a groan of pleasure when she pulled out the snickerdoodle. "Still warmmm," she muttered, sinking her teeth into the cushiony baked good. Steam billowed from the coffee cup as she removed the lid stopper and took the smallest sip, the smooth nutty coffee mingling with cinnamon on her tongue.

She marched out of her office, cookie and coffee in hand, to search for the thoughtful delivery man. The cinnamon sugar haze distanced her from her surroundings, and she entered the kitchenette unprepared for Zachary exiting it. Instead, her hands full of deliciousness bounced off his equally delicious chest, and she yelped, spreading her arms wide to avoid losing crumb or drop. His hands shot to her waist, skirting her coat. She thought she was steady, but once she felt the heat of his palms sear through her clothing, who was she to argue about the possibility of needing assistance? This unexpected breakfast treat was starting her day off on the right foot, after all, and to lose any of it would be a travesty.

Then came the onslaught. His subtle, woodsy scent swept around her, almost a citrusy element to it she hadn't noticed before. Compounded with cookie spice and notes of coffee, Charlie found herself frozen. It was an overstimulation, and she wanted to absorb it all. Absorb him. Eat him up alongside that cookie like the snack he was meant to be. She tried to stifle a giggle, and a whimper escaped instead.

The collision, the inhalation of deliciousness, all happened in a moment—a moment of silence—both facing each other, his hands on her, her grip clutching her cookie and drink tightly. But at the sound she'd let slip, Zachary's hands flexed at her waist, his eyes zeroed in on her mouth, and Charlie licked her lips.

She licked her damn lips, as though she were inviting him to take a closer inspection. Her heart pounded, and her brain became a floundering, broken record with the words *Coworker, hot*. It had been so long since she'd kissed a man, and his lips were just as tempting as his scent, drawing her closer, except his hands slowly let go.

"Guess it's a good sign you dove in before getting settled?" He gestured toward her body, and Charlie blinked herself alert—blinking through yumminess was difficult—and looked down.

Her coat was half unzipped, her purse still slung over her shoulder. She was, much like some of her patients, clearly food motivated. She shrugged away any embarrassment, taking another bite of her cookie and purposefully talking through the savored chew. "You've discovered my weakness. Not everyone is savvy enough to figure it out."

Zachary laughed, the sound shooting tingles to her toes as she struggled to swallow. Good Lord, but those laugh lines, pushing their way through the stubble on his face. She liked the way it had grown in over the week.

"I think I've discovered mine too." He stepped even closer, watching her face carefully, his hand reaching for her wrist and raising it up.

Charlie's feet stuttered forward, her eyes locked in his trance. Her lips parted as his focus flicked back to her mouth, and she inhaled sharply. *Holy shit. This is happening. Now. Zachary. At work.*

He guided her hand, still holding one half of the cookie, and took a bite. Her mouth dropped open farther, air escaped in a gust, and her eyes narrowed. He grinned at her reaction, chewing away happily. It was a chewing grin, for God's sake, and it was *sexy*?

"I can't believe you just did that," she said.

He shrugged, releasing her from his warm grip, and swiped a knuckle at the corners of his mouth. For *fuck's* sake, even that was hot!

"We have a shared weakness," he said. "Those are way too tempting."

Charlie sputtered. "You bought it for me!"

"I'm surprised you didn't inhale it on the five-second walk over here."

"I was savoring it!"

"Well, that's just smart."

"Exactly."

"Coming to find me while doing so wasn't."

She stifled a laugh. "Who manages to buy *one* snickerdoodle, anyway?"

He looked away, expression sheepish.

"Did you eat my other cookie?" she asked, voice low.

He scratched his head and winced. "Uh...that one was for me."

His nervous laugh made her shake her head, but she was grinning so wide, her cheeks brushed her glasses. "You owe me another one."

"I barely took a bite!"

"You ate an entire cookie before this! You know as well as I do, every bite counts."

"True." He tilted his head, looking at the floor. "Tonight? We could grab dinner first?"

Her inner teenager executed a series of backflips. Charlie bit her lip and wished she could fan her cheeks, the cookie and coffee limiting her movements. She suddenly had a new understanding for "zoomies."

Zachary cleared his throat. "I wanted to go over stuff with you. Discuss the books and Dad, fill you in on all that."

Business. Of course.

She stepped back toward the hall. "I have plans tonight. Let's schedule a meeting next week, though." She made a show of looking at the clock, lifting her coffee. "Thanks for this!"

Charlie hurried back to her—*their*—office and shrugged out of her coat to reveal standard navy scrubs. Laundry had taken a backseat lately, so all of her fun workwear was buried in the hamper. Zachary would be pleased, a thought that made her chuckle. He didn't try to hide how ridiculous he found her work attire, which only made her more proud of the pieces. In fact, holiday sales were happening. Maybe she could find one with a cat dressed like the Grinch.

"What's so funny?" Zachary came into the office and set down his coffee.

"Oh, nothing." She stood with her palms on her desk as she scanned her list for the day. Once she reached the end of her notes, the Zachary jitters, as opposed to those caffeine-induced, had calmed—until she walked by him on her way out of the office.

"What are you wearing?" He frowned, scanning her up and down.

"Last resort today, Lee," she said, feeling his eyes bore into her until she was out of sight.

***

"To shaming assholes!" Amber raised her glass and clanked it against the others, then took a large gulp of her whiskey cider.

Charlie giggled, watching her cousin from across the table. "How've you had three of those already? Too sweet, even for me." She hiccuped and sipped her old fashioned.

Amber sighed with a lazy grin, slumping against the booth in her caramel blazer and snug white top. "I even had a large slice of cake before coming here. To take the edge off."

Cleo made a gagging sound beside Amber. "Your reliance on sugar is concerning."

"Hey, you know sugar and sex are my favorite remedies. I was already seeing you lovely ladies, so sugar won out. This time." Amber wiggled her eyebrows, her simple eyeliner making her honey-brown eyes pop. She added a shake to her perky ponytail.

Magnolia laughed beside Charlie, her fingers tracing the condensation on a glass of whiskey on the rocks. Her natural, dark brown curls slid just over her shoulders, and a small gold nose stud winked against her light golden brown skin. "I'm picturing you in bed, post sex, pulling a cupcake from your nightstand drawer, taking a bite like a drag from a cigarette."

"That sounds like her dream scenario," Cleo murmured, grinning.

Amber had her hand over her chest, eyes closed in feigned ecstasy. "Give me a minute," she whispered.

They all laughed, the relief tangible following Amber's story of the latest asshole she'd removed from the restaurant where she worked, who'd found it perfectly acceptable to grab her ass while she took his order.

"I wish extra shifts at my shop could replace you having to work there," Cleo said with remorse. Amber had stories like this on the regular.

"Unfortunately, the tips are insane. At least my managers follow through on dealing with shit. I've almost saved enough to rent a workspace, though, and then I'll be able to take on more custom orders." Amber shrugged, appearing nonchalant, even though she'd had to move slowly with her woodworking launch. "In time. Speaking of your shop, did you tell them the latest?"

Cleo's grin was almost shy as she set down her old fashioned. Her curls, pinned back on one side, artfully grazed the wide-neck indigo top that exposed a delicate clavicle. "We've officially launched the events calendar. So far, we've selected dates for our art show night and the free painting class for the youth group. Mainly Books also agreed to a joint effort for a writing class. They're so excited, said they know of a few relatively local authors who'd love to do a guest spot."

They were a chorus of excitement and support. Charlie beamed at her friend. Cleo's shop had been open for two years, but her dream of expanding within the community had always been a goal. Her top priorities were interacting with youth and providing ways for those who couldn't afford extra training to have access to additional classes for the arts. The Village shops all had basement storage, but Cleo's had a bonus back room as well. It was a blank canvas, perfect for staging events.

"When's the first one?" Charlie asked.

"Mid-January. A little breathing room after the holiday craze."

"Oh, God, the holiday open house!" Magnolia yelped. "I don't know why I keep forgetting about that." She opened her phone and brought up her calendar. "When is it again?"

"Two weeks before Christmas," Cleo said.

"Shit, right." Magnolia tapped furiously, pausing to shimmy out of her jacket and briefly tug at her black silk blouse with giant flowers in creams and golds. She gave a thumbs-up to Amber, who'd picked up the menu card from their table and fanned her dramatically.

"I think we need another round of drinks," Amber said, signaling for a server.

"You've been a bit busy prepping for the store *opening*, Magnolia," Charlie said. "It's okay if you don't do anything special for the open house."

"Yeah, people will still come by," Cleo reassured.

Magnolia winced. "I'm already nervous we won't open in time. My boss just informed me that a couple vendors are changing. I also have to make extra of my products to send out to the flagship in Ojai *and* have ready here. I should be working right now," she added in a strained tone.

"When's she letting you hire people?" Cleo asked.

"Apparently, she has someone lined up already. Some daughter of a friend or something," Magnolia said.

"That you haven't met?" Charlie asked.

Magnolia hummed as she took another sip.

"Your boss is frustrating," Amber said.

"It's fine. It'll all work out," Magnolia said, brow furrowed as she stared at her glass.

"Can I help?" Charlie asked.

"Uh, don't you have enough going on right now, with Daniel being out and his son occupying your physical *and* mental space?" Amber challenged.

Charlie was known to stretch her time a little thin, but she could use the distraction. Besides, Magnolia had been under a lot of pressure since arriving in Elmwood Falls. She hadn't planned on moving across the country to open the shop's second location, only to face major construction mishaps. Plus, Charlie knew there was more on Magnolia's mind than she let on. Which was fair. They'd known her less than a year.

Charlie gave her cousin a look. "I'll need a new project, okay? Besides, I'm happy to help." She turned a reassuring smile to Magnolia.

Magnolia squeezed her arm in acknowledgment, then looked down. "Goodness, this shirt is soft. It's like butter."

"I know!" Charlie looked at her emerald-green wrap top, its neckline just daring enough to make her feel like she could evoke "I know how to use my body" vibes without drawing too much attention simultaneously. "It's from the company you told me about!"

"Really? That's where mine is from. Sustainable, washable silk right here." Magnolia tugged at her own blouse, then turned a pout at Charlie, her dark brown eyes glazed. "I'm so touched you ordered from them. Even my family is slow to jump on some of these businesses I tell them about."

"She'll probably buy one of everything in your shop when you open too," Amber teased with a loving smile.

"Alright, I really need to hear more about the young Dr. Lee, cause I don't remember. We barely talked about him on Halloween. Someone was too busy trying to score us free drinks," Cleo said. She smirked at Amber's playful shove.

"There's nothing to tell." Charlie dodged.

"I'll start!" Amber said. "He was the love of young Charlie's life—"

"No! He was *not* the love of my life. You're making it way more dramatic. Don't say shit like that!" Charlie sighed but couldn't help giggling at the tipsy satisfaction on Amber's face. "Fine. We met when I was in high school, working for Daniel as an office assistant. Zachary worked on weekends home from college and over school breaks, so we became friends. But when he graduated and finished up his residency training, he married his girlfriend and went to work for her father's veterinary practice in Chicago. I hadn't talked to him since he left. Now he's back and filling in for his dad."

Amber shot up in her seat. "You forgot to mention he's hot!"

Magnolia burst out laughing, and Charlie reached across the table to smack her cousin's hand, even though Amber was wiggling in her seat with a victory dance.

Cleo shook her head at Amber, amused. "You're such a menace. Though, Charlie, that's pretty much the gist I got from her already. With the detail of him being hot added in, of course."

"You're welcome," Amber said, flipping her ponytail.

"How long has it been?" Cleo said, eyes glittering with excitement. "Wait, is he still married?"

"Yeah, give us more dirt!" Magnolia's eyes were glassy with boozy consolation.

"Six years. And no, divorced."

Amber clapped her hands excitedly, causing all three women to turn their attention toward her. "What? Makes this the perfect opportunity. You adore Daniel, he adores you. Now you and Zachary have reconnected and get to share that cozy little office together, day in and day out. Things are gonna get juicy." Amber wiggled her eyebrows again, taking another sip of her drink.

Magnolia's face twisted. "I hate that word. *Juicy*," she added in a whisper.

Charlie and Cleo laughed as Amber grinned with satisfaction, gesturing for Magnolia to keep drinking.

"You're jumping to a lot of conclusions, Amber," Charlie said. "Seriously, there's no dirt. He's not as friendly toward me anymore. I mean, aside from yesterday. He gives very comforting hugs. And this morning, I guess. Getting me my favorite cookies to make up for my bad day was really thoughtful. What..."

Amber had both hands pressed firmly on the table, eyes mockingly wide. Cleo rubbed her lips together, trying to hide a smirk. Magnolia grinned openly.

"You guys touched," Amber said in a measured tone.

"*Hugged*," Charlie corrected. *Wow, the word* touched *sounded so intimate.*

"He bought you *cookies*?"

Charlie nodded. She bit her lip, remembering his eyes as they roamed her face. How close his mouth had been to her hand, how she'd ached for his lips to brush her skin. To move up her arm... It was ridiculous. Why allow herself to go down this fantasy road? It was different when she was young, when they'd actually had a fun relationship to make the fantasy enjoyable.

Amber's mouth gaped open, and she pointed a finger at Charlie's face. "You're blushing. Why's she blushing? Why are you blushing?!"

"Holy moly, Amber, the whole bar can hear you." Brooke sidled up to their table bundled in a charcoal peacoat, her ivory skin brightened by pink cheeks, her dusty-blue eyes piercing. She grabbed a cocktail napkin from the table to dab her red nose.

"Brooklyn Rose Marchand, where the hell have you been?" Amber turned her pointed finger at her older sister, and Charlie released a slow breath.

"My sister's name is Rosa!" Magnolia said, her cheeks and nose flush from her whiskey.

"Sasha loves roses!" Cleo said.

Amber turned her head toward her friend, keeping her finger pointed at Brooke. "Don't even get me started on Sasha," she warned.

Cleo snickered into her glass.

"You're all well ahead of me, I see," Brooke said with a smirk.

Amber dropped her hand, concern rushing over her face. "Hey. You alright, Brookie?"

"Mm-hmm," Brooke said. She picked up Charlie's old fashioned and took a long sip. "Chilly out there tonight. Wonder if we'll have snow before Thanksgiving."

"Ugh, don't say that. I'm not ready for it!" Magnolia moaned.

Charlie patted Magnolia's hand gently. Her friend was in for a treat. "You can't truly prepare. At least you'll get about six months of practice," she said helpfully.

"What do you mean, six months?" Magnolia whispered.

"I need a drink. Hey, did you see the new bartender tonight?" Brooke asked.

"You're changing the subject. Wait, who?" Amber strained her neck to look at the bar.

Brooke winked at the table as Amber stood for a better view and gasped, fanning herself.

Cleo strained to look. "Oh yeah, he's right up your alley."

Amber faced them and started slow steps backward toward the bar. "Okay, don't think I've forgotten what we were talking about. All of you." She pointed to each of them in turn. "Actually, Mags, yours is easy. Your sister's name is Rosa. Rose and Rosa...cool."

Magnolia tipped over giggling, grabbing hold of Charlie's hand to avoid falling off the seat, which set the whole table to laughing.

"Come on, next round's on me!" Amber turned and shimmied her way toward the bar.

They filed out after her. While this was a far cry from any drunken college night out, Charlie was thankful for the silliness of her friends just the same. It was exactly what she needed to keep her mind off the practice, off Daniel's health. Off Zachary Lee.

Who was *not* the love of her younger self.

Definitely not.

CHAPTER 12
Zachary

ZACHARY COULDN'T GET OVER the amount of white streaked through his dad's black hair. That and his mom lightening her tousled bob from its usual brown shade to what she called "caramel blonde"—the long game to lighten it and ease into her grays—glaringly reminded him of how long he'd been gone. One thing that was steadfast, though, was the commitment between his parents.

Leaning against the wall of the hospital room, arms crossed, his focus went from his mom fixing the sheets around his dad in bed every half hour to the rain pummeling the window.

"Get me out of this godforsaken place."

"Daniel, honey, the doctor said he's hoping in the next few days." Apparently, the half hour was up, as Jeanie set her crochet supplies on her chair and fixed the sheets again. His dad had grumbled when she'd said she was making him a blanket, arguing she only did that for the kids, but then he'd voted on the shades of blue yarn he preferred.

"I need to get back. The cookout's coming up—" Daniel stopped as soon as Jeanie's hand smoothed hair from his forehead.

"Dear, the kids are taking care of everything," Jeanie said softly.

Zachary simultaneously rolled his eyes and puffed up his chest.

"You know Charlie, she keeps things running smoothly. She's handled it all before."

"That was different," Daniel grumbled.

"Yes, this isn't really a vacation for you, that's for sure," Jeanie agreed. "All the same, they've got it under control. And since Zachary stepped in, they've been able to continue almost uninterrupted, right, sweetheart?" Jeanie looked at him, tired eyes pleading.

Zachary nodded. "Yeah, Dad. Schedule's busy, but we haven't had to cancel any appointments."

Daniel watched him carefully. "Jeanie, can I get some water?"

"Oh! Of course." Jeanie grabbed the cup off the bedside table and stood on tiptoe to kiss Zachary's cheek on her way to the hall.

Panic seized him. This was the first time he and his dad had been alone in years.

Zachary followed Daniel's gaze. They watched the rain as it slithered down the window and blurred the view of the flat roof of another hospital wing. A breeze whipped and rattled the glass.

It looked safer out there.

"You didn't run in and start changing everything, did you? Will I even recognize my own practice when I get back?"

Zachary gritted his teeth, laser-focused out the window. "No, Dad. Everything's as you left it."

Daniel grunted.

Zachary dared him a glance. "The place needs a lot of repairs."

His dad's face scrunched as if he'd bit a raisin thinking it a chocolate chip. "What are you talking about? It's fine."

"There's a chunk of tile missing in the kitchenette, a peeling floor. Paint chipping off the lobby walls. Not to mention the equipment. I heard some of it's been repaired multiple times—"

"Yes, well, not all of us can afford replacing the equipment every few years. Or being one of the first to order state-of-the-art technology."

Zachary paused as his dad described the exact details of his ex-father-in-law's practice.

"It's not for you to worry about, Zachary."

Zachary shifted his feet. "The place looks old, Dad. It's falling apart. I think something might be wrong with the heat—"

"It may not be as fancy as your place in Chicago, but the care is top-notch."

"This has nothing to do with the St. James Veterinary Clinic."

"Of course it does. As soon as you met that family, our place hasn't lived up to your standards."

Zachary took a full step back. The anger, the hurt on his dad's face, took him back to when he'd married Anna. To when her father gave a speech at the reception, welcoming Zachary into the family *and* his veterinary practice, even though Zachary hadn't officially accepted. That was how his dad had found out, in front of all their guests, when Zachary had wanted to talk with him first.

Beeping increased, his dad's heartbeat rising as he struggled to boost himself higher on clenched fists.

"Dad." Zachary moved forward just as Daniel relaxed into the pillows, holding up a hand to ward him off.

Daniel's eyes were squeezed shut, his breathing deep and slow. Zachary placed a hand on his, waiting for the beeping to return to normal, and the contact drew Zachary's attention. His dad's chilled fingers, long and thin, similar to his own. The veins he'd traced curiously as a kid, still prominent, though surrounded by more wrinkles. It was the first physical contact they'd had in years.

"The place is fine, Zachary," Daniel said softly.

"Dad, I'm just saying I've noticed a few things I could help with while I'm in town."

"How long are you *in town*? A few more days?"

"I'll be here awhile, actually. Helping out until you're better."

His dad's eyes blinked open in surprise. The dark brown irises Zachary knew so well, that matched his own, were dim, the exhaustion so pronounced it choked him.

"Don't worry about repairs, there's no room for that right now. I'll see to them when I get back. Just help Charlie," Daniel said, voice low.

"What do you mean, 'no room'?" Zachary asked.

Jeanie blew back into the room, renewed energy surrounding her.

"Got some good water cooler gossip," she said, rounding the bed to hand Daniel his water. "There was a proposal here the other day. A nurse and a doctor who met working the Halloween shift years ago—yesterday was their dating anniversary, and they both planned a surprise in the break room. How sweet is that?" She named the staff involved, Daniel acknowledging with apparent interest.

Zachary shook his head. He wasn't against other people's happiness. It was the gestures, though, the tiny acts of love and attention that couples shared so early in their relationships that chafed. He and Anna had been that way once. He'd believed in it. Couldn't imagine them ever stopping, growing apart, or looking back on their life together to find it was all a fabrication, a giant lie, a staged production of young love truly being naive.

What he'd really been was an idiot.

"Our son here thinks he can go in and fix all the 'problems' in the practice," Daniel groused.

His father thought he was *still* one.

Zachary shook his head, unsure how the conversation had switched back to work. "Dad, I was just offering my help."

"Did you know he'll be home for a while?"

Jeanie looked at Zachary, her pale blue eyes hopeful. "How long, sweetheart? Will you be here for Thanksgiving?"

"Mom..."

"You know you're welcome to stay by us."

"Yes, Mom, I know."

"Jeanie, leave him be."

Jeanie turned narrowed eyes at her husband. "*I* should leave him be, you say?"

Zachary watched his parents exchange a silent conversation, surprised to see his father's expression turn sheepish. Daniel picked up Jeanie's hand and pressed a light kiss to her knuckles, softening.

This visit had gone on long enough, Zachary thought as he pulled out his phone. There could only be more disagreements if he stayed, and one riled up moment for his dad was enough.

"I have to get going. I'll see you both later," Zachary said as he moved to kiss his mom.

"Oh, okay." Jeanie snuck in a hug.

He gave his dad's hand a gentle tap, surprised when his father wrapped his fingers into Zachary's with a small squeeze, so quick he almost missed it.

He swore he heard a soft, "Be careful," as he went out the door.

Zachary stopped to pick up Maple and continued to the vet hospital, dissecting his conversation with his dad. It was clear his father had to delegate more, get assistance finding a general contractor to repair problem areas, allow Maura and Charlie to help with the financial side. Daniel needed them, plus, it was smart business sense for Charlie to slowly take over. What he couldn't shake was how there wasn't "room" for repairs...and the envelope he'd discovered in his dad's desk the night before. He'd set it aside, confused more than anything, deciding to dig into it later. Seemed like a harmless decision at the time, but now its importance shot up a notch.

He parked next to their building and released a breath. What got him out of the clinic the night before was a plan to meet Jordan for dinner—something Zachary had arranged to compensate for Charlie's rejection. He hadn't meant to ask her out, but quickly covering it up under the guise of work had felt wrong. Especially after holding her close, feeling her silky wrist against his thumb. He'd surprised himself completely when he bit the cookie right from her hand, but what had overwhelmed him was the desire to suck her fingers into his mouth and remove every speck of sugar from her skin.

The employee door burst open and swung back to bump Charlie as she exited, nose buried in her phone.

Maple buzzed around the back seat, whimpering with excitement.

"Yeah, girl, I see her," Zachary said, getting out of the car.

Charlie jumped at the sound of the car door, hand to her chest. "Holy crap. Hi!"

"Hey, sorry," Zachary said. He kept his attention on Maple, lifting her out of the compact gray SUV. The old girl couldn't jump like she used to, but she always made a move like she was, as if pretending

Zachary's arms were really her, leaping high. Once on the ground, she bumbled over to Charlie, tail swishing, and greeted the woman with kisses.

Charlie cooed and asked Maple about her day, and his dog sat proudly at her feet.

"What are you doing here?" Despite his aloof tone, his emotions were having a field day, punching his insides around like a tetherball. He asked to fill the brief silence, or at least the lack of conversation between *him* and Charlie. She was wrapped up in Maple, granting loving pets and soothing sounds, and he almost squatted to get in on the attention.

"Had to check on a few things for the cookout. One of our vendors backed out, and my list of other options was here." She stood, hair hanging loose just past her shoulders. A breeze lifted the strands and pasted them to her lips. She swiped at her mouth. "Why are *you* here?"

"Needed to keep busy. This vendor, was it a big one?"

"Unfortunately. They make great dog treats. There was a supply issue, and a large account of theirs took precedence. So they can't commit to our event. They've been with us since we started inviting other businesses."

"Oh." Her noted her shoulders were hiked.

"I have a few others I've been meaning to reach out to, so apparently now's the time." She held up a notepad.

Zachary nodded. "Let me know if there's anything I can do."

She pulled her jacket close against the crisp air, regarding him. Maple nudged her thigh, and Charlie smiled and patted her head in return. "Thanks. Though, it seems you're keeping yourself pretty busy as it is. You know I'm happy to help with all those files, right?"

"Trust me, it's best I sort through the mess myself. Also, this from the woman planning a community event. A forty-year celebration at that." A feat he kept allowing himself to forget, one he truly wanted to recognize his father for.

"Yeah," she murmured.

He shrugged. "Just trying to do what I can while I'm here. Much as Dad might hate it."

She tilted her head. "I'm sure he doesn't."

He scoffed, unable to look her in the eye.

"How is he?"

"Ready to get out of there."

"I bet. Do they know when that'll be?"

"Doctor's hoping this week."

"I can't imagine him staying there all this time. He could barely sit at his desk long enough to enter notes."

"Yeah. He's really antsy. Visitors are a good distraction actually, you can stop by anytime." It would make Zachary feel better, knowing there were more people with him. Even though his dad had already grumbled about how no one left him alone.

Her eyes darted around the quiet parking lot. "Uh, yeah. I've been meaning to. Lot going on, you know..."

"He'd love to see you. Both my parents, actually."

Her eyes locked with his, and just when he thought he caught a glint of tears, she blinked her gaze away.

He didn't want her upset. He was on a high—yesterday morning he'd achieved an entirely new reaction from her, sparked by a gesture he'd meant as friendly, but then it had escalated into suggestive. Quite literally by his own hand.

He wanted to at least make her smile again.

"My mom is crocheting him a blanket."

Charlie put a hand over her heart. "I love that."

"He's pretending not to care, yet he keeps making sure it'll be big enough."

"Those two. Sounds like he's making sure there's room for both of them."

"What? No."

She laughed. "You're reacting like I mentioned them having sex."

When he gave her a look, she laughed again. Maple's tail wagged from her seated spot on the concrete, and he agreed with his dog—they should make Charlie laugh as much as possible.

"I adore their relationship. My mom has always been happiest on her own, but my aunt and uncle had that kind of love before she passed. Pretty amazing to see what it can grow into." She swallowed. "For their last anniversary, your dad brought a change of clothes to work, bought her favorite flowers, and picked her up for their date. Seriously, how cute is that?"

"That's sweet," he murmured, while Charlie squatted to pet Maple's ears. He appreciated her point of view, despite its glaring contrast to where else he'd failed in life. "How was your evening?" He immediately felt frustrated with himself for mentioning the night she'd turned him down.

"My evening?" She grinned, and he suddenly felt lighter. "Really good, actually. Haven't hung out with my friends like that in a while. We all needed it."

He ran a hand through his hair, oddly satisfied.

"We used to do that a lot more, but Cleo's been working to expand her shop. And my cousin Amber, well, she's got three jobs right now." Her words tumbled faster with each new name mentioned.

He watched her rifle through her coat pockets and purse until keys emerged.

"Then there's Magnolia. She's prepping to *open* a shop. It's on Main Street too," she added, pointing with a key as though he didn't know where she meant. "Like Cleo's."

He bit back a smile, teasing her hard to resist. "Don't worry, Harris. I get it. You had 'plans.'" Adding air quotes as he motioned for Maple to follow him to the door paid off.

"Wait, no, I'm serious!"

"Yeah, it all sounds very true. You had some names in the chamber."

"People I was *with*."

"Mentioned their jobs. No info on what you did last night, but I'm assuming they're real people. And that you actually saw them." He propped open the door with an outstretched arm, and Maple lumbered inside like it was her second home.

"Zachary."

He turned, grinning, unaware she was directly behind him, and the door jolted him forward an extra inch. Which wasn't enough, he realized, as he looked down into her face, a conflict of emotions playing across it. A tendril of hair brushed her cheek, enticing him with its flutter. Hugging her had unlocked a new level, inviting physical contact into their relationship. He resisted, wondering when he'd get the opportunity again.

Just bring her more cookies.

Swallowing, he tried to figure out why he was feeling this way. Why his body warmed with her near, or why her scent seemed to imprint on him. Why it made him happy that Maple adored her. He also wondered why he got excited to come to work and see her every morning, or why he saved his least favorite shirts for Thursdays when she might be off. He was curious as to why he looked forward to seeing which scrubs she'd wear and which color in her eyes they'd highlight. The brown tortoiseshell pair of glasses she wore, paired with a green jacket, shocked the hazel swirl of color in her eyes now.

She chewed her lip, and the longer he locked at her, the farther a flush traveled down her neck.

He chuckled, attempting to shake himself away from fantasy territory. To the reminder that he'd like to regain her friendship, and that was all it should be. "I'm just messing with you, Harris. Besides, even if you had been making it up, you'd have every right to."

Her attempt to look stern was thwarted by a grin breaking free and a small shake of her head. "I wasn't, it was real."

"It was real," he repeated softly.

Her eyes flitted between his. "I'd still like to take you up on your offer," she added.

His body hummed. "Sounds great."

"To go over things, of course."

He winced, and when she raised an eyebrow, he went for broke. "Or not," he said.

Her eyes widened.

"I've missed this. Our friendship." He scrubbed a hand through his hair.

"Me too," she said. "Though, until yesterday, I was starting to think I'd imagined us ever being friends."

Yesterday. When he'd bit a cookie from her hand, her fingers a breath from his lips.

"No," he replied. He hated she questioned it. "We were."

He remembered her favorite sandwich from More Than Bread on Birch Street. Certainly a friend thing to know. He'd gone to her graduation party, which was a very friend thing to do. And he didn't know what she used to smell like—a very good friend boundary.

Lavender. She smelled like lavender. Sometimes coffee and cinnamon in the mornings, if he was lucky to be near her before lunch.

He stayed silent, since he was spiraling down a bright stairway of broken boundaries.

Her nod was slow, likely trying to decipher whatever she saw on his face. Had his stomach fallen to his feet? Because it felt like it.

"Well, good." She smiled and backed away, pulling more strands of hair from her lips as the wind whipped it around her. "So, I'll see you tomorrow?"

He nodded, made sure she got in her sedan, then shoved inside the building.

Tomorrow. Not soon enough. How was that possible?

He yanked off his coat as he stepped into the office, Maple on alert. "Fuck, what am I doing?" With a groan, he sat and plugged his face in his hands. Maple waited a beat, then settled.

As he picked through the pile on his desk, his mind picked apart his behavior. How pleasantly surprised he'd been to see her. What his reaction to her meant.

His hand hovered over the envelope at the bottom of the pile, tucked there in haste before he'd left the office the night before. Its return address shouted at him, the font clean, exact. Thick, rounded letters stamped out the name *Neptune Corp*, a candy company diversifying its assets by buying up privately owned veterinary clinics around the country. While they weren't the only business doing so, they were known to be overly involved in the day-to-day, micromanaging until the clinic fit their mold, with barely a hint of the old practice left.

Zachary pulled out the contents, finding brochures of the company and pamphlets of practices transformed claiming positive experiences. A glossy file geared toward convincing the seller that this was the best decision they'd make in their life.

The seller. *Dad*.

A small piece of paper floated onto his desk, the scrawled handwriting unsettling:

Daniel, Looking forward to the cookout!

The signed name was illegible, and every other document was generic to the company and not the rep communicating with his father. But it was clear—Zachary would find out soon enough how big a deal the cookout would be.

CHAPTER 13

Charlie

BROKEN!

"Damn." Charlie stared at the note stuck to the coffeepot, the words *just like our spirits!* added below it in different handwriting. She smirked. "Hey, Maura?"

Maura met her in the hallway and followed Charlie to her office.

"Can you order a carafe or two from Village Coffee until we get our situation figured out?" Charlie handed over her credit card.

Maura smiled. "Sure thing."

"Thanks," Charlie said.

She settled at her desk and scanned lab results, noting which clients to call during lunch and which could wait until end of day. A buzz of excitement raced through her, and she couldn't help glancing over her shoulder repeatedly, watching for Zachary, even though he had surgeries that morning. Even a glimpse of him would do. She was eager to see what today would bring after what felt like their friendship returning. A sense of normalcy.

Actually, better than that. But she didn't dare allow herself to consider what it meant.

"Dr. Harris?" Their vet tech, Sheila, stood in the doorway, expression urgent. "Swallowed rubber band. Mrs. Roberts thinks it happened within the last half hour."

Charlie nodded and followed Sheila to the patient's room. Kicking the day off with an urgent situation, right at their opening hour.

Getting cats to throw up was difficult, swallowed rubber bands especially tricky to rescue. For some reason, Charlie felt today would be different.

***

"Oh my goodness, he swallowed *that?*"

Charlie pointed at the baggie with a grin, a slimy yellow rubber band on display. "Can't believe we got it. *Very* glad we got it though, this was a big one."

Maura shuddered. "Doesn't matter how many years I've worked here, I don't have the same level of excitement about it as you do."

Charlie laughed and left the room. "Mrs. Roberts was grossed out when we showed her."

Maura followed close behind her. "I'll bet. She was so grateful Homer avoided surgery."

"Me too," Charlie said.

"Coffee is here, by the way."

"Ooo, great." Charlie detoured toward the kitchenette.

"I have a new machine ready for pickup. I'll grab it after lunch."

Charlie nodded as she prepped her coffee, but Maura hovered. With her first sip, Charlie pivoted to face her, eyebrows raised in question.

"I wanted to give you the heads-up," Maura said softly. "Already handled Mrs. Delaney this morning."

"Oh no. What now?"

"She called to say that she 'found better care elsewhere and we can all go to hell.'"

"She said that." It wasn't a question, knowing the woman behind the words.

Maura nodded. "Apparently, after getting the same answer you gave her from *three* other clinics, she finally found one willing to tell her what she wanted to hear."

Charlie stared into her mug, watching oat milk swirl and blend. "Which clinic? Downtown?"

Maura grimaced at the mention of the clinic who'd become their rival once Neptune Corp had purchased them. "Yes."

"Damn it," Charlie muttered. "How many have we lost to them now?"

"At least ten percent since June."

"Seriously?" Charlie rubbed her forehead. "I didn't realize it'd gotten that high. Last Daniel told me, it was nearing five."

"Well..." She looked around.

"Maura, you can tell me."

"About five percent have left since Dr. Lee's heart attack."

Charlie opened her mouth to speak, but nothing came out. How many had left before Zachary arrived? All 5 percent? Was it her? Many of the recent accounts had probably been Daniel's, but that was a lot, and quick.

"Most people who've given a reason said it's because of cost," Maura rushed to add.

"Sure..." Their prices already hadn't changed much in recent years in an attempt to fight the corporate model. Still begged the question, how many would leave when Daniel retired? Would there even be a clientele list to serve?

"I have to get back to the lobby. Good news is we still have a full day of appointments, and two emergency walk-ins."

Charlie blew out a breath. "It's not even nine."

"And we're already behind."

"Of course," Charlie said, as they parted ways.

Every day was playing catch-up as soon as the doors opened, with the threat of losing clients close behind.

She looked over notes acquired by her technician for the next patient, the high from the rubber band rescue faded. As she scooted her chair to stand, it bumped Zachary's, the domino effect knocking papers from his desk. She picked them off the floor and set them down beside a notebook scratched with Zachary's all-caps handwriting. Her brow narrowed at the header: REPAIRS.

She leaned closer, moving a file out of the way to reveal a list ranging from equipment to busted kitchenette flooring. Most she recognized as concerns she and Maura had brought up to Daniel over the years, only they were likely written on various pieces of paper, scattered in the boxes surrounding his desk.

So Zachary thought they didn't have time to follow through with the cookout already in motion, but making a list of things to fix while he was here temporarily seemed reasonable? She yanked up the notebook, nearly pressing her bespectacled nose against the page. A small header labeled CHANGES was followed by online booking, online pharmacy refills, tech scheduling, and the dreaded uniforms. If one thing was abundantly clear, it was that Zachary Lee was making himself quite at home. He wasn't acting like a temporary fill, or even just the owner's son. He was trying to take charge.

"Dr. Harris? Room two?"

Charlie dropped the notebook like it had burned her fingertips, the way the words had seared her insides.

It would do her best to remember this wasn't the same friendship as in the past. Seemed like Zachary needed a reminder too.

***

Charlie gasped at the boxes of Dorothy's cupcakes squeezed onto the cramped counter. "Who sent us these?"

They were a welcome sight after a morning that had quickly gone downhill. One of her favorite senior dogs was sick, dropped off for her to check on in between patients, and while Charlie was able to test for a UTI, she had to do an ultrasound for a suspected mass. Then a client had brought in her dog for the third time in two months for gastrointestinal issues, and Charlie had explained again that they really recommended the prescription diet over the boutique brand the breeder was pushing.

She sighed. Taped to a cabinet was a note with the words:

Thanks for all you do for EFVH and our family.

—Dr. Zachary Lee

Well. So very fancy. Such a boss move.

She looked at the to-go box of coffee she'd ordered, nearing room temperature.

"Everyone's just doing their job, not like they're waiting for recognition from the boss's son," she mumbled as she yanked her lunch from the fridge, all while eyeing the desserts.

"Hey."

She yelped and spun around. Struggled for a neutral expression.

Zachary raised a brow, then walked past her. "Make sure you have a cupcake." He pulled a sparkling water from the fridge.

She held up the paper bag. "I'm all set."

Wait, no. The bag felt light. She peered inside, then shut it quickly. *Shit.* Only a container of hummus and celery inside. Her peanut butter sandwich was definitely on her counter at home.

"Everything okay there, Harris?"

"Great. Yep." She reached for the fridge and rummaged around, taking an extra second to nab her bottle of iced tea. When she turned, she smacked back into the fridge door, finding Zachary standing close, a plate in his hand with a single cupcake.

"Here. Have one."

"Could always send leftovers home with everyone."

"This is a little something for the whole team, and that includes you. I'm at a loss for what to do. People are showering my family with food. Everyone's working their ass off. You've put in a shit ton of overtime."

"I haven't—" Her voice broke as he pressed closer, and she sucked in a breath.

"Everyone's been through a lot. And things have been operating like normal here. That, for sure, is due to you."

She scanned his face, from his deep brown eyes to the laugh lines that were dimmed by a frown, and she found herself frowning as well.

When her eyes traveled back to his, she discovered he'd been doing his own mapping of her.

"Take the cupcake." A beat. "Please."

She slowly took the plate from his hands and waited for him to step back. "Thank you," she said quietly. When she had enough clearance to get around him, she started toward the hall, angry at her stomach for rumbling in excitement. She didn't want his food. They needed to talk. After she ate though, because with the way the day had been going, it'd be safer for everyone that way.

"It's snickerdoodle," he said.

She stopped, looked at the cupcake, and inhaled discreetly. Her body hummed *hell yes* in response, but she didn't look back as she continued down the hall. With each step, she vacillated between the appreciation of his nice gesture and the annoyance that he was somehow usurping her team.

But she wouldn't let that stop her from eating the delectable treat.

What she needed to stop? Thinking about how nice it felt to be close to him. Again.

"I need to get out more," she muttered. She shoveled some cupcake in her mouth, eyes rolling in delight at the first bite, and wrapped up her break determined and a little more confident, feeling like her day had turned around.

Until her last appointment.

The appointment itself wasn't the issue—it was that she was the doctor assigned to it.

"God damn it, Zachary, you cannot switch our patients!" Charlie stormed into their office and slammed the door shut.

All patients were cleared for the day, clients gone, and only a few staff remained. Might as well have it out with him now.

Zachary's eyes were wide with surprise. "It was just the one this afternoon—"

"Not 'just the one.'" She released a wild laugh. "You did the same thing last Friday, without explanation. And you know, I let it pass. That was a rough day, not sure if you recall, but your kindness was enough for me to let it slide." So much so, she had forgotten until this moment. "Now another one? No."

Zachary turned his chair to face her completely. "Trust me, it was better this way."

She crossed her arms, shifted her stance. Waited.

"Today's was a follow-up appointment. A quick one."

"I'm well aware. Which means whatever you had to do wouldn't have been delayed much. Or *you* should've talked to me, not gone through our staff."

He rubbed his palms over his thighs. "I didn't recommend a follow-up appointment. I think she just wanted to ask me out again."

A burst of incredulous laughter erupted from her. "Are you fucking serious?" Her arms flew out to the side. "Grow the 'F' up, Zachary!"

He was watching her with such an amused expression, it pissed her off. He made it worse by speaking.

"Do you only allow yourself one F-bomb a day or something?" he asked.

"Oh my *God*!" She spun toward the wall, grasping her hair. When she turned back to him, she felt crazed. "You've been acting like a...a..."

"An idiot? My sister likes to use that."

"No, no—don't you dare help me call you out! It makes you even more of an—"

"Ass?"

"Ugghhh!"

The man had the nerve to smirk at her.

"This isn't funny!"

His smile immediately dropped. "Sorry."

She huffed, pacing the small room, then pivoted and took firm steps toward him. "Stop undermining me. I don't care that Daniel is your dad. I don't care that you used to be in charge of me. That was years ago. You haven't worked here in *years*. I'm not about to let you come in and change whatever the hell you want." She heaved out deep breaths, his notebook of lists somehow waving in her hand.

He looked from it to her.

She lowered the notebook and her voice, tossing the pad in front of him. "If you have an issue with a client, come talk to me."

"Okay. I have an issue with my client."

She gritted her teeth. "Too late now, isn't it?"

He clenched his beautiful jaw, their eyes locked in an even louder war that was interrupted by a rapid knock.

"Doctors?" Sheila poked her head into the room. "We have kittens."

Charlie blinked her gaze back to Zachary, then spun around to follow Sheila to the main desk, Zachary right behind her.

"Oh my heavens, this is the cutest package I've ever seen," Maura cooed, standing over a cardboard box on her desk. "We have five little sweeties here with their mama," she said as Charlie reached her.

She peered inside, a spread of sleeping kittens nestled together and a cat that looked around two years old curved around them, watching carefully. One gray tabby lifted its head and squeaked, then burrowed against its neighbor.

"I called Jasmine. She's getting things set and will come back for them," Maura said.

Zachary let the mother cat sniff his hand, and after an approving lick, picked up a squirming black fuzz ball. He gently rubbed its head with his thumb. "Does she foster?"

"Yes," Maura answered. "Just cleared out her last litter, in fact."

"What do we know about these?" Charlie pulled her gaze away from the purring poof licking Zachary's chin.

"A woman brought them by, said she found them living under her front porch a few weeks ago. She's been trying to get them to a rescue, but so many are at capacity. Someone told her to come to us."

The kitten squeaked and promptly fell asleep in Zachary's hand.

"Alright, let's bring these cuties to the back for a quick check," Charlie said.

Sheila nodded and scooped up the box. "I'll help out until Jasmine gets here."

"You sure?" Charlie asked.

"You want one, don't you?" Zachary said with a small grin.

"I already promised my wife I wouldn't bring home another animal, even to foster," Sheila said, her cheeks pink. "That's how we ended up with five!" Her laughter filled the hallway as she carried the kittens to an exam room.

"I'll lock up on my way out after Jasmine arrives," Maura said.

"Thanks, Maura," Charlie called, making her way toward the back.

She ignored how Zachary still carried the kitten, whispering to it the whole way.

Positioned at the exam table across from one another, they assigned codes to each cat, and Sheila created their charts, entering notes as Charlie and Zachary called out vitals and details.

Charlie ignored the way their hands brushed when they both reached into the box, the heat that shot up her arm and through her core.

Charlie ignored the grin on Zachary's face, the little greeting he gave each new kitten as he picked it up for inspection.

Seriously, she worked with animals, and she saw people loving on their pets every day. Seeing him like this shouldn't be a turn-on, and yet, she was imagining those hands stroking her body, that voice whispering in her ear.

Finally, Jasmine swooped in, eyes bright as she calmly approached the litter, and Charlie and Zachary returned to their office.

"It's freezing in here," Zachary murmured, pulling on his fleece as he sat to finish paperwork and phone calls.

They'd started having problems the winter prior, but Charlie didn't want to mention it. He'd add it to his list anyway.

His chair creaked behind her, and she sensed Zachary's heat as he leaned back. "You're right," he said softly.

Her shoulders loosened, but she didn't turn around.

"I walked in here acting exactly like the son of the owner instead of a new hire—and a *temporary* one at that." He sighed. "Not that it makes a difference, but the appointment last week was an old family friend. He'd sent me a wedding card that basically told me off for bailing on my dad. Didn't think either of us would want to see the other."

She turned at that, watching as he scrubbed his face with his hand.

"That's my problem, though," he added.

"You can't keep avoiding them, Zachary," she said softly.

His eyes found hers again. The pain, the distance in them, tugged at her instincts to comfort. She felt her face soften the longer they sat, staring.

He seemed to struggle over what to say next, his mouth opening and closing a few times. Finally, he said, "Let me make it up to you?"

She looked away, out at the dark sky, the cold wind whipping past the windows. "Cookies?" she mumbled softly.

He chuckled, and she couldn't help herself as her gaze whipped back to catch him smiling. Now she saw he had more laugh lines on his face, ones that suggested years of happiness, someone who still enjoyed laughing. She ached to trace each and every one.

His smile shifted to a nervous uncertainty. "Cookies are a given. I still owe you, remember? Dinner, tomorrow night?" He blew out a sigh. "Let's get to know each other again."

CHAPTER 14

Zachary

"I DON'T KNOW WHAT to make of you in plain scrubs. Two days in a row. It's really throwing me." Zachary scratched his head, wishing the statement wasn't so true. "I'm used to them being loud," he added, an attempt to recalibrate.

"They're cheerful, not loud." Charlie slipped on her army green jacket, her grin almost proud, like she knew he was rattled. "You still like burgers?"

"Yes."

"Perfect." When they reached the parking lot, she swung open the door of her sedan and stretched inside, her scrub pants molding to her body nicely in the process. Honestly, he'd never paid attention to how scrubs fit anyone until now.

He cleared his throat and shoved his hands in his pockets.

"I can follow you," he said. "Al's Burgers?"

"No, no." She emerged with a periwinkle scarf and scrunched her nose. "Not Al's. There's a place up the road, if you don't mind walking?" She flipped the scarf around her neck in various ways and gripped it close to her chest, looking at him expectantly.

"Great." All that mattered was fueling his body, no matter what type of food apparently, since he would've followed her to the cheap burger joint he'd hung around as a teen.

Charlie shut the car door, swung her arm out to guide them, and started walking.

They moved in silence, Zachary trying to distract himself with their surroundings. Six years away from his hometown was longer than he'd realized. He appreciated the draw of the quaint Elmwood Falls Village, its historic buildings offering a century-old charm that had faded from surrounding neighborhoods. While the buildings were the same as he remembered, there were quite a few new businesses occupying them, denoted by modern signage and freshly painted doors. As close as he'd been to Main Street for the last week and a half, he hadn't taken the time to just absorb it all. Even on Halloween, he'd been in too much of a daze to really process everything around him.

Zachary zipped his jacket to keep out the crisp breeze, not minding the sting to his cheeks. Dried leaves crunched beneath their feet, and wrought iron lamps adorned with greenery and gold bows glowed. Shop windows were lined with twinkle lights, setting a holiday mood. Charlie was probably the type to go home and curl up under a blanket after enjoying an evening like this, with a mug of something hot to drink. He pictured her place outfitted with blankets of varying colors and fluffiness. The mug would have a minimalist-style drawing of a human curled like a shrimp on the couch next to a cat sitting like a human, or some cheeky shit.

He snuck an anxious glance her way, the conjured image way too appealing.

She was busy looking at the shops, at ease with their leisurely pace. Her hair was in a low braid, one she'd redone while they were finishing up notes at their desks. He'd turned just in time to see her fingers deftly twist and twine the strands while she stared out the window. As the wind swept up around them, the wisps of hair that always broke free danced across her cheeks. He was oddly grateful she didn't brush them away, and wondered how their softness compared to her skin.

She gripped his bicep and pulled them to a stop, halting his thoughts. *Were these daydreams?*

"This is my friend Cleo's shop," Charlie said, pointing to the black awning beside them that read Cleo's Local Goods in white script font.

The store was lit brightly, its front picture window showcasing a well-loved oak buffet and hutch cabinet, featuring teas, candles, towels, and pottery. Princess pumpkins were nestled on top and below the buffet, with sprays of dried florals.

"Now," she said, her hand still on his arm as she breathed deeply. When she looked up at him, the street lamp glinted off her eyes. "Smell that?"

He sniffed on command. Sugary sweetness hit his nostrils, the cinnamon spice blending with the autumnal air. Sure enough, they were one shop down from Dorothy's Bakery.

"Fuck. I forgot how that place filled the block."

Charlie laughed. "You didn't soak it in when you stopped by the other day?"

He took a moment to enjoy her laugh, missing it after her blowup the day before—even though he was enthralled to see that side of her too. "I'm embarrassed to admit, I called in a to-go order and was only inside for a minute."

She gasped, her hand sliding from him, leaving behind a warmth that made him shiver. "We'll have to fix that," she said with a small smile. "Magnolia's new place will be opening there soon," she added, pointing across the street at the storefront with a teal door before she continued walking.

"Ah, right. Magnolia, Cleo. The names you came up with the other night," he teased.

She nudged his arm with hers. "Cleo couldn't believe her luck when the space next to Dorothy's became available. She leaves her front door open on beautiful days so the bakery smell wafts in, but when they're all buttoned up in the summer or winter, get this, it carries through the vents. Something about how this connected strip of shops was originally built, I don't how it works. But it works, and that's the main thing."

Zachary salivated as they passed the bustling bakery, then realized the time. "How late do they stay open?" he asked.

"Oh, a couple years ago, they extended their hours to 8 p.m. Dorothy still bakes regularly, but her daughter runs the day-to-day and pushed for the change. The grandkids have taken an interest too, so they cover post-school hours and busy seasons. It's pretty neat, actually."

The words sank like a rock. All these family businesses were hanging on in this tumultuous economy, passing down through generations. It was what his dad had hoped for until Zachary had followed Anna. Dorothy's Bakery had been around as long as EFVH. Zachary remembered visiting his dad at work as a kid and running over to the bakery, his fist wrapped tightly around every dollar he'd scrounged together from his allowance. The woman had the biggest heart, always giving kids more than their money covered.

They reached the end of the block and crossed the street, the Menomonee River in front of them as they veered slightly, until Charlie announced, "Here we are."

He followed her into the gastropub, the name Gourmet Buns stenciled on the wood-paneled wall by the hostess stand. Once settled in their booth, he looked around at the open space decorated with cedar, steel, and iron.

"Trendy," he said.

"And delicious." She pointed to the menu. "Best burger I've ever had."

"In Elmwood Falls?"

"Ever," she said, leaning forward with a playful smirk.

"What about Chicago?"

"Well, I haven't been. Isn't it known for pizza, though? Or hot dogs?"

He grinned and leaned closer as well. "So I won't be disappointed we skipped Al's?"

"Good God, I hope not." Charlie laughed.

"Wait, you've never been to Chicago?"

"Nope. School and rotations took me through Northern Wisconsin and Minnesota. Never really had a reason to go to Illinois."

"Alright, we can definitely make an excuse to drive down for pizza one day. Maybe a burger too, depending on how this goes." The words fell easily, the thought exciting him, and yet, he straightened in his seat like he'd made a mistake.

Her smile faded, and she cleared her throat and grabbed her menu.

Rubbing a hand over his mouth, he stared at his menu, wondering what his reaction had looked like. Could she tell he felt her laugh ring through his entire body? That he wanted to do whatever he could to make her laugh again? He wanted to forget that she loomed over the business, that he was working there while his dad was recovering, that the financial hit the practice had taken was worse than he'd imagined. That hanging out with her again, outside of the office, was more than appealing.

He'd rather focus on the hints of their old friendship returning. Forget they even worked together. They deserved a night without anything between them—business shit could wait.

"How's your dad?"

He fell back against the seat. "Fine. Ornery. Toward me that's nothing new though, so seems we're on par."

"Ah." She returned to her menu, the din of the restaurant emphasizing their silence.

When the waitress arrived, they ordered their burgers—caramelized onions for him, cheese and pickles for her. Each with a side of fries, per her encouragement.

Then they were alone, no menus to distract them. No kittens in need of care—a situation that had launched him down memory lane to when he and Charlie had helped his dad with a litter of puppies as students.

He grabbed a packet of sugar from the little tray on the table, tapping and flipping it, his eyes following the motion.

"I know you two don't have the best relationship—"

"That's putting it mildly."

"Look, I'm sorry to bring him up. I didn't want to bother your mom, and Sandra's been swamped."

"I get it," he said, now disappointed he was a last resort. He tossed the sugar packet to the side and took a giant gulp of his beer right as the waitress set it down. "He'll most likely go home by the end of next week. Beyond that... His heart attack was really serious. It'll be a couple months before his doctor clears him to work." He took a deep breath. "Even then, he's pushing for Dad to retire."

Charlie's head bobbed up and down slowly, eyes wide as the words registered. "Wow."

"Yeah."

She took a small sip of her iced tea, then slid her finger through the condensation on the glass. "He must've hated that news."

"Yeah, well." Zachary scratched his head. "Apparently, Dad moved past the idea as if his doctor hadn't even mentioned it."

"Shit," she whispered.

"Basically."

She leaned on the table and looked out the window. "He's not ready to retire."

Her voice was scratchy, and Zachary almost reached for her hand, as though the comfort would help. As though *his* comfort would help the woman who would take over the practice.

The one spiraling beyond both their control, she just had no clue.

"Well, that's good for me to know. Best to have the heads-up that we might be looking for a more long-term replacement, then."

The thought of someone like Dr. Fletcher stepping in to do a job he could do better grated. "I don't think that's necessary right now. Let's give it a little time. We'll see what the word is when he goes home and go from there."

"We have to prepare for when you'll be leaving us too."

Leaving us.

"I won't leave you in a lurch, Harris."

"What about your job in Chicago, *Lee*?"

"Like I said, I had a sabbatical planned."

The waitress appeared with their food, setting down plates piled with fries next to giant burgers. Perfect for a distraction from Charlie's prying gaze.

He took a large bite of the burger, the flavor of the meat mixing perfectly with the onions and sauce. "*Damn*." He shoved another bite into his mouth, glancing up to see Charlie pushing fries around her plate. "Definitely better than Al's. I would've regretted going there."

Charlie allowed a small nod. "You'll have plenty of time to fit in a visit there, I guess."

Zachary grabbed a couple fries and popped them in, watching her as she picked at her food. "That bother you? That I'll be in town longer?"

"No." Her answer was immediate.

"Trying to drive me out of here, Harris?" He struggled to keep his tone light, despite the tension coiling in his chest. Business politics aside, he wanted her to *want him here*.

"Your family is thrilled you're home. Not to mention the clients."

"Not you, though." He set his burger down and pressed close, lowering his voice, the aged pain resurfacing. "You just want me out of the way. Get the practice to yourself. A little sooner than you were expecting, sure, but why waste time? Right?"

"What are you even talking about? I'm not the one sitting around making lists of things to fix as soon as Daniel's gone."

He narrowed his eyes. "You *should* be. Sign of someone who knows how to run things."

She gasped.

He swallowed hard, but continued. "What made you look through my things? Didn't trust me to not make more mistakes?"

Her face flushed as she appeared to calculate his words.

"Charlotte, I thought that was you! Goodness it's been a while. How are you, dear?" A woman swarmed their table and wrapped Charlie in an uninvited hug, stepping back to barely leave a foot of space.

Charlie's eyes widened, her cheeks still burned red, and her fingertips were white against the table. She stared at the woman in front of her, most likely in her late fifties, with her chic coat and tight bob of gray hair.

It took an extra moment, but Charlie softened her eyes slightly and forced a tight smile. "Hi, Mrs. Hampshire. Now isn't the b—"

"Oh, you know you can call me Loretta, Charlotte. We're long past the Mrs. Hampshire days. I'm doing very well. Here for a little night out with my sister, you remember Gloria? We are *so* excited for the holidays. You know Bobby's little one is two this year? What a sweetheart she is, my word. Let me show you." She whipped out her phone as quickly as the words were out, swiping the screen until she was satisfied enough to shove it in Charlie's face.

"Adorable," Charlie said with barely a glance, her voice quiet. "Lore—"

"Isn't she? She is the absolute *cutest*, but I'm biased, I suppose. She went as a little cupcake for Halloween, I just died when I saw the costume. Here, you have to see it. We joined them for their little trick or treat this year, what a delight."

"Sounds wonderful. Loretta, if you don't mind..."

"Oh! I hope I'm not interrupting a date?" She placed her hand on her chest, various rings sparkling in the dim light of the restaurant as she turned her body toward Zachary. Even without knowing her, he knew she'd been aware of his presence. "Though I suppose you wouldn't be in your work scrubs for a date now, would you?" Her laughter singed the air as she tapped a hand to Charlie's shoulder.

Charlie clenched her jaw. "Loretta Hampshire, this is Zachary Lee."

"Hello, what a pleasure. Of the Lee family, from Charlotte's clinic?"

"Yes." It was all Zachary felt was necessary, since this woman knew everything anyway.

"I see. I'm so sorry to interrupt your *work meeting*. What a lovely place you have, Dr. Lee. I remember the stories Charlotte shared when she and my son were dating."

Ah, that's why the name *Bobby* stood out. He remembered hearing about him when they worked together, a layer to the guy that sounded exactly the opposite of what he pictured for Charlie. He'd even met Bobby briefly when he came by to pick her up after a shift, and one handshake was all it took to solidify that gut feeling.

He saw a bit of where he got it from.

"Have a good rest of your night, Loretta," Charlie managed.

"We will! I'll make sure to tell Bobby you say hello."

"No need," Charlie said, voice firm.

Loretta blinked rapidly, mouth falling open with a silent gasp. With a nod his way and a final glance at Charlie, Loretta Hampshire zipped toward the front of the restaurant.

Zachary waited, watching Charlie's face as she looked everywhere but at him. Her pinched expression didn't lessen, despite the distance between her and Loretta.

"Could I get a to-go box? Thanks." Charlie caught the waitress on her way by, then busied herself with scooting her fries together, as if that'd help save time when the box arrived. "I need to go. It's been a hectic...God, only a couple weeks, but it sure feels like a month. Anyway, lots of prep to do yet for the cookout."

"Charlie—"

"We'll talk more about the practice later." She nodded a thanks to the waitress, then dumped her plateful of food into the container. Standing, Charlie rifled through her purse and pulled out her wallet, throwing a twenty on the table. "Um, let me know what else I owe."

"Wait—"

"I really do need to go. Oh, but Zachary?" Her eyes focused hard on his, face determined.

He swallowed. "Yeah?"

"The thought of your dad retiring makes me sad, for many reasons. I love working with him, and for him. Honestly, I know I still have a lot to learn. I'm not ready for him to hand over the reins. The fact that you're jumping to that conclusion is really painful, you know?" Her voice cracked. She shook her head. "Regarding you staying in town longer? What I'm struggling with the most is *working with you*."

Zachary stared at the space where she'd stood long after she left, kicking himself for not prying more about what had just happened with Loretta.

No. Kicking himself for accusing her of waiting with bated breath to take over the vet hospital. As though she'd been clamoring for it, or forcing it to happen somehow. She didn't conjure his dad's heart attack. She hadn't made Zachary leave town in the first place and abandon the one thing his dad had been so proud to pass along to him. She didn't make him come back, dead set on improving everything to try to make up for where he'd failed.

He owed her an explanation.

He glanced at the table and saw her box of leftovers.

Looked like he owed her dinner too.

CHAPTER 15

Charlie

CHARLIE SLAMMED THE DOOR to her flat. Toothless sprinted off the couch and hid under the arm chair, yellow eyes glowing. Once she determined there was no threat, she inched out and rubbed against Charlie's ankles.

Charlie scooped the cat into her arms and sighed, nuzzling her silky black fur.

"Ughhh, what is wrong with people?" she groaned into Toothless's back.

Zachary and his hurtful accusations. Loretta and her blatant entitlement. Her ex and his douchey manipulation.

Like a boomerang, Charlie ran into Bobby's parents often in the Village, never quite escaping that part of her past she so desperately wanted to retire. A past that solidified how much she didn't fit into the storybook happily ever after.

A sharp knock made Charlie jump. She turned and looked out the peephole.

"Whoops," she said, the volume of her voice loud enough to be heard through the door.

"I've got sustenance." The gruff reply made Charlie grin.

She opened the door, and her neighbor Levi entered, covered paper plate in hand. He looked relaxed in worn jeans and a green-and-blue plaid button-down, the sleeves rolled up his forearms to reveal the edge of an intricate tattoo that traveled up his right shoulder. His dark brown hair was rumpled, with silver strands peppered throughout it and the short beard growing in thick over his olive skin. He looked ready for a singles ad for people in their thirties, his deep blue eyes adding a layer of mystique many found irresistible.

That was ironically the most Levi thing about him—the man was a vault. Charlie could talk his ear off for hours, he'd offer a few key, insightful sentences, then return to his apartment, never to bring it up again. Their friendship formed a flawless system—their opposite traits for communicating was bound by their mutual appreciation for space.

"It fell down, didn't it?" she asked. Toothless leaped from her arms to follow their guest as he leaned against the arm of the couch.

"Sure did. The glass broke this time." Levi granted Toothless an awkward pat. Satisfied, she curled at his feet.

Charlie gasped, a small laugh bursting out. "Are you serious?"

The shared wall of their flats mirrored each space, from the front door that opened on the living room and led back to the kitchen. From time to time, whenever someone closed their door too hard—Levi from a frustrating day, or Charlie from holding too many bags of pet supplies and kicking her door shut—a frame fell off the wall.

"I've never closed it that hard before."

Levi held up the plate. "Figured you must've had a fucking bad day."

"Is that...?" She walked over and pulled back the foil, elated at the reveal of homemade peanut butter chocolate fudge. "Yesss." The first bite was in her mouth fast, eliciting a chuckle from Levi.

"Paul and the girls were over earlier, and they made sure to bring extra for you. They were disappointed you weren't home. Though, I'm not gonna lie, it was probably because they wanted to see Toothless." He looked down at the cat, who gave him a throaty meow in reply. He lifted his rugged waterproof boot closer, and Toothless rubbed her face against it lovingly.

"I don't care," Charlie said. "The girls brought me fudge because they know how much I love it." She reached for another piece, then thought better of it and grabbed the entire plate from Levi and ate over it. "They can see Toothless anytime. I told you, I don't care if you let them in."

As owner of the duplex, Levi had a key to Charlie's place. Actually, as one of the few in his trusted circle, she had a key to his. Still, he took his landlord duties seriously. While Charlie would argue that fudge counted as an emergency worthy of unscheduled entry, he'd disagree.

A slight smile quirked as he shook his head at her obsession with the treat. "Yeah, they're thoughtful, those two. I'm pretty lucky."

"Mm," Charlie said with a sticky mouthful. She swallowed the peanut butter chocolate goodness and grinned. "I want Paul to be *my* brother."

"He'd be happy to have you." Levi thumped his hand lightly against the couch. "He and Damion keep bugging me about dating again. They're using the girls as an excuse, saying they want an aunt but... Well, guess it's better than them asking for cousins."

Mid-chew, Charlie's shoulders dropped. Levi had been single for as long as she'd known him. They'd bonded over their shared avoidance of romantic relationships, and over time, she'd slowly gotten him to open up, albeit in tiny increments. She didn't have the whole story, but he didn't have hers either. He knew nothing of her physical struggles. However, he'd heard enough about Bobby to earnestly refer to him as her "fucker of an ex."

Either way, they gelled. They both worked a lot, had their small circles of close friends. He occasionally shared food with her, and she offered time with animals that he wouldn't admit to wanting. She didn't judge his no-strings approach to hooking up with women, and he didn't judge her limited interest in the dating arena.

For two people not in committed relationships, they didn't feel lacking, especially when their families seemed so focused on it being the key to happiness. They both knew it had the equal ability to cause heartbreak.

"They only bring it up 'because they love you,'" she parroted.

"You bet." He cleared his throat and stood, crossing his arms over his chest. "So the door slam. Want to talk about it?"

By saying what he already had, he'd reached his threshold for the day. Maybe even the month. Yet, she wasn't in the mood to share either.

"Nothing this delicious fudge can't fix," she said.

He gave her a smile, a bigger one this time—no teeth, but it actually produced the little crinkle at his eyes, which was a plus.

Another knock at the door had them both staring at it.

"Who in the world is that?" Charlie mumbled.

She opened it without looking, something she rarely did, perhaps comforted with Levi standing there.

Or maybe she sensed who was on the other side.

Zachary searched her face, lingering on her mouth, then jumping back to her eyes. His brow was creased, his hair mussed from the wind, strands falling freely on his forehead.

She shivered, a little weirded out that he knew where she lived and simultaneously happy he'd found her. Sensing Levi standing up behind her, she asked the question that should've popped out immediately. "What are you doing here?"

He held up a to-go box—*ah*, *leftovers*—and then lifted the other hand, holding a bag from Dorothy's. "Peace offering?"

Charlie bit her lip, trying to quickly sort through her feelings. Levi's hand on her shoulder pulled her attention to him.

"You good, Charlie?" he asked.

"Oh. Yes." She looked at Zachary, whose hands had dropped slightly at the sight of Levi. "This is Zachary Lee. Zachary, this is Levi."

Levi held out his hand, waiting as Zachary piled the Dorothy's bag on top of the to-go box so he could shake it.

"Hey," was all Levi said. Then he leaned over to Charlie's ear and whispered, "Got some chocolate on your upper lip."

Her eyes widened, remembering Zachary zeroing in on *that exact spot*, as she wiped furiously at her mouth.

"I...sorry, Harris. I didn't mean to interrupt," Zachary said, his eyes darting from Levi down to Charlie's hand clutching the plate of fudge.

"I was just leaving." Levi stepped into the shared mini alcove and went to the door across from hers. "Talk to you later, Charlie." He gave Zachary a nod as he stepped into his flat.

"Thank the girls for me, Levi!" Charlie called out, getting a small wave of acknowledgment from him before his door closed.

Leaving her and Zachary alone. At her apartment.

Silent.

Zachary gestured with the bag over his shoulder. "Close neighbor."

"I knocked his frame off the wall," she blurted.

Zachary looked rightfully confused. "Okay." He cleared his throat. "I reached out to Maura for your address, I hope that's alright. You forgot your leftovers. And this, though maybe I'm too late." He gestured to her hands, one with the plate and the other smudged with fudge.

"No! No. I never turn down Dorothy's. You owe me, remember?" Charlie snatched the bag from his hand and peered inside at a pile of snickerdoodles. "If this is how you handle arguments, you alone could keep them in business."

"Now, hang on, I don't think what we had necessarily qualifies as an argument."

"Mm..."

"Misunderstanding, maybe."

She squinted at him. "No denying there will be more *arguments* in the future."

Zachary took a deep breath. "Look, I need to clear the air on something."

His serious tone threw her. She stepped back reluctantly and gestured him inside. She could at least hear him out while she ate. "Okay, come in." She settled on her couch and shoved aside a stack of mail on the wooden coffee table, making room for the fudge. She waved the bag of cookies at him to continue. "You can sit if you want."

"Um..." He looked around her living room and frowned at the blanket crumpled at one end of the couch, then quickly returned focus to her. "Do you want some dinner?"

"This'll do," she said, already digging into a cookie.

"You hardly ate—"

"Zachary."

He was nervous. Still, she couldn't let his sweetness overwhelm her or him being in her home soften her anger. Her favorite fuzzy blanket was right there and perfect for two people.

Crap.

"Why would you bring me cookies and then tell me not to eat them?" she challenged.

He scratched his head, fighting a smile. She knew he wanted to let it free, to acknowledge what she was saying.

"Actually, you know what." She wiggled her fingers for the to-go box and snagged two fries before setting the container by the fudge. "There. My Nana always encouraged a good salt and sweet combo."

He chuckled nervously, then steeled himself with a deep breath. "I've been acting a bit off toward you since I've been back."

Charlie paused her chewing, surprised.

"Okay, here's the thing. After vet school, I left. It was my decision. When I told my dad I was going to work with my father-in-law, he didn't waste any time saying he was going to transfer the practice to you. As though it had always been his plan."

Charlie furrowed her brow, but he held up a hand.

"Let me explain myself, please," he said softly. He slipped off his shoes and started to pace. "You and I were friends, and I really enjoyed hanging out with you. Because of that, I felt good leaving, like my dad was in good hands. Like I wasn't leaving him high and dry. When I stopped by that last day, and he told me his plan though—giving it to you—I immediately questioned everything. Whether he thought I could run my own business. How much he actually believed in my ability as a vet. If he minded that I'd be gone." He paused, stared at the floor. "I even wondered if you'd just been acting friendly with everyone to weasel your way into the family business yourself."

"Ouch," Charlie whispered. While that stung, begrudgingly, his other admissions tugged at her heart. Brought back the memory of him storming out of the clinic all those years ago, without saying a word. "That's why you left so upset."

"Yeah." Zachary looked up at her, expression serious. "I'm sorry, Charlie. I blamed you this whole time, and I didn't realize it until I was back. Seeing you again. It hasn't been good between me and Dad, obviously. But I'd cut myself off from you, and somehow, that'd been my way of sticking it to you, I guess. Instead, I was only punishing myself. Our friendship keeps forcing its way back. It's a fight to hate you when really, you're *you*." He shoved his hands into his pockets. "Okay, I'm done."

"Wow." Charlie leaned back against the couch. "That's...wow."

"Yeah."

"I mean, it explains a lot."

"Good."

"Not quite how you could hate me so hard because, let's face it, I'm a delight," she said matter-of-factly.

He shook his head, that grin breaking free. "I know."

Charlie squirmed at her teasing bravado, unnerved by the tingling that burst through her with his agreement. At those creases by his mouth that let her know his smile was heartfelt. She braced herself to be real. "You know I love your family, right? Like, I would do anything for them, Zachary. I mean it." She nudged her glasses farther up her nose as though that exposed the truth in her eyes.

Zachary kneeled in front of her, placing one hand on the arm of the couch and one on the cushion beside her. "Charlie, I wish I could deny ever having that shitty thought. Believe me, I know there's no ounce of truth in it."

She tilted her head, earnest. "*All* those thoughts were shitty. Even the ones where you doubted yourself," she whispered.

His eyes softened. He swallowed, looking down at his hand beside her, his long fingers smoothing the cushion, the motion causing a slight vibration that tingled her thigh. "You know, you've been a part of my family for years. It didn't take long for that to happen." He hesitated, his eyes skating back to her face. "I found myself looking forward to summers home once I knew what it was like to work with you."

"Really?" Her voice was raspy, soft. She hated it. Wanted him. Could barely process what he was saying.

Her heart raced, her breathing tripped, and she realized she was dipping closer toward him.

He wasn't touching her, but his heat pulsed around her. The anticipation of his hands sliding over an inch to brush her thighs made her forget all concerns from earlier that night. The thought of his hand on hers, of their bare skin against one another, sent swirls of excitement through her body.

"Are you okay?" he asked softly.

"Hmm?" *Yes, if okay means a sugared-up, turned-on ball of energy.* She tipped closer, their faces inches apart, his breath mingling with hers. Her pulse raced through her ears.

"Do you want to talk about that woman who stopped by our table?" He asked the question quietly, but he may as well have shouted it.

The thought of her ex and his mother was enough to douse her arousal. "Ha!" She gently pushed his shoulders back, giving herself room to stand. "Nope. I do not."

"I thought we—"

"Don't ruin what you just said by turning this into some tit-for-tat situation, Zachary. You were ready to explain. I'm not." She guided him to his shoes and then the door, opened it, and scooted him into the alcove.

"Harris, I'm sorry, I shouldn't have brought it up—"

"I appreciate everything you said. Goodnight, Zachary."

"Wait!"

She paused, moments away from slamming the door in his face. She'd replace as many frames for Levi as she needed to. The thought actually made her giddy.

"What?"

"I'm off tomorrow."

"Yeah. What about it?"

"Do you want to go over stuff for the cookout?"

"No."

"No?"

She huffed. "Why do I have to keep repeating myself?"

"Your answers keep surprising me."

"Well, enjoy being surprised then. Go home, Zachary. Or wherever it is you're staying." She pushed the door closed, more gently than she'd have liked, considering she would've smashed his face. She used extra emphasis to lock it instead and watched through the peephole. Zachary stared a minute at her door, glanced over to Levi's, and left.

Toothless wound through her legs, so Charlie picked her up. "Where'd you run off to? Not much of a guard cat tonight, are you?"

Not that it would've been any help in warding off her emotions. Because despite what he'd revealed, Charlie had caught feelings, and she wasn't sure she'd be able to let them go.

Chapter 16

Zachary

"Put the damn phone down, Z," Sandra hissed. "The kids are trying to tell you a story."

Zachary clicked off his phone and slid it into his coat pocket. "Sorry, guys."

He looked up at his niece and nephew, who were making the most of their waiting room time until they were called back into his dad's room.

"Uncle Zachy." Vivi took hold of his hands, her long hair falling loose from a ponytail and topped off with a princess crown. Sparkly blue and purple plastic necklaces were piled around her neck, hanging to her stomach. "You hafta hear about the princess."

"I'm ready. I want to hear all about the princess," he said.

"Dun, dunn, dun, dunnn!" Alex cried, creating his own coronation song. He was draped in a blanket—to emulate royalty—and bopped around with his toy sword, tapping it on the floor. He wore a sparkly purple necklace Vivi had graced him with in an earlier ceremony.

The kids regaled them with a surprisingly short story about a princess and a prince, who were traipsing through the halls of a castle where lots of doctors and nurses worked. They had to whisper when they passed by the rooms of all the people living there, and their mission was inconclusive. But they knew there would be ice cream at the end, so it all worked out.

Then they settled into a waiting room chair to watch a show on Sandra's phone.

With their eyes glued to the screen, Zachary pulled out his phone again. "I love that you let them out of the house like that," he said quietly. "They look like little tornadoes."

Over jeans and an emerald sweater embroidered with robots, Vivi wore a bright yellow tutu that fluffed over the sides of her chair. Alex, whose short black hair was in a perpetual state of "I nap hard," wore his woodland creatures' blanket over a sweatshirt with neon green ABCs and fuchsia hand-me-down snow pants. One snow boot was inexplicably on the ground below his dangling feet.

"They wouldn't have come otherwise. But whatever, they're expressing themselves. If I act embarrassed about it, who's that going to help?"

"Mmm." No new messages, as he flipped through his texts and emails.

"Want to tell me what's going on?"

He tapped his phone in his hand, debating. Lying to her was useless—his sister had always been able to read him. Telling her exactly what was on his mind wasn't at the top of his list either, so he opted for the middle ground.

"Trying to figure out what else I can do to help Charlie. Feel like she's still taking on more than she needs to. You know, with me in town."

"That sounds like her."

"Yeah. She hasn't changed." He smiled, remembering how ready she was to tackle anything and everything when she first started at EFVH.

She'd arrive early or leave late from front desk shifts so she could shadow techs or his dad. Her eagerness had rubbed off on him a bit—the ability to discuss his career with someone so passionate who wasn't his father reminded him it wasn't a requirement to go into the business, it was a choice. One he really wanted.

Sandra tugged the cuffs of her crewneck sweater and tucked her hands between her knees. "How are things coming along for the cookout?"

"I'm not sure. Sounds like she has it under control."

"You're going?"

"I'm grilling the food."

Sandra practically tipped from her chair. "Seriously?"

"Yep. Talked to Mom a bit about Dad's setup."

Sandra blinked, the shake of her head slight as she processed the information. "You're literally filling in for him. At work. At the cookout."

"Yep."

"Wow. I'm surprised."

Zachary raised his eyebrows. "It's obvious."

"Can you blame me? After carefully carving your own path in the same career as Dad, you left town for what's-her-face"—Sandra said as she scrunched her nose—"and now, here you are, stepping in as though it was all ready and waiting for you."

It unsettled him, that everything locked into place so naturally. Instead of feeling honored to step into his father's shoes, Zachary felt guilty. After the choices he'd made and the hurt he'd caused, he didn't deserve things to run smoothly. For his father's sake, he was glad it did.

For Charlie too.

"You know which brand of these items Dad would get? Don't want to drop the ball." He showed the grocery list to Sandra, a photo of the handwritten list with Charlie's cheerful loopy penmanship. The one he'd convinced her to text him that morning in an effort to soften the night before and keep contact positive. He wanted her to accept his help, even if she didn't want to open up to him just yet. He knew there was more beneath her cheery exterior, and for some reason, he was hellbent on getting past it.

She shrugged. "I have no clue, we just show up. I'm sure Charlie has some ideas?"

He was surprised she hadn't included more details to make sure he followed things exactly. If it gave him an excuse to reach out to her though, he'd take it. She wouldn't deny a conversation about the cookout.

He tapped out a text.

Zachary: *Pretend I'm five. What specifics/brands etc should I get?*

He waited for those little dots to indicate she was responding.

"What are you grinning about?" Sandra asked.

The text that buzzed through made him smile even wider.

Charlie: *A five-year-old shouldn't be doing the shopping. Did you rope in Vivi and Alex?*

She didn't even accuse *him* of being five, which was a good sign.

"You're a genius, Sandra," he said.

"It's exhausting sometimes," she replied.

He ignored his sister, too busy arguing with the little voice in his head that proclaimed this was all a ruse to stay on Charlie's mind.

She was definitely on his.

***

Zachary piled meat, vegetarian patties, and toppings into the fridge, took a picture of the goods, and texted it to Charlie.

Charlie: *I'm surprised you didn't send me a picture of it in your car.*

Zachary: *?*

Charlie: *Got individual pix of the items, the full cart, now the fridge. I missed the transportation stage.*

Perhaps his attempts had turned desperate, but he wasn't ashamed. Now that he was home, alone, the hospital visit and grocery shopping behind him, he didn't need to simply text her. He looked at the clock. She had to be finishing up notes at the office.

Determined, he coaxed Maple into his SUV, the poor girl giving him a look that made him promise her it'd be worth it. He muttered to himself the whole drive there about how this was a good idea. Once he arrived in the Village and slowed, his shoulders relaxed. Wreaths and holiday lights dripped from awnings, street lamps showcased sparkly bows. Storefront windows were incorporating winter displays, the mood cheery, happy, *warm*.

He parked and stared at the employee exit. Twinkle lights framed the front windows of the otherwise dark clinic. Their end of the lot was quiet, Charlie's car the only one left. Maple popped up and panted excitedly as she recognized where they were.

"Pretty good surprise, huh? Let's go inside and say hi," he said. He helped her out of the car and into the building, the lights low, the space quiet. Maple did her version of hustling down the hall and into their office, where he heard a yelp of surprise.

He rounded the corner to see Charlie accepting kisses from Maple, her laugh breathless.

"She scared the crap out of me," she said.

He winced. "Sorry, I should've called out."

With one final kiss, Maple lumbered over to the bed she now claimed as her own and hunkered down.

"It's okay." Charlie stood, an adoring look on her face as her gaze left Maple and met his.

He stopped short, caught off guard by her soft expression, one she gave so freely to animals as though they all stole her heart. Maura was on the receiving end quite a bit as well. There was one time he thought he'd caught it directed at him—when they'd helped the kittens. He'd been holding one of the little guys in his hands, saying how lucky it was, only to look up, directly into Charlie's eyes. A sheen to their hazel warmth, her smile had made him feel like a hero.

The glow of the office lamps created a halo effect around her now, the space as cozy as a cabin up north. A pink hue rose to her cheeks and skimmed down her neck, and she bit her lower lip. When his eyes followed her action, she cleared her throat and turned back to her desk.

"What are you two doing here?" Her voice cracked.

What am *I doing here?*

"Thought I'd swing by to finish our conversation. About the groceries. Maple and I were running out anyway," he hastened to add as she turned.

One eyebrow raised above rose-gold glasses. "Was there a problem with them?"

"Problem? No. They're all tucked away in Jordan's fridge." He cringed at his words.

Her voice was laced with humor. "Do you need me to tell the food a bedtime story?"

His laugh shook, and he scratched a hand through his hair. He was *nervous*.

"I'm afraid it'd be grim," she continued. "All about what they're in for in a few days."

He groaned. "Harris, that's dark."

She chuckled. "Hey, I warned you, Lee." She lifted her purse to her shoulder, and he finally registered her coat.

"You're heading out?"

"Yeah. Running home to feed Toothless and then helping Magnolia at her shop."

"You're doing that tonight?"

"Yeah. She's got a fair amount left, and she's basically here alone."

"How are you managing that in the midst of everything else?"

She shrugged. "Good to have a change of scenery, I guess."

He nodded and looked at Maple, head resting between her paws, eyebrows seesawing as she watched them. "Think Toothless and Maple are on a similar schedule. Need to get her home for dinner too."

"I thought the two of you were heading somewhere?"

"We were?" What had he said? "Oh, right. Well, just a quick stop. The fridge! I left stuff in this fridge earlier." Not as smooth as if he'd mentioned it up front, but it was true.

"Oh, you'll find quite a few things in there. More deliveries came this afternoon."

"Seriously?"

She nodded.

"Right. If you hang on a second, we'll walk you out?"

She tilted her head, then nodded. "Okay."

"Great." He hurried out of the office, telling himself to cool it the entire way to the kitchenette and back, meals piled in his arms. "All set," he said.

"Want some help?" She turned off the lamps and walked toward him, Maple at her heels.

"No."

She locked their door, gave him another glance, then shrugged, leading him out.

"So...is Toothless missing all her teeth?" he asked.

"A fair amount, yes. She actually reminded me of the dragon though, that's where her name came from."

"What dragon?" The only dragons that came to mind were from *Game of Thrones*.

"You haven't been introduced to the world of *How to Train Your Dragon*?"

"Definitely not."

She sighed dramatically as she held the door for him and Maple, and he grinned.

"You'll score major uncle points with the kids if you ask to watch it with them. Vivi couldn't stop talking about it after she saw the movies. Asked me if anyone's brought in their pet dragons for me to take care of."

He thought of the kids and their play earlier.

"Thanks for the tip." They moved quietly toward her car. "You only have the one cat then?" he asked.

"Yeah. I foster from time to time too."

"Ah, making up for lost time?" She spun toward him, brow furrowed. "I, uh, remember your mom not being an animal person?" He phrased it like a question because he didn't realize he'd stored that detail.

She was quiet a moment, and he leaned closer to Maple to keep from saying more.

"Yeah. It still overwhelms her, even though she doesn't live with me." She opened her car door and tossed in her purse, then stared at her keys. "Toothless would love Maple. She's a great snuggle buddy. Recognizes a good soul."

Zachary looked down at the old pup who gazed back with her happy frosted face. "Maple too. I uh, I didn't see Toothless last night."

Charlie cleared her throat. "Yeah, I'm not sure where she ran off to. She was out when Levi came by."

"Ah." Seeing another man in Charlie's apartment wasn't on the list of things he'd been hoping for when he stopped by. Knowing that man had watched her drag chocolate all over her mouth made some weird jealous thoughts kick into gear.

She didn't let the silence last for long. "I really should get going."

He scrambled for something else to say, realizing that hearing her voice, seeing her, had been what he needed.

The admission was too much to process.

"Right, well, let me know if there's anything else I can take off your hands."

"Alright." She paused a moment. "A lot has changed, but I think you'll really enjoy it. I'm glad you'll be here."

"Me too. Wow, another Charlie Harris event. The first one I attended was your graduation."

"Oh, going way back, are we?"

He shrugged. "I remember a lot of really detailed decorations and multiple stations to keep people entertained."

"Mmm, well, the decorations were courtesy of my cousins."

"They put cutouts of your face everywhere. Even on the bathroom door."

She winced. "I blocked those from memory. It's all just a perfectly bright color scheme with pretty signage in my mind. The stations were my idea, mostly as a way to distract people from any embarrassing activities my mom had in mind. She managed to pull some off anyway."

"I remember the large poster board she made everyone sign with a memory of you growing up. Then she picked her favorites to read out loud."

Charlie groaned. "You were still there for that, huh?"

He laughed. "A little, maybe." He'd enjoyed it, hearing endearing stories about Charlie from those who loved her. Funny thing was, he could picture each one. Despite a professional approach at work, she was still Charlie.

She shifted her keys along the ring. "That was the one and only time I met Anna."

He scrunched his face in thought. "That's right. I forgot I brought her."

"Yeah. Even then, she wasn't your type." She looked away quickly, but not before her eyes widened into saucers.

Zachary straightened, the half-dozen casseroles heavy. "You don't think so, huh?"

She slowly looked at him. "Nope. Not warm enough for you. Or genuine, really."

Zachary didn't say anything. Hearing it from Charlie, who'd met Anna once, surprised him. She'd never met any of his previous girlfriends, and he'd never discussed them at work. Apparently, Charlie had considered what type of person would be good for him.

Then he zeroed in on the other detail, that she'd said "even then." What all did she know about how things went down with him and Anna?

"Thanks again for shopping. I'll see you tomorrow, okay?" She slid into her car, gave Maple a wave, and closed the door before he could say anything else.

No chance to ask who she thought would be a good fit for him. Not that he was looking. Instead, all he could do was let his imagination run with it, and he found that was almost as good.

CHAPTER 17

Charlie

CHARLIE HAD TRIED TO limit communication with Zachary. It seemed safest to put distance between them. Then he'd dropped by unexpectedly, all handsome and eager and seemingly happy to be near her. She couldn't have been misreading that, right?

There wasn't time to dwell on it now. Not here, not after her appointment that morning.

She turned off the car, parked in the small lot behind The Refill Mill. Releasing a slow breath, her forehead sank to the steering wheel.

It shouldn't surprise her. The city was big, yes, but Charlie ran into people she knew all the time. While personal experience proved that meant no place was off-limits, she hadn't been prepared to see Magnolia step out of an exam room just as she was leaving the PT office. They'd locked eyes, a look of shock passing over her friend's face. Charlie had bolted, as though her secret was printed across her forehead.

She had no clue Magnolia was going to physical therapy, and no one knew Charlie was. There might have even been a way to ignore it, shove it under the rug until they both "forgot" about it. With everything going on, Charlie had added an extra maintenance appointment, to make sure stress wasn't undoing any progress. She'd never expected to see her friend there at the exact same time! What were the odds of that?

It was pointless to put it off any longer. She trudged toward the door, a sense of relief washing over her when she heard Amber's voice carrying from the front. Dodging Magnolia with extra people around would be much easier.

Magnolia stood, hands pressed in front of her mouth, as she stared at a long table in the middle of the shop. Amber was sliding her hand over the wood as she walked around it, barely pausing to breathe.

"A friend from college grew up on a farm north of here, and she told me they were tearing down their old barn. Gathered up as much of the wood as I could over the summer. I was so grateful to her because people *love* handmade products from repurposed wood, but it's hard to get your hands on it because people snatch it up quickly. And especially from a barn? It's amazing, really. Even if you don't live near one you want something connected with it. I mean, the wood is great, and the pieces look beautiful. So that makes sense. When you told me what you needed for the shop, though, I knew this was the perfect project for it."

Another tug to Charlie's heart. Amber was named after Nana, and for good reason.

"Hey," Charlie said, her approach slow.

Amber glanced up. "Hey." She bit her nail, waiting, then put her arm around Magnolia. "Do you like it?" she asked softly.

The sheen in Magnolia's eyes glittered as she peeled her focus from the table. "Are you kidding?" she whispered. "It's beautiful." She squeezed Amber into a hug, and Amber blinked her own wet eyes.

Charlie looked at the long table in front of her, the wood sanded smooth, glowing a golden honey brown. Down the middle stretched another tier, tiny etchings shaped into the supports to match the ones down the legs of the table.

"Amber, you made this?" Charlie asked.

Her cousin nodded.

"It's absolutely perfect. I have to send this to my boss," Magnolia said, positioning her phone. The women stepped back so she could get a clear photo. "This will look amazing with all the light from the windows."

"It's gorgeous," Charlie added.

Amber smiled, a rare flash of embarrassment crossing her face. "I think it fits in well."

"Definitely." Magnolia scanned the store as though she'd been dropped back into reality. "Holy shit, there's still a lot to do."

"We're ready, Mags," Charlie said, offering a small smile.

"Only you, actually. Cleo's closing the shop, and I got called into the restaurant for a couple hours. Sorry," Amber added to Magnolia.

"It's okay. This is a great help. Next level of setup can be done," Magnolia said.

Amber turned to Charlie. "Before I run, any updates on your hottie vet? You've been shit at texting me back lately."

Charlie rolled her eyes on a laugh. "I've been distracted."

"Ooo, I love hot distractions," Amber said, rubbing her hands together.

Charlie laughed but gave herself an extra moment, taking off her coat and setting her things down near the checkout counter. She could tell how badly Zachary wanted to smooth things over from the previous night. Seeing him after he'd texted with her all day, everything had sunk in—and all she wanted was to hang out with him more.

She needed to talk this out.

She let out a slow breath. "He apologized to me."

Amber and Magnolia glanced at each other, then Amber leaned forward. "What did he do?" Her voice was low.

Charlie waved her off. "Remember how I said he'd been different? Not really letting our friendship come back? Turns out he was harboring some resentment for how things went down with his dad, and how Daniel wanted to pass the practice on to me."

"What!" Amber shouted.

"That's not your fault at all," Magnolia said.

"Which he acknowledged," Charlie continued. "We talked through it, he admitted I was kind of a symbol for all that. But that he can't, you know, resist our friendship."

"So, what, just like that he's back to being cool?" Amber didn't hide her skepticism.

"It helps a lot, to know what was going on. I'm sure we'll still disagree over things, workwise, but on a less personal level..." Charlie said. "He stopped by the office tonight, though, to say hi, when he could've just texted me." It hadn't been necessary at all. He'd come because he wanted to see her.

"Okay, that's cute," Magnolia added.

"Well, I still say keep an eye on him," Amber said.

"It doesn't sound like that'll be hard," Magnolia fake whispered.

Charlie grinned while they laughed, Amber in spite of herself.

"Okay, damnit, I have to go, but call if you need backup," Amber said as she wrapped Charlie in a hug.

After she left, Charlie and Magnolia slowly looked at one another, the occasional sounds from the street carrying inside the shop.

"I'm gonna turn on some music," Magnolia said. "Then let's put this magnificent table to work, shall we?"

Songs from the eighties onward played over the speakers as Charlie helped scoot over various boxes and totes, arranging it as a workstation. Over the next hour, they set paper wrappers around bars of soap, placed labels on bottles of handmade perfumes, sealed lip balms with compostable tapes. Little plaques were written to denote the items for display.

The lights in the shop glowed softly, a contrast to the darkness outside, the street lamps and twinkle lights dim through the window. The refinished, original wood floors creaked as they moved around, the echo of the space dimming as they arranged products on the shelves. As Charlie organized jars and bottles, Magnolia wiped down the cleared table.

"I had a double mastectomy."

At Magnolia's statement, Charlie turned away from the shelf, an empty mason jar in her hand. Magnolia set product markers on the table, eyes focused down as she went.

"I found a lump when I was twenty-five. Fortunately, we caught it early enough, but I decided then to just take them both. In my mind, that was helping me get past it all faster. And lessen the chances, you know?"

Charlie nodded, even though Magnolia didn't look at her. She lowered onto a crate and sat, waiting.

"I opted for reconstructive surgery, a smaller cup size than I'd been...before. I've had two surgeries since. The implants kept shifting, so then I had them removed altogether." She shrugged, finally looking at Charlie. "I had my last surgery about four months before I moved here. My physical therapy had been going well, but I guess I aggravated it carrying things around the shop." She glanced around, wincing. "That helped put me behind schedule, actually, I overdid it. Anyway, my PT back in California helped me find one nearby."

"Wow. Magnolia, I'm so sorry," Charlie said.

She gave her a small smile. "Felt weird not to tell you after this morning. I hadn't intentionally kept it from you all, it's just..." She bit her lip. "I went from trying to stand out among the praising of my older sister and the coddling of my younger sister, to having way more attention than I could handle. I'm talking, like, somehow my whole family knew what I ate each day type of involvement. Being in a small town where we pretty much knew everybody meant all our neighbors weighed in too. It was refreshing coming here, kind of finding a bit of me again. From before. If my boss hadn't planned on opening this location where she grew up, I would've moved somewhere else eventually." She swallowed, blinking her eyes rapidly as she picked the white cloth off the table and turned toward the stand-alone, brick bar counter she had thrifted and repurposed as a checkout station. "Anyway. That's that. I'll tell the others, too, but you're the lucky first." She turned to wink, her movements a little jerky.

"Magnolia, I'm sorry. I hope you didn't feel obligated."

"It feels good to share, actually. It's part of me, I'm not ashamed of it."

Not ashamed of it. Charlie stared at the jar in her hands, twisting the lid back and forth. To be able to acknowledge it like that, to own it, was something Charlie hadn't even allowed herself to consider. It seemed far from possible, after burying it so deep in high school. She didn't have anyone to talk to about it, or at least, that's what she'd thought. What if she simply shared it? Like Magnolia?

"I've been going to PT for a few years now, but no one else knows," Charlie said softly.

Magnolia moved closer and squatted down to meet her at eye level. "Hey, same thing to you—just because I shared, doesn't mean you have to."

Charlie swallowed. "Is it okay if I do?"

"Oh God, yes, of *course*." Magnolia sat on the ground, crossed her legs.

Charlie let out a shaky breath. "I've been seeing Ali there for pelvic floor therapy. For vaginismus. As far as we know, it's something I've always had, compounded by stressors and anxiety and all that. I say that because some women experience issues after surgeries or injuries, physical traumas, that sort of thing." She swallowed, her heart pounding in her throat, speeding up her words. "I had extreme pain, with no form of penetration allowed, even a tampon. I didn't really know what was going on for years, and I went from doctor to doctor until I finally found someone who knew what I was talking about, who wasn't just going to prescribe me medication and move on, and recognized that it wasn't all 'in my head.' Once I finally found her, I was referred to a PT, and a therapist who was familiar with it as well. These last few years have been pretty intensive in going through it all and so... Yeah." She said the words in a rush.

"Damn. That sucks, Charlie. I'm sorry. That's had to make romantic relationships pretty difficult. Or even scary?"

"Yes," Charlie choked. "How do you explain that to someone, when that's such a major part? Hard to get past feeling like something's wrong with me."

Magnolia's eyes welled, her nods slight. She rushed onto her knees, wrapping Charlie in a hug.

Neither of them made a sound, but Charlie felt the force of Magnolia's tears match her own, their breath hitching as they held tight.

"I know that feeling well," Magnolia whispered. She pulled back, swiping at her cheeks. "The others don't know?"

Charlie shook her head and wiped tears off her glasses. "No."

Magnolia tilted her head. "Not even Amber?" she asked softly.

"No, I haven't been able to bring myself to admit it, beyond my therapist. And now you."

She squeezed Charlie's hand. "I'm here if you ever want to talk about it."

Charlie squeezed hers in return. "Thanks. Same."

Magnolia stood and cleared her throat. "I think we deserve to wrap this up and get something delicious."

That brought a genuine smile to Charlie's face. "You know the way to my heart."

CHAPTER 18

Charlie

CHARLIE HUNCHED OVER HER desk, busying herself with files for the day's lineup. Soft footsteps carried down the hall as techs prepped for morning appointments, but the nudge of a wet nose against her hip pulled her focus.

"Maple, sweet girl, how are you?" She crimped the old pup's soft, floppy ear and received a lick on the wrist. Greeting complete, Maple curled up next to Zachary's desk.

Zachary's desk. When had it switched to that?

Dark gray tennis shoes came into view. Charlie's eyes traveled up the long legs and torso to find a clean-shaven Zachary. He pulled on his jacket, the muscles of his forearms twisting as he flipped it over his back. She followed the motion of his hands as he adjusted the strap of his watch, his long fingers moving with swift and gentle motions. That same hand moved up and passed through his hair, which was when she noticed him watching from the corner of his eyes.

The night before, she'd basically revealed she'd thought about him in a boyfriend sense, imagining what type of person she pictured for him. Breathing room was important to get her head on straight. It couldn't start now, not with him calling to ask that she cover him while he helped with his dad.

Hearing his voice in the early morning, somehow deeper through the phone, was a new favorite way to start her day.

"Something wrong, Harris?"

Oh. Her mouth was actually hanging open. She jolted to close it and her teeth clamped loudly, her brain and motions nowhere near in sync. Here she was, gaping at the man, newly aware that strong, lean hands were a major turn-on, and they should be all over her. Preferably while feeding her snickerdoodles.

A small laugh bubbled out as she replied, "No." *God, Charlie, that was almost a whimper!* She cleared her throat. "No. Everything is good. All good. Great, even."

He nodded slowly. "Sure."

"Maple reminds me of Dale the Dog." *Ah, yes.* Common ground, bringing up the sweet dog. *Nope, just another way to show how long you've known each other, Charlie. This isn't safe territory at all!*

Someday, she'd address why she scolded herself in the third person.

His smile was soft. "Thought the same thing when I saw her picture on the rescue's website. Couldn't imagine her not having a family during her golden years."

"How long have you had her?"

"About three years. Waited a little after Dale passed. Anna was so pissed."

"That you adopted again?"

"That I adopted a *senior*. She'd wanted a puppy, something about it being better for her 'brand,'" he mumbled, then crouched to give Maple a belly rub. "She didn't even really care for Dale when he was around."

"That's impossible! He was a natural heart stealer."

"I guess you'd have to have a heart for him to steal in the first place."

"*Woah.*" Her delivery was soft, with the impact of a punchline.

A laugh shot out of Zachary, but there was pain in his eyes when he glanced back at her. "It's the truth. She wasn't always that way." He looked back at Maple. "I don't think."

"Well, she's missing out." She watched Zachary dote on Maple, and found herself gazing at him with the same adoration as the old girl. Before Zachary caught her staring awkwardly *again*, in the span of minutes, she quickly added, "Maple's a very lucky girl."

Adding the sentiment had seemed like a way to soften Anna "missing out," but now the whole conversation felt more affectionate. Why did she keep revealing she was fond of him? *God, 'fond'? Own up!*

Zachary stood, walked over to her. She tipped her head back, sucking in a breath filled with the scent of warm, crisp woods. She swallowed, an attempt to capture it while not being obvious she'd just inhaled the man—except she swallowed too much air and choked.

Turning away, she squinted tearing eyes at the window. The red and gold leaves of the park blurred like a watercolor blend. His warm hand patted her shoulder a few times.

"You okay?" Zachary asked.

She swallowed carefully and looked at him. He appeared to have no trouble with *his* breathing and, instead, dared to look sexy and cool in his jacket.

"*Cool*" was something she was not. "All good."

A slow smile spread across his face. "Did you choke on air?"

"It happens sometimes!"

His laugh filled the room, its deep rumble zinging between her legs. *Oh my.* So far, he'd only given her small chuckles, a tease. She'd forgotten how full-bodied his laugh was. It lit her up inside until she felt like she could power every marquee of Broadway. She wanted to wrap her arms around him, feel it roll from his body to hers.

"Dr. Harris?"

Charlie peered around him, feeling privileged he was so close. She felt his gaze on her.

Jasmine stood in the doorway. "Room three is ready."

"Great, thanks." She cleared her hoarse voice.

Zachary's fingers pulled back from her shoulder, pinching her fabric lightly before taking slow steps back. The material *poofed* against her clavicle, and she shivered, the chill heightened by the warmth his hand had left behind.

"Thanks again for covering me. I really appreciate it." He scratched Maple's head. "I'll come back for you later, sweet girl."

"Hope everything goes alright," Charlie said.

"I like your scrubs today." He winked, signaled Maple to stay, and left the office.

Charlie stared at the door as her heart raced after him—she felt the pulse in her throat. She looked at Maple just as the old girl turned her gaze from the door to Charlie.

"He sure keeps me on my toes," she whispered. The dog slowly lowered her head onto the bed with a sigh. "Yeah, I know. He can do no wrong in your eyes."

She gathered up her stuff and straightened her scrubs, which were printed with line drawings of cats and dogs in baking caps, cupcakes, and, of course, cookies.

***

"I was really hoping I'd get Dr. Lee today."

Charlie glared at her cousin. "I actually had someone tell me that earlier and mean it."

She continued her inspection of the scruffy gray dog Amber had brought in. The small stray had to be around one year old, but its mange suggested it'd been on the streets for a while.

"I definitely mean it." Amber leaned on the exam table across from Charlie and grinned. Her thick, plaid coat draped over her frame. "When can I meet him?"

"The cookout. Unfortunately."

"Hmm." Amber straightened and pulled her long hair up into a messy knot, tugging the longer bangs into place.

"I can't believe you scheduled this, knowing I wasn't supposed to be here," Charlie muttered. She made little sounds of encouragement to the pup as she continued her exam.

"Don't blame me, this sweet guy needed looking after." Amber shook her head. "This actually works out, though, since you haven't returned any of my texts. Good thing I found a stray dog so I could talk to you."

Charlie rolled her eyes. "You're so dramatic. I just saw you."

"Ooo, maybe I should go into acting."

"And sarcastic."

"You're only listing reasons supporting that career choice."

The dog settled onto his belly, brown eyes drifting closed as Charlie inspected his ears.

"Oh my God, this little guy is so freakin adorable. Did he just fall asleep?" Amber leaned closer, drooping her lips in a little pout. "Is he okay?" she whispered, gently nuzzling the top of his head with a maroon-painted finger.

"He needs food and a bath. Looks pretty malnourished. We'll run some panels on him, though. What did Cory say when you called him?"

"He's hooking me up with a groomer since this pupperuni is in rough shape. They'll hopefully have someone to foster him by the end of the week, though. Going through the vetting process."

"Who's going to watch this little guy until then?"

There was no reply. When Charlie looked at Amber, she found her cousin gazing at him, her eyes practically bursting with hearts.

"I'll sneak him into my place." She looked up at Charlie and held out her hands. "It'll be fine! Only for a few days, and look—he's so tiny and chill, no one will know."

"Whatever you say." Charlie went to the computer in the room and added notes to his chart. "I'll have Sheila grab him for tests." She hesitated. "If it doesn't work out, call me, okay?"

Amber rolled her eyes. "It'll be fine. *We'll* be fine."

"Last time—"

"Last time, I tried to sneak in a forty-pound dog that liked to bark at dust bunnies. Definitely not as stealthy."

Amber's heart was in the right place, but it hadn't been the first time Charlie had needed to bail her out. This little puppy needed a lot of attention, and hopefully, his chill demeanor would, in fact, last. "Alright, well, keep me posted? I'll see you this weekend." Charlie opened the door to the hall just as Zachary approached.

"Oh! You're back!" Charlie's cheeks heated, the happiness in her voice as cheery as if he was holding boxes full of Dorothy's, all for her.

How her cousin had managed it, even *sensed* the opportunity, she had no clue, but suddenly, Amber was next to her, keeping the door to the employee-only hallway open.

"Are you Dr. Lee?"

"Amber!" Charlie hissed.

Zachary slowed, his gaze bouncing from Amber to Charlie and back again. "Yes..."

"Knew it."

"Wild guess. He's the only other doctor here right now, you know that," Charlie groused.

Her cousin ignored her completely. "Wow, you look just like your parents. Good genes."

"Okay, seriously. That's enough." Charlie forced her way into the hall and tried to pull the door closed, but Amber kept her body in the way.

"I'm Amber, Charlie's cousin." She stuck out her hand.

"Nice to meet you." Zachary shook her hand, then gave Charlie a look. "Taking personal meetings during the workday, Harris?"

"Yeah, sounds like me, when I barely take time for lunch." She let out a nervous laugh, which sounded more crazed than anything. Now she was overheating.

"Why so defensive?" He replied softly, with a grin that made Charlie bite her lower lip. His eyes zeroed in on the action, and his grin grew wider.

Those laugh lines would be the end of her. *Shit*. He. Was. Sexy.

"Well, it's nice to finally put a face to a name. I've heard a lot about you over the years, it's been a long time comin'," Amber said.

He raised his eyebrows. "That so?" Zachary asked Amber, his gaze fixed on Charlie.

She flapped her top to cool down. "Sheila!" she yelled, way too loudly, and spun around right into the woman. "Sorry. God, this hallway. Can you please take care of...Amber, what's the pup's name?"

"Charlie."

Charlie glared at her cousin.

Amber shrugged. "Might call him Chuck. Not sure yet. He's got this hidden feistiness about him, seems fitting."

"I hate you," Charlie muttered.

Zachary grinned, looking at his feet, but Amber stood proudly, smiling with ease.

"Sheila, please get Chuck the pup squared away with his tests. Then let's get Amber out of here." Charlie started toward her office.

"See you Sunday, Charlotte!" Amber called out, putting the final dig in as Charlie closed her office door behind her.

Knock, knock.

"Dr. Harris?" Jasmine called through the door.

"Yeah?"

"Room one is ready."

"Thanks!" Charlie gave herself a minute, staring out the window at the long shadows in the park.

She knew what she was doing. She could manage her work life with a personal life. Handle her *feelings*. Sure, this was a unique situation of the two colliding, but at the same time, it was only temporary. Zachary wasn't going to be in Elmwood Falls forever. Nothing aside from innocent flirting had happened, anyway. She was probably blowing it out of proportion.

Another knock sounded at the door, and she collected herself and whipped it open.

"Sorry, Jasmine, I'm coming."

Zachary stood in the hall, his thumb swiping slowly over his bottom lip. His eyes ticked up to hers, those dark eyebrows luring her. "You good?"

"Great!" She hurried past him and shoved into her next appointment room.

Relationships? Yeah, she had no clue what she was doing. In order to keep her cool, she had to find it in the first place.

CHAPTER 19

Charlie

CHARLIE SET HER GLASSES on the desk and leaned into her hands with a moan. Rain pummeled the windows as unrelenting as her migraine. The panes of glass glowed with the dreary gray of outside, her desk lamp angled at the wall to soften its slash of light. She pinched her forehead with her pointer fingers and dug her thumbs into her temples. Nothing soothed it.

She had three more hours of appointments, an afternoon where she and Zachary were booked solid. As unpleasant as it was, she'd worked through migraines before, so either way, she'd power through. It made her reliable. A picture of self-care, she was not. If she was lucky, the pain would dissipate by evening so she could tackle the final cookout details. Fortunately, most things were in order for the event the next day.

"Have you guys—what's wrong?"

Zachary's deep voice jolted Charlie from her sad attempt at massaging pressure points, but she kept her head in her hands. His question echoed in her head, and she shivered, the pain dulled for a split second. *Must be the deep breathing. Damn near sucked all the air from the room when he spoke.*

"Headache," Charlie mumbled.

"It looks like something knocked you out."

"Thanks. Always nice to hear."

The shift of his scrubs stopped, and a teasing nudge woke her shoulder. "Migraine?"

"Mmm," she mumbled again, shoving her fingers in desperation. "What were you asking?"

His subtle scent filled her nostrils—thank God it wasn't sweet because her head would explode. His body was so close she wanted to tip to the side and curl into him. If she hadn't been acutely aware of him filling her space, she might've thought he'd left. He released a resigned sigh just before his fingertips brushed her hand.

Charlie jolted at the contact, her hands dropping to the desk as she looked up at his concerned face. Her heart galloped, the pulse in her head increasing enough to make her wince. His eyes, an even deeper brown in the low light, tracked the movement.

"Aw, Charlie," he said, voice almost tentative. He crouched. His hand brushed aside wisps of hair and tucked them behind her ear. He placed the other along her jaw, cool fingers cradling her like she might break if he held on too hard. "Bear with me, okay?" Both his hands slid until the back of her head rested in them, fingertips squeezing her nape, thumbs pressing her temples.

She searched his face while he focused on his ministrations. He hadn't shaved again, the scruff on his jaw annoyingly arousing. Why did he have to walk around so effortlessly...*Zachary*? Emitting that "oh I'm so sexy but don't know it but really do" vibe that reeled her in willingly. Wearing his white coat over navy-blue scrubs, all clean and sharp and hot. She huffed in her head, closing her eyes lest they roll right out of their sockets. But then she kept them closed, nearly whimpering at the comfort. Her body was *fully* aware his hands were on her.

"Is this helping?" His voice was low, almost raspy.

Pressure increased, so every digit was actively trying to dull the pain. The scrape of his fingers in her hair, against her scalp, sent tingles down her spine.

Charlie cleared her throat. "Um." *Real clear, Charlie. That'll get him to stop. Or continue. Whichever the hell you want because, really, you don't know!*

"Anna used to get these all the time. When she couldn't get into acupuncture, she'd have me work certain spots. I don't really know what I'm doing, I'm just trying to put pressure everywhere."

Charlie's eyes opened as his hands, now warmed from friction, relocated. Heat traveled down her neck with the path his fingers took until he dug into the muscles by her shoulders and clavicle.

"Fuck, Harris. You're so tight. Is this good? Tell me what to do."

Oh, those words. He had no idea they triggered a different kind of tightness in her body. She squirmed, trying to ease the tingling zipping from her stomach. The thought of his hands on more of her bare skin was too much.

"This is the best I've felt all day," Charlie whispered, not wanting to disrupt the progress. Not wanting him to leave.

His eyes locked on hers, bounced between them. Her breathing was uneven, the thought of the woods had never been so sexy, and her stomach did a flip it hadn't done in years.

Maybe six.

Zachary glanced at her chest in its paw print scrubs as it heaved, then locked on her lips. He hesitated a fraction of a beat, then leaned forward, his hand sliding up her neck.

"Dr. Harris? Oh! Sorry to interrupt."

Charlie shot back in her seat as Zachary bolted to stand, and they both turned toward the neglected open door to see Maura standing there with a pinched expression.

"Oh! Oh no, what is it?" Charlie forced her jostled brain back in the game, while her body cried about the interruption.

"Mrs. Bergman is here."

Apparently, a consistently panicked client was as effective as stepping into a freezing shower. Mrs. Bergman had been a client since Daniel first opened his doors. She remained his client specifically, save for the rare appointments where he was unavailable and she was desperate. Neither woman was a fan of that situation, and she swore Mrs. Bergman felt personally insulted that Daniel had dared have a heart attack.

That migraine was back to full force without Zachary's hands on her. At least now she knew the cure.

The sigh escaped her before Charlie could stop it. "What is it today?"

Maura straightened and cleared her throat, trying to maintain a professional composure that her eyes betrayed—probably dying to comment on the scene she'd witnessed. "Pickles hasn't stopped sneezing yet."

Charlie closed her eyes and took a deep breath. She prided herself on the patience she carried with patients and clients, though, clients provoked her more. Today, however, was not one of her better days. Especially considering the woman had been in with her precious Pickles the day before. "Is she in a room?"

"Out front. We didn't have one available anyway, and I tried to avoid bringing her back for something I know you can tell her in two minutes." At Charlie's raised eyebrows, Maura chuckled. "Okay, maybe five to ten for her."

"I'll follow you." Charlie motioned Maura ahead, leaving Zachary behind and letting her frustrations duel in her head so they'd be out of her system before speaking with Mrs. Bergman. When she caught sight of the woman, though, she felt a stab of guilt.

Mrs. Bergman stood at the counter, the tiny Pomeranian Pickles cradled in her arms. The white ball of fluff matched Mrs. Bergman's own wispy hair, but to ensure an even deeper familial connection, Pickles wore a sparkly pink leopard-print collar and tutu that coordinated with Mrs. Bergman's large purse. It was evident to anyone Pickles was her pride and joy, and since Charlie knew she was a widow with a daughter living out of state, the care and concern she felt for her pup ran into overcompensating territory. It was eccentrically sweet.

"Goodness gracious, Dr. Harris, I've been waiting forever. Didn't Maura tell you it was urgent?"

Charlie's guilt eased slightly. "What seems to be the concern, Mrs. Bergman?" She came around the counter and reached out to stroke Pickles under the chin.

"She hasn't stopped sneezing. You said the medicine would help. It's not. I'm worried she has something else going on."

Keeping her focus on the dog, Charlie examined the fluffy ears and kept her tone professional. "She got her first dose at dinner yesterday, correct? We like to give it a full twenty-four hours to ease the sneezing."

"That's almost now."

"She's much more relaxed than she was yesterday. That's a good sign. I'm betting later this evening you'll notice an even bigger improvement."

Mrs. Bergman shifted Pickles to her other arm. "Dr. Harris, I don't believe this medicine is working. When Dr. Lee prescribed stuff in the past, it worked like that." She snapped her fingers for emphasis.

Charlie straightened her stance and looked the woman in the eye, her headache pulsing. "I know you're concerned, Mrs. Bergman. Everything checked out yesterday, so there's no need to worry. It's just a little cold that should pass over the next couple of days. In the meantime, give her extra snuggles on the couch, curl up together with her favorite blanket, anything you can do to add to her comfort. Make sure she continues to get plenty of water, and I guarantee she'll sleep better tonight."

"Was 'giving snuggles' part of your official schooling, Dr. Harris? Dr. Lee would be appalled to know you're running his practice into the ground."

Charlie blinked back at the surprisingly snide tone. *Difficult* was common for the woman, but her stubbornness had never evolved into such rude behavior. Or tapped so directly into Charlie's fears.

"Excuse me, Mrs. Bergman?"

Zachary emerged from behind the front desk. It didn't matter how scruffy his jaw was or how rumpled his hair looked, he walked confidently toward them, like a younger version of his father. Which should've prepared Charlie for the reaction that followed.

"Why, Dr. Zachary Lee!" Mrs. Bergman exclaimed. *Exclaimed*. The woman's entire demeanor shifted, worries of Pickles floating away on a judgmental cloud. "It's so good to see you! I heard you were filling in for your father. How wonderful, he must be relieved."

Charlie bristled, but before she could interject, Zachary replied.

"I can assure you everything is in Dr. Harris's very capable hands," he said. "I'm merely here to assist."

"Perhaps you wouldn't mind taking a look at Pickles?" Mrs. Bergman urged.

"I default to Dr. Harris here. I trust her diagnosis." He locked eyes with Charlie, and satisfaction bloomed. Her tension didn't dissipate, it only magnified with the realization that Mrs. Bergman wasn't taking her word for it, without the assistance of Daniel's son.

"Since you're here—"

"Mrs. Bergman, the reason I came out here at all was because I overheard someone speaking rudely to my father's coworker, one he not only trained personally but also trusts completely."

"I realize Dr. Harris is valued here. I just don't think she's the right vet for me and Pickles personally."

How very diplomatic. Though Charlie didn't disagree, public display aside. She knew better than to handle Mrs. Bergman in the front. She could blame her judgment and slow reactions on her migraine, currently orchestrating a marching band behind her eyes.

"Is that why you're insulting her in front of a room full of other clients?"

Mrs. Bergman leaned back in shock, eyes wide, mouth moving without forming words. She flirted a glance toward the full room.

Charlie regained her voice and stepped between the woman and Zachary. "Mrs. Bergman, like I said, Pickles looks much better. While you're here, though, let's have Jasmine take her on back and check her temperature. Maura will give you my number, and if anything seems suspicious, call right away. Okay?"

Mrs. Bergman finally pulled her gaze away from Zachary and registered Charlie's words. She settled Pickles into her bag and raised her head high. "Yes. Alright."

"Jasmine," Charlie called to her tech, who was standing nearby. "Would you please help Mrs. Bergman?" Charlie hightailed it back to her office.

She shut the door and leaned her head against it. She hated that flicker of a moment where she'd felt small and weak, where she'd questioned herself and her abilities. Mrs. Bergman's fading trust in her was disheartening. When the business fell to her, there'd be numerous people who didn't trust Charlie and her abilities, both as a vet and a business owner. She couldn't rely on the staff to support her all the time—their own trust would wane. And she didn't want Zachary to have to vouch for her. How embarrassing, a temporary doctor, owner's son or not, having to step in for her. She'd been here for *years*.

Animals were her world. They were straightforward, needed love and care and attention, and they managed to give all that back in return. No grudges, no judgments, no analyzing your choices, no forcing your actions. True love. They were her haven, the facility her safe space. Breaking up with her ex years ago had allowed her to focus all her energy on her studies, to commit extra time to volunteering at shelters and fostering animals. She focused on building her confidence professionally, hoping it could somehow balance her physical insecurity. Dating took a back burner. If she made time for anyone, it was her mother and close friends.

Zachary had defended her, stood by her and what she'd said. He hadn't changed course or overruled her. He believed in her and was ready to tell Mrs. Bergman off if he had to. He'd actually taken the brunt of the conversation, giving Charlie the chance to make peace with their client. Though he never said it outright, she felt his support in running the day-to-day. It didn't matter how stubborn he was, or how he insisted on wearing his white coat every day. It didn't matter how much he wanted to fix everything in sight—he held off.

She thought of his caring touch, her migraine faint with the rush of adrenaline. Her hand flew to her stomach as it flipped. She wanted to go back to that. She wanted to kiss him, damn it. It didn't matter how terrified she was to pursue *any* sort of relationship with him, considering her condition and lack of experience. He could actually make her believe in a healthy, mutually intimate relationship. Enough of these interruptions, these conversations about the business that really shouldn't affect what was going on with them. *Right? Right.*

Charlie turned and whipped the door open, only to collide with a ruffled Zachary.

He shoved inside, his hands on her biceps as he moved her backward with him. "After the way she spoke to you, you go and offer your num—"

She stood on her toes, arms pinned to her side by his hands, and smashed her lips against his. It was brief, the momentum tipping her back down to her heels. It certainly wasn't as romantic as imagined—she was pretty sure she'd bitten her own lip.

But she'd done it. She'd kissed him.

Broken the seal.

He stared down at her mouth in shock, his own stunned lips open. Charlie's breath came out in little pants, hands balled into fists, as her heart tried to leap from her chest and run for the door. Fear was coming in hot. A man like Zachary didn't want a woman to slam her lips into his like she didn't know what she was doing. Charlie knew how to kiss, but suddenly, she felt like an awkward teenager. She hadn't even seduced the man! Hadn't even *asked* him! All this while they were working! The "moment" had passed, and here she was, barreling in like they were both on the same page, as if he knew she was turned on by his support and recalling their "almost kiss" earlier.

"Zachary, I'm sorry, I..." She panicked, struggled to think of what to say, but words collided in her brain until the letters scattered like a game of Pick-Up Sticks.

His fingers flexed on her arms, and his gaze roamed her face. His eyes narrowed briefly, trying to decipher answers in hers. Charlie licked her lips, begging her mind to think of more than the scolding she was chanting of *Brain? Braaain!*

Zachary zeroed in on her mouth, and "Charlie" was all he whispered as he pressed his lips to hers.

CHAPTER 20

Zachary

HE SAVORED HER.

Charlie Harris was in his arms, his lips were on hers, and fuck it about Mrs. Bergman. With one arm at her waist, the other flailed until he found the door and flipped it shut. He nestled his hand along her jaw, tilted it, his kisses slow. Mint from the lip balm she used every day tingled, his senses heightened until all he smelled was lavender, her warm *Charlie* scent.

Their bodies flush, he curved over her to accommodate their height difference, and with the shift, deepened the kiss. His tongue traced the seam of her soft lips. She parted them on a moan, shoved her hands into his hair as their tongues tangled. It spurred him on, his hands roaming her back, her waist, skimming her ass and sliding up again. Her fingers skated up and down his arms, but when he grabbed her lower lip between his teeth, she stilled and gasped.

They parted, foreheads together as they caught their breath. Their kiss was sloppy, her mouth shiny and wet. Her chin was red from the scratch of his scruff, and he leaned forward to press another gentle kiss, only it escalated into a seductive match.

Her back bumped her desk, and she sat, opening her legs to keep him close. She flicked her tongue playfully at his. The groan that escaped him was guttural, and the strokes of his tongue made her whimper. He gripped her, and when she wrapped a leg around him, he pressed his pelvis into her instinctively, wanting to hear that sound again.

Her hands grasped his shoulders, slid up his neck to cradle his jaw. It was then he remembered his earlier plan: *Don't mess with Charlie, the woman who wouldn't want a one-night stand.*

The woman he didn't want for only one night.

He released her, stumbled back a step, their lips the last to break contact.

It should end here. They'd satisfied their curiosity, now they could move on. He was about to say as much when the quick knock on the door startled them both. He leaped farther from her, and she hopped into her chair.

"Yes?" Charlie asked as Sheila opened the door.

"Room two is ready for you. And room one for you, Dr. Lee."

"Thank you," they replied together.

His eyes darted back to Charlie's as the tech closed the door. They stared at each other as rain pelted the window, cocooning them from the outside world.

"We should get to it," he said abruptly. Later. They could talk later.

But he wouldn't stop thinking about her.

***

He didn't *intentionally* avoid her for the rest of the day. It just happened. Or so he told himself.

The afternoon powered on, fueled by the intensity of their make-out session. Routine checkups were interspersed with a feverish kitten and a dog finding poison ivy on a hike, but nothing fully distracted him from that kiss. They'd both been aching for it, that much was clear—they were practically climbing into each other.

But the panic on her face after initiating the kiss told him she'd been concerned about making the first move, and it reminded him she wasn't the type to go around kissing guys. His insistence on keeping her firmly outside the "one-night stand" camp was warranted. Charlie Harris deserved care and attention from someone who'd be there for her every day. Definitely not a man who'd be leaving in a few short weeks.

A frustrated breath shot out of him as he finished sorting the days' files. It was best to let them cool off, have space to really think about what happened, what it meant.

His phone buzzed on the desk, announcing a text.

Sandra: *Heads up, it's chaos over here.*

Zachary raised his eyebrow.

Zachary: *It's always chaos at your house.*

Sandra: *No, Mom and Dad's. Stopped on my way home to check on them, and it's...*

Zachary: ...

Sandra: *Just tread carefully when you stop by tonight.*

Fuck. Being told to rest was already a struggle for his dad, but being told he couldn't work, possibly ever? It was a life sentence.

Zachary: *How long will you be there?*

Sandra: *Trying my damnedest to get out the door, but Mom needs help. He's having a rough day.*

Zachary: *I'll head out in five.*

Sandra: *K. I'll prob still be here. Maybe forcing Dad to FaceTime the kids while I ply Mom with wine.*

Zachary: *Sounds like good counseling tricks.*

Sandra: *A lot of clinical rules are flying out the window. See your ass in a few.*

Zachary grabbed his things. When he stepped into the hall, he found Charlie heading his way. Her steps slowed, and she stopped a foot from him. The satisfaction that coursed through him as her cheeks flushed only made him scold himself internally. *She's not a toy.*

"How's your head?"

"A little fuzzy, but better than earlier." The pinch in her brow lessened as she gave him a soft smile, then the smile slipped. "You okay?"

"Fine."

"You look upset."

"Just my face."

She shoved her hands on her hips. "You have 'upset resting face' now?"

He shrugged. "It's a thing."

She glanced around, then stepped closer. "Really, Zachary. Are you okay?"

The concern in her voice tugged him toward her, and before he realized it, his hand was brushing a wild strand of hair behind her ear. "Sandra just texted. Guess Dad's having a rough day." It was half of what weighed on him, but it was the half he understood most.

"Oh." She blinked multiple times as his hand left her. "Anything I can do?"

"You mean aside from offering your personal number to every client that comes around? I think you've done your good deed for today. Maybe even longer. Probably for the life of Pickles."

She chuckled lightly, capped it with a shrug. "It's through our texting system, she won't have my direct number." She shifted her feet, a guilty expression falling across her face. "She's lonely. I wanted her to know I heard her. She's not my biggest fan, so if I can go an extra step to win her over, I'll do it."

"Why does she need to be on Team Charlie? She can go somewhere else if she's not happy. Or going to be a constant pain in the ass." He already counted her in the "most likely to leave" column when they raised their prices—a detail he'd have to discuss with Charlie soon, though now wasn't the time.

"She loves your dad. Really, she represents numerous clients with a similar devotion to him and not the woman who'll take over the practice. No matter how much he mentored me."

That he thought she could ever manipulate things to get into the family business when she lived and breathed the work made him disappointed with himself.

"They'll come around. Some of us need a little shake to get our head out of our ass."

She gazed up at him with a smirk. "Maybe a little more than a shake, huh?" She wiggled her eyebrows, then stepped around him. Her back practically slid along the wall, giving as much space as she could in the narrow hallway, like she was afraid with one touch they'd combust. "Give your dad my best, okay? I'm assuming they won't be coming to the cookout tomorrow."

"Not sure. You don't want to swing by and see him now? He's in a mood."

"Ha, tempting. I need to turn in early. Try to get rid of this. Big day ahead."

He stopped her, his hand grazing hers, and she inhaled sharply. His own pulse kicked up a notch. He took a small step closer. "Can I get you anything?"

She gave him a small shake of her head. "I'm good. Thanks." She twisted her hand and squeezed his, then continued backward toward their office, in those ridiculous paw-print scrubs with the squiggly hearts as berry pink as her shoes. His fingers flexed with the memory of pulling her close.

"See you tomorrow." She gave him a full smile, so bright it seemed to imprint on his eyelids when he blinked. Then she disappeared into the office.

Well, fuck him. Zachary had his first adult-sized crush.

CHAPTER 21

Charlie

"You're here early." Zachary's deep timbre vibrated beneath her skin.

Charlie shivered and turned from the window. "So are you."

Maple shuffled over with a happy greeting, then settled onto the dog bed. Charlie inhaled sharply when she looked up, watching Zachary's slow approach. He wore one of the clinic's long-sleeve navy T-shirts, the name and logo printed in white across the chest, with little paw prints floating on the top left. It was the same one she wore, and it looked way better on him than it had a right to, especially paired with his well-worn jeans.

"I had a feeling you'd be here before anyone else," he said. "How are you today?"

"Much better. Sleep helped." His texts in the evening to check on her had also put her on a euphoric cloud that had lulled her to said sleep.

"Good." His gaze traveled over her face, roamed her body, his mouth twitching when he reached her feet. "Those sneakers..."

She threw her hands on her hips in mock annoyance. "What about them?"

"I like them. Part of your uniform. But they say a lot about you."

Charlie glanced down, her berry sneakers their normal selves. "What do they say?"

"They're bright, obviously. Matches your personality."

"Well, that's sweet," Charlie mumbled, her heart rate picking up as Zachary inched the final distance toward her.

"They're clearly a go-to."

"True. When these finally wear out, I'll just buy another pair."

"Same color?"

"Most likely. Predictable?"

He chuckled, his fingers brushing hers as his warm scent invaded her space. "Reliable."

"Oh." Charlie's mouth twitched, the game amusing and somehow extremely titillating.

"Charming," he added.

"You know, they do wink at me daily." Her eyes darted away from his, down to their hands as his fingers clung more boldly to hers, despite her bad joke.

"Strong."

"My shoes are strong?" Her voice was strained, his closeness interrupting her brain waves with thoughts of *closer, please.*

"Kind."

"Okay, now I'm questioning your observational skills."

"Feisty."

She sighed. "I can see that one."

"Charlie."

Her eyes locked on his instantly when her name fell softly from his lips, her stomach executing a clumsy flip of excitement. His use of any part of her name held a weight no one else could replicate.

"Yes?" It was a whisper, her heartbeat so fast she could jumpstart his.

His fingers tangled with hers as the other hand traveled her arm, sending rays of heat over her torso, until he cupped her jaw in his palm. Their feet nestled together, his closeness a calming blanket that made her want to curl up inside him.

His brown eyes caught a glint of light from the window, small flecks of gold more visible the closer his face inched toward hers. The rugged stubble on his face marred his normally pressed look in a sexy way he surely underestimated. She bit her lip in anticipation.

Zachary brushed the backs of his fingers against her cheek and tucked her hair behind her ear. "Want to have dinner with me tonight?" he asked.

"Yes."

He smiled, breaking out those laugh lines. She gave in to temptation and traced her finger over one, pressing into it when his smile grew, effectively deepening the happy crease.

"I've wanted to do that for a while," she admitted.

His eyes widened, then softened as he pressed closer. "Have at it."

"Mm, they're good," she hummed, grinning when he chuckled.

The faint echo of the employee door to the clinic sounded, voices filling the air. Zachary stepped back, and Charlie instantly missed his body against hers. She watched him squat by Maple to give the pup some pets. When he looked back at her, he grinned, and she realized her smile had never left.

"Ah, of course, you're both here." Maura appeared in the doorway and glanced at her watch. "I hope you haven't been here for hours already." She tossed a motherly look at Charlie.

"Not too long," Charlie replied.

"Well, I've put on some coffee to get us through setup," Maura said.

"Amazing, I didn't get that far."

"I'll see you out there." Maura returned to the kitchenette.

Charlie grabbed her clipboard, the plans for the day set out in a much clearer way than the top of her desk looked. "How'd everything go with your dad?" Her mind had volleyed all night—thinking about Zachary helping Daniel, thinking about Zachary, thinking about kissing Zachary. Then her heart would dive as nerves for pursuing anything with him would take hold, fear looming that they'd only have that one kiss.

One *luxurious* kiss.

Zachary sighed and stood. "Mostly well. By the time I got there, Mom was kinda tipsy, thanks to Sandra. So that was amusing. Pretty sure that's the first I've witnessed it. Put Dad in a better mood for a while." He shrugged. "It's sweet, though, both dogs stay by him all the time."

Charlie pressed a hand to her chest. "Keeping an eye on their guy."

Zachary dragged a hand through his hair. "He wants to come today. I thought it'd be too much, but...he's going to do what he wants. Sandra encouraged him to stay home, but I feel like she'll give in too."

"It sucks, not being able to fully celebrate right now."

They were quiet a moment, Charlie watching his brow furrow and twitch.

"We'll keep an eye on him if he shows," she finally said.

Zachary straightened and opened his desk drawer, pulling out a piece of mail. "Yes, well..." he said, voice tight as he folded the envelope and tucked it into his jeans. "Hopefully, he won't show. Best he gets his rest," he added.

Charlie nodded, watching him look everywhere but at her.

"Charlie! We've got vendors!" Maura called.

She blinked to attention, smiling as Zachary finally looked her way. "Well, let's get started."

***

The late afternoon air smelled of crushed leaves and the grill Zachary managed. Charlie pulled up the hood of her cornflower-blue puffy vest and pressed against the Lee's SUV, shivering as the driver's side window rolled down.

"Hi! Look what the bakery made!" She held up a plate and waved a hand over dog-and-cat-shaped cutout cookies, decorated with bright royal icing.

"Oh! Look, how adorable are these?" Jeanie took the plate and swiveled to the passenger seat to show Daniel, a flicker of happiness nudging through his tired features.

"I, um, wanted to make sure you got some," Charlie said.

When Sandra and her family had arrived, she'd mentioned her parents were parked, watching, debating on whether to walk through the cookout. There was only a little over an hour left, so Charlie had taken it upon herself to pay them a visit, if only to satisfy the need to see Daniel at his own event.

"That was sweet of you. You know, we were trying to decide if we should walk over or not, but it's gotten so cold," Jeanie said. She glanced at Daniel, then back at Charlie. "Know what? I might get us a hot drink and maybe grab a little something from the grill. Do you mind keeping him company?"

"I don't need a babysitter," Daniel grumbled.

"I don't think I could pay anyone enough *to* babysit you, honey," Jeanie said, smiling once he snorted a chuckle.

Charlie stepped back as Jeanie maneuvered from the car and gestured for her to sit. She moved almost in slow motion, taking the plate back from Jeanie, scooting into the vehicle, next to Daniel, where they'd have time to talk. Alone. Without doctors or nurses nearby...

"I'll be back in a few," Jeanie said, shoving the door closed.

Or Jeanie.

Charlie and Daniel watched in silence while she waved and shouted greetings to people as she approached the cookout, her bright red and white winter coat a beacon.

A brisk breeze whirled through the car, and Charlie rolled up the window. The sky had darkened throughout the day, gracing them with a nice, crisp cookout and promising a storm as soon as it ended. Sweatshirts and coats increased in size to accommodate, but it didn't stop anyone from attending and taking their time to visit every booth, to meet the dogs up for adoption, to chat in line at the food tent. Families huddled together to eat, bundling up with blankets until they could move their bodies again.

The support from the community warmed Charlie, and watching each year grow was electrifying. There were folks who attended every single one, no matter the weather. It didn't matter if people had pets or not, showing up and participating went a long way. It was evident the man who started it all was the force behind it.

She slid back her hood and shifted. Daniel was way more lucid than her last visit to the hospital—he'd dozed off and on, giving her time to focus on how tired and worn he looked. She'd hated it, seeing him like that. It had felt like a dream, watching nurses walk in and out of the room as they checked on him while he gave them small smiles of appreciation for their lighthearted approach, as they told Jeanie to make sure she stuck around for a hospital dessert actually worth enjoying with him. She'd merely been part of the scene, waiting for someone to wake her up, tell her he was okay. That the concern of it happening again was gone. But no one had.

Sitting beside him now, it felt like a later scene of the same dream, with a facade of normalcy. There was no longer a hospital bed. He was at his anniversary cookout—parked yards away and staring from the safety of his SUV. He was awake, alert, and available to talk. Which meant she should say something of substance.

"How are you feeling?" Immediately, she dropped her head and closed her eyes, cursing her small-talk inabilities.

Daniel grunted.

She smirked. At least they were on the same level of communication. She opened her eyes, the plate of cookies beaming up at her.

"Did you see the bow tie on this one? They put the number forty on it," she said, tilting the plate toward him. "Shoot. I'm sure sugar isn't on the 'approved' list from the doctor."

As if in challenge, his eyes went from the plate, to her, and back. He picked up the cookie, removed its cellophane wrapper, and bit, chewing as he looked out of the front window.

Charlie stared at the plate. She really needed to be better at looking out for him. This wasn't helping at all, encouraging unhealthy behavior.

"One cookie won't kill me," Daniel said softly.

She blinked rapidly, cleared her throat. "Everyone's been asking about you. It's the busiest year yet, I think. So many people sending their congrats on forty years, and well-wishes that you...that you get better soon."

His gaze stayed on the cookout.

"We even had a couple vendors run out of stuff a little while ago, can you believe it? And the raffle entries have been steady. We've raised a lot of money so far."

"Damn it," Daniel grumbled, as cookie crumbled all over his lap.

"Oh, here." Charlie pulled a small wad of napkins from the zippered pocket of her fleece.

"Thank you," he said, the veins on his hand more pronounced, the joints of his fingers stiff and slightly bent as he took them from her. Focused on cleaning up his mess, he continued, "Zachary looks comfortable out there."

She found Zachary with a magnetic pull, a gray fleece over his T-shirt, the sleeves shoved up his forearms as he worked the grill. His smile was gentle as he talked to an older couple, nodding and laughing with them as though he hadn't been gone for years. Fitting right back in, while everyone felt the significance of his presence.

Working alongside him again made her happy. He'd been smiling all day, embracing everything with such love and care. He'd brought her food when he noticed she hadn't stopped moving all morning. And well, there were a few times their eyes met across the way, when his smile turned mischievous and his eyes scanned her body in a way that let her know he was thinking about their kiss too.

Charlie nudged the vent, directing the heat away from her face. "Mm-hmm," was her reply.

"Has he been following orders?"

She chuckled. "Yes."

"I was preparing myself for the building to be repainted or something," he muttered.

"Just the inside. Ocean blue. One wall is bright stripes, surprisingly," she said, smirking.

"Oh, *that* sounds like *your* doing," he said, gifting her a small smile. "I can't go in there yet. I'm not..." He shook his head, forced a small cough into his fist as he tripped on the words.

"That's okay, Daniel," she said softly, watching him. His focus was on the trees, the sky, everywhere but her. "We don't have a 'welcome home' banner up yet anyway."

He smiled at his lap. "Thank you. For taking care of everything."

"Of course." Charlie bit the inside of her cheek. She gripped the steering wheel, the cool leather sturdy under her hands. "Daniel, I'm really sorry." She sensed him turn toward her. "That this happened, what you're going through. I feel like it's my fault. Things have been so nonstop, and I could've been doing more."

His hand on her shoulder stopped her, and she looked into his tired eyes. "Charlie. This wasn't your fault."

"I mean—"

"No. Don't take credit for something so spectacular," he said.

Her laugh was short. "I hear you, and *shit*, I didn't want this to be about me. I—"

He shook his head. "So many factors went into this. Even I...even I can't take full responsibility. Genetics, and life, and all that."

Her nods were small, her blinking rapid. "I just feel like I let you down," she whispered.

His fingers squeezed her shoulder, firm in their gentleness. "No. You never have, Charlie. It's not in your nature."

Her nose pricked, her eyes welling up when she saw the same in his. She stretched across the seat and hugged him, carefully, awkwardly, a small sob escaping her as he squeezed her tightly. "I'm so glad you're home," she whispered.

He choked out a sound in reply and kissed the top of her head, a gesture he'd done after her graduation that had made her feel like the familial bond between them was mutual. It had carried her through until now, yet this one was worth even more.

When they separated, she dabbed her eyes, and he did the same with the corner of a napkin. They both chuckled in relief.

"I hope Jeanie grabbed more cookies, if there were any left," he said as he gestured out the window, where his wife approached.

Charlie laughed and stepped out to help her settle in the driver's seat.

"Here, my love, I got us both some tea," Jeanie said, handing him a cup. "Our son grilled veggies for us to bring home too. And look! Little popcorn balls shaped like animals." She held one up, then tossed it into a canvas tote.

"Where did this come from?" Daniel asked, looking at the bag itself.

"One of the vendors. Picked out a few things for the dogs while I was at it. They had the cutest bandanas—"

"Did you get more cookies?" This, while he started rifling inside like a kid trying to contain his excitement.

She squinted at him. "Yes."

He winked at Charlie.

The picture of the two of them warmed her as the wind howled around them. "Alright, kids. Get some good rest tonight, yeah?"

Jeanie patted Charlie's hand. "You too, sweetheart. Stay warm!"

Charlie shut the door with a wave before she walked back to the cookout. She felt lighter, now that she'd cleared the air with Daniel—or at least done a light sweeping. Seeing him here, as he observed his son helping out in a way he probably never dreamed possible, brought a new wave of hope.

"Dr. Harris?"

She had just reached the first tent when she heard her name, looking up to find a man who looked a little younger than Daniel holding a cup of coffee, standing alone. His fair skin was pink with cold. With a *swish* of his puffy coat, he reached out a hand.

"Ned North. Nice to meet you."

"Oh, well..." She shook his hand, racking her brain to place him. "And you."

"I've heard a lot about you." He gestured around. "You've put on a nice event."

"Thanks." She hesitated. "Is this your first time here?"

"No, no." He grinned, like she was missing out on some joke. "First time here, but I know what a great place it is. How lucky for Dr. Lee he was able to have such a wonderful veterinarian on staff with him."

She gave a small smile. "You're a friend of his?"

"Hope to be." He stepped closer, holding out a business card. "Our company owns a few clinics in the area, and we're actually looking for a veterinarian to lead one of our teams. Not too far from here actually, we hope to be a sister clinic with this one. But my research has been pointing me in your direction."

"Oh, I'm not looking to leave."

He held up a hand. "Things change. Please keep us in mind, is all I'm asking. I won't take up more of your time, but you have my info."

She shook his hand, his rough grip firm. As he walked away, she flipped the card over to see Neptune Corp in thick, bulbous letters. Her head whipped up to locate him, but he'd disappeared among the groups of people wandering between the tents. She could find him if she wanted, but what would she say? *I hate your company. Why are you here?*

It was shady, to compliment her, to have learned about her. To try to poach her at her own event? Especially now, when they needed her most, she had no intention of leaving.

As she watched Zachary talk with patrons at the dog adoption tent, she couldn't help but feel lucky. Things were falling into place in a way she hadn't dared to imagine.

Their practice was in good hands, because of the great team they made.

CHAPTER 22

Zachary

ZACHARY STEPPED AWAY FROM the rescue's tent with a happiness he hadn't felt in years. He was grateful Cory had called him over to answer questions from interested people, if only to witness a family lean into their consideration of adopting a senior dog. Their six-year-old daughter had fallen in love with a sweet old cocker spaniel, and the two had been cuddled in the grass ever since.

"Sheila, thanks for covering for me," he said when he returned to his station.

"No prob, Dr. Lee," she said, adding patties to prepped plates. "There's a guy over there looking for you, though. I didn't catch his name. I'll hang here until you're back."

"Oh." He looked at the cluster of tables where she pointed, spotting someone sitting on his own, surveying the crowd around him. "In the gray hat?"

She nodded, so he wound his way over, spotting Charlie at the raffle booth, talking with Jasmine animatedly. He smiled at her unfazed, bouncy spirit, but his grin grew when she noticed him watching, and that blush raced over her face and neck.

"Hey there, I'm Dr. Lee," he said, a chipper energy in his voice he hardly recognized, as he reached the lone guest. "I believe you were looking for me?"

The middle-aged man stood. "Dr. Lee!"

"Hope I'm not interrupting," Zachary said as the man held out his hand.

"Not at all. You're stopping me from going back for more sweets, in fact," he said with a grin. "Ned North, from Neptune Corp. Nice to finally meet you." He gestured to an open chair across from him.

Zachary's descent into the seat slowed as he remembered the letter in his pocket. He swallowed. "Actually, you must be looking for Daniel Lee. I'm his son. Zachary."

Ned leaned back in the chair, his green coat puffing around his shoulders. "I didn't realize you were working here too. What a surprise! Well, I'm happy to talk with you as well, if your father can join us."

"He's out sick at the moment. I'm filling in for him."

"Oh. Sorry to hear that."

"I can have him contact you when he returns?" Zachary offered reluctantly.

"I was hoping to meet him in person. I'm passing through on my way to Illinois and Ohio, so this cookout seemed like a good opportunity for us to meet in a more casual capacity."

"I see."

Ned tapped his fingers on the table, a slow, studying rhythm. "You've heard of us? Beyond our candy line, I mean."

Zachary nodded. "Have friends whose practices were bought out by your company because they could no longer compete with large corporation prices."

"We rescue struggling clinics and allow them to keep serving their community."

"Some of them might look at it that way." Zachary said.

"Some?"

"Not all."

Ned's smile was too wide—perfect for a second set of teeth. "I'm gathering which way you lean."

Zachary shrugged. "As you can see, we have a large community supporting us already. We don't need you to *save* us."

"Your father might have a different view on it."

"My father and I often do."

Ned's nod was slow. "Well, I am sorry I missed him. If you could let him know I stopped by, I'd appreciate it. When he's feeling up to it, I'd love to chat with him over the phone at least. I'm not sure when I'll be back in the area."

Zachary clenched his jaw, released a quiet breath through his nose. "Of course."

They stood at the same time, Zachary stretching his height as they did the perfunctory handshake. He didn't like to use his stature against people, but Ned didn't seem like "people."

"Cute event, by the way," Ned said, gesturing around them. "Nice to see such great turnout in this weather."

Zachary's nod jerked. He watched Ned meander through the booths, even stopping by the adoption tent, as though he was a participant instead of a leech. He scrubbed a hand over his mouth as he mumbled, "Fuck."

"Dr. Lee?"

He sighed, straightened, and turned. "Dr. Zachary Lee, yes."

The woman in front of him grinned, rubbing her sable-brown hands together for warmth. A rust-orange silk-and-knit headband showed off a knot of curls and dangling earrings that swayed as she nodded. "You're the one I'm looking for. I'm Cleo, Charlie's friend." She held out her hand, metal from skinny rings cool among her chilled, slender fingers.

"Cleo," he repeated. "Right, you have a shop on Main?"

"I do. Welcome back. It's great you could attend this year, especially for Charlie. I was worried she'd overdo it what with everything."

"She still might have. I don't know that I helped very much."

"She's interacting with people instead of running around, so that's a good sign. And a lot less stressed than a few weeks ago."

"Good," he murmured. Somehow, his eyes had found Charlie, showing off a vendor's bandanas to a client and their husky.

"I have something for your parents, if you don't mind?"

Zachary turned at the amused tone, finding Cleo grinning as she held out a small kraft bag. Her eyes darted to where his had been, then back.

"It's some local tea I know they like, and one of your dad's favorite candles."

Zachary blinked rapidly. "He has a favorite candle?" He noted the sticker on the bag with the shop's name and pulled out the candle and studied it as though it held secrets.

Cleo shrugged. "Sometimes your parents mix it up and try new ones, but I figured old reliables would be best right now."

As sweet as the image sounded, it conflicted with childhood memories of his dad coming home from work after staying late, only to recount the day with his mom or go into the basement to research solutions for his patients.

"Right, okay. I'll make sure to give it to them. That's very kind of you."

She shrugged. "It's the least I could do. I was relieved to hear his recovery's going well."

"Thanks." He paused, fiddled with the handles. "So my mom comes in often?"

"Both your parents. I'd met your dad briefly over the years, but when Charlie told him and Jeanie about my shop, they came to the grand opening to show support. They've been regulars ever since, it's very sweet."

He rubbed his chest, a pressure the weight of Maple's head setting in. His parents had always loved attending games, watching him and Sandra compete through high school. His dad had missed a few but made a huge effort in spite of his work schedule. And his mom had adjusted her hours at the bank, rarely missing an event. A memory long forgotten returned though, of his parents making a point to attend some of Jordan's major track and field meets, cheering in the stands alongside Zachary.

He realized he was watching Charlie again as she chatted with local pet hotel reps. She had on a striped knit hat, her hair in a loose ponytail over her shoulder, cheeks pink from the snapping breeze.

"Oh, helloooo there, Doc." Amber loped into position next to Cleo—who was studying him—and nudged his arm with her knuckles. "Pretty great work our girl did, huh?"

"Yeah, amazing, actually." He looked between the two women, Cleo huddled in a bulky gray sweater, Amber wearing a black fleece and standing hands on hips. "What?"

Cleo grinned.

Amber adjusted her black ball cap. "We didn't get to chat much the other day, since my cousin so rudely rushed me out of the clinic."

"You mean, had your dog examined," he supplied, fighting a chuckle.

She waved away the detail with her hand. "How's it going, working under Charlie?"

He cleared his throat. *Under Charlie.* "Going well."

"Are you following her protocol?"

"Yes."

"How long will you be in town?"

"Not sure."

"Are you trying to take over, kick her out of the running?" Amber ignored the elbow jab from Cleo.

"What?" He looked between Charlie's two bodyguards. "No, that's definitely not my intention. Does she feel that way?"

"She works her ass off and would do anything for the people she cares about." Cleo gave Amber a look she clocked but continued anyway. "She loves your dad. And this place. She doesn't need someone else coming in with their Jedi mind games."

Cleo shook her head, and with reluctance, said, "Mind *tricks.*"

"I know, Amber," he said. "Wait, who used mind tricks?"

"Just, don't be a dick. I know you're"—she flicked a hand up and down as she scanned his body—"*tall.* But you'll have to answer to us. Not *just* us two, there are others."

"Okay, maybe a little less moxie in your morning coffee tomorrow," Cleo said.

"Trust me." When they both looked at him, he continued. "I admire the hell out of Charlie. Sure, the arrangement was awkward at first, but we've sorted it out. We..." He saw her by the adoption tent, squatted next to that little girl and the cocker spaniel. "We work really well together. The last thing I want to do is hurt her. She's my friend." The word sounded insufficient.

He watched as Charlie coaxed the dog to stretch for a belly rub, and the little girl's face lit up when she got to try. Charlie beamed, and she stood, spotting him. Her smile was contagious and grew as they stared at one another.

It was hard to remember why he'd told himself not to pursue whatever this was with her. Not when she locked genuinely happy to see him. That morning, his resolve had crumbled instantly. All he wanted was to stay in her orbit.

Her expression faltered when she registered Cleo and Amber.

Cleo waved as though there was nothing unusual about the three of them together. Amber stared at him with a frown, but as she scanned his face, a smile broke free. She laughed, almost maniacally, as Charlie hustled over.

"What are you saying to him?" Charlie demanded, slightly winded, reminding him of her strong dislike for running.

"She was being supportive," Cleo said as she unwrapped a piece of gum.

"That doesn't make me feel better."

"Nonsense, little sugar butt," Amber said. She threw an arm around Charlie. "Only making sure our guy Zachary knows how amazing you are. And he does."

Charlie's eyes widened.

"Yes, he told us quite frankly that he admires you as a veterinarian," Cleo supplied.

Eventually, Charlie softened. He wasn't sure if it was from those words or if it was relief that he hadn't spilled the news about their kiss. That had to be at the root of her panic. It wasn't his place to share it anyway, though he wondered what intensity Amber would aim his way once she found out. She'd probably pull the classic "*If you hurt her...*" threat, which he'd fully expect and appreciate. He was feeling the same way—about himself.

He swallowed, his throat dry, his breath stuttering. No one else noticed he had tripped himself up. That he'd realized for certain his feelings for Charlie were more than friendly, and not just a one-off. That he'd been searching her out all day like a sunflower seeking the sun.

Her light touch pulled him back.

"Um. What?"

"Cleo and Amber are leaving," Charlie said.

"It was nice meeting you," Cleo said.

"Doc, keep up the good work," Amber added.

Charlie rolled her eyes as they hugged her goodbye and left. She faced him, keeping a respectable distance. Which felt too far.

This is bad.

"Everyone will be packing up soon. We'll store tents inside for tomorrow's early pickup, but most of the staff is here so it should go quick."

"Okay."

She looked tired and windblown, but her pale skin and red cheeks made the green of her eyes sparkle. "We kicked ass today," she whispered.

"I don't have the final count from all the booths, but it's the best year we've had. I can't wait to tell your dad."

"Harris, that's awesome." He wanted to hug her. "You should be proud."

"Thanks." She beamed. "So you admire me, huh?"

"Hell yes."

Her blush overpowered her wind-kissed cheeks.

"You deserve to hear that," he added.

"I admire you too," she said softly.

He straightened, felt the confidence that had dwindled that last year or so trickling back. Felt like he belonged.

He stepped closer, grinning as she looked up with wide eyes.

"We still on for dinner?"

She nodded.

He couldn't wait.

CHAPTER 23

Charlie

CHARLIE MANAGED TO TURN off her car, unbuckle her seatbelt, and step halfway out the door all at once. Initially, her excitement at having Zachary over had bubbled and fizzed into a champagne party for her stomach. But reality had quickly swept in on the short drive to her place. Was it clean? How cluttered was it? Was underwear on the floor?

Was *she* clean?

At least they'd both been working all day, and not in sweltering heat, but a quick touch-up would be ideal.

The garage door closed as she hurried inside, knowing full well Zachary would be at her front door in no time, even with dropping Maple off at Jordan's so the old girl could sleep. The living room was decent, aside from mail on the coffee table. She pretended the knit blankets spilling off the couch were a carefree artistic choice and tossed throw pillows from the floor onto the couch and armchair. Then she half-kicked, half-carried the laundry basket full of clothes into her bedroom.

A quick scan of the kitchen showed a sink with some of the morning's dishes and a pile of mail on the counter—not terrible. Oh, and another pile of mail on the small table tucked by the window, along with the open shipping box of treats and food for Toothless.

"Whatever," she muttered, and moved back to the living room.

She glanced out the window—there he was, parked, inside his car. She squinted through the darkness, and from the faint visor mirror light, saw him shove his fingers through his hair.

"God, he's cute." She spun around and nearly stepped on Toothless, who called out a warning meow. "Sorry, little peanut!" Charlie yelled, racing to the bathroom.

With a pump of lavender lotion, she rubbed her hands together and patted behind her ears. She pulled her hair free from the hat and ponytail and fluffed it. "Nope," she said, loosely plaiting snarly sections as she stepped out of the bathroom, the timing perfect with the knock at her door.

She flipped the hair band around the end of the braid and opened the door.

Zachary walked in with a cooler. "Easier to bring the whole thing in, hope that's alright. Maybe we could make it a picnic right here?"

"Love that idea." Charlie scooted the coffee table farther from the couch and flipped a lightweight teal blanket onto the floor. *Chill, Charlie.* "Um, what can I get you to drink? I have wine and...water. That might be it, actually."

"Wine or water?" Zachary grinned.

"I'm really good at keeping the essentials around," Charlie said, smiling back. "I do have oat milk, if you wanna go wild."

Zachary tossed his jacket on the arm of the couch, effectively closing the distance between them. "Wine sounds great."

She nodded, her head tilted to look up at him. "Great."

He brushed a strand of hair from her face. Whenever she was around him, those flyaways didn't bother her so much.

"You just did this?" He asked the question softly, his fingers toying with her braid.

"Mmm," she replied. Words escaped her, especially when he tugged lightly, urging her closer.

Her stomach growled, and Zachary chuckled. Her desire to stare at him was strong, but her hunger game was stronger. She gestured toward the blanket.

"Have a seat, please. I'll be right back."

"Why, thank you."

She looked back at his teasing and laughed nervously at her formal tone.

"So awkward, Charlotte," she hissed as she tore into her wine selection. She grabbed one of her favorite reds from the small collection in her cabinet and a chardonnay from the fridge. With a bottle and glass entwined in each hand, she made the short trek back to the living room, stopping short.

Toothless was curled up on Zachary, eyes closed and head back as he scratched under her chin. She'd secured the best seat in the house. Levi would occasionally hold her in his burly arms, but curled up in Zachary's *lap,* she looked precious. And he looked even more delicious.

She emitted a strange sound, a mix between clearing her throat and forcing out a chuckle. "Looks like someone made a new friend," she said, walking into the room. *Great, that's something Mom would say.*

"She's sweet," Zachary said.

"Oh yeah." Charlie settled on the blanket across from them. "She is not shy when it comes to affection. Red or white? I brought both."

"Red." Zachary gave Charlie his full attention while he absentmindedly pet Toothless, who purred like the happy cat she was. "Your place is nice. Very you."

She opened the bottle and poured. "Thanks. Levi owns the building actually and rents out this apartment."

"Ah. Convenient to live next to the owner."

"It is. He does a lot of the handiwork or ropes his brother-in-law to help out. Damion's in construction," she added, as if he cared to learn extraneous information about her friend. She handed him his glass and raised hers in a toast before taking a sip.

She looked around the small living room, the intricate molding original but painted white for a more modern look, accented by gray walls. The space was large enough for her couch and coffee table, a small stand for her TV, and a cozy navy armchair. Narrow built-ins on either side of the picture window held books and picture frames. She loved the charm of her place, the old bones intact and blending with the cosmetic updates Levi had incorporated. It was cute, with character that relieved Charlie from the stress of interior decorating.

"Looks well taken care of."

"God yes. I'm lucky. Plus, his family brings me delicious fudge." She shook her head in mock dismay and took another sip of wine.

"Like the other day?"

"Yeah. His nieces insisted on making me some. The girls love Toothless and meeting whatever fosters I have. His brother and brother-in-law aren't looking to adopt a pet right now, so it's a good arrangement." She took another sip, while Zachary looked around.

"So fudge and cookies are the way in, huh," he said softly.

After only a few sips of wine, a slight buzz was kicking in, but his words pulled her upright. Suddenly, talking about her neighbor was the last thing she wanted to discuss.

"Cookies for sure. Snickerdoodles win every time." She answered just as softly, her voice surprisingly husky. Zachary's eyes flew to hers, then down to her lips.

Her stomach growled, interrupting the silence, and she slapped her hand to her abdomen.

"Speaking of food?" Zachary said.

"Yes. We should eat."

They both reached for the cooler and lifted the lid together. They set out the meal, the burgers still warm since Zachary had cooked and wrapped them at the end of the day. By the time their plates were set, Toothless was splayed on her back, presenting herself to Zachary like the little hussy she was.

"You're ridiculous," Charlie said to her cat, though she understood the feeling. If she hadn't been so hungry, the thought of laying herself out on the floor for Zachary's eyes to feast on her would've overpowered any other thought.

"I'll have to bring Maple over to meet her," Zachary said.

Charlie took a bite of her food, humming in agreement. "She did well today," she said through her bite.

He laughed. "You've got something there," he said, pointing at her mouth.

She felt lettuce between her teeth and gave him an exaggerated smile to showcase it. "What? I have something stuck?"

He shook his head. "I'm seriously flashing back to when you were in high school and did that to me the first time."

"The first time? Right. I guess I've done it often enough. Yikes." She laughed nervously.

Zachary, on the other hand, cracked up. "I get the joke. I've always gotten it."

Charlie felt her cheeks warm. Smooth and sensual, she was not. Laying herself in front of Zachary probably wouldn't go as planned.

"Your sense of humor has always gotten to me. In the best way," he hurried to add when she looked up at him. "Don't know how Anna's aversion to...*everything* didn't stand out more after being friends with you."

She swallowed a large chunk. The thought of their friendship being that vivid to him was a lot to process. "Love makes you do crazy things," she said. Her eyes narrowed at her food as she pulled a piece of the bun and ate it slowly. "Been there."

Memories swarmed of trying to keep her ex happy, sacrificing her needs, instead of the idea that they make each other happy by being themselves.

"I hate that you were hurt," Zachary said.

Charlie forced a smile, but when she looked at Zachary, she felt the sadness show through, her attempt at hiding behind it much more difficult. She shrugged. "I learned a lot, you know how it goes. Granted, my therapist would confirm that I'm *still* working through it. But I'm much better for it now."

"You're in therapy because of it?" His voice was laced with concern.

"It's a combination of things. I didn't realize how much it messed with me, mentally, you know? Until we started digging into everything."

"Ah, yeah. I get that."

Charlie picked at the thin weave of the blanket and released a quiet breath. "There was a lot of manipulation. My self-confidence took a major hit." She tipped her head from side to side. "I mean, you met his mom. That's a pretty good glimpse into life with him. Little self-awareness and a whole lot of selfishness. I was just going through the motions instead of recognizing what it was."

"That sounds like a huge revelation," Zachary said. He stretched onto his side, leaning on an elbow. One hand traced hers lightly as he listened.

"It was a giant shock to my system too. I'd been ignoring signs and kept getting sucked further and further into this spiral, until it felt normal. I felt exposed and vulnerable, and he was laser-focused on what he needed and wanted. Anytime I tried to tell him something was wrong, he'd make me feel bad. Say he felt guilty, and then *that* was my fault, and I needed to help him feel better. It was at my expense. Every time." So much of it had revolved around physical intimacy limitations.

His knuckles clenched.

"I don't know what made me launch into that," she said. They both stared in silence, watching his finger soothe her veins, her knuckles, and her joints. She shivered. Zachary gave her hand a little squeeze.

"I'm really sorry you went through that...Fuckin' pisses me off." He released a shaky breath. "I'm trying really hard not to push. Emotional scars can take a while."

"They do. Time and therapy have been huge."

"Good." He waited a beat. "Do I make you anxious?" he asked softly.

Charlie shook her head. She realized she'd been leaning closer and closer, lured by his warmth and comfort.

"You make me nervous," she admitted, "in a good way."

Zachary's eyebrows twitched, then he smiled. "You make me nervous too."

Charlie pulled her mouth into an *O*, making Zachary laugh, her playful reaction more a defensive move than anything. When she realized it, she took a deep breath, and decided to go for it. "I...feel good when I'm with you," she said.

Zachary tucked his fingers between hers, tugging lightly.

"You make me feel good too," he whispered. Then he pulled his other hand up to grasp behind her neck and kissed her, his lips firm, gentle.

They broke for a moment, and Charlie grinned. "I just want to point out that this all started with me showing lettuce in my teeth."

He chuckled softly, shaking his head. "You underestimate its power."

She laughed, but it was muffled when he kissed her again. This time, she kneeled, her body curving over his. Six years ago, Charlie would have been losing her shit, making out with her insanely attractive coworker in their matching work T-shirts like some real-life rom-com. Present-day Charlie was too focused on this inherently sweet, hot man, who listened carefully to every word she said. A man who gripped her with a need she felt in her bones. His free hand roamed her body, sliding toward her ass, but hovered at her waist. She felt his hesitation, and wondering if it was because of their conversation, decided to show him what she wanted. That she was more than okay.

With their mouths fused, she slid one leg over to straddle him, and wiggled her ass into his hands. He squeezed, lifted his head to kiss her deeper, for his tongue to claim her. She rotated her hips and pressed down, unable to stop herself from feeling him hard beneath her. He groaned, his kisses traveling her jaw.

"God, Charlie," he murmured.

Charlie tilted her head back, then stopped, her eyes landing on Toothless, who sat perfectly, staring directly at them.

She sputtered a laugh.

"What?" Zachary asked, his mouth finding the sensitive spots along her neck.

"Toothless. She's...entranced."

Zachary craned his head, laughing when he saw the cat's curious gaze.

"She doesn't see much action around here," Charlie said.

She swore Zachary growled and gasped when she felt his tongue trace her collarbone.

"Should we move?" he asked, right before his mouth took hers again, tongue plunging and tangling and tasting.

Charlie gripped his hair, tugged his ears lightly as she pressed closer. She wanted him. Need coursed through her, desire coiled her tightly. She had to tell him she needed to go slow, as much as her body was leading her otherwise.

His hands slid up her ribs, cupping right below her breasts. He tore his lips from hers and kissed down her neck, and she held her breath in anticipation, gasping when his thumbs brushed lightly over her nipples, their sensitivity skyrocketing. His thumbs went back and forth, her breath coming out in little pants, until his hands grabbed hold her of her breasts, kneading, his groan matching hers.

Jesus, and this wasn't even skin on skin!

Like he'd read her mind, Zachary's hands flew down her sides then up under the hem of her shirt, his warmth sending tingles of awareness to her core, his touch gentle and still on her ribs.

She yanked her shirt over her head and tossed it at the couch.

"Fuck," Zachary groaned, his grip skimming up, fingertips slipping under the fabric of her basic black bra, the backs of his fingers sliding back and forth as they slowly inched closer to her nipples.

Charlie rolled her hips, throwing her head back. When she looked back at Zachary, his eyes were scanning her body, his teeth were digging into his bottom lip, and he looked hungry.

"God, I need more of you," he said, shoving up into a seated position.

Charlie tipped back and grabbed hold of his shoulders, but they rocked off balance, and her legs flailed until they tipped onto their sides. The wine bottle went down, spilling on the rug, and that's when Toothless decided she'd had enough, slowly cat walking out of the living room.

"Shit," Zachary said, straining for the wine with Charlie still wrapped around him.

"Here." She slid off him and righted the bottle.

Zachary had a bundle of paper towels in moments. She dabbed the damp end of the blanket while he pressed at the carpet. She grabbed the baking soda and scooted his hands away, pouring it over the spots.

"Will that do it?" he asked.

"Probably not. It'll help, though. I think I might be missing a step," she said.

They locked eyes and grinned. Zachary reached out and brushed a loose strand of hair behind her ear, his fingers tracing her neck and shoulder. He leaned back, forearms resting on bent knees as he looked at the ground, a smirk playing.

Charlie's heart was still racing, and as much as she longed for his body against hers, now was not the night. Not the night to test herself, not the night to dig into it all with him.

He seemed to sense the moment was on pause and reached for her shirt, holding it out to her. Without a word, he started cleaning up, taking things to the kitchen. They worked in silence until they were by her front door, staring at the floor, the only trace of what had happened confined to a splattering of baking soda on the carpet hiding what was surely a permanent stain.

Zachary leaned in and kissed Charlie on the cheek, then pressed his forehead to hers. "See you tomorrow?"

She nodded but couldn't resist pressing one final kiss to his lips. It was supposed to be small, but soon her arms wound around his neck, and his hands pulled her close.

Finally, he stepped back, with a small shake of his head. "See you, Harris."

He was out the door before either of them could delay it anymore. It was for the best, because if this was going to go any further, she'd need to tell him what was going on.

CHAPTER 24

Zachary

THE CRISP BREEZE SWIRLED the scent of pine and impending snow through the crowd at the edge of Village Park. Thirty-degree weather wouldn't stop people from attending the Elmwood Falls Village Tree Lighting, but as more groups arrived, it helped cut the wind. A family closed in, nearly separating Zachary from his own.

"Uncle Zachy!" Vivi stretched out a dramatic arm as though she'd lose him forever.

He chuckled and squeezed closer. "I'm right here, kiddo."

Theatrics done, she gripped his hand with both of hers, her purple mittens soft and floppy. "Don't forget, we're getting fudge next!"

"I wouldn't miss it," he said.

"They've been talking about it all day," Sandra said. "This is one of their favorite nights. Sweetie, pull your hat down." She tugged on Vivi's matching cap.

"You remember doing this last year, Vivi?" He looked over at his mom and Jay, who was holding Alex as he pointed at storefront displays.

Vivi nodded. "Mom let me get two fudges. Peanut butter and mint. That's what I want."

"We're not eating it all tonight. Some of it's to bring home," Sandra reminded her.

"Who sells fudge?" Zachary asked his sister.

"The Door County shop. Have you been in there? Really cute."

"No." He followed where she pointed. "I haven't thought about Door County in ages."

"We're thinking of taking the kids next fall. Rent a cabin, like we did a couple times."

"Oh, right. Hard to remember Dad taking time off for that."

"They usually paired it with a Monday holiday. Drove up after Saturday closed. Mom kinda dragged him out of the office."

The memory was faint, waiting for his dad in the car so they could make the three-hour drive north. The last time they'd gone, he'd been fifteen.

"Mommy! Look!" Vivi tugged Sandra's coat, then Jay's. "Alex! It's almost time!"

Alex squealed in delight as they all faced the compact stage in front of a giant Christmas tree, its decor muted without the glowing lights. A handful of people huddled around the podium, and a buzz went through the crowd.

"I feel like they keep doing this earlier each year," Sandra muttered.

"Well, stores started with Halloween decorations in July," their mom said. "This is nothing."

"This used to happen after Thanksgiving, though, right? It's just a few days away, why not wait?" Zachary asked, tuning out any reply as he spotted Charlie in the crowd.

She stood with a few of their staff, hugging her large coat tight. There had been talk of attending as a group that evening—and he'd been tempted to join—but felt like he owed his family the time. Besides, as much as he wanted to see Charlie outside the office again, which hadn't happened since the cookout, he still didn't know what the hell he was doing. Though the urge to return to Chicago grew smaller.

He considered that thought as the mayor and other city council members addressed the crowd. Fortunately, there were a lot of clinics hiring due to the smaller numbers of veterinarians in the field. Unfortunately, the locations often consisted of burnt-out employees, not enough employees, and high-stress situations because of low funds. If there was a place he felt good fighting for, it was here.

He looked back at Charlie just as the tree lights twinkled, and the crowd cheered. She clapped her hands above her head, shimmying to the holiday music that blared over the blocked-off Main Street. A family approached with their small dog and stopped her, and her genuine happiness shone through the sea of people.

"Uncle Zachy, let's go!" Vivi shouted.

His family was already walking toward the shop, but he didn't make it far.

"Zachary Lee!"

A young woman launched herself into his arms as he turned.

He pulled back and looked down into her laughing face. "Holy shit! Bella Mazzolari," he said. He bopped the puffball on top of her forest-green knit hat and scanned the rest of her. She had a matching scarf and gloves, a cream down coat, and her jeans were tucked into a tan heeled boot with a furry lining. "How many layers do you have on? Is your body already adapted to LA weather?"

"It is *no joke*, Zachary. Also, where's this mild winter everyone's been talking about? I feel like my family tricked me into coming home."

He grinned. "Has it been a while?"

"A couple years, for Christmas at least." She glanced around at all the moving bodies. "Are you here by yourself?"

"No, my family's getting fudge. You?"

"Everyone is here." She pointed to a large group of adults and a couple of kids, standing near the tree. "My older sister lives nearby and invited me, but then everyone else found out."

"That's nice," he said.

"Yeah. My mom jumped at the chance to have us all together outside of the Thanksgiving meal." She peered around him, then looked up with her light brown eyes, makeup flawless, olive skin rosy from the cold. "Is your dad here too?"

"No. Too cold. And too busy."

"Mmm, yeah. How is he?"

"A little better every day. He's, uh, probably going to retire."

Bella blew out a breath. "Oh my. Lots of things to process."

Zachary nodded. "How are you?"

She shrugged. "Pretty good. For getting dumped on national television."

"Aah, Bella..."

She chuckled, her smile wide. "Seriously. It was rough for a bit, but I'm in a better place now. The producers are even talking to me about hosting a new reality show," she added in a lower tone.

"Another dating one?"

She held a finger to her lips.

"Did the experience not deter you from the relationship scene?"

Bella rocked between her feet, swinging her arms to keep warm. She stopped, head cocked. "No. If you'd asked a few months ago, it'd have been a different story. I dunno, the journey of the relationship is part of the fun. Even in such a compressed time, I learned things about myself and what I want in a partner. And for his many, *many* flaws, there were moments when I was really happy. Pain and all, I'd rather go for it than regret not trying."

"Bella!" The chorus shouting her name startled them, the power of five siblings plus.

Bella waved a wild hand. "Yeah, I'm coming!" She rolled her eyes. "It's like we jump back twenty years when we're all together. Okay, I promise we'll grab food while we're both home. I'll text you!" She hugged him tight.

"Good to see you, Bella."

She blew a kiss, then scuttled across the street, shouting indiscernible things to her family. A man, probably a brother, looped an arm around her neck in a loose headlock, and one of the little kids jumped on his back.

Zachary smiled at the mayhem, and the thought of Alex's and Vivi's faces watching the festivities lodged something quite uncomfortable in his throat. It seemed to grow in size as his family emerged from the Door County shop down the street. Vivi immediately sat at the curb to eat her fudge, with Alex wrangled by Jay to do the same. Sandra stood behind them, sipping a hot drink, and their mom came out of the store moments later and handed each kid something. He watched Sandra protest, but then she handed her a trinket and Sandra burst out laughing. Whatever she handed Jay next made his face light up like Alex.

Zachary didn't want to watch from the sidelines anymore. He wanted to be up close to witness his mom's glee as she spoiled her grandkids, see what old joke Sandra's gift referenced, learn something his brother-in-law loved. He wanted to be there. In the thick of it.

Even if he and his dad stood next to one another in silence, he would make this time home count.

*****

Zachary moved past clumps of people as they enjoyed the blocked-off Main Street like it was a special treat. When he spotted Charlie, alone, staring up at the tree, he maneuvered her way, stopping at her left shoulder. Bella's words had echoed the entire night—"*I'd rather go for it than regret not trying.*"

"Hey." He leaned close to her ear. Her breath hitched, and when she turned, their faces were inches apart.

"Hey." Berry glasses today, to match her shoes. She looked back at the tree. "Well?"

"Good show. Though I'll admit, Vivi and Alex were the most fun to watch." *Her too.* How to say it without making her uncomfortable?

"I don't doubt it."

He lilted forward, his chest brushing her back. He grinned when she pressed to him. "It's nice to see you," he murmured. He looked down at her head as she stared at the tree and saw her cheeks perk into a grin.

"We just saw each other."

"Yes, but out of the office."

There was a beat, then "It's good to see you too."

He reached for her hand, threaded their fingers, and tucked them in the folds of his coat, hidden from everyone else. It had been years since he'd held a woman's hand. He hadn't realized the urge still existed.

He swallowed. "You're freezing."

"Forgot my gloves this morning."

He warmed her fingers in his as they faced the tree. Her skin against his was his new favorite thing.

Gentle flurries fell, steady, as though on cue. Charlie chuckled and looked up, the snowflakes landing on her face, melting on her cheeks, her glasses.

"You've gotta be kidding me," she murmured.

"What is it?"

"I mean, this is perfect timing. *Magical.*" She gestured up. "High-school Charlie would be freaking out right now." She blinked rapidly, her smile freezing. Her eyes darted to him.

He chuckled. "High school you?"

She groaned and removed her hand from his so she could flip up the hood of her coat. With a quick tug at the strings, she cinched the hood briefly, then released the strings and turned.

"I may have...had a crush on you. When I was younger."

"You did, huh?"

"Why don't you sound surprised? God, was I that obvious?"

"I, no, I..." He scratched his head. "I guess I wondered once or twice. It's not like I thought about it a lot."

She put her face in her hands and groaned.

He laughed, peeling one finger away from her eye and stepping close. "It's not a bad thing."

"Easy for you to say," she grumbled.

"Okay, true. I'm flattered. But I'm...I'm glad the me I am now is still...someone you're interested in."

"Oh, I'm definitely interested," she said, her voice adopting a husky tone.

He shivered, clenching his jaw to keep from tugging her close. Instead, he leaned down and whispered in her ear, "Oh, I'm definitely interested too."

Her eyes were closed when he straightened, as though she were absorbing a kiss, her lips parted slightly. She blinked them open and looked around with a surprised giggle, shaking her head to herself. Finally locking eyes with him, her smile softened into one he hadn't seen, one that made him want to sit in her affection and simultaneously whisk her away to somewhere private.

"So, um...ready for the holiday festivities?" Charlie asked.

He snorted a laugh.

It had been a long time since he'd shared a holiday with his family. He'd never experienced it with the kids around, either, to see what excited them, what foods they liked or hated. His mom had told them they were skipping events with relatives this year. A day together, relaxed in celebration, could be really nice.

He looked down at Charlie, and she grinned back, turning to completely face him. She kept their bodies close and brought her hands up to meet his in the coat cocoon. Looking at her under the twinkling lights was dangerous, her eyes sparkling, her mouth inviting. The thought of seeing her in Christmas-themed scrubs was as appealing as being with her now, close together, only them existing in this holiday fanfare.

He'd enjoy it all while he could.

"I'm ready."

Chapter 25

Charlie

"When are you two going out again? Don't get me wrong, I like your mug, but I figured you'd jump at any free time to spend with him. I know you guys are there together long hours, but I don't see you getting frisky in that office." Amber chuckled, following Charlie into her apartment.

Charlie hung up her coat and settled onto the couch, Toothless sauntering over for a pat. She'd invited her cousin over with the sole purpose of talking with her. After telling Magnolia, it had been a little easier for Charlie to picture sharing her vaginismus with Amber, and with the way she and Zachary were advancing, she needed the support.

"I don't know. We've been swamped, plus he's helping with his dad. We see each other almost every day, though."

"That's not the same as going out! How are you keeping your hands to yourself?"

They had trouble keeping their hands to themselves. Each day was part of a painstakingly sexy foreplay, and Charlie was an excited participant.

Amber squealed. "You're blushing! What happened with the sexy vet?"

"Well, he knows I had a crush on him."

Amber gasped. "Did he figure it out?"

"I kinda let it slip." She laughed at Amber's pained groan. "It ended up being a good thing. He was very sweet about it."

"I'm excited for you. I know he's a big deal, but you're so happy. And you *deserve* to be happy. Also, I'm surprised you haven't jumped his bones already." She chuckled.

Charlie bit the inside of her cheek, glancing away. "I can't just do that," she said quietly.

"Yeah, I know, that's not your style. Totally get it," Amber said, squeezing her arm.

"No, I mean." Charlie took a breath. "Physically. I can't just go and do that."

Amber was silent, her eyes searching Charlie's as Toothless walked across their laps.

"Wait. Charlie. Are you...?" Amber shifted, the crease between her brows deepening. "Are you still a virgin?"

"Well, technically, yes."

"*Oh.* Oh, shit. Wow, okay, yeah, I didn't know."

"That's not the whole deal, though."

"I'm confused."

Charlie huffed out a laugh. She gave Amber a rundown, similar to her conversation with Magnolia. She let her talk, listening quietly.

When Charlie stopped, Amber said softly, "I had no idea."

She shrugged. "How could you? I never told you."

"Why?"

"It got to this point where...everyone had gone well beyond tampons and losing their virginity. I thought by college, I'd have some answers. When I didn't, it became too difficult to bring it up." She blew out a breath. "I was extremely embarrassed."

"It's nothing to be embarrassed about—"

"Try thinking that when everyone around you is talking about getting laid, hooking up with strangers, trying new positions, or kinky things with their boyfriends." Charlie shook her head. "It made me feel *dumb* somehow. Naive. Like I couldn't chime in about anything because I didn't have the experience. No one ever talked about having pain that never went away or being unable to stick *anything* in. I felt very alone, like something was wrong with me. Bringing it up to someone I'm interested in is the last thing I want to do. Even Bobby couldn't wrap his head around it."

"What did that asshole say?"

Charlie waved her hand. "He got tired of us not really progressing. We did other stuff, but I had a hard time even being in the mood. I mean, he was more concerned with getting off, anyway. Said I was a tease for having wants and desires but then being too nervous to follow through. Made me feel guilty if I didn't participate, that he couldn't do it solo for religious reasons..."

"Motherfucker." Amber tapped the armrest. "We tell each other everything."

"We did. When we were younger."

"We still do."

"Amber, it's not like it used to be."

Amber crossed her arms and looked away from Charlie, no doubt thinking of her own mother. How much she'd pulled away once she'd passed.

"All those times I talked about hooking up with guys..." Amber shook her head. "You must've hated me."

Charlie reared back slightly. "Hated you? Why?"

"It was like throwing it in your face. Taunting you."

"I never thought of it that way."

"I would've."

Charlie smirked. "No you wouldn't."

Amber sighed. "You think too highly of me sometimes."

Charlie snorted.

Eyes pinched with worry, Amber leaned closer. "Is it hard to talk to me about stuff?"

"No, it's not that. It's just...I've had a hard time processing it. And accepting it myself. It's been me and my doctors, which kept it in this strange little bubble. Telling Magnolia was the first time I felt like I was actually admitting it aloud."

Amber leaned back. "You told Magnolia?"

"Only recently. She happened to see me," Charlie fumbled, not wanting to reveal anything of Magnolia's before she did. "It just sort of came out. I think it bubbled to the surface or something."

"We hardly know Magnolia."

"Come on, that's not true. She fit in immediately, like we'd known her forever, you even said that yourself. Why would we all have been helping her with the shop this whole time?"

"Still."

Charlie rubbed her forehead. "That doesn't matter."

"Maybe not to you."

"Look, I'm still figuring out how to process all this. How to not feel embarrassed, to be able to say the words to people close to me. To try and not worry about what people will think, like my therapist says, even though all I can do is spin my wheels with ways people won't understand or will tell me it's not real, when it's been *very real*, and for most of my life! And to top it off, I'm wild about this amazing guy, and I have *no clue* how to talk to him about this because the last time it came up for me, the relationship didn't go too well. How do you tell someone you want to be with them in *all the ways*, and then add on that you're broken? That...you feel like your value is somehow less as a person, and a partner? What if I'm...what if it's not worth the effort to him, and the patience, and he wants to leave?"

Charlie's voice shook. Her frantic eyes found her cousin's, Amber's glistening with tears.

"Is that how you feel? Like you're...broken?" Amber finally asked.

All Charlie could do was nod. Amber launched herself forward, wrapping her arms tight around Charlie, crying with her. This time, Charlie's tears came out in sobs, the force of them racking her body. Amber squeezed her tighter, whispering over and over again that she had her, that it would be okay.

It shocked Charlie to realize that this time, she believed it would be.

CHAPTER 26

Zachary

"JEANIE, FOR THE LAST time, I'm fine," Daniel grumbled from the passenger seat.

Zachary's mom held up her hands as she sat back in her seat behind him, surrounded by their two dogs and Maple. "We have a lot to be thankful for, Daniel. I'd like us to look our best."

"This is as good as it's gonna get." Daniel huffed, pulling the end of his flannel shirt over his sweats. "Probably putting on my sweatshirt as soon as we get there anyway. Always freezing in their house," he grumbled.

Zachary felt for the man, even though words between them were limited. He also knew his mom was fretting because she wanted this gathering to feel as normal as possible, but his dad going at all was effort enough.

His dad's eyes were heavy with exhaustion, a detail Zachary glimpsed before his father turned his face toward the passenger window.

"Mom, it smells like the entire dinner in here," Zachary said. "I'm surprised the dogs aren't going crazy."

"Oh," came her simple reply.

He glanced in the rearview to find her holding food in her hand, breaking off little pieces at a time for each dog in turn. Maple was tucked to her side on the bench seat, and his parents' boxer and yellow lab were behind them, stretching their heads around the head rests. He shook his head with a chuckle, careful not to draw his father's attention. Feeding table scraps had been an argument their entire marriage, Daniel constantly concerned about the dogs' diets, and Jeanie constantly concerned about their happiness.

She bit her lip, fighting a grin. Her bob looked chic, her makeup brightening her face.

"What all did you make?" Zachary prompted.

She winked. "Oh just a few things. Cheesy corn casserole, sweet potatoes, this new squash recipe Maura told me about—it smells amazing—and sweet red-bean soup. I also picked up a cooked turkey this year."

"That's a lot," Zachary said. His dad grunted in agreement.

"No, no. Sandra and Jay made the roasted duck, mashed potatoes, oyster stuffing, and sticky rice dumplings. And other desserts."

"Jesus, how did you all have the energy?" Zachary asked.

"One of my favorite things to do. Extra special since you're home too." She reached forward to pat his arm, just as he eased into Sandra's driveway, shaded by a white pine tree.

"Allowed her to have a break from me but still hover," Daniel grumbled.

"Oh look, the kids were watching for us," his mom said, ignoring Daniel.

Jeanie opened her door, and the dogs hopped out just as Vivi and Alex burst from the two-story, red brick colonial house and down the stone front steps with their fluffy Maltese, Puff. The front yard had a large maple tree with straggler leaves remaining, its branches spanning the lawn. Puff hopped around, barking commands at all the guests, weaving between the other dogs. Zachary helped Maple out of the back seat, then scooped up Alex and flipped him over his shoulder, his peals of laughter ringing through the neighborhood.

"Zachary, carry this inside." Jeanie set a stack of dishes in his free arm.

"Okay, buddy, let's bring in the food," Zachary said, still toting his nephew.

"Doo, do, do, DOO! To the castle!" Alex sang his toddler tune.

"Oh my apologies, *Prince Alexander*," Zachary said as he reached the midnight-blue front door. It framed the three-quarter glass window, and he saw his sister as she approached on the other side.

Sandra opened the door, hair in a low ponytail, sleeves rolled on a teal blouse, and a black apron tied around her waist. She reached toward the dishes and wiggled her fingers. "Gimme."

"You guys went all out," Zachary said.

"What are you talking about?"

He gestured at the food. "Mom made a ton of sh—stuff." He caught himself and tickled Alex. "Sounds like you did too. You'd think this family wasn't going through something right now."

"Jay and I cooked together, so it wasn't that bad. Besides, it calms me. Really."

"You sound like Mom," he murmured.

"Well, it's true." Sandra shrugged, then lowered her voice. "I could tell it was really important to her. She wanted this to be...special."

"I could've done more than bring beer. I feel like a jerk." Alex squirmed for freedom, so Zachary set him down, watching as the little guy kicked off his shoes and ran through the house.

"Aw, you're not a jerk." Sandra started to walk toward her kitchen, then glanced over her shoulder with a mischievous grin. "Just an idiot. But don't worry, it's only from time to time."

Zachary called after her, "Watch your back, Sandra. Plenty of pies around looking for a face!"

"There's only one pie today, and your niece made it!"

"Damn," he muttered.

Sandra's burst of laughter followed as he stepped outside to grab the beer from his trunk.

His dad sat on a bench near the front door, rust-colored leaves piled on the mulch at his feet. Zachary swallowed the thick ball of emotion in his throat, registering his dad for the first time as an older man, a grandfather. Daniel's shirt was a plaid of light blue and gray, the material heavy against his frame. He had one arm draped over the back of the bench, fingers tapping the wrought iron while he watched Jeanie and Vivi play with the dogs. Vivi giggled as she leaned toward Maple, getting kisses all over her face in return as the dog loped around with her slow-motion gait.

Zachary smiled, glancing back to his dad, only to do a double-take. His father had the smallest of smiles on his face, but it showed an immense amount of love for the scene before him. His eyes glistened, his frame and posture stoic. Zachary moved toward his car, barely catching movement as his dad wiped his hand across his cheeks.

"Uncle Zachy, did you watch the parade?" Vivi asked as she bounded over.

"I did not. Was it awesome?"

She nodded solemnly. "We recorded it. Wanna watch it with me?"

He closed the trunk, smiling. Ah, to have the enthusiasm of a child who could watch a parade over and over. "I'd love to."

"Yes!" She pumped her fist in the air for emphasis, then took off for the front door, the pack of dogs following after her.

Zachary bent to pick up the beer and saw his mom leaning over his dad, their voices too soft to carry. Jeanie pressed a kiss to Daniel's head, and his dad smiled, a look of devotion between them like they were the only ones there. His mom held out her hand as his dad stood, and they walked up the front steps and into the house.

Zachary cleared his throat, overwhelmed by the affection he witnessed from his family within mere minutes of them all being together. He had to admit his mother was right—today was special.

***

"Vivi, it's time to set up your pie!" Sandra called from the kitchen.

Vivi bolted off the couch from her spot next to Zachary and ran to help.

"You sure you don't need help, honey?" Jeanie sat in the tan swivel arm chair next to Daniel's while they all watched the parade, now dulled without Vivi's commentary.

"We're good, Mom!" Sandra called back.

Jeanie pushed her chair with extra emphasis while she muttered about children treating her like an old woman.

Zachary rolled his eyes. "She's trying to do something nice for you, Mom. She and Jay have it covered."

"You weren't supposed to hear that," Jeanie replied haughtily, straightening her plum cardigan over a floral blouse.

"Speaking of children knowing everything," Daniel chimed in. He'd been quiet the whole time watching the parade, unless spoken to directly by his grandchildren. Now his gaze pierced Zachary. "How are things going at the clinic?"

"Everything's fine. We've been able to maintain a full schedule, it's almost like they didn't miss a beat," Zachary said.

Daniel gave a quick nod. "People have been receptive to you being there?"

"Much to Charlie's chagrin, yes." Zachary smiled, thinking of her throwing down the gauntlet in the beginning.

"I've always loved her," Jeanie said.

Daniel grunted.

Zachary knew his dad loved her too. "She keeps things running smoothly, Dad. You'd be proud."

Daniel looked away. "She's fantastic. Perfect for the practice."

Zachary cleared his throat. "I agree."

"There's something you need to know, though." Daniel's face was twisted with concern.

"No, not today," Jeanie said urgently, her hand landing on his forearm.

"We're approaching the end of the year, Jeanie. With Dr. Kamath's orders, I need to make sure things are moving in the right direction."

Zachary looked at his parents. "What's going on?"

Daniel turned his gaze toward him. "The practice is in trouble."

Zachary nodded slowly. "I found a few things I'd wanted to discuss with you."

"There's a lot of...debt. I had to take out another loan recently, and I'm behind on payments."

"Wait, another loan? I didn't come across any of that paperwork."

"You wouldn't. I've had the documents at the house."

"How bad is it?"

"I can show you later."

"Dad. What about your accountant? Hasn't he been involved with this?"

"He's a SOB who took off and left us high and dry," Jeanie chimed in.

Daniel looked away. "I fired him, Jeanie."

"What?" Jeanie sat higher in her chair.

"It's true, he's a son of a bitch, and he was screwing things up," Daniel said in a harsh whisper. "So I fired him. I never got around to hiring someone new this year."

She sank back against her seat.

"I've held my prices for years, working with our clients to make sure they could afford the care they needed, but with these other clinics getting bought out and lowering their rates, it's become too much. The point is, I have a large amount of money due at the end of the year, otherwise, the practice will close. I've started to pursue options to sell."

Zachary's stomach lurched. "You mean Neptune, right? He came to the cookout to see you," Zachary added when his dad's eyebrows rose.

"Yes. Neptune is a very likely possibility. They've already drawn up an offer."

"You've heard what's happened to the clinics they've bought. They're taking over, making them all the same. Driving out places like us."

His dad paused, then continued softly, "I'm running out of options. If I can get a partner, that could help offset some of the money."

"Charlie wouldn't be able to do that?"

"It's not right. It needs to stay within the family right now. I can't in good conscience transfer this over to her. It's like giving a gift of debt. The practice would hardly be part of it."

"I thought you considered her family," Zachary spat the words through gritted teeth.

"You know it's not the same," Daniel said.

Silence hung over the room. If Charlie learned about the dire straits of the clinic, she'd be crushed. Financially, emotionally...

If she heard the words they'd just exchanged, it'd do her in just as badly.

"I can't keep this from her," Zachary said.

"Find a way. Until I can convince you to buy into the practice with me. Those are our choices."

Zachary stared at him. Selling to Neptune was an adamant *no* from him. *But buy into the practice?* The one he'd chosen to leave? The one he'd been removed from without a second thought? That'd mean moving back to Wisconsin. Uprooting his life in Chicago. Taking the practice right out from under Charlie.

It meant working *with* Charlie. As her boss. As the owner. Seeing each other every day, no longer in a temporary situation. What would that mean for them? When things finally fizzled out between them, then what?

She wouldn't want to leave, and he'd hate to be the reason she did. He couldn't shatter her dreams.

"Dinner's ready!" Sandra appeared at the living room entrance, a proud Vivi by her side.

"Uncle Zachy, you're sitting by me!" Vivi exclaimed.

"Perfect," Zachary said, forcing a smile.

Unfortunately, the table wasn't going to be enough distance between him and his father.

CHAPTER 27

Charlie

"THANK GOD YOU'RE HERE." Amber yanked Charlie inside Brooke's house and closed the door. Her maroon dress with tiny cream flowers floated around her knees, the sleeves cinched at the wrists.

"You look awesome. Look at those cute booties." Charlie trailed off and looked around.

The house was quiet. It smelled of turkey, rosemary, and simmering spiced cranberries, but the small front living room was unusually empty. On any other Thanksgiving, the gray wool couch would house Brooke's husband, Elliot, and their daughter, Mina, along with Brooke and Amber's dad, Carl. Today? No one.

"Am I the first one here?" Charlie asked as she took off her coat and smoothed her verdant shirt dress.

"Carl, stop testing the turkey. You're going to eat it all!" Penelope's voice rang through the house like a siren.

"Jesus, Pen, I'm not gonna eat an entire ten-pound turkey myself!" Carl yelled back.

"Never mind. The kids are bickering already, I hear," Charlie said of her mom and uncle.

Amber rolled her eyes. "I got here with Dad right before your mom showed up. It's been about twenty minutes of that while doing what Brooke asks of them."

"Brooke hasn't kicked them out of the kitchen yet?"

"She's been surprisingly okay with the help."

"Where are Elliot and Mina?"

"Right. So." Amber glanced toward the kitchen and lowered her voice as if they could be heard over the sibling squabbles. "Brooke answered the door and said, 'Elliot's not coming today.' Then she went back to the kitchen and kept making pie."

"He's not coming?"

"No explanation. Haven't been able to get anything out of her either. Charlie, she made five pies. You heard right. Technically, a pie for each of us."

"I mean, I like pie. But that's not what you're getting at," Charlie said.

Amber shook her head. "Correct. Something's wrong."

Brooke bustled into the living room holding the baby monitor, sleeves of a lightweight black sweater shoved up her arms, hair smoothed back into a low bun. "Oh! Hey, Charlie. Happy Thanksgiving." She pecked Charlie's cheek. "Can one of you get Mina? She just woke up from her nap. I'd like her to wear the outfit I set on the rocking chair."

"Sure, I've got her," Amber said, raising her eyebrows at Charlie as she left the room.

"I've got those fancy carrots you requested." Charlie held up her ceramic dish.

"Wonderful. Come on in." Brooke headed to the kitchen before Charlie could say more.

"Charlotte, hi, sweetheart." Penelope leaned over from her station at the counter to plant a kiss on her cheek, then smudged away the mauve lipstick print it left behind. Light pink painted the fair skin of her cheeks. Her golden-brown hair hung in loose curls to her shoulders, the way she'd styled it for years. "Carl, seriously, stop being an ass."

Charlie grinned. The rare occasion when her mom cursed was toward her own brother.

Carl snickered at Penelope's playful swat to the shoulder while savoring the bite of mashed potatoes he'd scooped from her bowl. The two stood side by side, similar in height, with Penelope's low black pumps, in her classic look with black pants and a light blue button-down, whether she was going out or working at the department store. Carl, on the other hand, wore sneakers with jeans and a long-sleeved gray shirt with the Packers' emblem.

"Hey, Uncle Carl," Charlie greeted, scooting into his side for the best bear hug.

"How are you, sweetie? How are the animals?"

Always the same question. "Good. How's the team?"

He winked. "Good."

"Can't have one day without them, even if they aren't playing," Penelope muttered.

"Hey, I wore my dress tee today." Carl pointed to the emblem, small over his pec. "See? Subtle."

Charlie, and her mom with reluctance, laughed. Brooke, on the other hand, stayed focused on shuffling around the kitchen.

"So put me to work, Brooke—"

Brooke's hands guided Charlie by the shoulders to a handful of apples on the counter. "Peel, slice. The rest is already mixed together. Crust is here."

"Apple pie?" Charlie asked, remembering what Amber had said.

"Mmm. Almost forgot it."

"Yum," Charlie added, getting to work, though she sent a few glances Brooke's way. She noticed her mom and uncle were doing the same.

"I think we'll be okay on the pie front, Brookie," Carl said.

"What? Oh. Well, I thought it'd be nice for everyone to have their favorite. I have an extra pecan though, Charlie. Maybe the Lees would like it?"

Charlie straightened, surprised at the mention of Zachary's family. They'd sent each other simple texts that morning. Today was family time. A holiday. Too serious for whatever it was brewing between them anyway.

"That's sweet of you, Brooke," Charlie said.

"It's nothing." Brooke forced a chuckle. "Forgot I made one yesterday. Was on a roll."

"I'll say," Penelope muttered.

Charlie shot her mom a wide-eyed look, and Penelope gestured at the food and mouthed "*What!*"

"Someone's ready to eat!" Amber walked in holding two-year-old Mina's hand.

They doted on the little girl, her strawberry-blonde ringlets clipped away from her face with a rust-orange barrette that matched her sweater dress. Following Aunt Amber's lead, she turned around and wiggled, showcasing the embroidered turkey feathers over her butt. She clapped along, unsure of the joke but happy to be part of it. Brooke scooped her up with a kiss, then gave instructions to finish setting the table. Finally, they found themselves seated, a colorful feast in front of them on the tan linen tablecloth, a trio of pillar candles burning in their mismatched brass holders, flames dancing tentatively.

"Well, shall we?" Brooke said. She stood to serve turkey, and dishes made their way around, among bits of chatter about the meal.

"A little toast, Brooke?" Carl said, raising his glass.

If Charlie hadn't been watching her closely, she would've missed the glimmer of irritation on Brooke's face as she grabbed her glass of pinot.

"Sure, Dad," Brooke said. "Go for it."

Carl looked surprised at the green light to take the lead. Brooke ran many a show ever since her mom had passed. Carl had been lost without Charlie's Aunt Dana, and Brooke had stepped into the role of problem-solver so quickly, Charlie didn't know when she found time to handle her own emotions.

"To family," Carl started. "I'm grateful for all of you, every day. And to Brooke, for hosting this wonderful meal."

"Hear! Hear!" Amber said, leading the charge for everyone to take a sip. "Let's eat."

"Where's Dadda?" Mina asked. She kicked her little legs up and down in her booster seat next to Brooke, large blue eyes staring as she chomped on a roll.

"Not here, honey," Brooke said, looking at her almost empty glass of wine.

"Soon?" Mina asked.

"Nope," Brooke said tightly.

Charlie's eyes flew to Amber's across the table.

"The turkey is delicious," Carl said.

"You know, the recipe group was talking about ways to cook your turkey. Someone mentioned this thing called...shoot, what was it?" Penelope snapped her fingers a few times, trying to jog her memory. "The Egg? Yes, I think that was it."

"Green Egg," Amber said through a mouthful.

Penelope pointed at Amber in acknowledgment. "Yes. Green Egg. Thank you. You know about it?"

Penelope regaled them on various cooking topics from her online neighborhood group. It diverted conversation away from Brooke, who remained silent, forcing an occasional smile.

By the end of the meal, everyone was relaxed in their seats, pants loosened, dresses fanning.

"Amber, good Lord, what are you doing?" Penelope asked.

"Food sweats," Amber groused. "I'm metabolizing." She continued to flap the fabric away from her body like she was cooling herself down.

Charlie chuckled. This conversation happened most holidays. Penelope conveniently forgot it was a thing.

"What are you talking about? Just...digest it," Penelope said, getting up and clearing plates.

"Oh, yes, good call, Mom. Easy as that," Charlie said with a roll of her eyes.

Penelope swatted Brooke's hands away as she grabbed the plate in front of her. "You sit. You've been on your feet all day. Your father and I will start to clean up." Carl was about to sit, having just come back from starting a movie for Mina in the living room, but stood again. Penelope gave Charlie and Amber a pointed look, with a tilt of her head toward Brooke, before she and Carl walked to the kitchen with loaded arms.

"Punky Brookester?" Amber said. "What's going on?"

"Nothing," Brooke said, finishing her glass of wine. She pulled the bottle close and frowned, finding it empty. "Damn. How many bottles did we go through?" she muttered.

Charlie touched her hand. "You can talk to us. We're worried about you."

Brooke yanked her hand back. "Nothing to be worried about. I'm fine! If there's anyone you should be worried about, it's Elliot." She scoffed. "Bastard could've acquired a bunch of STDs by now."

"Wait, what?" Amber whipped her head back and forth between her sister and Charlie. "What are you talking about?"

That sinking feeling slammed into Charlie as she watched red creep along Brooke's neck.

Brooke feigned nonchalance. "That's what happens when you start sleeping around, right? When you start sticking it into someone who isn't your wife?"

"Shit," Charlie whispered.

"That. Mother. Fucker. *Elliot*?" Amber said. Charlie noticed that Amber ignored the first part, her taste for dating around always misunderstood by her more calculated sister.

"Whatever. I'm not going to worry about him anymore. Told him not to bother coming back here. He's her problem, now."

"Brooke, I'm so sorry," Charlie said. "When?"

Brooke folded her cotton terracotta napkin, its pristine appearance not a representation of how neatly Brooke ate, but that she hadn't eaten much at all. "Yesterday."

"Yesterday?" Amber whisper-cried. "Jesus, Brooke. Why are we even here right now? We should be curled up on your couch, bashing his name, and eating loads of ice cream. Not at the table for a nice Thanksgiving feast. Most of which you cooked!"

"I needed to do it," Brooke said softly. "Kept me from thinking about it. I already can't get the image out of my head. Making food stopped it."

"Ugh, don't think about him with this other woman," Amber said.

"Can't unsee it," Brooke murmured.

"You *saw* them?" Charlie asked.

Brooke nodded. "I stopped by his office yesterday on my lunch. I was bringing him some jam my coworker makes every fall. He loves it, says it's always a hit at his office. Thought they'd enjoy the treat before the long weekend. Except he and Monica had lunch plans of their own." She tapped her light pink nail against the table, the sound dull through the linen tablecloth. "Walked by them in his SUV in the parking lot."

"Woah," Amber said. "Ballsy."

Brooke shrugged. "Guess he didn't care if anyone caught him. Though, he didn't want *me* to catch them. He succinctly said, 'Brooke, you weren't supposed to find out like this.'"

"Bastard," Charlie whispered.

Amber sat with her arms crossed, fuming. "Such a fucking weasel."

"I should've known. Things haven't been the same since Mina was born." Brooke swallowed.

They all knew—ever since she found out she couldn't have a second baby. It'd been devastating for both of them, and Charlie and Amber had noticed a shift in Brooke, saw a change in the two of them. In Brooke's availability, her presence with them. Something hadn't felt right.

"Okay. I say, let's get those two out of here, after they're done cleaning up, of course," Amber said. She managed to get a small smile from Brooke. "We'll all put on stretchy pants and curl up with Mina, and eat pie until we can't move."

Brooke blinked away tears. "That's not how you want to spend Thanksgiving."

"Eat pie on top of pie on top of pie? That's what today is for!" Charlie said lightly. She stood and wrapped her arms around Brooke's shoulders, and Amber enveloped them both.

A shriek from the kitchen made them jump.

"Carl! What are you doing!" Penelope cried out.

Mina's laughter got them up and over to the kitchen threshold.

She squealed on the floor, loving the live entertainment. Carl stood at the sink with the nozzle in spray form, aimed at Penelope's shirt and hair. Penelope scooped bubbles from the sink and swiped them over Carl's nose, and Mina's laughter tipped her over, which sent Carl and Penelope cracking up.

"I'm not going to tell them today, okay?" Brooke said, watching the scene.

"You got it, babe," Amber said, looping her arm over Brooke's shoulders.

Charlie swung her arm around Brooke's waist.

There were no guarantees in life. Sometimes, college sweethearts grew apart—or one of them really took a leap onto the asshole train. Sometimes, a man like her uncle lost his wife after over twenty years together and never recovered. Sometimes, a man only existed as a biological father and child support check, a preference that worked best for people like Charlie and her mom. And sometimes, a man became a father-figure to an employee, and reminded her that good can come from anywhere.

With her own struggles, Charlie knew there were limits on romantic relationships for herself. Even though he was only in town for a little while, she was grateful she had Zachary. Loved being with him. Felt cared for, even in the simplest terms.

She trusted him.

For however long they had before he left Elmwood Falls, she wanted to *be* with him. It was time to let him know.

CHAPTER 28

Zachary

WHERE DO YOU LIVE these days?

Zachary couldn't text back fast enough as he typed out Jordan's address.

Charlie: *Perfect.*

Charlie: *Wait, are you there now?*

Zachary: *Yes... Should I be expecting you?*

Charlie: *:)*

He laughed.

Zachary: *Helpful, Harris.*

"Hey, wanna grab a drink with me before my shift?" Jordan asked.

Zachary looked at the time. "Uh, I'm kinda waiting on someone..."

"Waiting on someone?" Jordan peered over, trying to read his phone. "Whatcha got?"

"Charlie's coming by," Zachary said.

"I see, waiting until I'd be working to bring her here, huh?"

"She asked me where I'm staying. I have no idea what it's about."

"You two couldn't go two whole days without seeing each other?"

"Yeah, it's not like that."

"That's what they always say. Why don't you both join me for a drink? If it's so low pressure and all?"

"I don't know," Zachary said, walking toward the guest room while he tugged his shirt over his head.

He did know. He liked the sound of that. Hanging out with one of his best friends, having him meet the woman in his life.

Except, *was* she the woman in his life?

Would you be trying to screw over the woman in your life by buying a business out from under her? And lying about it?

His conversation with his father hadn't continued at Sandra's, and by the time he'd dropped them home, Daniel had been exhausted. There was a lot left to discuss.

The doorbell rang just as he closed the final buttons on his dark green button-down, but no amount of hustle could beat Jordan. The man must've been standing there, waiting.

"Hey! You must be Charlie," Jordan said, gesturing into the house. "Come on in."

"I am. Jordan?" Charlie said.

Zachary's heart raced as she came into view, her hair loose as it brushed her winter coat. She shook Jordan's hand, her smile genuine, warm. Jordan's was equally warm. Suddenly he hated being left out of the moment.

"Hey," he said, going up to her with a kiss on the cheek.

She turned, her eyes wide in surprise behind thin blue wire frames, smiling as the pink of her cheeks spread. "Hey," she said. She held out a round dish. "This is for you. Well, for your family. My cousin made it and thought you all might want it."

He tipped his head to the side with a smile. "But you brought it to me. That's dangerous, you know," he teased. He peeked under the foil. "Pecan?"

"God, that smells good," Jordan said.

Zachary moved the pan away from his friend's nose.

"Yeah, well, last night didn't go quite as planned. Hence, me bringing it to you today." She twisted her hands together. "Will you guys eat it?"

"Yes," he and Jordan said at the same time.

"Believe me," Zachary added.

"Oh, I'm convinced," Charlie said, her eyes sparkling.

"My mom and sister made a shit ton of food anyway, so they're all just fine." Zachary made his way toward the kitchen. "Want a slice?" he asked her, pulling out silverware while Jordan grabbed plates.

"You're going to have some now?" she asked.

"Why not?" Zachary asked.

She laughed. "I'm good. Still recovering from mine last night."

"So listen, Charlie," Jordan said, already digging into his piece. "Shit, that's good. We were gonna go to Whiskey Nights for a drink. Want to join?"

Zachary narrowed his eyes at his friend and got a smirk in response.

"Oh, I love that place!"

"Yeah?" Jordan smiled. "My sister owns it."

Her mouth dropped open. "You're kidding. We've been crushing on it since it opened."

"Well, Mel will be there tonight, so you can meet her."

Charlie clapped her hands, and Zachary realized he'd go wherever she wanted.

Which is how he found himself in his car twenty minutes later, with Charlie in the passenger seat, as they followed Jordan to the bar. Holiday music played softly in the car, their hands twining together.

A buzz filled the air as they drove through the village, shoppers starting on checklists and treating themselves in the process, but they somehow found parking not too far from the bar.

With his hands in his pockets, Zachary nudged his body against Charlie's on their short walk. "You're quiet today," he said.

"So are you," she countered, offering a small smile.

Their companionable silence was as familiar as it was new. Though his thoughts were preoccupied with his dad's news, his desire to be near her overruled any warning of how close they were becoming.

He held open the door to Whiskey Nights, and Jordan beckoned them over to the bar.

"What'll we have to drink?" Jordan asked, waving over a bartender.

"Mel doesn't make you mix the drinks when you show up early?" Zachary asked.

"Nah," Jordan said. "She knows better than to squeeze more time from me."

"Jordan's a nurse at the children's hospital during the week," Zachary said.

"Have you told her nothing about me? I'm hurt." He pinched his lips together and drew an imaginary tear path with his finger.

Charlie smiled. "He doesn't make a habit out of sharing stories of his charming friends. I think he's trying to hide something."

"See, she already called you *charming*," Zachary muttered.

"Well, that's because she can see it. Though, next to you, I'm not surprised," Jordan said. "He's gotten a bit surly in his old age."

"I've noticed. He was much more easygoing in college," Charlie added.

"You knew him in college too? How did we not meet?"

Zachary rolled his eyes. "She and I worked together at the clinic. You know this, Jordan."

Jordan winked. "Oh, I know."

Charlie blushed, and Zachary straightened in his seat, looking at Jordan over her head.

Jordan laughed.

"Well, look at you, having the time of your life over here. Enjoying my fine establishment before I put you to work, huh?" A woman with dark brown skin propped her arms on the bar across from them, the rust-colored curls of her Afro catching light from the Edison bulbs around the bar. She grinned, a deep red lipstick pairing well with her silky black sleeveless top, the V-neck dipping low. "Oh my God, you did it, you got Zachary Lee in here!"

"Hey, Mel," Zachary said as she cut around the counter.

"Give me a hug!" She wrapped her arms around him as she rocked back and forth.

"You look great."

"Aw, stop," she said with a pat to his shoulder. "Hi, I'm Mel." She stuck out her hand to Charlie, who grasped it.

"Charlie. It's so nice to meet you. My friends and I love your place," Charlie gushed.

"Thank you," Mel said. "Very happy to hear that."

"She was raving about it before we got here. Couldn't get her to stop," Jordan said.

"Whatever." Mel nudged Jordan's shoulder as she went back behind the bar. "Alright, Zachary, fill me in. Jordan's so happy to have you home. Though, I know it wasn't planned. How's your dad?"

"Doing okay. Home, antsy. Wants to get back to work, but his doctor wants him to retire."

"Oh, no," Mel said.

"Yeah. He's not happy about that either."

"I'm glad he's home, but shit, he must be driving your mom nuts."

"Yeah, they're getting to that point," Zachary said. He caught Charlie's glance of concern and shrugged.

"Well, you know you're welcome here anytime. And friends of these two idiots are friends of mine," Mel added with a smile at Charlie.

"Why does everyone keep calling me an idiot?" Zachary murmured.

Mel patted his hand patronizingly. "You forget who I'm friends with, Z."

He groaned on a laugh. "Sandra."

Mel laughed, her eyes traveling to someone on the other side of the bar. "Okay, enjoy. Great to see you," she said to Zachary, then to Charlie, "Great to meet you. Jordan, you're mine in twenty!" She smacked the bar and walked away.

"How do you manage working with your older sister?" Zachary asked.

"She's a great boss, I'll admit. And I'm an awesome baby brother." He leaned closer to Charlie. "I bring in a lot of extra customers."

Charlie laughed. "I believe it."

Jordan grinned. "So, Charlie, tell me more about what this asshole is like to work with."

"Oh yes, happy to." Charlie straightened in her seat and cleared her throat dramatically, while Zachary groaned.

Zachary listened as she traded stories of working with him for Jordan's of growing up together. He watched them bond over what could be deciphered as a goal to humiliate him, had he not chimed in with his own side of the story. By the time Jordan was pouring drinks during his shift, there'd been enough shared humiliation to have them all laughing.

As Jordan left them to tend to other patrons, Zachary huddled close to Charlie at the bar. He was happy. He couldn't remember the last time he'd described himself as such. Hanging out with her and his best friend...It felt like the next step in a relationship.

One they had to talk about.

Charlie spun herself on the barstool so her feet rested on the rung of his. "Well, now it's out in the open, how anal we think the other is in the workplace."

"We already knew that," he said, turning his seat, shifting his legs to box in hers.

"True." She looked up at him, her eyes glazed over a bit. She propped an elbow on the bar, inching his way. "I should stop drinking. Otherwise, I'm going to be useless tomorrow."

"Good thing it's a late-start day."

"Mmm, good thing." She toyed with the sleeve of his shirt.

He slid his hand to her thigh and squeezed.

Her eyes darted to his lips, and he followed suit. When she leaned closer still, he met her, their tongues tangling instantly in a slow dance, his hand squeezing her thigh tighter as she inhaled sharply.

Charlie pulled back, her breathing rapid. "Want to go back to my place?"

"Yes."

They shoved off their stools, and he pulled his wallet out just as Jordan came over.

"On the house."

"No—"

"Boss's orders." Jordan pointed toward Mel, who gave a wave. "Just make sure you come back again. That's the only request."

"Ahh, here just take it as a tip then." Zachary threw some bills on the counter, then grabbed Charlie's hand.

"Nice to finally meet you, Jordan."

"Same. Be good to our guy, yeah?"

"Oh, I will," Charlie promised.

He suppressed a growl as he looked down into Charlie's face, her mischievous twinkle meant for him, especially when she pinched his butt.

"You'll pay for that," he whispered in her ear.

She giggled. "Can't wait." She waved to Mel, then hurried out of the bar, with Zachary right on her heels.

"Wait!" She spun toward him, her hand going to his chest. "What about Maple? She needs dinner, or—"

He kissed her. "She's at Sandra's. Vivi asked if they could have a sleepover."

"Oh my God, that's the cutest damn thing," Charlie said, pulling him down for another scorching kiss. "Take me home."

CHAPTER 29

Charlie

CHARLIE SLID HER HANDS up and down her thighs, pressing her back against the passenger seat of Zachary's car. Her attraction to him vibrated through her body, ready to burst from her fingertips if they didn't do something about it.

The closer they got to her place, the more nervous she became. Zachary's light touch on her shoulder made her jump, pulling her focus from the window to find his gaze on her.

"You okay?"

"Of course!" It came out high-pitched, immediate proof of her lie.

He nodded toward her hands, clenched into fists on her lap. She stretched her fingers, sliding them down her legs until her upper body was flush to her thighs.

"Fuck," she mumbled. She lifted her head. "Can we go inside and...talk?"

Zachary nodded. "Whatever you want."

She gave him a small smile, then bolted from the car, hurried up the walkway, and through the alcove to her apartment. Two small lamps glowed from the built-in shelves. Toothless was perched just inside, waiting to greet them, and wove between their legs. Charlie used the distraction to feed the cat and mutter sweet nothings at her.

"Feels so much later, but I guess we got to the bar early," she said as she pulled the curtains and joined Zachary on the couch.

The darkness of late November added a chill to the air. She shivered. Zachary pulled the blanket from the end of the couch and draped it over their laps, then silently grabbed her hand, tracing her knuckles. She watched the motion, building up the courage to speak.

He waited. His patience, his care, went so much further than he could ever realize.

"I have something called vaginismus." The admission fell from her lips, no bullshit, no dance. Her heart rate picked up, and Zachary gripped her hand. She dared to look him in the eye. "It's a physical limitation. A sexual dysfunction, more specifically."

His hand relaxed slightly, but he stayed focused on her. "Okay."

She took a deep breath and let it out slowly. "There are different causes, based on the person. Some experience it after trauma, some after medical treatments...which I guess is a form of trauma. Some, as far as they can tell, are born with it—that's my scenario, by the way. Nothing happened, it's always been like this."

Zachary nodded, still quiet.

"Umm. Right. So I've been in physical therapy for years. Actually, it took years to find a doctor who understood what I was going through. I cycled through a bunch, most of them telling me it was in my head. Others saying that, with time, I could work through it—without giving me guidance, by the way. Oh, so I suppose I should explain more of what it is, huh? That might help." She cleared her throat, nervous, emotions clawing their way out.

Zachary gave her a small smile. He didn't move closer, but he still held her hand.

"Basically, it's difficulty with penetration. There's immense pain, a burning that, no matter what you hear, is *not* normal to experience—it should *not* bring you to tears from pain any time you try to put a tampon in, or even a finger. If anything, you want to cry from happiness. Or pleasure. Anyway." She waved her hand to move forward. "Some women have it so bad that sitting is too painful, or clothing rubbing against them is awful. I fortunately didn't have it like that. But for the longest time, I couldn't get anything in. It amped up my anxiety, and it became this snowball effect, where my mind knew there was pain—not this made up pain that some doctors like to pin on women as if we were still in the 1950s—so fear added this extra layer to any attempt at figuring things out. I was just...lost. I couldn't talk to anyone about it. My mom and I don't talk about sex. All my friends started talking about tampons, and by the time they were having sex, it felt too late to bring anything up. I was extremely embarrassed. I didn't know what was going on or who to turn to. No one talked about issues like that, at least, not in my circle of friends."

Her breaths were heavy. "This is way more information than I planned on saying. Almost feels like I'm giving excuses for why I'm... I've hardly told anyone this yet. Maybe that's obvious. Feels like it might be." She swallowed.

"It's okay," Zachary said softly.

She gave a firm nod. "Eventually, I found a doctor who knew what I was talking about. She was amazing, took extra time and care with me, referred me to this amazing physical therapist who does pelvic floor therapy. It took some time for me to trust her, but she's been awesome. It started small, but I've made a lot of progress. The pain is almost gone. I've been working through layers and layers of protection I've built around myself, and that's not something that can be rushed, you know? I've carried it with me my whole life."

Zachary pressed a kiss to the inside of her wrist. She reached out her other hand and brushed his cheek with her fingers, keeping her focus there as she avoided his eyes.

"What I'm trying to say is," she said softly, "I haven't slept with anyone before. I mean, I'm not completely innocent." She forced a wink. "My ex and I tried various things, but I haven't really dated much since then. Nothing serious. Nothing that really got physical."

"How was your ex with all this?" Zachary asked, his voice low.

"Um." She pressed her lips together. "I didn't really understand what was going on at the time. Neither one of us did. But he was far from being the right partner while I figured it out."

Zachary's grip tightened on her hand. "I don't want you to feel pressured, Charlie. You're in control here. This is...well, it's a lot."

She sank back against the couch. "Did I scare you off?" Her tone was light, her attempt to be playful about a topic that had ruled her life in all too serious a manner.

"What? No." Zachary scooted closer. "I'm here with you because it's the only place I want to be, not because I want to get you naked." He paused, picking at the blanket. "Okay, full disclosure, I've thought about you naked plenty of times."

She smiled. "Same."

His eyes locked on hers. "Yeah?" He grinned, his focus trailing to her mouth, then back up to her eyes. "You pretty much pawed your way under my skin, Harris. I don't know how, it's like you burrowed in and took over." He patted his chest softly as he spoke. Swallowed hard. "Like it's been your spot all along."

Her heart flipped. His analogy hit home, the comfort she felt with him the only reason she'd divulged everything she had. She pressed a gentle kiss to his lips. His hand slid up to her face, cradling her jaw, and he kissed her tenderly.

When his fingers slipped into her hair, a tingle shivered down her spine, and Charlie was reignited. The weight of the conversation was off her chest. She didn't want it to rule her anymore, and that started immediately. It wasn't going to stop them from enjoying each other—as much as her body and mind would allow. With how turned on she was, both were clearly on board.

Mouths locked, Charlie clambered onto her knees and straddled Zachary. Her hands gripped his shoulders as she set herself down, their lips slipping and searching fervently with the movement.

"Wait, wait, wait," Zachary said, pulling his mouth from hers.

She trailed her kisses down his neck and settled her body lower on his lap, feeling him harden beneath her.

"Harris, baby." He held her away from him, then touched her cheek. "Charlie. We don't have to do anything tonight. Really."

She pressed a kiss to his nose, then whispered, "I thought you were following my lead?"

He shivered, and she grinned.

"Yes, but you just unloaded a whole ton of heavy shit. Don't you need a minute, or a night, or...something?"

She shook her head, then gasped. "I'm sorry, do *you*?"

"No." He sighed as she continued her kiss trail, and when she bit his earlobe, it earned her a groan.

She breathed into his neck. "I don't want it to overrule what we had going. Like I said, I've made a lot of progress. I just wanted you to know that I couldn't just spread my legs and say, 'Put it in me.' Much as I might want to."

He snorted. "Jesus."

"I've had orgasms."

He clenched his jaw.

"I really like them."

He cursed softly.

She pulled back slightly, smiling that they could be light about it. "Are you uncomfortable with doing anything tonight?" Her eyes searched his.

"No." He shook his head firmly. "No, I'm good if you're good."

"Good," she said softly against his lips. "I trust you, Zachary."

His palms curved to her cheeks as he pulled back, eyes soft as he scanned her face. Her stomach flipped at the intensity of his gaze. It was a look she'd fantasized about, but the feeling it elicited was beyond her imagination. She was light enough to float on a cloud yet heavy with need. It was a gut punch of desire, a mutual want. Tenderness.

They moved at the same time, and when their mouths fused, they held. Charlie touched his jaw lightly, then tugged his bottom lip between her teeth.

Zachary groaned, and one palm engulfed her nape and angled her head. The kiss was deep, the strokes of his tongue long, slow, playful, like he was letting her know he could make these kisses count, that they could be enough if she wanted. His hands mapped her hips and slid to her ass, following her movements as she ground herself against him.

Her whole body was ignited, sparks shooting everywhere that she wanted to chase immediately. Naked.

He tugged his mouth from hers. "Are you okay?"

"What? Yes. I'm so okay." She pulled at the bottom buttons of his shirt and slipped her hands beneath his undershirt, the feel of his warm skin against her energizing. To feel it against her body would be...

She gasped, his hands trailing under her shirt and up. She raised her arms, and Zachary slipped the top over her head and tossed it to the floor. She shivered and finished his buttons, shoving at the shoulders until the sleeves slid from his body.

"So...many...layers!" she griped, grabbing the hem of his undershirt to tug it off. "Ugh, I don't even want winter to come, that'll mean more." She slammed her mouth against his, smoothing her hands over his pecs, his ribs, around his back.

Zachary laughed against her lips, then trailed kisses down her neck to her chest, slowing over the swells of her breasts. His hands reached behind her, finding the clasp of her bra, and freed her from the restraint. He guided the straps down her arms with extreme patience, bit his lip as he tossed the bra aside. His hands kneaded her breasts, taking his time. Fingers brushed her nipples, then pinched them lightly.

Charlie moaned, the sound growing as Zachary crashed forward, his mouth capturing one nipple, fingers working the other. She arched her back, gripped his head to hold him against her.

Her body was on fire. She reached for his jeans, scooting back on his thighs to give herself room as she tugged at the button and zipper. Her hand found his boxer briefs, and she slid her palm down, his hard length straining. Zachary's breath hitched, an arm tightening around her waist. Then she was on her back, pressed into the couch cushions, as Zachary kneeled over her.

"Fuck, Charlie," he said.

She whimpered, the loss of his mouth on her, her hands on him, too much.

He kissed her, tongue diving into her mouth, hands splayed over her body. His fingers trailed along her stomach, tracing lower between her thighs. Her heart raced, but then his hand was on the move again. After two more rounds of the same, she realized he wasn't going to go any further unless she wanted him to. And she wanted him to. Wanted release, from him.

She held his hand in place when it once again flirted between her thighs. He stared at her, their breaths heavy. She nodded.

"You sure?"

"Yes. Please. Touch me," she whispered.

"Fuck," he said, his forehead falling to her shoulder. "I don't want to hurt you."

She shook her head. "You won't. Just...go slow."

He lifted his head and nodded. Then he kneeled beside the couch, a sly grin forming. "Oh, I can go slow."

She bit her lip, the tease as hot as it was concerning because she had no doubt this man could make her beg.

Carefully, his eyes monitoring her every breath, Zachary undid her jeans and tugged them down, the well-worn denim harsh against her sensitive skin. His hands slid up, with a squeeze to her calves, then thighs. His thumbs grazed over the edge of her plain berry bikini-cut underwear. *Did* not *think this far ahead. These are so boring.*

He grinned. "Perfect color for you." His thumbs skimmed the fabric, right over her clit, seeming to emphasize his point.

Charlie arched from the couch with a gasp.

He pressed kisses to her thighs, on the inside of her legs, over her hips, slowly working his way up until he was back at her breasts, tongue swirling over her nipples, making her crazy with want. Every inch of her was tingling, the brush of his chest against her causing rippling shocks through her body.

"God, Zachary," she breathed.

"Mmm," he hummed over her breast.

His hand worked its way down, brushing over the only scrap of fabric left. The touch was featherlight, back and forth, until she was squirming, whimpering. She held her breath as he finally slipped the fabric off her legs.

He groaned, his hands sliding back up her legs with deep, firm squeezes. His eyes took in her bare pussy, a grooming routine she'd started in recent years as another way to reconnect with her body. His excitement as he took in every inch of her turned her on even more.

He squeezed his tall frame onto the edge of the cushions, his body stretched out beside her. She started to turn toward him, but he held her there.

"Tonight, I'm going to touch you," he whispered, his fingers doing the featherlight dance again. "We'll go from there. Okay?" He trailed his kisses to her neck, and she hummed in reply.

He traced over her smooth skin, groaning as his touch got closer and closer to really feeling her. To discovering how wet she already was. She panted, grabbed for him, fingers slipping into his hair and tugging lightly, his grunt of approval spurring her on. Her legs rubbed together, and his hand squeezed between her, the need for pressure growing.

"God, Zachary, please," she pleaded.

His finger reached her slit, gliding slowly, and they both groaned.

"You're so wet," he said, voice low.

She could only whimper in reply.

The tip pressed in.

"Yes," she whispered. *No pain*. "Hold there a minute," she whispered.

"Anything," he grumbled. He bent forward and sucked her neck.

She gasped, relaxing even as he wound her up. "Okay, a little more."

He pushed his finger farther, pausing when she put her hand on his. "You alright?"

She nodded. His thumb skimmed her clit in response, and she arched her hips off the couch. "Mmm." The hum of pleasure grew into a chuckle.

"Feel good?" he asked with a sly grin.

"Oh yes." She gasped as he did it again, then lightly pressed his hand. "More, Zachary."

His nostrils flared, and he eased farther into her. Her breath shook. *No involuntary muscle creating a wall.*

She squeezed her eyes shut, tears pricking. All she felt was *need*.

He continued, intent on her face, and she felt his finger deep inside her. He twitched it, and she quivered, her eyes locking on his.

"Oh, fuck," she said.

"Ohhh, fuck," he said, slamming his mouth to hers.

He pumped his finger in and out of her slowly, eventually adding another at her plea. When his thumb paid attention to her clit again, she went off, her body tightening around him as the orgasm pulsed through her.

She gasped for breath. When she opened her eyes, Zachary slipped his fingers into his mouth, gaze on her, and sucked.

"Holy shit," she breathed out.

She pounced on him, throwing her body on top of his and knocking him back on the carpet. She removed his jeans completely, his underwear following.

Her hand gripped his shaft, sliding up and down, and her lips went right after.

Zachary cried out.

She hummed, overcome with desire, her fist working below her mouth as she slid up and down him, her tongue swirling the tip. In the past, she never looked forward to this. It was expected—in her experience—but with Zachary, she couldn't wait to taste him.

"Fuck," Zachary whispered, then pulled her up toward him. "Not tonight," he groaned, as her hand continued to touch.

"Oh, not at all?" she asked, hand frozen in place.

"What? No this is good, just not—" He groaned, because she immediately resumed.

She straddled his leg, getting the chance to watch him overcome with pleasure.

"God, Charlie, I can feel how wet you are. So warm."

She wiggled against his thigh, pleased at his groan, one hand on his shaft as the other teased his balls.

"Fuck. Charlie."

His body tightened, and Charlie watched him cum, a pleasure she gave him that she wanted to repeat over and over again.

In many ways.

They cleaned up, and she settled into Zachary's side, nestled against his chest. He tugged her leg over him and covered them with the blanket. His hand toyed with her hair while her thumb traced his warm skin.

"How are you?" he whispered.

She smiled against him. "Amazing," she whispered back. He squeezed her, and she adjusted to look at him. "Happy. I might cry later, from relief? Right now, though, I am just so, so happy. Thank you," she ended on another whisper.

He lifted his head and kissed her gently, his hand cupping her cheek. When she nestled back against him, he added one more kiss to her forehead.

She closed her eyes and sighed. "Let's not move, ever."

"Okay."

"I'm glad we agree." He chuckled adoringly.

They cuddled in comfortable silence, the minutes passing.

"So how was your Thanksgiving?"

He laughed. "What, are you hungry?"

"No. Hm, maybe. But you mentioned earlier everyone was getting a little restless."

"Yeah, well." His finger trailed her back. "Mom and Sandra both cooked enough to feed the neighborhood. They wanted to make the day special, since Dad was doing better...What?"

Charlie had popped her head up as he spoke. "Weird. Brooke was the same way. Cooked a shit ton of food. Definitely was using it as a distraction, we found out later." She bit her lip. "She caught her husband with another woman."

"Shit."

"Yeah." She put her head back down, her pointer finger learning his chest. She wiggled closer to him, his body comforting, until she felt him harden against her.

"Just ignore it," he murmured.

She grinned, lifted her head to look at him again. Then kissed him lightly, over and over.

CHAPTER 30

Zachary

ZACHARY DROPPED HIS HEAD in his hands, paperwork spread across his father's desk. He'd come in early Saturday morning to sort through it all, needing a space away from his dad, who'd been almost angry to share the documents. Zachary knew it was his dad's pride getting in the way, but that didn't soften the aggravation of him watching over Zachary's shoulder.

No, best to take care of it away from his parents altogether. It felt risky bringing it all into the office, which was why he went in early, hoping for time alone before Charlie's arrival. He'd been trying to find another solution somewhere, but even paying Mel's accountant for a meeting came up empty. Nothing besides giving it to Zachary or finding a buyer looked promising.

Charlie would be devastated. They'd been avoiding conversations about transferring over the practice, keeping things running and not thinking about Daniel retiring.

And being with each other.

Most nights after work, they went back to her place for dinner. Continued exploring each other. Nothing much beyond what they'd done the previous weekend, but Zachary saw her comfort growing each day, a fact that made him honored and determined to keep her trust.

She even shared a book with him that had helped her learn about her vaginismus, so he'd been reading that in spare moments too.

He ran his fingers through his hair. Buying the practice himself would do exactly the opposite of what he wanted—it would lose her trust and their relationship. This whole time, she'd been under the impression he was only here temporarily, without interest in running things. If he changed his mind? She'd be crushed. After all the years she'd put into this place, working toward it becoming her own, how could she then just sit back and let him have it? She was way too ambitious for that, her dreams too big. She deserved to have her own practice. She'd probably even leave. Besides. If he stayed in town, it would mean defining what they were, and he hadn't planned on going down that road again.

But selling to Neptune was worse.

"Oh! Hey." Charlie's footsteps stuttered in the doorway. "You beat me today."

"Catching up on some financial stuff for Dad." *Not a lie.*

"What a coincidence. I actually wanted to talk to you about money."

Zachary turned back to his desk, busying himself so she didn't see the worry on his face. "What about?"

"Each year, we take up additional collections for our Dale Fund during the holidays. People tend to give a fair amount around this time. I was thinking, what if we partner up with one of the rescues too? See what their wish list is. Sometimes people have extra leashes lying around that didn't work out, or prefer to contribute new goods instead of donating money. We can have a collection bin going."

Zachary had turned to watch her excitement. With her feet planted on the ground, she swiveled her seat this way and that. Her scrub top matched her energy, printed with snowflakes and animals wearing winter hats, tongues out to catch the crystals. "That's a great idea. You thinking the rescue you work with?"

She nodded. "They're always looking for supplies."

He smiled. "I love it."

She grinned back. "Great."

They sat for a moment, looking at each other. Charlie glanced at their open doorway, then stood, placing her hands on the arm rests of his chair. She leaned in for a peck, but his hands shot up to cup her face, and she giggled. Short, sweet. Their kiss deepened, and all Zachary wanted was to pull her on his lap. When voices carried down the hall, she stepped back, a smile on her flushed face. She started to prep at her desk. He knew he should do the same, but found it harder to tear his eyes from her every time they were together.

***

"Thought I might not get a chance to see you while you were in town." The gravelly voice dripped with admonishment.

Zachary glanced over the head of the Bernese mountain dog stretched on the floor to the client, an older man who was one of the select few who held the title of original customer at EFVH. Also, the man Zachary had pawned off to Charlie early on in his return.

"How've you been, Mr. Sandalli?"

The man shrugged in his seat, golden-brown skin creased, one long, skinny leg resting by its ankle on the other knee. "Can't complain. Not too cold yet."

"Mmm. Think it'll be a mild winter this year?" Weather was one of the easiest tools of communication, and in Wisconsin, the winter especially.

"Who knows anymore," Mr. Sandalli groused. "Laurel keeps praying that we'll have a white Christmas with the kids and grandkids in town. And that if a blizzard should hit, that it comes immediately after they arrive. Thinks it's a way to keep them here a little longer."

Zachary chuckled. "How is Mrs. Sandalli?"

"Doing fine. Knitting mittens for the grandbabies. We've got five of them, you know."

"I didn't. That's great, congrats." Zachary continued his checks on the dog.

"You giving your dad grandbabies anytime soon?"

He coughed, moving to the computer to jot some notes, the slow computer that was extending his time in this room. "Uh, no. No kids. Sandra's two keep them plenty busy right now. Any other concerns about Boscoe here?"

"Nope. Still eating like the horse that he is. Just want to make sure there's nothing wrong, since the stool's been so loose and all."

Zachary nodded. "We'll test that sample and get his round of bloodwork taken care of. He's due anyway, so let's start there, see what it might tell us about his change in weight. Should have the results back to you in a couple days." Zachary held out his hand. "It's nice to see you, Mr. Sandalli. Please say hi to your wife for me."

Mr. Sandalli kept his grip firm. "Sorry to have missed you when I brought Whiskers in. Your dad must be thrilled to have you home and handling things here. I'm sure it's a major weight lifted. Nice to see you taking care of things, son."

Zachary swallowed. Was that what was required to be considered a good son? To do the job his father had hoped for him? Was everything else considered moot otherwise?

He gave a small nod. "One of the techs will be in shortly for Boscoe. Take care." He squeezed out of the room and hustled down the hallway for the kitchenette, needing something fizzy to quench whatever guilt had just wrung him dry.

"How'd it go?" Charlie asked behind him.

He turned, the sparkling water a shake to his system. "Not terrible."

"Good." She rummaged in the fridge and pulled out a protein bar.

"You had that in the fridge?"

She bit, eyes wide. "So good. It's got dates and little chocolate chips. Tastes like dessert." She wiggled her eyebrows.

He shook his head, amused.

She tilted her head. "You sure you're good? You look a little...?"

He took another gulp. *Pressured? Annoyed? Overwhelmed and afraid of disappointing everyone?* He went with "Tired?"

"Constipated."

He fought off another laugh as a ridiculously pleased smile lit up her face.

"Want a bite? Maybe this'll help." She held up her bar, but he waved it off.

"I've got a lot on my mind," he said.

"Anything you want to talk about?"

So many things.

"No. Not now."

He startled when her hand lightly touched his arm, but seeing her soft eyes and furrowed brow, his shoulders relaxed.

"I'm good, really. Thinking about Dad, and the practice...You know, the usual."

She nodded. "Want to grab a drink tonight?"

He sighed. "That sounds perfect."

"Great. Because your sister wanted to go out, and I kinda told her we would."

"You told her *we* would?"

"Yeah. Well. We were texting about your dad, and you came up, and I mentioned I met Mel last weekend, and all of a sudden, she planned a night with us. Your mom is going to watch the kids, I guess. She needs out of the house, and your dad wants to be left alone. So Sandra jumped on the chance to have a night out with Jay. Apparently, Whiskey Nights has a holiday spritz or something he wants to try."

"Jay and his mocktails." He scrubbed a hand through his hair. "They want to spend their night out with us?"

She shrugged. "Why not?" She gave him a little punch at his shoulder. "Her baby brother's in town. And she knows we're friends."

"We're more than that," he grumbled.

Charlie blinked rapidly, her lips parted. Her tongue darted out as she stepped closer, but before she could speak, before he could find out if she was wetting those lips for him, Sheila came in, alerting Charlie of her next appointment.

Without a word, Charlie's fingertips brushed his on her way out of the room. Which left him with a little more time to determine what all of this even meant.

***

"I know it's barely eight, and this is our one stop, but I feel like we're getting a night out on the town." Sandra raised her glass to acknowledge the group, then took a sip of her old fashioned. She smiled with plum-colored lips, her hair falling in soft curls. A skinny gold bracelet matched the necklace hanging over her black turtleneck. "So good."

Charlie laughed. "How were the kids?"

"Alex was very focused on the bedtime story he picked for Gram, and Vivi was just excited they had Gram to themselves," Jay said. His black sweater was a sharp complement to his wife. He took another sip of his smoky cider mocktail, then handed it to Sandra to try.

"Gram was excited too. For time away from her grumpy husband," Sandra added.

Zachary sat quietly, fingers tapping his pint glass, listening. Hyper-aware of Charlie's leg against his as they sat side by side, their scrubs a beacon that they'd stayed late at the office once again. He wore a gray zip fleece over his, neutralizing the work image. Charlie had busted out a bulky maroon cardigan that looked soft to the touch. He wanted to test his theory.

"He's having a difficult time, huh?" Charlie asked.

"That's putting it lightly," Sandra said. "He's struggling with some depression, but neither one of them want to talk about it. He wants to get up and go like he used to, but his energy is completely drained. So he's frustrated he can't do much of anything without having to take a break, or a nap. And when Mom tries to help, he claims she's treating him like a child."

"She did try to feed him the other day," Jay said carefully.

Sandra rolled her eyes. "Mom was letting him taste the soup she made! You have to get the *full* story from him." She turned from her husband to Zachary and Charlie. "God, he's ridiculous, going to Jay and trying to drum up support. But he leaves out very pertinent information. He's like my teenagers at school!"

The comparison launched Sandra into a story about some of her students, and eventually Vivi and Alex, which in turn had them laughing. The knots in Zachary's neck slowly loosened, and he sat comfortably, arm behind Charlie, his fingers occasionally grazing her shoulder. The sweater reminded him of Maple's silkiness—though nothing could beat the softest pup's head in the world. He smoothed the contour of her shoulder, dragged his fingers absentmindedly. It was a natural movement, one he didn't realize he was doing until he caught the raised eyebrow of his sister across from him, her pointed look clueing him in on his less-than-subtle affection. When Charlie left the table for the restroom, Sandra pounced.

"What is going on with you two?" she hissed.

"Nothing. We're friends."

"Friends who can't seem to keep their hands off each other?"

He winced. He thought it might be obvious that Charlie was placing her hand on his thigh beneath the table, but he had cared little to worry about it. He should've known his sister would catch on.

Then there was his shoulder grazing. *Much more obvious.*

Oh. And brushing her hair over her shoulder. He'd caught himself off guard with that one.

"No use lying to her, man," Jay said solemnly.

Zachary held out his hands. "It's nothing serious. We're enjoying each other's company."

"Ah, yes, and while you're 'enjoying each other's company'"—she added air quotes and adopted a classic sister tone for the words—"do you happen to be shoving your tongue down her throat? Because then we have a problem."

"I don't want to talk to you about this," Zachary said.

"We're all adults, Z. But that woman is like family to us. Not to mention a major part of the practice. Mom will plan your wedding as soon as she finds out, and Dad will make you sign some sort of agreement to ensure you don't scare her off when things go south."

Jay mouthed *yikes*. "That might be jumping ahead a bit, babe," he said calmly before taking another sip.

"Seriously. And thanks for the vote of confidence, sis."

"I'm just saying, you're playing with fire. This is Charlie we're talking about. This is a huge deal!"

"I know who she is. Like you said, we're adults. She and I are on the same page."

"So, what, she knows you're going to leave soon, and she's okay with that too? Charlie's not the type of person to have a fling."

"I know."

"She cares *so* deeply, Z. Like, heart on her sleeve."

"Yes, *I know*." His annoyance spiked. "No concern for me, then? It's okay for my heart to be broken?"

"Holy shit, is your heart involved?!" Sandra hissed.

He swore the organ stopped beating in that brief moment, waiting for his answer, before she continued.

"What if Mom and Dad find out? Then what? They'll want you to stay and keep working together. How's that going to go if things end between you guys?"

"Who knows what they want? Dad wants me to buy the practice from him now."

Jay straightened as Sandra leaned forward.

"But Charlie's taking over the practice," she said.

"Not with the state it's in."

"What are you talking about?"

He gave them a brief rundown.

"She has no idea?" Sandra asked.

He nodded grimly.

"Zachary. You need to tell her."

"Sandra. I just told you, I can't."

"But this is what she's been working toward—"

"I know! Sandra, fuck, I know. This is shitty. Someone or everyone will be hurt. I'm trying to figure out the best solution before she hears the news. There's gotta be a way."

They sat quietly.

"Are you considering it?" Jay asked.

He scrubbed his hand over his face. "I don't know where my head is at right now."

"But you guys are seeing each other," Jay supplied.

"Honestly, that's the one thing I look forward to most."

Sandra's eyes widened, but she said nothing.

"Good God, women take a long time at the bathroom," Charlie said, sliding back into the booth. "So I met this woman in line, and she was telling me about the new restaurant moving in around the corner."

"You met someone in line again?" Zachary asked.

"What else are we going to do while we wait?" she asked.

"Last time, she came back and told me all about this poodle, I thought it was a patient of ours. Turned out, it belonged to someone she'd just met in the bathroom," Zachary said.

She laughed lightly. "I think she scheduled with us afterward, so technically, that poodle *is* a patient."

He felt it on his face, his affection for her. It must've shown, because even in the dim light of the bar, he saw the blush spread across her cheeks. She leaned closer, and he grabbed her hand to keep from running his nose along her neck.

"Babe, I think we still have time to get food from that place we were talking about," Jay said as he nudged Sandra. "Make this a real night on the town...thing."

Zachary looked over to see his sister's eyes bouncing between him and Charlie.

"Uh, yes. Good call. Rare night out, you know how it goes. Well, yeah. You get it." Sandra scrunched her face as she reset herself. "It was great hanging out with you both, thanks for joining us." She scooted from the booth. "See you later!" She grabbed Jay's hand and tugged him away, giving the man only a moment to throw a wave behind him.

"That was weird," Charlie murmured.

Zachary shifted in his seat. "Wanna get out of here?"

Her smile was coy, and she trailed a finger down his arm. "Come over?"

He pressed his lips to her temple and murmured, "Right behind you."

CHAPTER 31

Charlie

SUNLIGHT SEEPED IN AROUND Charlie's bedroom window shade, the white sheer curtains softening the glow. Last night, she and Zachary hadn't quite made it to her bed—in fact, they'd only made it to her floor. She rolled over, grateful they had spilled their boneless bodies into bed to sleep, at least. Zachary was sprawled on his stomach, face nearly consumed by the berry-and-white-striped pillow, hair askew. She scanned the contours of his arms, bent underneath the pillow, the muscles in his back exposed by the soft sheet that went up to his waist. He looked *right* in her bed, especially in the morning light. A shift near his feet caught her eye, and she found Toothless changing positions on the navy down comforter, curled between his legs. A small sleep-bark sounded, and both Charlie and Toothless popped up their heads, glancing over to see Maple asleep on her orthopedic bed, chasing squirrels in her dreams.

Charlie chuckled and flopped back on her pillow.

"What's so funny?" Zachary's muffled words emerged without opening his eyes.

Just absorbing how much I love this.

"Them," she said instead. "Toothless is sleeping on you, and Maple had no problem staying here overnight."

He opened one eye. "Maple can sleep anywhere."

"It's nice." Her fingertips skated along his face, then coasted through his hair. She reveled in his *hum* in reply. "How about you? You also had no problem sleeping here."

He chuckled. "And I'm very picky about where I sleep."

"This was night two for you."

She rolled onto her side, wearing his white T-shirt, tucking the sheet right below her breasts. He followed her movements, heat zipping along every area he scanned, and her nipples tightened in response. He bit his lip.

"I...yes. It was the second night. Sleeping. Here." He blinked rapidly, seeming to clear his eyes. "How do you feel about that?"

She leaned close and kissed his cheek. "I'm looking forward to night three."

"Mmm." He flopped out a hand toward Charlie, his fingers landing on hers unceremoniously.

She laughed, and he groaned.

"My hand's asleep," he moaned. "I was trying to do...this..." He shoved his fingers between hers.

Her laugh softened, and she kissed his fingers.

He grunted, a smile tugging as he buried part of his face into the pillow again. Sleepy Zachary was terribly adorable.

"I have to step out of the office tomorrow afternoon, by the way. Had to schedule PT at a different time this week." She'd increased appointments to get her mind ready.

"Oh, okay." He was quiet a moment before he asked, "What will that be like?"

"She'll check on how things are going. How much pain I'm experiencing. How my tissues feel. How well my dilator work has been going. Which, you've been providing me another exercise." She wiggled her brows, and he smiled.

"How often do you use your dilators?"

"I try to at least every other day. In the beginning especially, it was hard. I had to get past some of my more depressed stages. Thankfully, my doctors understand that there are multiple areas that need focus—not just the physical, not just the mental. All of it."

"I'm glad you found them," he said quietly.

"God, me too." She turned onto her back, stared at the ceiling. "I'm so grateful for them, and so extremely frustrated for women that don't have access to the same kind of care."

He traced his fingers up and down her arm soothingly. "If there's anything I can do, you know, let me know."

She smiled at him, then turned it playful. "I can show you my dilators, if you want?"

He shrugged. "Okay."

"Oh." She should've known he'd be okay with it. "Yeah, okay." She turned toward her nightstand and pulled out the size she was working with, the largest one she'd been able to use successfully. The one that was helping her mentally prepare for actual intercourse. "Here it is."

He frowned at the solid tube of hard plastic. "Looks less fun than a vibrator."

She snorted. "Um, definitely. I think they have slightly better options now." She tapped it against her hand, thinking. "Maybe at some point, I could, I don't know, maybe I could try it with you here? Might be a way to help us move forward."

311

"Whatever you want, Charlie. I'm game."

She nodded, still staring at the unassuming tool in her hand. "How about now?"

His head lifted slightly. "If you're sure."

"Yeah." She nodded, an effort to build up her confidence in the moment. She grabbed her small jar of coconut oil from the nightstand and coated the dilator.

Zachary propped himself up on his arm. "Where do you want me?"

"Right there is fine," she said. She slid the bedsheet down, then her underwear. Wearing only his shirt made the moment feel more intimate. Less clinical.

Her heartbeat picked up, and she realized she wasn't nervous about the exercise, but actually excited. For as calm as Zachary's expression struggled to be, she felt his gaze as it traveled over her, lingering on her breasts, traveling her stomach and lower. His hands clenched, and she realized he wanted to touch her. His focus on what she was about to do was truly sincere. Witnessing his struggle was genuine, personal, endearing.

A major turn-on.

Charlie's breath quickened. She grabbed the towel she kept with her supplies and placed it underneath her. She bent a knee, straightened her other leg, and lined up the lubricated dilator, inserting it slowly. Zachary watched as she slid it in farther and farther, until she was just gripping the end, then as she slowly worked it around, stretching the inner tissues.

Finally, he spoke, his voice strained. "So this is how you do it, huh?"

Charlie nodded, unable to speak. Her hands were shaking, from the control of the exercise to the desire coursing unexpectedly through her.

His gaze was intent, all on her. His fingers trailed ever so lightly on her side, and he glanced down and froze, as though he'd just discovered it.

He swallowed, his eyes darting to Charlie's. "Sorry," he breathed.

"Fuck," she whispered. The hunger on his face, the want, sent tingles through her body.

"You okay?" he asked, voice low, hoarse.

She nodded, cleared her throat. "I've never enjoyed this before."

He grinned, the smile crooked, mischievous. "Should I get closer?"

She bit her lip, nodded vigorously.

Zachary flipped the sheet off his body, wearing his black boxer briefs, and shifted lower, lining himself up with her waist. He inched up the white T-shirt and traced her skin, over her hips, across her stomach, down her thigh. Her breath hitched when his fingers went between her legs, their path close to her hand, but not touching it.

"God, Zachary." She blew out a breath. "I am so turned on right now."

He chuckled. "I like the feedback." He leaned forward and pressed a kiss to her belly, his tongue coming out to trace a path lower.

"Yes," Charlie hissed. She slid the dilator out, flopping it onto her nightstand. Her hand tangled in Zachary's hair as he continued lower. His eyes looked up at hers, and she nodded. She cried out, her body arching as his tongue made gentle contact with her clit.

"Sweet," he whispered, his tongue tracing around it, keeping the touch light as it traveled back over the nub. He slid his hands over her thighs to keep them still and chuckled.

"Sorry." She breathed. "Did I almost crush you?"

He settled between her legs and held her thighs open as he grinned. "Again, it's good feedback." When he pressed his face to her this time, his tongue slid up along her slit. He started off slowly, moaning at the sounds of pleasure she made. When her cries got louder and her hands gripped his hair harder, his tongue dove deeper. One hand stretched to pinch her nipple over the shirt, and she arched her back with a gasp, her hand flying to squeeze her other breast. Zachary groaned in response, his tongue moving faster.

Waves of pleasure coursed through Charlie's body, her core tightening with each moment, breath shuddering. Her mind was consumed with it, free of concern, of pain. There wasn't time to think, she only felt.

"Oh God," she cried. "Zachary."

"Mmm." He slipped a finger inside her, turning to that spot he'd come to know so well the past few weeks, and sucked her clit.

She detonated. Her body stiffened, shook, tightened on him as her pleasure skyrocketed until she was boneless. Her eyes were closed, chest heaving, and she smiled as Zachary placed a kiss on her stomach, slowly trailing kisses up her body, one to each breast over the shirt, until he nuzzled against her neck. His hand scooted under her, and he held her close. Tight against him. Almost lovingly.

"Thank you," he murmured.

"For what?" she whispered, staring at the ceiling.

He hesitated, pressed a kiss to her neck. "For sharing that with me. Trusting me."

Charlie blinked rapidly, tears burning. She trusted Zachary completely. The weight of what they'd shared hit her as she realized that was the first time without pain and involuntary muscles—or fears—getting in the way.

She squeezed him closer, wishing they could stay like that forever.

***

Charlie looked at the stack of pet supplies piled near the front desk. The collection had been going for a week, and the response from the community was extremely positive.

"That there came in today," Maura said.

Charlie turned toward the woman, her mouth open. "Only today? That's amazing."

"Yep. I contacted Cory and arranged a pickup since we have so much. He was thrilled. I guess they've had a few bites from some of our folks looking to adopt too."

Charlie clapped her hands together. "That makes me happy."

Maura gave her a squeeze on the shoulder. "We've received quite a few donations for the Dale Fund. Daniel will be touched."

Charlie's smile faltered, wondering what Daniel would actually think. She hadn't talked to him in weeks.

"Alright, I'm off. Have some baking to do for tomorrow's church reception," Maura said, tugging on her coat.

"Okay. Thanks for handling this, Maura."

Charlie's wheels turned, trying to decide a good way to bring it up to Daniel. Maybe coming from Maura, it would be more well received.

She walked into her office, the sight before her now familiar, as Zachary hunched over his desk. He glanced up, forehead etched with creases.

He'd been going over documents so rigorously, coming in earlier than her to dive into whatever project had been keeping him busy. A project he hadn't shared with her, which she tried hard not to take personally.

"Hey." He stretched.

"Was just talking to Maura. We've had a lot of people donating to the Dale Fund. And the contributions for the rescue are amazing. Did you see the pile out there? That was from *today*. Cory is going to freak."

A corner of Zachary's mouth twitched.

"Hey," she said softly, settling into her chair. "What's up? Something's stressing you."

"Uh." He tapped his pen on the desk.

She waited. When he said nothing, she leaned forward. "I like helping."

He glanced at her. "I know, Harris. It's not something I can talk about right now."

"Oh. Okay." She tried to ignore how that stung. Right when she was about to spin toward her desk, he sighed.

"He asked me not to."

Her head jerked back. "Who? Your dad?"

He gave her a single nod.

Daniel didn't want her to know what was going on? What could be that extreme?

"Oh my God. He's not giving me the practice, is he?" The words were a whisper.

Zachary looked at his lap.

"Wow." She melted into her seat, spinning to look out her window, the trees a blur.

The wheels of Zachary's chair churned the short distance, and he reached for her hand.

"It's not that. He wants you to have it." He cursed under his breath.

Charlie looked at him, saw his anguish as he struggled between telling her or not. She couldn't bring herself to ease his worry, couldn't tell him not to bother. She needed to know.

"The practice is completely tapped out." He brought his gaze up to hers and held it. "He even took out another loan. I guess a number of pro bono things turned into too much, and in order to cover expenses and keep prices low with the competitors...Well. He's in too deep."

Charlie blinked slowly, the words sinking in. "Okay. What can I do to help?"

He huffed out a soft laugh and squeezed her hand, releasing it so he could pace the room. "That's the problem. He doesn't want your help."

"Why not?"

"Many reasons. But he'd rather let this place sink than pass it to you with a mountain of debt."

Charlie swallowed. "How bad is it really? I have some money saved. I could still buy in, help alleviate some of it."

Zachary was already shaking his head. "No. He doesn't want you to cover it."

"Well then, what other option is there?"

"Getting a buyer."

She threw her hands out wide. "I could be a buyer!"

"He doesn't want it to be you!"

Her stomach dropped, his next words hitting her harder.

"He wants me to take over the practice, Charlie. Transfer it through family means."

She narrowed her eyes. "Then what, kick me out?"

He shook his head. "No. He wants you to be part of it, but I know you'd hate that. You don't want to work for me."

"No." *Right?*

"See, no hesitation. Not that I blame you. But the other thing is..." He scrubbed a hand down his face. "Neptune Corp has given him an offer."

Charlie pushed out of her seat. "No, he can't sell to them. This won't *be* EFVH anymore. It can't become part of some corporate machine. Our clients didn't ask for that!"

Zachary's nods were slow. She stepped toward him and set her hands on his shoulders. They finally locked eyes, and she felt it, deep in her gut. A hum of energy was buzzing through her, and she hoped she was interpreting it right.

"What if we buy it together?" she asked.

"That's not—"

"If it's truly a 'mountain,' why should only one of us deal with it?"

"Charlie."

"Think about it! We've already worked through a hell of a lot to find our rhythm, and we work really well together." She wiggled her eyebrows, then went for it. "Besides, I like seeing you here. The thought of sharing this with you is *way* nicer than it was in the beginning, when I thought you were vying for it. Wait, this isn't all some ploy, *right?*" She was teasing, though there was a small part of her that worried about its truth.

"God, no. You know my plan wasn't to stay."

She swallowed, nodding. "Right. Right. You have a job to get back to."

"Shit." He shook his head. "No, I don't. I was let go. My ex-father-in-law let me go."

Stepping back, she asked, "Why didn't you tell me?"

"I thought if my dad found out, he'd use it as a way to rub it in my face, how I was burned, which he'd warned me about. He felt burned by me, I know. Plus, I thought he'd try to keep me here." He laughed, unamused. "Guess that didn't matter, did it? Worried myself about something that happened in a way I hadn't planned."

"That...really sucks," she said.

"Oh, and my replacement is Anna's new boyfriend."

"Seriously?"

He grumbled.

"Zachary," she said softly.

"Wasn't an ideal situation there in the first place," he said, turning back to his desk.

"Well, okay. There are a lot of things to think about...How about you consider my offer?"

"Charlie—"

"Daniel will hear us out. He loves this place. He won't let it crumble. And we won't stand by and watch it become unrecognizable by a company like Neptune." She paced a moment, desperate for time to create a solution. "Just think about it, okay? Maybe there's another buyer out there who secretly wants to revive a struggling veterinary hospital."

He snorted.

"I'll think on some things we can incorporate to help alleviate the weight," she added. "Can't hurt to have a few more ideas in mind, right?" She forced a grin, trying to ignore the building panic.

"True." He stood a beat, looking at her, or maybe through her. "I actually have to head out," he said. "The kids have a holiday concert thing."

That's when she registered he had on jeans with his fleece.

"Oh! Right. Okay, yeah, cool." She shuffled papers around. Without looking at him, she asked, "You want company?"

The beat of silence felt long, like a distance wedged between them in that instant.

"I would, but...They had to reserve seats, and each family only gets so many."

She faced him, waving her hands to shove the words aside. "All good. I get it."

He scratched his cheek. "I was going to tell you, it just didn't seem like a big thing."

"Or we'd be making it a big thing. If I went with you, I mean."

"Yeah, that too," he said softly.

"Yeah," she said, the word barely audible. She cleared her throat. "We downloaded a lot of information. We can talk more later."

"I'll call you."

She forced a smile. "Have fun."

He clenched his jaw, stepped forward to peck her cheek, then left.

It's what they signed up for—his time home was temporary. Even if he bought the practice, it didn't mean he'd stay. Didn't mean they'd stay together.

Everything was...temporary.

CHAPTER 32

Zachary

"SHE WANTS TO BUY it with me."

"Holy shit," Sandra hissed.

The woman in front of them turned around, eyes narrowed, frown lines deep. Sandra smiled sweetly, and the woman huffed her attention back to the stage. The school gym was transformed into an auditorium with lined up folding chairs. Families packed the seats, abuzz with conversation as they watched one class leave and another assume their positions.

"So what did you tell her?" Sandra asked softly.

Music started, the kids on stage shifting from side to side in anticipation. Jay nudged Sandra and leaned over.

"Did you see your son up there?" Jay asked.

"Oh!" Sandra's eyes flew to the stage, her grin wide as she noticed Alex waving madly. She waved back. When Alex blew her a kiss, Sandra melted into her chair. Chuckles and *aww*s from the audience surrounded them as the children began the opening words to their song.

"Oh my God, that was the cutest thing. He's never going to do that again in his life. Did you get that?" Sandra smacked Jay's arm, which was holding his phone, trained on Alex.

"Yeah, knock it off, Sandra, I'm recording it," Jay said.

"Oh, good."

"Now he'll be able to hear how obsessed his mother is with him," Zachary said.

She smacked him on the arm, and he chuckled, watching Jay fight his own laugh.

They watched Alex and his class sing three songs, with one final wave from Alex as they were guided offstage.

"Hi, Uncle Zachy!" he cried out with all the might of his little lungs.

A laugh erupted from Zachary in surprise, drowned by more laughter from the crowd. He threw back a wave, swallowing hard.

Sandra gripped his arm, her other hand flat to her chest. "That kid. He's the absolute sweetest."

He heard the sentimental tone but didn't dare look at his sister, knowing it would take away any grip he had on keeping it together. They were a couple of emotional adults, loving acknowledgment from the cutest little guy up there, in a sea of people chuckling at how adorable it all was. How was the whole room not in tears? This was precious!

Being part of this was more important to him than he'd expected. He'd missed these events before, but with the strain between him and his dad, he hadn't allowed himself to dwell on it much. He'd viewed FaceTimes, videos, and pictures his sister and mom sent him as enough, never stopping to consider what else he was missing. In Illinois, it was just...him.

He couldn't deny the overwhelming feeling that being back felt right. Like he was meant to be in this seat, meant to attend more of these cute and chaotic events for the kids. Watch them grow up and change each year—hell, day-to-day—to remind them of embarrassing moments from previous years. Cheer them on if they played sports or got involved in theater or some other shit. Grab a drink with Sandra and Jay.

Sit with his parents at their kitchen table for a quiet meal.

Zachary zoned out on the performances while Sandra leaned across Jay toward their mom, no doubt rehashing what had just happened. If he bought the practice, he wouldn't necessarily have to stay in town. He could still return to Chicago, hand over the reins to Charlie—if she'd even consider it at that point. Or he could buy it, stay here, and start fresh. In his hometown. Whether he and Charlie continued their...*fling* or not, it didn't have to factor into his decision. They had an immense amount of respect for each other, professionally and personally, and that would only continue when they moved on.

Calling it a fling minimized it. Their connection, their trust, went well beyond that. He didn't even want to picture them eventually moving on. The thought of Charlie finding someone else to share herself with so beautifully made him want to rush out of that gym and go to her.

He'd shied away from the idea of inviting her to the concert, afraid it would be too serious a step for a relationship that couldn't go much further. But Chicago aside, why he'd ruled out a serious relationship was no longer clear.

"You'll have to finish updating me later, Z. I'm too hopped up on emotion at the moment. I'll just end up telling you to stay in town, buy the practice, and marry Charlie or something. Better to wait." Sandra patted his knee. "I'm really glad you're here," she whispered. She smiled, then pressed against Jay, content to watch the rest of the performances before her children returned to her.

He faced forward, staring through the jingles and shouted songs. *Marry Charlie?* He almost laughed, that idea—that possibility—so beyond any realm of consideration. He wasn't getting married again, he and *Charlie* weren't getting married. His parents didn't even know about them, and if they did, they'd be more concerned about how he'd mess things up again.

While that panic brewed, the rest of Sandra's words sank in—how glad she was to have him back. He couldn't deny how much he'd enjoyed spending time with her and the kids. How calm he felt being home, the energy more his speed. Or the instant sense of community that working at his dad's practice brought, the familiarity comforting. In Chicago, working for his ex-father-in-law, he'd felt like an impostor. In the way. Here, he wasn't on the periphery anymore. This was his family, his home.

Watching his niece and nephew perform with their classmates warmed him.

So, yeah. What if he stayed?

***

"This. Is. Amazing." Cory surveyed the collection of items currently piled in the waiting area. "And did Maura tell you? We had two adoptions and two new foster families who learned about us from your clinic. Such a great group of people here."

"I'm so glad!" Charlie clasped her hands, the sincerity written in every gesture of her body. A body Zachary hoped to explore more later that night, if she let him.

"It's all Charlie," Zachary said. "As I'm sure you know, anyone who meets her wants to help however they can."

She beamed, exhibiting the closest real-life interpretation of the "hearts-for-eyes" emoji.

He craved more of it. Quite possibly he was starved for her affection, considering they'd hardly communicated since he'd left for the concert. He'd texted her after, but she'd been with Magnolia, and then had only sent a brief message when she was home. When they'd both arrived at EFVH, she'd immediately handed him stuff to prep and move before Cory showed. Professional Charlie had been in full effect, but he knew it was for both of their benefit. Best to tackle personal shit later.

"You're right about that. She's been at the rescue, by chance, when people come by to meet the dogs, and they always leave with one. Every time."

"Okay, now you're going too far," Charlie said.

"I'm just saying, we don't have that kind of record normally. Maybe you should be stationed there all the time," Cory added in a light tone.

Charlie laughed, nudging Cory's arm. "Well, I'm happy to help. This community is very giving, and they really stepped up."

She reasoned it out, but the truth was, she was as invested in the good of the community as the people who'd stepped up to help. He'd witnessed her interactions with too many people, seen her care and the welcome response from those she affected.

They did a tally of the supplies acquired. When Cory's fiancé Brian arrived, everyone carried the items to their vehicles, and the front waiting area was empty once again.

Charlie closed the front doors behind them and turned to Zachary.

"I was thinking, maybe in the summer, we could do another one of these. It's always great to have successful events around the holidays at the end of the year, but pets are always in need, right? Maybe we could do a Holidays in July drive, or—"

Zachary cut her off, sealing his lips over hers. She let out a muffled chirp of surprise but quickly softened, winding her arms around his neck and tugging him closer.

He kissed her for her kindness, for her passion for animals, and her job. He kissed her because her mind never stopped working on new things they could implement, ways to help the community. She embodied what his father wanted for his practice, in spirit and in action. He kissed her because he couldn't hold himself back anymore, because going almost twenty-four hours without her in his arms was too long. And he desperately wanted her to feel the same way.

He pulled back and rested his forehead against hers, her breath warm against his lips.

"What was that for?" she whispered.

"Couldn't wait any longer. God, Charlie, I'm sorry about the concert. I wanted to ask you, and that freaked me out. I was trying to be careful with...us...with me living in Chicago and all. But I also want to *be with you*."

She pressed closer. "I want to be with you too."

"I feel bad for not telling you about everything with Dad and all the debt. Really. You have a right to know what's going on around here."

She nodded, took a moment before speaking. "What are we going to do about it?"

"I have no clue."

She slid her hands down his chest, her fingers digging into his wool sweater. "Come with me to the Open House?"

His hands paused their journey over her back. Out in public, wandering through the Village Holiday Open House with their community felt openly intimate.

"I promised Cleo and Magnolia I'd stop by their shops. It's pretty cute. The stores go all out, and Dorothy's has special cookies for this. Of course, eating them usually means you'll end up inside buying at least a dozen of something while you're there. Oh, and the coffee shop releases latte and hot chocolate specials. Do you like hot chocolate?"

"Charlie, you're rambling."

"Oh, am I? Hmm. Must be because I panicked, seeing your face." He chuckled. "Okay, I'll admit, I was thinking about how it might look."

Her eyes widened then narrowed in such rapid succession he couldn't interpret what she was thinking. All she said was, "What, like the local veterinarians supporting their neighbors?"

He swallowed. He was all over the place with what he was saying to her. "I do like hot chocolate, actually," he said.

She gave him a small smile, not as Charlie-esque as normal, but it was something. "Perfect." She zipped her coat and tugged on a hat and gloves. "We'll start there, end with Dorothy's." She winked and held open the door for him to follow.

He watched the strands of her hair blow against her shoulders, a soft, thin veil of snow on the ground behind her. Her cheeks were already rosy, her eyes bright behind her glasses. She did a little shimmy of excitement, waving him on, and locked the door behind them.

The biting cold knocked sense into him immediately—for a minute there, he'd started imagining future holidays, and Charlie was definitely in them.

CHAPTER 33

Charlie

"WAIT, SO, YOU MAKE your own soap, with lye and everything? Like, *Fight Club* style?"

Charlie grinned at the excitement in Zachary's voice as he surveyed the products on the display table outside The Refill Mill. Magnolia was wrapped in layers, her California blood unaccustomed to the cold weather, evident by her thick turtleneck sweater and scarf, popping out from underneath a heavy wool coat. Her gloved hands were shoved deep into the pockets, her hat pulled as snugly as possible, her curls in a loose braid.

"Yes, we make our soap. These three my boss makes, and mine are right here. I also make these." She held up small glass bottles filled with a liquid and dried berries. "Natural perfumes. I source the ingredients from urban growers, actually. Not as exciting as the soap, I take it?" she added, grinning at Zachary's inspection of the bars of soap.

"I mean, it's all impressive," he muttered.

Charlie nudged his shoulder. "Maybe Sandra or your mom would like one?"

He lit up at the excuse to buy some. He looked at Charlie. "Help me choose?"

She nodded, ignoring Magnolia's eyebrow wiggle while they smelled the soaps and admired the raw edges, pressed with dried botanicals or coffee beans. In the end, he picked one for each woman, along with bath fizzers and bubble bath made by other small businesses.

"Now make sure you let them know they can come back and refill these jars when they run out." Magnolia pointed to the bubble bath as she rang up the total. "Or any jar."

"If they haven't stopped by already, I'm sure you'll see them soon," Charlie said. "I've been raving about your shop to them."

"Oh, well, thank you for telling his family about us," Magnolia said, her eyes widening for emphasis.

Zachary gave Charlie a small smile. He opened his mouth to speak, when someone called out his name.

"Oh, wow, hey!" He touched Charlie's elbow. "I'll be right back."

Charlie watched him approach a man and shake hands.

"So. This is kind of a big deal for you two, huh? Going out together, shopping around all the super cute local shops, decked out for the holidays."

"He freaked out a bit when I suggested it," Charlie admitted.

"He did?"

Charlie nodded. "He looked like I'd told him his mom wanted me there with them Christmas morning or something super intimate."

"She didn't invite you to that, did she?"

"No!"

"That'd be a pretty big deal."

Yep. Even if Charlie had gone to bed disappointed at not being at the kids' concert—the sort of event Sandra or Jeanie would have invited her to before Zachary was back in town—attending it with Zachary would've given it an entirely different meaning. Unfortunately, it also made her feel like a placeholder for the Lee family by not including her, now that they had Zachary back.

Especially since Daniel wanted him to take the practice.

"Charlie!"

She turned to Sandra's voice, who appeared as though Charlie had conjured her out of the frosty air. The woman toted Alex on one arm, the other lined with bags from multiple shops. Jeanie was right behind her with Vivi.

"Hey!" Charlie said.

"What's this?" Vivi was already holding up the perfume on Magnolia's table.

"That's a perfume," Charlie said. "This is my friend Magnolia. She runs this shop."

"Hi there. You can smell it if you'd like. Here, let me help you," Magnolia said, opening one for Vivi to sniff.

"Magnolia, this is Zachary's family." Charlie made introductions.

Magnolia steered them toward products not selected by Zachary, as the man himself came back to their table.

"When did you all get here?" he asked.

"Uncle Zachy, look!" Vivi held up a bath fizzy. "Flowers will float in my bath!"

"Wow, that's fancy," he said. "Perfect for a princess."

"I'm a superhero now!" Vivi proclaimed, throwing her arms in the air.

"Oh, so sorry," Zachary said.

"Keep up, baby bro," Sandra said, busy putting every item Alex had grabbed off Magnolia's table back. Finally, she tugged him away from the temptation.

"Hello, dear," Jeanie said, kissing his cheek. "Are you two walking around together?"

Zachary went rigid next to her.

"We were meeting with the rescue earlier, so we decided to pop on by after we finished," Charlie supplied.

"How nice," Jeanie said, eyeing the cups of hot chocolate in each of their hands, the tiny bags of items they'd purchased so far lining their arms.

Then Charlie remembered Zachary had draped her scarf over his shoulders earlier in their walk, after she'd worked up too much heat. It wasn't quite like carrying her purse, but the bright berry color stood out as signature Charlie.

He seemed to register it at the same moment, sliding it from his neck and casually draping it around her.

"Looks like you've made a few stops already," Zachary said, gesturing at the bags in his mother's hands.

"Oh, yes. I usually get a little head start on my Christmas shopping here. We've had to be a little sneaky with the kids, but we've made it work."

"We've done well for ourselves, I'd say," Sandra said. "Cleo had some super cute T-shirts. Charlie, have you seen them?"

"We haven't made it over there yet," Charlie said. "Kinda working our way around to end with Dorothy's." She smiled at Zachary, whose eyes were darting between the women with concern, as though they were deciding the relationship status without him.

"She was telling us about the artist events she'll be hosting next year," Jeanie said. She rooted around in a bag and pulled out a flyer. "First one in mid-January."

"Yes! I'm so excited for her," Charlie said. "She's got a great lineup already."

"Seems like every time I'm there, it's busier than the last. How have things been going for you so far?" Jeanie asked Magnolia.

Charlie tuned out their conversation, too concerned with the whispered one happening between Zachary and his sister. When he caught her watching, his face softened, a smile peeking out.

"I'm ready for some cookies. What do you say, Harris?" he asked.

"I want cookies!" Vivi cried out.

"Me, me, me!" Alex chimed in.

"You already had cookies," Sandra said. "But we still have one more stop to make."

"Hot chocolate!" Vivi called out, arms in the air as she zipped around the sidewalk, weaving between pedestrians.

"Sure that's a good idea?" Zachary asked.

"They'll get about two sips in before we get to the car and zonk out. Works out perfectly. They'll finish it tomorrow."

Charlie laughed. "Sounds very sneaky."

"Have to be, with these two little monsters. Crap, I've gotta catch up to Viv before she convinces someone else to buy her drink. Come on, Alex. Mom, I'll meet you there. See you later!" Sandra and Alex hurried off.

Zachary placed his hand on Charlie's arm, the contact light through the weight of her coat, but sending electricity through her body. He added in a small nod across the street, and she stepped closer, calling over her shoulder to Magnolia.

"I'll call you later, Mags. Good luck today!"

Magnolia waved, but Jeanie turned abruptly.

"Charlie, you're still having the employee holiday party on Thursday?" she asked. Charlie nodded. "Daniel and I want to come by."

"Oh, that'd be wonderful."

"And you should join us at the house on Christmas Eve."

Magnolia's eyes widened behind Jeanie, though she scooted items around on the table. Charlie had to give her credit because it was subtler than Zachary's stiffening frame beside her, once again, and calmer than her own racing heart.

"Mom..." Zachary said.

Jeanie continued. "It'll just be us, nothing fancy, of course. We're all so grateful to you, for guiding the practice the way you have. For keeping this one in line." She gestured to her son. "A little chance to say thanks without more people around, you know?"

"Thanks, Jeanie, I appreciate it."

"Your mother's welcome to join if she'd like."

"Uh." Charlie looked at Zachary, then back to Jeanie. "That's sweet, but she's working."

"Well, all the more reason for you to join us! The offer is there. You just let me know. We'll see you on Thursday." Jeanie waved them off, said her goodbyes to Magnolia, and headed down the street toward the coffee shop.

"You two go get some cookies. You look a little peaked," Magnolia said.

Charlie gave a faint wave and followed Zachary across the street, his steps quick. He held the door open for her, bypassing the holiday table out front and going straight for the indoor line.

She shivered, standing next to him in silence. He remained a picture of discomfort.

"I don't have to stop by on Christmas Eve," she said.

He glanced at her, then at the counter. "Mom wants you there, you should come."

She scrunched her face. "Yeah, see, that's the problem. If *you* don't want me there, I *shouldn't* come."

He scratched his head, taking an extra beat before he said, "No, Charlie, it'd be nice to have you there."

She nodded slowly. "If this makes you uncomfortable, I shouldn't go."

"I—"

"Next?" The cashier smiled, welcoming them forward.

She and Zachary placed their order, and as they stepped to the side of the counter, Zachary continued.

"You and I haven't talked about...us...in a while. Really talked. I want *us* to decide it before anyone else does."

"Okay."

"Truth is..."

Bodies in large winter coats bumped into them, shoved them together, then wove them apart. They glanced at each other in the noisy bakery and seemed to agree that they'd wait.

Their little bags of warmed cookies were ready, the holiday mint chocolate flavor in one, signature snickerdoodles in the other. They stepped outside to bells from a horse-drawn sleigh and flurries.

He held her elbow and led her away from the door, huddling close to the wall. "There's been a lot on my mind, obviously. Really, though, I'd love to have you at my parents' place." He stepped closer still, took a deep breath. "As for us? You're not a fling to me, Charlie. I don't take any of our time together for granted. It feels like we're dating. I didn't think I'd be interested in that again, but clearly, I underestimated you."

She grinned back at him, scooting herself closer. "It was my scrubs, wasn't it?"

He laughed, hard enough that he tipped his head back, and snowflakes dotted his eyelashes when he looked back at her. "Oh, they definitely helped."

She couldn't even think about things with the practice at the moment, not when Zachary Lee was saying he wanted to date her. Even after all he'd learned, with his patience and care as they slowly got more intimate. He wasn't running away. Yet she didn't want him to stay with her out of obligation.

"Zachary, I don't want you to feel like you need to...keep seeing me, after everything—"

"Charlie." He stepped her to the wall, one leg between hers, his hand cradling her face. "You sharing that side of yourself with me? I'm honored you trusted me. But I want to see you—*date* you—because I can't stop thinking about you. Or wondering what scrubs you'll wear the next time I see you. Or if you have a berry-colored bra to match your underwear," he murmured. "Or if you're happy."

"You don't need to worry about me," she whispered.

"Ah, but I do," he said, the backs of his fingers sliding hair from her cheek. "I'm realizing I don't want *you* to worry. That I hope you can finally release what you've been through and...hold me instead."

Charlie's eyes misted, and no sooner had she stood on her toes, Zachary leaned toward her, their kiss slow, sensual, as though they had all night.

***

Her head was reeling, not to mention that her concerns about paying into the business with Zachary didn't bother her as much as it probably should. Going into business with someone you were seeing, and barely had been, at that?

It had to be the holidays. They were messing with her mind. Because co-owning the business with the owner's son sounded like a great idea, if only she could get him on board.

And she was pretty sure she was falling for him.

CHAPTER 34

Zachary

A HOLIDAY PLAYLIST CURATED by the staff jingled through a small wireless speaker, filling the party room at Arturo's Restaurant with cheerful energy. They had closed the hospital a couple hours early, allowing everyone enough time to go home, change, and bring their families to their annual celebration.

The mood was certainly brighter than when he'd arrived almost two months ago. After his father's heart attack, there was a somber veil over the staff, his absence weighing on everyone's mind. Once he and Charlie found their own rhythm, though, things settled. Spirits lifted, especially with news of Daniel's recovery. The question as to his return to work came up less and less as time went on. Everyone adjusted to him and Charlie running things, to them being the go-to duo.

Mostly, though, it was Charlie. She kept things running like normal, despite his instincts to find things to fix and change.

He watched her now across the room as she laughed with Maura and her husband. Sure, he could take over and run things the way his father wanted. He'd incorporate a few of his own preferences into the fold—it was only natural, running a business.

What stood out the most was how much he wanted Charlie by his side as he did it.

She wore her cream sweater loosely tucked into the high waist of camel-colored pants that lengthened the look of her legs and showed off her round ass. He'd tugged her into the hallway when she'd arrived to express how much he liked them, and she had assured him he could help her out of them later.

"My God, honey, have you asked her out yet?" His mother's voice carried softly, her hand at his shoulder.

He turned, finding her in a bright red knit sweater adorned with snowflakes and puppies.

"I...what? When did you get here?" What expression had been on his face?

She smirked and squeezed him to her side. He put his arm over her shoulders, almost reluctantly.

"A little bit ago." She glanced over her shoulder, then back to him. "Everyone's very excited to see your father. He's barely made it past the door."

He hummed noncommittally, his gaze darting back to Charlie.

"So?"

He looked down at her. "What?"

"Never were that good at hiding your feelings. Have you asked her out yet?"

"I..." Charlie's gaze met his. She perked at the sight of his mom, then slowly raised an eyebrow at him. He couldn't help but smile at her, calming when she grinned back. "Yes."

Jeanie clasped her hands together. "Oh my, I never thought this day would come."

"No, Mom—"

"I won't say anything to your father."

"Definitely don't. We aren't...this isn't serious."

She pursed her lips.

"She and I are on the same page, before you ask. Sandra made sure about that too."

"Your sister knows?" Jeanie asked softly.

"Yes. It's not a big deal. This was all supposed to be temporary." Even as the words came out, he knew it was bullshit. As soon as he'd stepped foot in town, it was like his roots replanted. Seeing Charlie again had only made him more eager to stay. More curious. There was never going to be any "temporary" where he and Charlie were concerned.

"But the practice?" Jeanie asked.

"Yeah, well, that's separate."

Jeanie looked at Charlie, then back to him. "How?"

"It just is. We're being open with each other about it all. Don't worry. Don't say anything to Charlie either, okay? I don't want her to be embarrassed."

"Oh, honey. With the way she's been watching you this whole time, I'd say 'embarrassed' is highly unlikely. She looks completely smitten. She's almost as bad as you at hiding it."

Charlie was staring again and immediately blushed at being caught. She looked around, appearing to have just realized Maura and her husband had moved along and she was standing alone. Just watching him and his mom. She bit that lower lip and owned it. With a little wave, she lifted her head high and walked toward Jasmine. He chuckled softly.

"I don't think I've seen you smile like that in years," Jeanie mused.

He felt it in his cheeks, the strain of unused muscles there to prove his mom's point.

"Son." His father came up beside him, steps slow. "Nice little party you have here."

"Charlie and Maura. All them," Zachary said, taking a sip of the holiday punch.

"Of course. Can we go on into the hall for a minute?"

Zachary nodded, sparing his mom a quick glance as he followed his dad through the room and into the dim hallway.

"I talked to the new accountant." Daniel threaded his fingers together. "We're prepping the paperwork to transfer the practice to you."

He shook his head. "Wait. We're still discussing this. That I *might* buy into it."

"There's no more time."

"What do you mean? That was only a week ago."

"I needed to have the decision by the end of this month. It's financially the best way for us to solve it, and to help us avoid some other issues. Additional taxes and late fees, that sort of thing. Your guy was very helpful." He added the last statement reluctantly.

Zachary ran his fingers through his hair. "Dad, you should've talked to me about this. Charlie..." He hesitated.

"I already said I didn't want her to carry the burden. This should remain in the family. And I certainly wasn't going to discuss the Neptune offer with her, not when I know how she feels. There'll be more opportunities for her. Better ones."

"She wanted to buy into it, Dad. She was willing to share it with me."

Daniel's eyes widened. "You told her?"

Zachary paced.

Daniel grunted. "What, exactly, did you say?"

"The gist of it. That there was a hefty amount of debt, and you didn't want to pass that onto her." *But would willingly give it to me.* Again, he couldn't put all the blame on his father when he'd been ill-advised. Plus, Zachary had bailed instead of being there for him, instead of what his dad had dreamed of for years.

Daniel waved a hand in the air. "That wouldn't have been right. To start out like that."

"How is it 'right' for me? Better her and I teaming up, tackling this together."

"This was the smartest decision, Zachary. You're back in town, and with how well things have been going in my absence, I figured you'd be staying."

"But you didn't *ask* me if I was."

Daniel was quiet, his blinks slow as he studied every inch of Zachary's face. He asked softly, "Don't you want to stay?"

The pain etched in his father's face rattled him. "I hadn't thought through it yet. It's a big decision. Why doesn't anyone see that?"

"Is it the practice?"

Zachary shook his head.

"Me? That's why you left." Daniel's voice was strained.

"Dad, I left because I was getting married. I followed Anna to where she was from, because it was important to her. Yes, I put her plans first, no need to rehash all that bullshit. I recognize the choices I made."

"You decided to work for her father."

"It seemed like the right thing at the time." He hesitated, scrubbed a hand through his hair. "Things worked out fine because, like you said, you had Charlie, so you didn't need me here. You know what, though? At our wedding, during his speech? I hadn't even told him 'yes' yet. I wanted to be the one to tell you the news. That was my plan. I'm sorry for how that happened."

Daniel was silent long enough for Zachary to replay his words. Then his dad shook his head.

"You staying here would've been me forcing you. But don't think for a second that I wouldn't have been thrilled to have you back. I'd always dre—" Daniel swallowed. "Working alongside you was something I'd looked forward to since you told me you wanted to be a veterinarian. Having you here now, I thought maybe it was time for you to come home."

Zachary sighed. "I was let go, Dad." He spread his arms wide. "I didn't have anything to return to. Seemed like the right thing to do."

"Oh, I see." Daniel nodded slowly. "And now?"

"Well. I'm not necessarily looking forward to leaving."

Daniel's eyebrows raised slightly.

"I just need time to think through it all."

"You've been here two months—"

"I didn't know *this* for two months. Puts a different spin on things, don't you think?"

Daniel waited a moment. "So you're not happy about this plan? Taking over?"

"I don't know what I am right now. Look. Let's talk more about this later. We need to be in there."

Daniel nodded, waited a beat. Then walked back into the room.

Zachary pressed his head to the wall, whispering, "Fuck." Then turned and followed.

It was like being beamed to a joy-filled dimension. The holiday music seemed loud, as carefree kids danced. The food filled tables in artful displays with candlesticks and wood tiers draped with greenery, a train weaving through as people piled their plates. Techs surrounded his dad, laughing as though there hadn't been an immense health scare. No one knew the state of things, how drastically everything could change.

Charlie's laugh. It pulled him in, softened everything. She stood with his mom, listening with rapt attention as Sheila and her wife spoke to them. His chest tightened, his steps lighter as he found himself physically drawn to her, moving her way.

Things were spiraling again. It wasn't just the practice he was losing a grip on. It was also his feelings, because somewhere along the way, Charlie Harris had grabbed hold of his heart, and he feared she wasn't about to let go.

He didn't want her to.

CHAPTER 35

Charlie

CHARLIE TUGGED THE HEM of her evergreen tunic sweater underneath her coat, its thick neck blocking the bite of the wind. The gray leggings and lined boots kept her warm, but she was far from overheating, considering the plummeting cold that had snapped the night before. She woke to a chill so silent and intense, it felt like her eyeballs were frozen.

She juggled a bag of wrapped gifts in one hand and a bottle of Brunello in the other as she approached the stoop of the tan brick Tudor. Cleo had hooked her up with some last minute things for the Lee and Wang families, so while she looked prepared, she didn't feel it.

A fresh evergreen wreath with a sparkly gold bow stared back at her from the rounded-top, black front door. Why was her heart racing? This wasn't even the first time they'd invited her to a family holiday gathering.

She set the bottle on the ground to knock, and as she bent to pick it back up, the door opened. The breath rushed out of her as she straightened, her eyes eagerly eating up Zachary. The bulky gray sweater and dark jeans hugged his frame and made him look cozy all at once, especially when capped with a thick pair of gray socks with what appeared to be a face of a reindeer knit into the fabric. His toes wiggled as she stared.

"The kids picked these out for me," he said sheepishly.

She smiled, not looking at him. Her racing heart paused long enough to skip multiple beats. *This is why I'm nervous. He is what's different.*

"Come on, Harris. Get in from the cold," Zachary said, gently tugging her by the coat.

She let him guide her into the foyer and close the door, the warmth of the house, the heat from him, burning her up instantly. Music carried from the kitchen, a TV murmured from the living room, and the gleeful shrieks of the kids seemed to bounce around the walls. His hand on her lapel, he tugged her closer still, leaning for a kiss.

"Charlie!" Vivi ran into the foyer, her arms flailing. "Look what we got!"

Charlie laughed, Zachary's face mere inches from hers. He stepped back with a small chuckle, shaking his head as Alex appeared next to his sister. Beaming, the two held up their small hands, clutching tiny LEGO knights and dragons in their palms.

"Wow, look at that!" Charlie said.

"Uncle Zachy gave them to us," Vivi said. "There's a castle too!"

"Yeah!" chimed in a proud Alex.

"Those are pretty cool..." Charlie trailed off, as the kids cheered and zipped away. "Seems like they're having a good day so far."

"Yeah. For Christmas Eve, they've made out like bandits."

"Hey," Sandra said, her arrival perfect. "Don't pretend like you aren't partially to blame. This guy has been their personal elf."

Zachary shrugged. "Look, it's a bit addicting to shop for them."

"Well, be prepared, because they won't forget it. Are you going to let the woman in? Geez, where are your manners? Charlie, give him your coat."

Zachary shot his sister a look as Charlie laughed, the comfortable chaos easing her heart.

"I've barely said a word to her since she arrived! Keep getting interrupted," Zachary said. Kinda grumpily.

"Well, *excuse* me," Sandra said, rolling her eyes. "If you would've picked her up, you wouldn't have had that problem."

"I had to swing by my mom's this morning," Charlie rushed to add. She held up the stuff in her hands. "I brought a few things."

"How sweet!" Sandra took the gifts from Charlie. "I'll set these under the tree. Everyone's in the living room, join us when you're situated. I'll keep them occupied until then." With a sly wink, she sauntered out of the foyer.

"God, it smells amazing in here," Charlie said as Zachary helped her out of her coat.

"Mom's making roast pork," he said.

"Ohmigod, amazing," she groaned.

Zachary chuckled and hung Charlie's coat on a hook by the door, watching as she yanked off her boots.

"So. Welcome to the chaos," he said with a grin. "Sure you want to stay?"

"I like it. Puts the hustle and bustle into the holidays. *Ooof.*" The second boot took extra effort to remove, and she flopped against the wall with an exaggerated sigh, thrilled when his hand grabbed her waist, even though she didn't need the help. What she did need was his touch, and it seemed mutual. "It's nice. Cozy."

She glanced around the foyer. A narrow black console table opposite the coats and shoes had a mini-Christmas tree with fairy lights on top, propping up a plush gnome wearing a Fair Isle stocking cap.

The iron banister to the second floor had fake pine garland wrapped around it, gold bows every few feet. The archways on either side of the stairs—leading to the dining room or the sunken living room—had holiday cards taped around them.

He hummed, stepping closer. "You look cozy," he said, fingers toying with her sweater.

"You do too." All she wanted was to curl up with him on the couch under a blanket. Watch snow fall. Stare at the lights on the tree.

He leaned down and pressed a soft kiss to her lips, but it quickly turned heated. His hands curved to cup her ass, while her arms wound tightly around his neck. He swept his tongue into her mouth, and she muffled a moan. Their goodbye after the party the night before had been quick, and clearly, she was a deprived woman because of it. Wanted him more when she learned the kids had requested he sleep over, and she couldn't let him turn down the offer. Her fingers gripped his hair, and she pushed closer, standing on her toes to alleviate their height difference. He groaned, then pressed his forehead to hers, their breath quick.

"Charlie," he whispered.

"Huhnm?" she panted.

He smiled softly, pressing a light kiss to her lips. Then he tucked his face in the crook of her neck, wrapping his arms tight. And hugged her.

Charlie blinked. The garland wrapped around the stair rail blurred from tears building in her eyes. His smell washed over her, his sweater as cozy as she suspected. Being in his arms was amazing, each time far surpassing the last. She didn't want to move.

Her eyes squeezed shut.

She hadn't meant for it to happen, but it had. She'd fallen in love with Zachary Lee.

***

She was going to remember this—she, Charlie Harris, had the power to will her dreams into reality.

The thought made her chuckle to herself, mentally of course, so as not to disturb the perfect setting. After a lovely afternoon watching the kids open some gifts and entertain the adults with mini performances, Vivi and Alex had curled up with a movie by the big Christmas tree, while the adults enjoyed drinks and snacks in the four-season room. Garland was draped over the large windows and a second, smaller tree stood brightly in the corner, full of ornaments made by Sandra and Zachary growing up. Jeanie regaled them with her favorite Christmas stories of the two, with Jay promising to show her some of his favorite of their home videos.

Now she and Zachary sat alone, nestled on the loveseat, with Maple curled on the plush cream rug at their feet. Christmas tree lights sparkled as snow flurried softly, surrounding them in the early darkness.

Sandra and Jay had joined the kids in the living room, where Daniel had opted to take a nap in the reclining chair. Jeanie, meanwhile, had kicked everyone out of the kitchen. Which left Charlie and Zachary comfortable enough to share a blanket, for him to wrap his arm around her and snuggle her close.

It felt like she was spending the holidays with her boyfriend and his family. But she didn't dare bring it up.

Instead, she stared at the twinkling tree, breathing in pine and the hot cider in her snowman mug. The mug that was suddenly removed from her hands as Zachary stole it from her and took a sip.

"Hey!"

He smacked his lips for effect. "Had to see what the fuss was about." He took another drink, holding the mug out to the side when she reached for it.

She watched his tongue trace his lips, her stomach doing flips of excitement.

"You have a habit of sharing my food. And drink," she said.

He glanced down at her. "Tastes better that way." He grinned and handed back the mug.

She peered inside, satisfied he hadn't had too much, which would force her to leave their cozy love cocoon for a refill.

No, no, just "cozy cocoon," she corrected. As though thinking the word would somehow alert the man beside her.

"Never really liked apple juice or cider growing up. But Sandra's bragged about her recipe the last few years, I've just never been here to try it."

Charlie nodded. "And?"

"Pretty good."

"Want your own?"

"Like I said, tastes better from yours."

Charlie bit her lip, pleased when he groaned. Zachary glanced around, then pressed his lips to hers, his hand cupping her cheek while he devoured her in a hasty, satisfying kiss.

"Maybe we should get out of here," he said, voice husky.

Charlie shivered. "Extremely tempting. But your mom's making dinner."

"She has plenty of people to feed." He bit her earlobe, trailed his nose down her neck.

"Zachary..."

He kissed her nose. "I know." He sighed and flopped back against the couch, tugging her closer. "As soon as we're done, though." He threw his thumb over his shoulder. "Outta here."

She nuzzled against his side. "Tomorrow afternoon I'll be at Brooke's. We're going to watch movies in our pajamas all day. Something simple, hopefully enough to keep her and Mina distracted." She picked at his sweater. Tried to think of an excuse to see him.

His fingers grazed her shoulder. Finally, he said, "I'll be at Sandra and Jay's."

"Right." Too much to expect they'd spend the entire holiday together. Why rush this non-relationship thing anyway?

"Maybe we could meet up tomorrow night?"

She slid her head along his chest to look at him, her heart doing a tap dance.

"Could have dinner, watch a movie. If you're not sick of that by then." He played with strands of her hair as he waited for her answer.

"That sounds perfect," she said. They had a lot to discuss, but it could wait. 'Til after the holidays, maybe.

His eyes locked on hers, his smile bringing back those deep creases she loved so much. She traced them, his eyes softening.

She had to tell him *something*. This moment was too perfect. Her heart was in it, and it felt right to put it on the line—that she cared about him, deeply.

Zachary's gaze moved, and he straightened, effectively sliding Charlie to his side. She looked over to find Daniel entering the room, his steps slow as he took in the two of them.

"Hey, Dad," Zachary said, clearing his throat.

Daniel said nothing, instead taking a seat across from them, his eyes still calculating.

Charlie tugged her legs out from under her and Zachary shifted some more, sliding the blanket from his lap.

"I wanted to talk to you both."

She braced herself. Daniel was probably about to tell her the practice was in trouble, not knowing Zachary already had. She was prepared for this, she would tell him she'd still buy in, that it didn't matter—

"Charlie, I've transferred the practice over to Zachary."

"Dad," Zachary choked out.

Charlie blinked at Daniel, shooting a quick glance at Zachary before looking back at her boss, her mentor, once again. "I'm sorry, what?"

"I had the paperwork drawn up this week. EFVH is now in his name. It was best for everyone, believe me. I understand you're aware I was in some financial trouble."

She swallowed hard. "I had heard, yes, but I don't understand."

"There are certain tax laws and breaks that come with it moving between family."

"Right, family..." Charlie said absently.

"Dad, you couldn't be a little more gentle with this?"

Charlie turned to Zachary, registered his lack of surprise.

Zachary looked at her. "I'm sorry, Charlie, I didn't ask for—"

She looked at Daniel. "When was this decided?"

"I had the paperwork finalized yesterday. This doesn't mean anything about your work with the practice, Charlie. Your dedication has been above and beyond."

"Just not family level," she said. It was the most brash tone she'd used with Daniel in all the years she'd known him.

"This has nothing to do with your ability to run things, Charlie." His gentled tone didn't matter.

She felt her heartbeat in her throat. "Then why not talk to me about what was going on? You owed me that, Daniel."

He firmed his lips. "It was something I had to take care of myself."

"You didn't think you could even talk to me about it?" Charlie scooted to the edge of the couch. "After all this time?"

Daniel looked to Zachary, a gaze passing between them that Charlie didn't understand. Zachary held up his hands.

"This isn't my thing, Dad. You surprised me too."

"So now I'll have you both mad at me," Daniel said.

She was fuming. She couldn't remember *ever* being mad at him. He'd only ever guided her with a kind hand, been there for her throughout all those years of schooling, of learning. Was someone she could consult, could securely admit when she didn't know something—because, like he'd always reminded her, how could she know everything? There was always something new to learn.

A lesson he must have forgotten.

It was a major reminder that their respect didn't go both ways.

"Charlie, I still want you there. This doesn't change that."

"You know it's not what we agreed to, Daniel. It's not what we've talked about all these years," Charlie said. She choked up, tears threatening, but she was too angry to let them spill.

"That can still be an option. Right now, things will shift over to Zachary until we can get on more solid ground."

She looked at Zachary. "So, you *are* staying?"

"I haven't actually agreed to or signed anything yet." Zachary looked between her and his dad. "I'm still trying to figure all this out."

She nodded slowly. "Yeah." She blew out a loud breath. "This forces you to stay in town, take over for your father, see me when we were supposed to be temporary. That must be really throwing you for a loop." She huffed out a crazed laugh and stood, running her hands through her hair. "Um, I'm going to go."

She hurried out of the room and passed quickly through the living room, ignoring the sound of her name from other members of the family. She had to get out of there. Get some air, clear her head. Figure out what she needed to do.

Her coat and purse in hand, she stepped outside, shoving her heels the rest of the way into her boots. The snow fluttered in a whimsical dance, cool on her face, melting on the war in her chest. She tugged on her coat, feeling sobs threatening to escape.

"Charlie!" Zachary turned her to face him. "Charlie." He swiped at her cheeks, removing evidence of tears she didn't know were there. "Let's talk this out. I'll come over, and we can sort through this mess together—"

"I'm in love with you," Charlie blurted.

His hand stilled on her face, but his eyes widened to hers. "What?" he asked softly.

"Shit," she whispered. "Zachary, I'm in love with you. It's terrible timing. I don't even know why I said it right now, it sort of fell out. It's been on my mind, and that doesn't help all of...*this*." She gestured wildly between them, the house, at the romantic snow. "I don't want us to be temporary. I haven't for a while now. But this complicates everything. You didn't want more, and now the business is yours. And for some reason, that isn't the part that bothers me the most, which pisses me off. *That* is what makes this complicated. I couldn't work for you, and not only because the thought drives me crazy. But I couldn't, knowing how I feel, and that you don't feel the same way." She swallowed, then sucked in a breath and went for broke. "Do you?"

His hand fell to his side. "Charlie..."

She waited until he didn't say anything else. "Right," she muttered. Her nods were frantic as she stepped back, tears streaming down her face. He reached toward her, but she held up her hands. "Don't."

"This was supposed to be temporary. We both..." he trailed off.

"Yep. Yes. That's what we agreed to. Initially."

He shifted on his feet, his breath a white burst between them. "You need to go experience more now, anyway. Now that you're free from all that shit. Date around. Do...what you want." His words were strained. "You deserve that."

"What? I don't want that." How did he not see? "I deserve you!"

His laugh was unamused. "I don't deserve *you*! You deserve better than I can give! Look at how I'm already crushing you!"

She shook her head, daring a step closer. "You mean I don't deserve someone who accepted me for who I am? Who never pressured me?"

He scoffed. "I constantly pressure you."

"In work, yes. We both do. I'm talking about personally, Zachary. You never made me feel like I was falling short. You made me feel sexy when it was the last thing I imagined being."

His throat worked. "Well, you are. I'm not the only one who sees it."

"I don't care about anyone else. I care about you!"

He scrubbed his hands through his hair, face pained. "Charlie, I don't want you to look back one day and regret this. To wish you'd had time to really find what you're looking for."

She was shocked at his words. Appalled at how differently they'd been viewing their connection. It didn't change how she felt, and she wasn't going to tell him otherwise.

She huffed. "You know what I'd regret? Letting you go." She stood a beat, working up the final strands of courage. "I know what I'm looking for. Us, together? That's when I realized what a relationship could be. The respect, the support, the need. I want to live out my fantasies and dreams with *you*, Zachary. As my partner."

The silence of the snowfall surrounded them, the blankets of white absorbing their words. Charlie sensed her cheeks were numb, but she could no longer determine if it was from the cold or from the look in Zachary's eyes. He lifted his hand, like maybe he wanted to reach out for her, but then crossed his arms.

"I'm sorry, Charlie," he said softly. "I can't be part of making your dreams come true. I'm only capable of wrecking them. Look how quickly I ruined the practice for you."

This was it. *Temporary* hit swiftly, Zachary staying true to their plan, and holding fast that he'd remind her if they strayed off course.

She gave him a nod and hustled toward her car, arms flailing wide for balance as she slipped on some ice. Once steady, she kept moving, undeterred. Nothing would stop her.

"Charlie."

Her back was to him as she reached her car, and she didn't look his way. Only waited.

"I'm sorry."

She closed her eyes and blew out a quiet breath, then climbed into her car. If she looked at him, she'd lose it. So instead, she drove away, without a glance in the rearview. Leaving her job, as she knew it, floating in the breeze.

And her heart buried in the snow.

CHAPTER 36

Zachary

"WHAT THE HELL IS going on with you?"

Zachary scraped his head along the thick beige carpet toward Jordan, his vision swimming despite lying on the ground for support. Maple rested her head on his stomach, determined to keep him anchored.

He raised the bottle of lager toward his best friend. "I've been drinking."

"Ah." Jordan flopped onto the oversized leather sectional in his sweats and hoodie. He stared at the ceiling, hands folded on his sternum. "What happened?"

Zachary shrugged, his shoulders restricted by the soft rug pile below him. "Life."

Jordan snorted. "That all?"

Zachary sighed. "My dad signed over the business to me."

Jordan lifted his head. "I didn't know you'd decided that. Shit, man. Are you staying?"

"That's the problem. It was announced *for* me. Again. I didn't decide any of it." He waved the bottle around. "Didn't say I was staying. Didn't say I was taking over. Didn't know it was an option. What about all the debt?" He lifted his head slightly to take another sip, then plopped

357

it back on the floor. "Didn't say 'I love you' back to Charlie. Even though I probably do." He sighed. "I do..."

"Woah, hold on." Jordan promptly sat and braced his arms on his thighs. "What did you just say?"

Zachary closed his eyes. "There's a mountain of debt. Well, it was a mountain, and that's why I got the practice instead of Charlie. I guess that trimmed down the mountain. Now it's more like a...hill. I can do a hill. But I didn't even want to do the hill. Well, before I didn't want to, but then I started to think it might be nice to, you know, climb the hill *with* someone."

"The fuck are you *talking* about?"

Zachary glared at Jordan. *Why doesn't he get it?* "The hill of debt. It's helpful to share it with someone. More enjoyable to swim in the money too." He paused. "Why don't cartoon ducks wear pants?"

Jordan rolled his eyes. "This isn't the time, Z. *Focus*. Now, the practice, we'll get to that. What's this about loving Charlie?"

"I didn't say that," Zachary grumbled.

"Okay, you've been a pain in the ass these last few days."

Zachary groaned, his gaze going to his friend. "I get it. I'm a dick."

"Now we're getting somewhere."

Zachary laughed, but it was forced. "She hasn't talked to me in days."

"Charlie?"

"Charlie. Charlotte Harris. Not since Christmas Eve, when she told me..." Zachary closed his eyes, but then the memory was front and center. Didn't matter, thoughts of her had flooded his mind every day anyway. He swallowed, trying to sort his thoughts. "Dad signed the practice over to me. Skipped over her. He told her on Christmas Eve. Then she told me she loved me."

"No way."

"Yeah. Said she was *in love* with me." He still couldn't process it. Especially since the words had been way more welcoming than scary. He'd wanted to hear her say it again.

"What did you tell her?"

"I...didn't."

"What does that mean?"

"I couldn't say it back, Jordan. It was supposed to be temporary. *That* I did say."

"No."

Zachary groaned. "Yes. And that she should date around." *Why the fuck did I say that?*

Jordan whistled, and Maple popped her head up. "You can hear that tone, huh, girl?"

Maple realized all was normal and rested her head down. Zachary petted it clumsily. "Softest head in all the land," he mumbled.

Jordan nudged Zachary's foot with his own. "So what happened after you said that?"

"She left."

Jordan nodded. "And then?"

"She didn't respond to my texts. Barely said a word to me at work all week. She has to actively avoid me. You've been there, that place isn't that big. We share an office!"

"I don't blame her. She said she loved you, and you told her it wasn't real."

"I never said that."

"You practically did. Telling her it's temporary? It's like...the adult form of make-believe."

"Fuck!" Zachary shoved himself to sit with his back to the couch, and Maple repositioned her head in his lap.

"What are you gonna do?"

"I don't know! I didn't ask for the practice, but now it's in my hands. That sounds shitty, but I'd been telling myself it wouldn't be mine for years now, you know? Then she mentioned owning it together, and that was actually appealing to me. Which scared the fuck out of me."

"She wanted to buy in with you?"

Zachary nodded. "Dad didn't want to pass on the debt. Felt too horrible, I don't know. I haven't heard all the details yet."

"Sounds like that would be good."

Zachary shot him a glare. "I hate when you're right."

Jordan laughed. "You'll get over it. Especially because we've found the way to fix this."

"I don't remember that part of the conversation."

"The practice is yours. You can do what you want with it."

He groaned. "I know this."

"Stop whining. Jesus. Here." Jordan took the bottle away from Zachary. "That means you can sign anyone on that you choose, Z. If you want a partner, you can have a partner."

"You're saying I should offer her what she had suggested," Zachary said slowly, thinking through the decision.

"Why not? If it's something that sounded good to you before, what's changed?"

"She loves me."

"I think she already knew that when she offered."

"No, I mean...what does that say to share the practice when I know how she feels?"

"Well. How do *you* feel?"

"I don't know."

Jordan sank into the couch. "So you'll own the practice, but return to Chicago? Or will you sell it?"

"No. I'm not selling it."

"And Chicago?"

Zachary looked around the living room, still petting Maple absentmindedly. "I don't want to go back to Chicago. Nothing there for me."

Jordan grinned. "First, I'll just get this out of the way and say, as your friend, that's awesome. You can crash here as long as you need while you figure shit out."

Zachary laughed, bracing his arms on his knees. "Thanks, man."

"You've clearly got a lot of shit to figure out."

Zachary sighed. "Yeah, I know."

"So the practice. You're taking it on. Do you want to do it alone?"

Zachary shook his head. "No."

"Do you want a random partner?"

"No."

"Who do you want? Your dad?"

"God, no. No. He's retiring anyway." Zachary thought of Charlie, how they enjoyed discussing patients together. How smoothly things operated, how fluidly they moved about the office. How they had each other's back. "I want Charlie. We work really well together, and she's amazing for the practice. It needs her."

"Those are all really great reasons," Jordan said almost gently. "Doesn't really address the 'love' element, does it?"

"Did you take counseling classes or something? You sound like my sister," Zachary grumbled.

Jordan shrugged. "I get to hone my skills at both jobs. Talking through things with children and straightening out drunk adults. Thanks for giving me practice on both. So?"

Zachary could hardly process the jab, more focused on Charlie. And his swimming head. "She won't work with me, after telling me how she feels."

"How do you know for sure?"

Zachary pushed up to stand and paced. Maple perked for a moment, then placed her head on the floor between her paws, promptly falling asleep.

"What if we do this? What if we go for it, and it starts off really great, because it's been really great so far? Then what if we don't work out? What do we do then? At that point, we're working together, and we know that is great. I don't want to ruin that."

"Uh." Jordan shook his head. "Let me see if I follow—you want her, you want her to be part of the practice, but you're worried what would happen if your relationship didn't work."

"Exactly."

"I don't know," Jordan said.

"I don't know either!"

Jordan watched him pace. Then he repeated slowly, "You want her. And you want the practice. So, I think the person you need to ask is..."

Zachary finally stopped in front of him. "Her."

Jordan nodded.

"It's stupid, isn't it? To sign into business together? Before, when she mentioned it, she said we would figure it out."

Jordan shrugged. "Fuck, it's risky as hell to go into business with anyone you care about. Look at Mel. She's got her bar, hired her best friend as her manager, and they fight all the time. They somehow don't let it affect anyone else though, they've made it work. You've gotta decide which risk is worth taking: being with her knowing your relationship could fall apart—maybe even the practice—or working with her without pursuing whatever it is you guys have going."

"I can't just ignore what we've got going."

"That sounds like a pretty big deal."

Zachary put his hands on his hips. "This isn't like Anna. I'm not making this decision, staying in town, with the practice, because of Charlie."

"It's definitely not like Anna," Jordan said.

Zachary blew out a breath. "I just feel like I've been down this road before."

"Look, you're the only one who really knows how this is different from your relationship with your ex-wife. From my perspective? It's very different. You're completely yourself around her. From the little I've seen of you two together, you push each other. Also, I haven't seen you smile that much in a really long time."

"My mom said the same thing."

"She must be freaking out, then. You guys have known each other for a long time, Z. Even with time apart, that's not nothing."

"I didn't realize how much I missed her," Zachary said. "Now that feeling won't go away."

"That sounds like something worth looking into."

He nodded. "Yeah. Yeah. Okay, thanks." He clapped his hands and hopped out of the room.

"Where are you going?"

"Got some work to do!"

"It's like, two in the morning!" Jordan called.

Zachary stalled, looking at his phone. *Huh.* He was wide awake.

"Love waits for no one!"

Jordan laughed. "Is this the kinda shit I'm gonna hear, now? You're an idiot!"

Zachary grinned.

Didn't mind being an idiot when he knew he was doing it for love.

CHAPTER 37

Charlie

"WHAT DO YOU THINK of our proposal?"

Charlie looked across the bistro table at Ned North as he sipped his coffee, his fleece bearing a small Neptune Corp logo. He'd seized the chance to meet at a café outside Elmwood Falls, willing to drive early on a Sunday at her request. It halved the chances of any familiar faces seeing her, though there was really only one who made a difference.

"A nice plan is in place," she said. Their offer to her was generous, though she was hesitant to say as much. The images of the revamped veterinary clinic on the east side of town looked chic and modern, sure to draw lots of attention.

It chafed, the way money swooped in to transform. In the wrong hands, it was only a disguise—it eliminated any heart in the process.

She had to remind herself why she was here in the first place. What mattered was considering her options, finding what was best for her. If that meant moving to another clinic, then so be it. She was still her, *that* wouldn't change. She could bring all the heart she could wherever she went!

"Their schedule is filling up nicely," Ned said. "The community is very pleased. A few other businesses have closed up shop, and this location is well-equipped to handle the overflow."

"What do you mean, which businesses?"

"Well." He shrugged. "There was another clinic not far from there. They shut their doors a couple months ago, so plenty of clients were looking for a new option."

"East Town Veterinary?" Her voice was barely above a whisper. Daniel knew the owner—they'd opened their practices around the same time and bonded through the process. He was a lifer. She wondered if Daniel even knew what had happened.

"Yeah." He waved away the name. "Owner was ready to retire. Worked out great. We were hoping the same would go for your boss, but no such luck...*yet*. Maybe in a few years." He laughed.

She blinked at the reminder that Neptune had made Daniel an offer.

"What that means for you though is that you'd be in charge of a solid team, overseeing a large clientele that we anticipate will grow exponentially over the next few years. Numerous partnerships are already in place, and the outlook for expanding the technology is huge. All we're missing is a strong leader who will win over everyone."

He grinned at what he surely thought was a compliment. Charlie, however, noticed her body coiled tighter the more he spoke.

She released a slow breath. "You have to understand. I know this *is* a business, but it's about more than that to me. I chose this career because I love it, and what has been most amazing is that I've fallen in love with all my patients, the community, my team. What I have at EFVH is family. That's not easily replicated. *That* can't be bought."

Ned leaned forward. "Or is it that wherever you go, family will find you?"

***

A tap on Charlie's shoulder made her shriek, sudsy water flinging from her hands onto the cat clock above the kitchen sink. Amber jumped back, hands out.

"Sorry!" she shouted. "You couldn't hear me over the music!"

"You scared the shit out of me!" Charlie yelled.

"Where the hell is your phone?"

"It's on the—" Charlie broke off when silence filled the air, Amber locating the phone on the counter and pausing the music.

Her cousin flicked her eyes at her. "Playing a concert for the whole neighborhood?"

Charlie returned to scrubbing. "You're channeling my mom."

"Levi was banging his head against the wall of the alcove when I arrived. I'm surprised he didn't knock a hole through to your side. Said he couldn't take the pop tunes anymore."

Charlie snorted. "He secretly loves pop."

"You may have ruined it for him."

She scrubbed harder at the Pyrex, muttering under her breath.

"What are you doing?"

"Dishes."

"Are you trying to wear through the glass? Turn it back to sand?"

Charlie stopped and huffed a sigh. "Did you just come over to antagonize me?"

Amber pointed to a grocery bag on the kitchen table. "Our New Year's Eve bash. Remember?" She slipped on a pair of plastic glasses and pressed a button to set the frames flashing. "It's gonna be a rager here at Chez Charlie."

Charlie returned to the sink.

"You do remember us talking about it, don't you? Magnolia and Cleo are coming..."

"Sure." She didn't remember. The last few days had been exhausting enough, dancing around to avoid contact with Zachary while she processed what to do with her life. No one knew about her meeting with Ned. Talking with her cousin on the phone earlier in the week was vaguely familiar, but all Charlie recalled was uttering random sounds of agreement. To something. Apparently, it had to do with hosting New Year's Eve, one of her least favorite holidays.

This year was no exception.

"Is that why your hair is a tangled mess? I see you busted out your sexy high school sweatpants that have lost all elasticity in the waist. Real hot."

"Aren't we going comfy?" Charlie said, in an effort to appear prepared and uncaring.

Amber laughed, her perfect bangs highlighting perfect eyeliner in her perfect oversized maroon sweater. Paired with leggings and cozy wool socks, she was the picture of winter comfort.

Charlie was a wreck, in a faded T-shirt that hid how far her gray sweatpants had fallen.

"Okay, hun, I think this dish is clean." Amber pulled it from her hands. "Why don't you go freshen up? The ladies will be here in a little bit, and we'll get you nice and drunk. Then you can tell us what's going on."

"I don't want to."

"That's the spirit. Brush your teeth." Amber shoved Charlie out of the room.

"'*Brush your teeth*,'" Charlie mumbled, stumbling into her bathroom to do just that. The lingering taste of onion in her mouth was from dinner...the night before.

She rinsed her face, ran a brush through her hair, then pulled on leggings and her favorite sweatshirt, berry pink with little paw prints embroidered over the heart. She wouldn't admit it out loud, but by the time she returned to the living room, she felt an ounce better.

"Here," Amber said, handing over a glass of red wine. "Sit." She shoved Charlie onto the couch, then sipped from her own glass and waited. She stood in front of her, as though to stop her from thinking she could get up and leave.

Charlie scooped Toothless off the back of the couch and into her lap, and dutifully drank.

"They'll be here any minute. Want to just wait for them?" As soon as the words left Amber's mouth there was a knock at the door.

Charlie watched as her cousin let their friends in, watched as they bustled about, shoving clutter underneath the coffee table so they could cram it with drinks and snacks. A business card fluttered to the ground in the process, *Neptune Corp* facing up. Then all too quickly, the women stared at her expectantly. Amber sat on the couch beside Charlie, Cleo in the arm chair, and Magnolia cross-legged on the floor.

"No Sasha?" Charlie asked Cleo, trying to fill the silence.

"Nope," Cleo said. "She's out dancing with friends tonight. No Zachary?"

Charlie scowled.

"Oh, nice," Amber said.

"Thank you," Cleo said with a smirk.

"I told you guys what happened on Christmas Eve."

"And since?" Cleo asked.

Charlie shrugged. "Nothing."

"How could there be nothing? You work with the man!" Amber cried.

"He hasn't said anything to you about that night?" Magnolia asked.

"I've been busy."

"You've been avoiding him," Cleo said.

"I found out the practice is his, then I told him how I felt about him! Just blurted it out like I was running out of time. He doesn't feel the same, in case anyone forgot that detail. He made that clear. What else is there? The practice isn't mine, *he* isn't mine." She stuttered out a breath and pet Toothless, who had lifted her head at Charlie's despair. "I'm looking into other clinics."

"What?" Amber smacked her hand on the couch cushion, then reached to give Toothless her own pat as an apology for startling her. "You're going to leave?"

"I don't know what to do right now." She shook her head. She glanced at the business card again. "I was offered a chance to run one."

"What do you mean?" Cleo asked.

"One of the nearby clinics was purchased, and they're hiring."

"Wait, who purchased them?" Amber challenged.

"Neptune," Charlie mumbled.

"Charlie, you can't be serious! You hate them! You were adamant that Daniel not sell!" Amber exclaimed.

"Maybe the dust needs to settle a bit? It's like you're recovering from shock or something," said Cleo, her voice even.

Charlie stroked Toothless's silky fur as she blinked away tears. Magnolia scooted closer to pat her knee.

"What is it you want, Charlie?" Amber's tone softened, her hand resting on Charlie's arm.

"What do I want?" Charlie looked at each woman, concern on their faces as they waited. "I'd always envisioned taking over for Daniel. In high school, I never thought it possible. If anything, I wanted to be partner. Work alongside him, even Zachary, before he left."

"So owning your own place is what you want," Amber said carefully.

Charlie considered it a moment, what that really meant. "I loved the idea of it, but being a vet is my top priority. Continuing the legacy Daniel has created. The community he's built, I want to stay a part of it."

"Is working for Zachary an option, then?" Cleo asked.

Charlie paused. If she worked for him, she'd continue on almost like they had the last couple months. If he even decided to stay in town.

That thought worried her more than anything—him going back to Chicago.

"I want to stay. I have some requests, but being there is most important right now."

"Even with him knowing how you feel?" Magnolia said, not hiding her surprise.

Charlie nodded. "If there's anything we've built over these last couple months, it's trust. Yes, our relationship became much more intimate, but I trust him with...everything."

Amber squeezed her hand. "We don't want you to get hurt, working with him after..."

"No." She shook her head, more certain than ever. "It's only strengthened our working relationship. I can honestly say I'd rather work with him, for him, than switch clinics or move. Besides, his friendship is too important to me. I can't let that go."

Amber blew out a breath. "You are much braver than I am. I don't think I could stomach working with someone I loved, knowing he didn't love me back." A napkin hit her in the forehead, and she looked at Cleo. "What? I'm just being real."

"You're never not real," Cleo said.

Amber narrowed her eyes.

"I think he does," Charlie said softly. "He's just not ready to admit it."

"God, I am so lost in all this love stuff," Magnolia said.

"Honey," Amber said carefully. "You can't pine after the man, hoping he'll fall in love."

"That's not what I'm doing. I have a pretty good idea of how he feels, but I'm not going to push. Just like he didn't with me."

The women exchanged concerned looks around her.

Charlie straightened. "I can't believe I considered working for Neptune!"

"You had to consider your options," Cleo said.

"Yeah, you have to do what's best for you," Magnolia added.

"Right...Staying is right. Oh my God. I have to tell him." She stood, Toothless hopping from her lap, and rushed toward her front door.

"Wait, I'm coming with, and you aren't driving!" Amber tripped herself to reach Charlie.

"Us too!" Cleo and Magnolia bolted up.

Charlie shoved her feet into her boots, nearly toppling over from the effort. "Damn things. Always such a nuisance."

"I don't know how you guys do this every winter," Magnolia grumbled, adding layer upon layer.

"You'll get used to it," Cleo said. "Eventually, you might even be able to forgo a layer or two." She looked at Magnolia, then added, "Maybe one."

"Ladies! Enough with the chitchat! We're on a mission!" Amber cried. "Everyone buttoned up? How about you, Charlie?"

Charlie turned, stiff in her bulky winter coat, wrapped in her scarf as she finished pulling her hat and gloves snug. "I'm good." She grinned.

Amber laughed, then pulled the door open.

Only to reveal Zachary on the other side.

"Zachary," Charlie breathed. The other women gasped, the sound muffled to Charlie's ears by her winter gear. "What are you doing here?"

His gaze traveled over her, a smirk tugging as his eyes locked on hers. "You heading out to play in the snow?"

"I was heading to you!"

"You know, we're gonna go bug Levi for a bit," Amber said, shoving past Charlie.

Cleo and Magnolia followed, arms suddenly loaded with drinks and snacks.

Amber rapped on Levi's door, and as soon as it opened an inch, she shoved her way inside. "Look out, buddy, we need to borrow you for a bit. Don't worry, you won't have to ring in the new year with us, but we do have alcohol."

Charlie saw Levi's stunned face as each woman entered, his gaze widening on Magnolia as she passed him without a glance. He looked over to Charlie, saw Zachary, then nodded and shut the door.

"Umm." Charlie looked behind her, then back to the man only inches away as her heart stretched to meet his. "Want to come in? I happen to be alone."

Zachary smiled and followed her inside, toeing off his shoes. "I didn't mean to interrupt."

"No, we were coming to see you. I was coming to see you. Well, I didn't actually know if you were at Jordan's, but I was going to start there. Because..." Her voice trailed as Zachary slid the hat off her head. She was on high alert, wanting him to keep going.

"You're going to roast in here," he said, handing her the hat.

"Right," she said softly, twisting it in her hands.

He opened his coat, but stayed near the door. "So you were going to find me?"

She nodded. Stumbled out of her boots.

"After avoiding me all week at work?"

"Uh. Yes..."

He unwound the scarf from her neck. If she roasted a little longer, he'd keep at it. She was desperate for any way to be close to him.

"Why were you going to find me?" he asked. He tossed the scarf at the couch, then took the hat from her and did the same. He focused next on her gloves.

"I...um." She let out a breath, watching his fingers slowly reveal hers. "I was going to tell you that I still want to work at EFVH, even if it's yours now, if you'll have me. The people there, the history of that place, it means too much to me to leave it behind. I'm extremely disappointed for how this all changed, but not at you. Except for the whole 'I love you and you don't feel the same' part." She laughed nervously, still watching their hands, his fingers intertwining with hers. "We'll figure it out. I'm willing to try. Working there, with you, it's worth it."

Zachary tugged her closer. "Charlie?"

She looked up at him, her eyes searching for what he was going to say, trying to protect her heart, even though it was screaming out that he had come to find her.

"Harris," he said, grinning when she did. "I'm in love with you."

"You're what?" she croaked.

"I'm so in love with you," he said. "I don't want to do this without you. I know it's not how you planned it—"

She jumped into his arms, almost bouncing off him from the puffiness of her coat. Her face smacked his and they laughed, but it didn't stop her lips from devouring him, her arms from winding around him as much as they could while he held her close.

She pulled back her head, her feet dangling. "You love me?" She was grinning so wide, her glasses pressed into her cheeks.

"I love you." He slid her to the ground, then reached inside his coat, pulling out some papers and handing them to her. "I had these drawn up. I mean it. I want to do this with you. If you're still interested, I want you to be half of EFVH with me."

Charlie stared at the papers in her hand, the words blurring in front of her eyes. "Thought we decided this was too risky, going into business with your partner."

He flung his arms wide. "Yeah, well, this is all going down differently than any of us planned, I guess. But it's only worth it if you're there with me. The practice needs you, Charlie. The community needs you." He stepped closer to her again, brushing staticky hair from her cheek. "I need you."

She smiled, but before she could speak, he interrupted.

"Not to pressure you. Fuck, you know how saying that sounds good in your head? I don't want me needing you to be the reason. I want you to want to be a part of it, be with me—"

Charlie laughed, cupping his face with her hands. "Zachary. I want this—this is perfect. It's messy and unexpected and exactly right."

He pressed his forehead against hers and sighed. "I have one request, if we're going to do this. White coats, five days a week."

She reared back, but then noticed the teasing smile on his face. "How about I wear it for you here, without anything else?"

He groaned, scooping her closer. "That sounds fair," he said, kissing her deeply. "Can we take these jackets off now?"

She laughed, tearing hers off, shrieking when he scooped her over his shoulder. When he set her down in the bedroom, he pressed a gentle kiss to her lips.

"I've missed you in my life, Charlie Harris," he said.

Charlie ran her fingers along his jaw. "Me too," she whispered. "Stay in mine?"

"You can count on it."

EPILOGUE
Charlie

THE MUSIC FILLED THE room, and Charlie swayed her hips. She set out two small plates, then carefully placed a snickerdoodle cupcake on each. She shimmied over to the wine, pouring two glasses.

It had been a couple of weeks since they'd made it official—she and Zachary were the proud co-owners of EFVH. Daniel had given his blessing, emotional that the two of them cared so deeply about his life's work to continue it, and relieved they'd found a way to ease some of the practice's struggles. The transition was smooth, considering everyone had been working under them for the last few months, but the positive reception from their team had been extremely important.

That morning in particular had been especially positive—Charlie's PT appointment being one of her most progressive yet. It had boosted her spirits the whole day, sending her humming all the way to the bakery and home. Zachary would be there soon, Maple and Toothless were curled up asleep, and she was as turned on as a live wire.

Arms circled her waist, and she yelped.

"You have a habit of playing your music so loud you can't hear the door," Zachary said, with a kiss to her neck.

"Easier to sing along and not have to hear myself," she joked. She tilted her head back and forth. "That would probably bother Levi more, to be honest."

Zachary chuckled. "What do you have here?"

"Snickerdoodle cupcakes. Final ones of the season." Charlie spun in his arms and wrapped hers around him.

"Your appointment went well this morning, huh?" he said.

She nodded and stood on her tiptoes to brush her nose along his jaw. "Mm-hmm. Best one yet." She nipped at his skin, and he inhaled sharply.

"That's great," he said, returning the favor. "I had to stop checking your texts today. They made me want to pack up and head right to you."

She giggled, then gasped as he sucked at her collarbone. "Zachary," she breathed.

He lifted her legs around his waist and walked slowly toward the bedroom.

Setting her on the bed, he stepped back to remove his scrubs. She slipped her sweater over her head and shimmied off her pants. Now only in boxer briefs, Zachary crawled over her, pressing his warm body against hers.

"I missed your body," he hummed, kissing down her neck, slipping her bra straps off her shoulders. "This morning wasn't enough." He tugged down her bra with a sexy force that made her gasp, then groaned as he sucked her nipple into his mouth.

She arched her back, hands gripping his hair. He switched to her other breast, unclasped the bra, and tossed it. His hand skated down her ribs and hips while his tongue circled her nipples. Charlie squeezed her legs against him, trying to ease the want. He knew. Zachary skimmed the silky bikini-cut material down and slipped two fingers inside her, groaning as she gasped.

"Fuck, you're so wet already," he whispered.

"God, I want you," she breathed. "I want you to do me against the wall." She wanted it, knew she wasn't ready for that—but oh, did she want it.

He smiled and bit her bottom lip. "Soon, baby. I'll do whatever you want me to do."

He kissed her, his tongue stroking hers. His lips trailed down her chest to her breast, back up, picking up speed. All the while, his fingers pumped in and out of her, his thumb slowly circling her clit. Charlie's pants and moans grew until she knew she wanted more. Needed more. She put her hands to his shoulders and guided him to the headboard. He sat with his back to it, watching while she tugged down his underwear, her kisses frantic as she moved up his legs, her fingers grazing him as she licked up his chest, moving to straddle him. He rolled on a condom while she grabbed the lubricant, then attacked him again.

She kissed him feverishly, moaning as his hands raced over her body, igniting her, pinching her nipples lightly as she rocked over him. She reached down, sliding her fingers around his shaft, and he moaned into her mouth. Charlie leaned back, her touch light, watching his face as he closed his eyes and pressed his head to the headboard, his breath fast, his lips swollen from hers.

She lifted herself and slowly lowered. Zachary's eyes popped open, his head tilting forward as the tip of him touched her body. They'd worked toward this numerous times already, the familiarity helping Charlie, and at the same time, building up their desire to pretty intense levels. Something about today, though...

She shifted, looking for the right angle, easing the tip inside. Zachary's hands were gentle on her hips, supporting her weight as she moved. Then he was in, her gasp strained, her hands flexing at his shoulder, his waist. She held for a moment, rose slightly, then pressed back down, feeling him stretch her farther as he went deeper. They both moaned, Zachary gripping her hips.

"Fuuuck," he whispered.

Charlie leaned forward and kissed him. His hands coasted her body, squeezed her ass, her tits, traced lightly over her back, turning on every switch until she was writhing, rocking against him, feeling him inside her. He tilted her, the angle hitting a new spot, and she gasped.

"Yes," she panted. "Move me."

He lifted her and pumped into her, their rhythm gentle, slowly picking up speed. Charlie reached down between them and touched her clit, sending shivers through her body.

"Oh fuck, yes," Zachary said. His gaze bounced between her touching herself, her bouncing tits, her face.

"Zachary," she breathed.

"Yeah, baby," he said. "Come for me."

"Oh God." Charlie gripped his shoulder, the convulsions rocking her, stiffening her, shaking her, as she felt the fireworks burst.

"Fuck," he groaned.

"Yes." She nodded to him, her aftershocks still rocketing. He joined her, biting his lower lip as he came, pulsing, squeezing her hips, and pressing her tightly to him.

Charlie flopped against his neck. Their hearts raced, skin damp, and Charlie wanted to laugh and cry but could only breathe him in, letting the pleasure roll through her in a whole new way.

Zachary tightened his arms around her, holding her close. After a few minutes, they cleaned up and settled on the bed. He tucked her against him, rained kisses over her face, a smile on his, and pressed a light kiss to her lips.

"How are you?" he whispered.

Her heart fluttered. "Amazing."

He grinned, then his gaze softened. He leaned closer, his lips grazing hers as he said, "I love you, Harris."

She smiled. "I love you, Lee."

THE END

Acknowledgements

Despite time away from writing, I knew deep down it was something I had to return to. That it was what my soul needed the most. In order to write, especially this story, there were many people who supported me, and I'd love to do my best to thank them.

First, to my parents, who worked tirelessly to provide for us, whose sacrifices to care for their kids have never gone unnoticed. You taught us to have pride in our hard work and encouraged us to follow our dreams. Thank you for always believing in me and supporting my writing!

My siblings, thank you for letting me boss you around and create stories that we could act out when we were young. You've always made me feel like I could accomplish anything—except sing in front of people, but I'll leave that to you! You were my first audience and cheer squad, and I'm forever grateful for your love.

To my in-laws, who've supported me wholeheartedly this entire time! Who've been eager for this book release, sharing in the excitement of each step. Your trust, love, and acceptance means the world.

To my friends, for their support even when I'd only share vague comments about my book; you waited with an eager patience that motivated me. Julia and Kim, your unwavering enthusiasm kept the spark alive, even when publishing day was still far off.

To JoHanna for your ear, support, patience, guidance, and the best push ever—encouraging me to write Charlie with vaginismus. To my doctors and physical therapists for believing me and helping me with my vaginismus (and the many others who've been lucky enough to find you!)

Veterinarians and vet techs—you're amazing. My family's personal experience at our local vet was the inspiration behind Charlie's and Zachary's careers. You care about our babies as your own, and you don't get enough recognition for all you do. Thank you for your tireless work, your time, your expertise, your loving ways. To Julie, for letting me pick your brain about life as a veterinarian. And to the wonderful rescues and shelters who are helping animals find furever homes.

To my Beta readers, my loudest cheerleaders and an integral part of bringing this story to life. My husband and Liz, you read the most drafts, saw the spark in this before I was even comfortable sharing it with anyone, and gifted me with your unwavering excitement, and I'm eternally grateful. Erica and Bea, my romance reading buddies, but you're my dearest friends first, always supporting me and shouting about HMI from the rooftops. Joey, Gina, Mez, Miki, I'm indebted to you for your enthusiasm and thoughtful notes as I dug out the best parts of this story. To my sensitivity reader Helen Li for your time, care and attention.

My editors! Jessica, thank you for learning about vaginismus before we even started working together. Your care and attention to something so important to this book set a great foundation. Sadie, your immediate support of my story and your own women's health advocacy made me feel connected to you instantly. You validated this story at a time when I needed it most.

Sam at Ink and Laurel, you designed the most beautiful cover, capturing the tenderness between Charlie and Zachary and infusing warmth and color that speaks to who they are. Lemmy and Luna Lit, for your amazing ARC management expertise and support of indie authors, I'm eternally grateful. And to fellow authors I've met along the way, thank you for your friendship!

To our pets. Our senior cat Emma—our sweetheart, our love bug, our protector, the one who made my love for animals grow exponentially, and the first being whom my husband and I cared for together. Our late dog, Poppy—the inspiration behind Zachary's dog, Maple. When she passed during the writing of this book, Maple slowly adopted more of her ways. It's become a tribute to Poppy as a result, and I hope Maple gives you insight to the amazing dog Poppy was, who she remains to be in our hearts. Finally our orange boy, Kermit, our hilarious rascal and cuddle-bug who keeps us constantly laughing.

To my son, who is our best thing. Your sweet nature, your playfulness, your sense of humor all amaze me and push me to be the best version of myself every day. Love doesn't feel like a strong enough word to encompass the gift that you are.

To my husband. The love of my life, my best friend. My amazing partner and the wonderful father to our little guy and animals. You're my rock, my anchor, you've believed in me when I doubted myself the most. You have loved me through it all—and never made me feel like it was "through it all." You've listened to me ramble (for years!) about this story, workshopped scenes and details with me, and cared for us extra hard when I was deep in edits and marketing. I love that we're growing together, and I can't wait for the decades more we have ahead. I love you.

Last but certainly not least—Readers, thank you for taking a chance on a debut author. I'm giving a piece of my heart to you with this book, and I already know it's in good hands. Thank you so much for reading.